SO LONG EARTH

SO LONG EARTH

MICHAEL BIENENSTOCK

Michael Bienenstock

CONTENTS

This book is dedicated to my wife, Debbie and
my hero, Sammy

I woudl also like to acknowledge the hard work of
my copy editor, Maria Lewytzkyj-Milligan

This book is also dedicated to all of the people in
the world who are trying to clean up the planet
and deal with the environment so that our
chlidren and grandchildren can enjoy life.

CHAPTER 1

Far From Routine

Prologue
Denver, CO, September 2017

Dr. Thomas Burns could not believe what he was hearing. He was sitting in a restaurant with his eight-year-old son Sam after attending a baseball game. The Colorado Rockies had just defeated the New York Mets by a score of eight to six. They were discussing the various players on the team. That was until the president started talking.

Listening intently to every word President Trump said on CNN, the environmental scientist shook his head several times. *He's appealing to every gawker of developers and brand-loving radicals rolling everything back—radicals who want to de-regulate, de-environment, just de-any-thing—and it was deflating*, thought Dr. Burns. Decades of work falling apart for a new consensus, it seemed. Depressing.

Not only was the president waging a permanent delay of just about everything, while making money for his backers, but he was hoping people were going to do nothing about it. He was buying time for some of his obscenely wealthy investors and developers; that was all. They somehow pinned their losses in the previous years from failed deals and investments on anyone but themselves, despite how their investments were only about money, not about the major concerns of the times that appeared everywhere you looked. Having had a great outing with his son only moments ago, Dr. Burns fumed as he sat there.

The president was like the suits many in the rural parts of the Dakotas, Tennessee, and his home state of Colorado worried about. They were all caught up in their excesses, mindless to what life outside their air-conditioned life was like. Who cared how his message on TV was going to benefit neglected areas? He just expected people to deal with it. Except, this time, this suit, staring at Dr. Burns on the high-definition TV screen, was the one barreling his way at anyone who gave him a microphone like a dusted wagon train full of barons with money bags who pulled into town. And he'd be building what he knew best, a wall of heat for struggling people. They were less interested in tackling the daily concerns in their lives, finding no areas of concern in common.

Dr. Burns shook his head again. *And the environment was a no-brainer!*

Sam looked up at him momentarily, and Dr. Burns gave a half-reassuring smile. Sam returned his attention to his cell phone.

The president was unconcerned about whatever no man's land was left in his wake of ruin while he doled out skepticism and disparaging comments when people needed reassurances and to feel confident that the authorities were doing their best to keep them safe and secure. In the old Wild West, they used to blame the Yankee, wondering if somebody up in the skyscrapers meant them more harm than good. They just wanted the top suite.

Dr. Burns couldn't stop looking from the TV to his son. He felt like he was falling into an abyss when he should have been feeling like he was there to share a moment of joy with his son.

He stood up, and despite his tall stature—he'd almost made it to varsity baseball years ago at six feet, two inches tall—he felt powerless. It was time to put the agreed-upon plan into action—at full speed. First, he gave his son some ice cream and told him to stay seated across from him, take out his Game Boy, and put his ear buds in, as he did not want Sam to be concerned about what he was going to discuss over the phone. He pulled out his phone and dialed a group text number, the specific code setting of a meeting of his peers. Tom raked his hands through his solid black hair, practically pulling strands out as he waited impatiently for everyone involved in the meeting.

Within five minutes, all of his colleagues around the world were on FaceTime. He'd been selective about which colleagues from Russia, Germany, Australia and America he involved in preparing the mission. Several of them had worked with him on projects at Boeing and others he had met at conferences around the world that had brought his attention to the staggeringly slow pace of applied research. He knew immediately what he wanted to say to the thirty people he'd reached. He trusted them. He sat back down as they met and discussed their plans.

Members from these four countries were going to be the first ones involved because they understood that to do nothing would ensure the end of the human race. These thirty people were the most esteemed researchers in their field of expertise. They published nearly 500 research papers researching climate warming and various environmental issues as well as future space travel. Russia, as the leader in space travel, was an obvious choice. Germany had some of the leading engineers in the world. Australians had suffered a great number of environmental disasters such as a deteriorating Great Barrier Reef and also had a large number of excellent engineers.

Tom, despite his anguish, spoke calmly. "I hope everyone was watching the president's disgusting speech. Obviously, he is not going to listen to any environmental scientists or reports. We have no choice but to go ahead with our agreed-upon plans. It is full steam ahead. We will have to speed everything up. Based on the environmental evidence and facts, the human race probably has 200 years—or less—to live. To survive, we need to find a new planet."

Several of his colleagues made comments agreeing with Dr. Burns. They all agreed they would go home and start implementing the agreed-upon plans.

With that, he ended the FaceTime meeting. He felt a spectrum of emotions including betrayal by the president's actions and fear for his children's future and the future of everyone else. He had hoped his family could grow up to lead normal lives, go to college, marry, have children and choose a career for themselves without worrying about the environmental disasters that were sure to take place. He also felt bad for just about everyone alive and every person yet to be born. Most people were going to face terrible hardships just trying to survive. Most of all, he felt determined.

He and Sam walked toward the exit. Tom waved goodbye to the woman behind the counter.

As his son closed the door behind them to the restaurant, Tom felt the cool night air, hoping his son wasn't too cold given the temperature had fallen quickly. It was September and although it had been a mild seventy-five degrees at Coors Field, they had to walk a block to get to their car. He didn't want to embarrass his son, so he just put his arm around him to keep him warmer. Sam didn't protest thankfully.

As they made their way to their car, Tom couldn't help but look at Sam's baseball glove that Sam held loosely in his hands. He'd given the glove to Sam after his son refused to use Tom's old worn-out one. Tom had used that glove as a teenager when he was about Sam's age. He laughed to himself when he remembered Sam's look on his face as he stared at Tom's old glove. It seemed so important to him to give it to Sam, but Sam wanted his own glove.

Tom knew that Sam had loved the game that afternoon. Sam had a fantastic baseball card collection and often recited stats that baffled Tom, who also felt proud of his son for knowing and memorizing all kinds of stats. Seemed like the type of thing kids should be worried about in high school, not what was weighing on Tom's mind. Tom shook away a bunch of thoughts. He still wanted to look like he was enjoying himself after he and Sam had watched their favorite team win and ate at their favorite restaurant. But that damn television and the news. He was overcome with concern and resentment, knowing that his son's future was going to be nothing like his own.

Sam said, "You know my good friend Kory just made varsity, and I heard that there were even some top university recruits watching. I hope when I get to high school, I'll play that well."

Tom stared at Sam momentarily, masking the welled-up feeling of regret and sorrow that threatened to silence him, before he said, "Sam, you're going to play with the best."

He unlocked the car door, and they headed toward Interstate 70. All the while, Tom was glad that he had reached an agreement with his colleagues that there would be no more delays, no matter what lay ahead.

And so, it began.

Part I

Preparing

2017-2024

Chapter 1 – Far from Routine

Dr. Tom Burns, Boeing Offices, Aurora, Colorado

Tom and his colleagues had decided to hire the best teams to build intergalactic spaceships to find a new planet to live on that was comparable to Earth. It was either that or face the possibility of seeing the end of life. Since it could take years, if not hundreds of years, to prepare and reach a destination or planet that was safe for human life, it was necessary to keep humans alive, active, and to be able to live as healthy a life as possible.

Tom, who had worked at Boeing for sixteen years, knew there was no way a spaceship would ever be approved by the government. Also, he could not ask a company such as Boeing to build a spaceship that would be necessary to their specifications. It took years for any new program to be developed at a major corporation that was mainly concerned about its stock price and shareholders. There was just too much red tape that Tom wanted to avoid at all costs.

When Tom had decided to implement the spaceship project, he had known he had to resign his position with Boeing. By the age of forty-two, Tom had worked on various innovative projects that attempted to help sustain the future of the planet. Under Tom, Boeing had reduced greenhouse emissions and noise created by airplanes. His latest work had been on a hybrid airplane like what was currently available in cars. This would decrease the need for gasoline and carbon emissions. He was sad that he was leaving all these research projects and certainly some of his fellow scientists, but the work had been drawn out too long and time was of the essence.

Tom lived in Colorado with his family near Denver in Aurora, not too far from work. Soon after his meeting with his colleagues on the phone, he had decided to meet with his boss, Dr. Frank Sullivan, who supervised his job as an engineer, to let him know he was leaving and explain his reason for resigning.

Frank welcomed Tom to his office. Tom came in, and they shook hands.

Frank said, "What can I do for you, Tom?"

"Well, Frankie, I need to talk to you about something."

Frankie, as everyone called him, had worked for Boeing for thirty-five years and generally was seen as a terrific boss and person. He had been through all the successes and failures, including a speedy rising stock price as well as a hustle to catch up with Airbus and build successors to their fifty-year old designs.

"Ok. What's up?"

"Frankie, good to see you. I came here because I wanted to tell you face to face that I will be resigning from my position with Boeing and moving on to another job."

Frankie looked aghast. He said, "Are you going to General Dynamics, Lockheed or any of our competitors? Is it because of your salary or stock options?"

Tom almost wanted to laugh, but since this was a serious discussion, he did not.

"No, I am not going to any of those companies. I will do my best to explain it to you. You are probably going to think I am crazy when I finish. First, I want to say that I have enjoyed the time I have spent working at Boeing. However, as an environmental scientist, I am very concerned that human life on Earth will come to an end soon. I believe in the next two hundred years, with one natural disaster after another occurring, the world will end. People are going to die horrible deaths. Now I know that the government environmental reports and scientific journals have reported that they, too, believe we are going to have major problems with the environment. Still, they predict we will survive for quite a long time, although it will become more difficult with all the man-made pollution. I just think these scientists and government workers are not willing to provide the dire warning necessary because it would set off a huge panic in the population. After all, where would everyone go if you knew the world was about to end?"

"You know Boeing's been in the news for wanting to beat Elon Musk to Mars over the years!" It was almost offhanded. Frankie gave his winning smile. "In addition, Boeing has been working on electric planes using a fuel cell. We were able to successfully fly one in 2008."

"Jousting news, you know that! I've seen the mockups. Look, they're mockups. Design stage stuff! Far from routine. First person to set their foot on Mars will get there on a Boeing-built rocket? Yeah, I saw that. Anyway, if Earth is uninhabitable, there will be no place on Earth that is safe from the destruction that is sure to come. Electric planes should have been developed a long time ago. I want my family, especially my children and grandchildren, to be able to live in a world where they do not have to worry. Why would you even have a baby if you knew the baby would die before they lived to be thirty years old? I have decided with the help of a special group of people from around the world to build a huge spaceship capable of reaching other galaxies in an attempt to find a planet to live on."

Tom waited for a reaction, which he knew was sure to happen.

"You are kidding me, right? Tell me this is a joke."

Tom said with a straight face, "No, Frankie, it is no joke."

Frankie stood up, rubbed his hands over his hair and looked down. Then he said, "Look; actually, I agree somewhat with what you are saying. Earth will have big problems, and people will pay the price for a lot of stupid politicians around the world. But this idea of yours to build a spaceship to reach some faraway destination is just pure fantasy. Maybe in a hundred years, we will be able to do it, but we do not have a clue right now. Why don't you stay here and help Boeing keep designing and researching this?"

Frankie looked pained. Tom couldn't help briefly sharing in his boss's concerns or even appreciating Frankie's gesture. In fact, he was proud of his work at Boeing. He'd spent years attempting to improve technologies, finding new ways to build sensors and develop applicable environmental assessments. Still, it seemed like they were drowning in data. Feeble improvements and politics were going to let politicians sit idly by despite it all and give his kids more explanations of how things *really* worked. What kind of message was being sent to his kids who hadn't had the benefit of years of discovery and evidence yet? He didn't only feel desperate; he felt like he would be shirking the contribution to the world that kept nagging at him, his calling.

"Also, even if you travel at Mach 4, which is the fastest rocket speed we currently have, it will take you an eternity to go anywhere near where you want to be. You will all be dead before you even become close to getting there. Plus, you have no funding. This is going to cost billions—if not trillions—of dollars. No company in the world would undertake such a project right now. They would be bankrupt before it was finished, and there would be no profit at all. What if it exploded right after take-off? Who will be your partners in this endeavor? No one has developed anything close to what you are planning to do, so it is going to take a lot of manpower and brainpower to accomplish this. There are just too many unknowns right now to succeed."

Tom said, "Your reaction is kind of what I expected, and you have every right to your own opinion, but listen to me. There have been many advances in technology since the last millennia. Just look at Thomas Edison, the wonderful deaf inventor, and the Wright brothers flying for the first time. I bet people thought they were crazy too when they decided to fly a plane. Yet, they succeeded. Their inventions led to generations of discoveries. Unfortunately, each positive invention seems to have an equally negative reaction that affects the environment. The number of positive results, which make our lives easier, seems to have an equal impact on destroying life. We could call our world *Man builds, Man destroys.*"

"Granted, you might have a point, but—" Frankie rubbed the inside of his palms with his fingers frantically.

"Just look at the cellphone, which is used by millions of people. Little did we know that the cell phone would lead to killing millions of bees and cause other problems. It is also causing thousands of car accidents. At a certain point, I am certain the only way we could actually survive here is to turn off all the electricity, go back to the horse and buggy, and see what happens. I really doubt that humans would ever accept that choice. Think of politicians and business people without the New York Stock Exchange. They would not know what to do with themselves. Yet, through the years our inventions have been advancing at a very rapid pace. Most of these inventors have also been told they would never succeed, but they do. Steve Jobs is a testimony to that. I have thought long and hard about this project, and I know many people will tell my colleagues that we will never succeed just like they told everyone else who came before us."

"I'm not saying you're doomed to fail, I'm just, well, it's a lonely endeavor without the proper sup—"

"For your information, several other countries will join this endeavor, including Russia, Australia, and Germany. There will be more than one spaceship. I know it will take many years to complete the building of a huge spaceship, but we will do it. I have faith and truly believe that I will find the right people to succeed at this. If we fail, I believe all humanity fails, as there will be no one able to tell the story of the human race on Earth."

Frankie had listened intently, not used to Tom being so expressive about his aspirations. He said, "That was a nice speech, but do you really think Russia is going to cooperate with you? They are only doing this to help themselves. Everyone knows they will not allow someone from the United States to beat them on a project like this. You know that is how they think. What about Putin and his puppet, Trump? Do you think they would sign off to a joint project of this magnitude? If you are so serious about this, maybe I can arrange for Boeing to have you lead a group of scientists to develop a project like this. We would not have to involve Russia. Plus, you would have a salary and a pension when you retire. Let me talk to the directors."

While Tom had thoroughly enjoyed working for Boeing, it was not possible to do both of these two jobs simultaneously. Since they were only going to build one ship and it was never coming back to Earth, there would be too many problems to overcome.

Tom said, "First, Boeing would have to approve the project, which could take years. In making this kind of proposal, Boeing would want to know the estimated cost to develop a spaceship like this and how they would profit from it. Patents would have to be filed. Companies—such as Lockheed—might challenge them. The courts could take years to settle a very minor issue, and the building of the spaceship could be delayed indefinitely. Also, there would not be any financial profit for this since we are not returning to Earth. We will have to do this using only private funds. I have scouted a list of wealthy individuals that I hope to meet to obtain the necessary startup funds for such an endeavor. Several venture capitalists are already invested. I've managed to get a global technology stock portfolio percentage figured into several wealth flagship assets and investment management advisors' pitches to navigate funds into our endeavor through small percentages of their stock choices. They gain, we gain. Additionally, we've set up a galactic superfund site."

"What? Superfund sites are polluted locations set aside for massive cleanup of hazardous material contamination."

"Exactly. Hope the point is well taken. It's what we're dealing with here. This is one big clean up, and although the contamination we're talking about on Earth is going to continue to be administered by the EPA, the contamination we're looking to focus on has to do with unknown hazardous materials that we might have to address if it ends up posing a risk to human health and/or environment. Not sure if you ever went on a trip overseas after college, but you could always rely on traveler's insurance to cover your trip essentials.

"Since we're not going to be able to get any evacuation by helicopters, we're going to have to deal with any exposure to hazardous materials that we find or that we end up carrying as a result of the long-term travel. Investors are interested in minimizing our waste-print in the galaxy even if we'll be living in hazmat suits at some point. What we keep learning is that the waste end of the equation is a constant afterthought in all the projects we've seen funded ever since the Industrial Revolution with a whole slew of apologies published as excellent PR in front of the cameras and in print. We're not interested in good PR and apologies. We're interested in preventing the same kind of serious errors we've had in our production streams here on Earth.

We'll be working off of some baseline new developments like NASA's trash-to-gas, plasma gasification, implementing research that shows that bacteria can combat dangerous gas leaks, and avoiding all the missteps. We've seen problems that are now serious problems for NASA as they try to handle long-term waste generation. We're shooting for hopefully converting waste into useful gases. Call it the 'Everything-we-need-to-do-to-not-have-to-have-another-Superfund-Site' as a national, um, stellar, priority. Stocks are already bringing in massive revenue streams. As is our own Amazon-like platform that allows people to purchase different parts and programs that we'll be relying on to get the journey accomplished. Which by the way—"

"Stop, Tom. I'm almost ready to buy a few of your parts."

"Well, you can. For a nominal price, you too may be able to reshape the future of space waste without turning everything into a giant trash pile, helping on the front end of production. We can call the part after you or Boeing or both—Frankie goes to Centauri-wood."

Both men looked like two metal detectors that had detected the metal in each other's words and were simultaneously beeping, testing each other's mettle; neither was willing to believe what the other was willing or unwilling to do given the state of things.

Staring in disbelief, and despite Frankie not having the heart to follow through when the going got tough. Tom was disappointed but had to stay focused on the issues he faced. He continued, "The second issue is the government red tape. I could care less about what Putin and Trump think about this. First, let me say something about President Trump. He is the main reason I am doing this right now. That man is totally ignorant about what is going to happen to life on this planet. All of his positions on the environment will make things a lot worse for the future of everyone. I admit this is not all the president's fault. The problem started years ago when we hit the Industrial Age. Also, I don't think Putin cares about the environment. I do know the Russian commander, and so far, he has been fully cooperating with my colleagues and myself. He has flown into space before and is fully confident he can build the Russian spaceship for the journey. I do think you are right in one way. It is not going to be easy to trust the Russians for a long-term project like this. The Russians and Americans have always been adversaries. I am fully aware at some point we may have minor or major conflicts with them, and I am going to have to be prepared to handle whatever problems arise. Our ship will be armed with the latest weapons and have the best personnel available to utilize them."

Frankie looked at Tom in disbelief. "Tom, all of your ideas are great, but you need the Boeing team to assist you with this. We have some of the greatest minds working here, and I am sure Boeing would be willing to assist you in developing whatever you need. We don't want to lose a person with your skills and fantastic ideas that may benefit everyone. We have a company that can mass produce whatever is created. I am sure we can come to an agreement that will satisfy everyone, including you."

Tom stood silent for a moment. He looked down at the ground and then started to shake his head with his arms crossed. He then continued, "Thanks for the possible offer, but my colleagues and I have decided to do this without going through all the red tape and decision-making processes. We have already decided what must be done and will begin work soon. I don't mind staying open to the possibility of you sponsoring some of the technology. Maybe that'll be beneficial for everyone. Please feel free. I wish you the best of luck."

"What about the conference tomorrow?"

"I'll be there and won't say a thing about my resignation. I'm sure what I have to say, with Boeing's blessings, since you've seen the presentation, will still make the impact we need."

Tom offered his hand to Frankie, who was agitated and angry.

Frankie raised his voice. "What a fool you are, Tom. This dream of an impossible project will surely fail. You will end up broke, and you and your children and grandchildren will never recover from it. Plus, you will drag down all the other people you plan to hire with your con job. Even if you succeed in building a ship like Noah's Ark, it will probably explode or end up not going anywhere, and you will still be broke. What the hell do you think you are going to accomplish with all this nonsense?"

Tom said, "We can only accomplish something if we try. If we try and fail, then we can die knowing we did everything possible to save the human race. If someone else comes along and follows up on this and succeeds in saving the human race, that would be great too."

With those words, Tom turned in his letter of resignation and walked out of Frankie's office.

He never spoke to Frankie again.

The Short Flight

Chapter 2 – The Short Flight

Tom Burns, Chicago-bound

During the flight to the climate change conference in Chicago, Tom reviewed his presentation. It was an early morning flight. He was ready for his mid-afternoon presentation. He felt great having talked to Frankie. He felt even better about the conference and the next few weeks. In the past one hundred years, people had done more harm to the climate than the last six hundred million years. This was unacceptable, but there was not much he could do about it. The United States government under Donald Trump had been resistant to accepting any report the environmental scientists had produced. Tom had become interested in saving the environment ever since his dad, William, died from cancer inflicted by Agent Orange during the Vietnam War. The United States government during the 1960s and 1970s had not only killed thousands of Vietnamese with these dangerous chemicals but also thousands of United States citizens. The military had been less than forthcoming about the effects of Agent Orange and tried to cover it up for years.

Before his dad died, his dad had made it clear that he was proud to have served his country and proud of his only son. He had wanted his son and grandchildren to enjoy life and have as many opportunities as possible. Tom believed in what his dad had told him. But now it was clear that the only way to enjoy a full life would be by leaving Earth behind.

After watching his dad die a horrible death in 2001, Tom had promised himself that he would do whatever he could to save people from the dangers that governments were inflicting on people of the world. He had decided to travel to places where climate change was having an impact on gaining as much information as possible. It was the subject of his presentation. Since the increase of cars, carbon emissions had increased significantly, causing the polar caps to melt, the ozone layer to disappear, and the oceans to rise. First, he had taken a job at Boeing, where he was one of the youngest engineers.

In 2008, Tom had met with a group of scientists to discuss climate changes happening in the world. Tom had left the meeting with a real sense of purpose. His daughter, Sophie, was only a year old, and he and his wife, Sarah, had been focused on building a family. They wanted three children. Once the kids were old enough, Tom would be ready to travel and gather first-hand accounts to prepare steps to help solve the problems beyond what he had been doing at Boeing ever since he was twenty-six years old.

Seven years later, Tom had traveled to the island of Kiribati. Jeff Tirortu, a native of the islands, had met him there. After having a meal, they had sat down to talk.

"Our people have lived mostly off the land and sea, building up our subsistence agriculture, relying on coconut trees since our soil quality is poor and we have great fishing grounds. Kiribati was once a much larger island than it is now. It is part of a group of islands called the Gilbert Islands that stretches hundreds of miles. Our ancestors have been living here for hundreds of years. During World War II, we were the battlefield for one of the bloodiest battles between Japan and the allies. In the Battle of Tarawa in 1943, nearly 6,400 soldiers from the United States, Korea, and Japan died. The villagers experienced terror, torture, and destruction under the Japanese. Forced labor, being forced to provide goods and homes to soldiers, and the destruction of canoes made them think the end of the world had arrived. Then they were evacuated."

"How dreadful," Tom had said.

"Yeah. And the American bombings left nowhere to hide. After the Japanese surrendered, the local people saw better working conditions and compensation and provisions with an end to the forced labor. Their traditional way of life was gradually restored despite how long it took to recover from the war's ecological and economic damage on the land and subsistence living. It's taken decades. And they still find remains of servicemembers in unmarked graves who were killed during the battle, providing some answers to the families who were left in the dark back at home. And, now, how are the latest damages to the environment affecting our people and our lives living off the land and sea?"

Jeff had slowly shaken his head, recalling stories he'd heard about how long it took to develop before a crop could be harvested again.

"Once the industrialized countries started to mass-produce cars, there has been a considerable loss of land due to carbon emissions. We're low-lying islands. Many smaller islands have had to be evacuated due to extreme flooding and drought as the sea rises. All of these evacuees have had to relocate to Tarawa, our capital. The losses seem endless to us. We haven't been able to isolate ourselves, between the war and the environmental damages, and struggle to survive. What kind of answers will ever be provided?"

"Good question. Is it overpopulated?"

"Yes, over 100,000 people. There are so many people living here now that the living conditions have deteriorated. It is almost like a can of sardines. We are forced to try to relocate our citizens in other countries. We try to relocate as many citizens as possible close to each other so that we can try to preserve some of our cultural traditions. Some have been sent to New Zealand. When we move to New Zealand, we are forced to give up most of our cultural ways. The graves of our great ancestors are left behind, and many are underwater now. Many structures and buildings which were built in the last forty years are also underwater."

"It's like watching something you love fall away and you'll never get to reclaim it. Some people have never experienced such a devastating loss. How do you rebuild? Where do you start?"

"Yes, I do not know how long our country will survive as the polar caps melt, and the oceans rise and cover our islands. When the ocean rises enough, it goes into our freshwater, contaminating it and making it unfit to drink. Most of our citizens are spending a lot of their time trying to build walls to keep out the floods, but it has proved very difficult. It is probably impossible to save the islands.

"And they don't want to leave. Their hearts and spirits are tied to the land and to our people. I don't think my mother and father would ever leave. They are our elders, and they can't imagine starting over somewhere else. Maybe when you are young, you can flee, but—"

"How long before you think all the inhabitants will have to be evacuated?"

"Definitely before 2040, unless the world changes its behavior towards destroying the climate."

After visiting Tarawa and several smaller communities, Tom had flown back to the United States. His next opportunity to gather first-hand accounts was Lake Ontario years later in the summer of 2016. Lake Ontario stretches 310 kilometers, spanning the U.S. border with Canada between the state of New York and the province of Ontario. The last in the Great Lakes chain, Lake Ontario, serves as the outlet to the Atlantic Ocean via the Saint Lawrence River.

There he'd met Joyce and Hilda Scott. They had sat in their living room. They had told Tom they would have loved him to have seen their backyard, 300 yards from the lake. Tom remembered looking outside the back and noticing there was virtually no backyard at one time. It was only a matter of time before their home was underwater. As a result, there was no way to sell the house. Who would want to live in a place that was going to be underwater? They were both retired teachers and had bought a small home northwest of Rochester, New York. They had purchased their home in 1980. Unfortunately, around 1990, they had woken up one morning to find the water was only ten feet from their house. Many of their neighbors' homes had been flooded and abandoned. The lake had risen due to the water release from the Moses-Saunders Dam, which also sent water into the Saint Lawrence River.

"Can you imagine what it's taken to get some common sense of water management? The water level of the lake is in the hands of the International Joint Commission, not the state. So, you can imagine the board of six people, with three Canadians and three Americans, have to compromise and are slow to react to flooding. Still, I keep hearing they're trying to increase lake outflows, over two million gallons every second leaving the lake. That's still not going to be enough of a drop overall, according to the experts," Hilda had said.

"We're just sitting ducks while public hearings and politicians smack their lips about the 'new normal,' creating reality TV-styled opinions about different plans minus their red tape and bureaucracies. So, we just prepare with more sandbags? Please! Now, the Army Corps of Engineers has stepped in."

"Took a while. There's no way for us to know how often this is going to repeat and how the adjustments are going to prevent devastating damage for everyone," Joyce had said.

Joyce and Hilda had no place to relocate at their advanced ages. All of their money was tied up into the house that could be flooded shortly.

Joyce said, "It would actually be better off if we died before the next flood came. We will be homeless if we live long enough."

Tom's next stop had been Tangier Island off the coast of Virginia, often considered America's first climate change casualty. This island has lost about two-thirds of its mass. Most of this has occurred in the past fifty years as the ocean levels rose and increased erosion. Many of the homes there are now underwater. Some families had lived there for 200 years. They were primarily fishermen. Some of the people living there had spoken to Tom about the erosion of the land. Most doubted that they could remain there after twenty more years. What was interesting to Tom was that, unlike other locations, most of the citizens left on Tangier did not believe that climate change was man-made.

After a few more visits to places around the United States and Canada, Tom had seen enough to know that climate change was real. He was appalled. Only a week before he'd left his job at Boeing, he had visited the National Weather Center in Atlanta. The data from the Weather Center had also shown considerable deterioration in the climate. He had studied the data compiled over the years. Hurricanes and tornadoes had been occurring with high frequency and strength. Summers were becoming warmer, and winters were becoming colder. Clearly, this was leading to more widespread damage both on the coasts and inland. Tornados in locations where there was no history of tornados touching down were suddenly happening and destroying homes and businesses. People had moved there years ago, thinking that they were free of natural disasters. Now, everything they owned had been destroyed.

Tom had decided to disclose many of his findings from around the world to various conferences dedicated to climate control he'd attended this past year that culminated in this conference he was preparing for in Chicago. Coupled with all of the human disasters being experienced, he couldn't believe the number of animals suffering in different climates and how powerless it made him feel, knowing that enough people didn't care about their welfare. While many people believed in everything he spoke about, others were too stubborn to admit that he might be right. Many people who agreed with him did not put forth ambitious enough plans to reverse the trends.

He couldn't stop thinking about what he'd seen in Tangier, Lake Ontario, and Kiribati—well, at least he could *believe* it. What he didn't *tolerate* was how politics had reversed course, and climate change had not, given how easy it was to see how many lives and lands were going to suffer the consequences. If his father had become a casualty of recklessness and concealment of the major harm he'd been exposed to, he sure as hell wasn't going to continue to wait and see what he, Jeff, Joyce, Hilda, and folks were going to be exposed to as tornados forged new paths.

He arrived in Chicago, headed to the conference, and delivered his presentation with many people impressed and happy that Boeing was one of the business executive delegates willing to convene with professionals from the government, academia, and non-profits.

He had booked an evening flight home. He needed to get started on his plans.

After a short flight, he drove home. Although Sam always loved greeting him when he returned from his travels, Sam would be asleep by the time he got home. Besides, Tom was more interested in seeing the expression on Sam's face when he showed up after talking to President Trump in person the following week.

All Part of Growing Up

Chapter 3 – All Part of Growing Up

Sam Burns, Aurora, Colorado

Sam was only seven years old at the time Donald Trump became president. Despite his age, he had noticed the change in his dad's behavior after watching Donald Trump. He knew almost immediately something was bothering his dad, call it son-father intuition. His dad was not going to tell him anything about the problem. Like most parents, his mom and dad wanted him to be happy and have a normal upbringing. Sam had no idea what the future held, not many seven-year-old children do, but he knew he could trust his dad to make decisions for him. His dad was always giving him praise and encouraging him to be better. It seemed his dad was more focused on him than on his sister, Sophie. Sam had asked his dad about that, and the response was always the same.

His dad would say, "Son, you are special and will be very successful one day. You are blessed with natural abilities, and I just want to be sure that you develop them. I also want you to live a normal life until you graduate from high school."

"Why am I so special?"

"Son, someday I will not have to tell you how special you are. Just work hard, and you will see it yourself."

Whenever his dad said that it made him determined to study hard in school and learn as much as possible. Sam formed friendships in elementary school with many of his classmates. It seemed every week, or so some new student joined his school from another part of the country. Sam would often ask them as they became friends and why they had moved to Colorado, but none knew why. Sam thought it was mysterious that so many children moved into his school, but he really did not mind. He enjoyed meeting all these new students and competing with them on school tests.

One of the first students he met was Sally McDaniel. When Sally McDaniel moved to Colorado from New York, Sam liked her right away. Sally was also seven. She was very smart. He always found her smiling and laughing. Like the other students, Sally did not know why her family had moved from New York. Sam enjoyed hearing Sally tell him about the Statue of Liberty and some of the museums she had visited. Sally, like Sam, seemed to make friends easily.

After he met Sally, he made friends with Jose Black. They became the 'three amigos'

and spent a lot of time together, studying and hanging out after school. They attended each other's birthday parties and spent a lot of time with their parents. To Sam and his friends, it was just part of growing up and having a good time.

He and his friends could not imagine what was in store for them later in life.

CHAPTER 4

Burning

Chapter 4 Burning

Sam Burns, Aurora, Colorado

Sam was only seven years old at the time Donald Trump became president. Despite his age, he had noticed the change in his dad's behavior after watching Donald Trump. He knew almost immediately something was bothering his dad, call it son-father intuition. His dad was not going to tell him anything about the problem. Like most parents, his mom and dad wanted him to be happy and have a normal upbringing. Sam had no idea what the future held, not many seven-year-old children do, but he knew he could trust his dad to make decisions for him. His dad was always giving him praise and encouraging him to be better. It seemed his dad was more focused on him than on his sister, Sophie. Sam had asked his dad about that, and the response was always the same.

His dad would say, "Son, you are special and will be very successful one day. You are blessed with natural abilities, and I just want to be sure that you develop them. I also want you to live a normal life until you graduate from high school."

"Why am I so special?"

"Son, someday I will not have to tell you how special you are. Just work hard, and you will see it yourself."

Whenever his dad said that it made him determined to study hard in school and learn as much as possible. Sam formed friendships in elementary school with many of his classmates. It seemed every week, or so some new student joined his school from another part of the country. Sam would often ask them as they became friends and why they had moved to Colorado, but none knew why. Sam thought it was mysterious that so many children moved into his school, but he really did not mind. He enjoyed meeting all these new students and competing with them on school tests.

One of the first students he met was Sally McDaniel. When Sally McDaniel moved to Colorado from New York, Sam liked her right away. Sally was also seven. She was very smart. He always found her smiling and laughing. Like the other students, Sally did not know why her family had moved from New York. Sam enjoyed hearing Sally tell him about the Statue of Liberty and some of the museums she had visited. Sally, like Sam, seemed to make friends easily.

After he met Sally, he made friends with Jose Black. They became the 'three amigos'

and spent a lot of time together, studying and hanging out after school. They attended each other's birthday parties and spent a lot of time with their parents. To Sam and his friends, it was just part of growing up and having a good time.

He and his friends could not imagine what was in store for them later in life.

Meeting Donald Trump

Chapter 5 – Meeting Donald Trump

Tom Burns, Washington, D.C.

Tom set up a meeting with President Trump for Friday, October 17th. The day before, he had told Sam he was taking off to meet with the president and had watched his son contort his face in disgust.

It had made Tom smile. He had rubbed Sam's head momentarily and had said, "Yeah, I know. I'll bring you a souvenir from the Capitol, though."

Sitting at the airport waiting to board, he thought about how his life had changed recently. They were boarding in ten minutes. There was a time he loved waiting to board and would strike up conversations. When Trump became president, everything had changed for Tom and his fellow scientists. Staying intellectually honest had become less of the usual when it came to talking to random people about environmental science. It was something he had thoroughly enjoyed over the years and went with the territory. Now it was something much more forceful, something that made Tom unable—or was it possible unwilling—to subject himself to. Instead of intellectual conversations, these were insincere diatribes or an inane constant dismissiveness. At first, he'd thought it was a few people who just didn't want to think about science, who were safely guarding themselves in their chosen beliefs. They were more interested in preserving some ideas about life and what they were entitled to.

To Tom, it became abruptly disheartening. It was the sign of the times. The shift had to do with people who were willing to sacrifice much more than he was in life and the responsibilities that came with knowledge. Gone were the days of reasonable conversations, measuring the effects of deforestation or increased pollution. The rising tide preferred the pursuit of narrow interests and class distinctions, extensively concerned about status. It seemed to trump turning any conversation toward any whiff of the common good.

Joe Simmons, one of his fellow scientists at Boeing and a technologist who'd spent hours a day testing an infinite array of new technologies, had once said to him, "We're over here hoping to recover and conserve resources. They're just interested in fist bumps over what a pain in the ass it is to make room for thinking about vehicle emissions." During one of their discussions leading up to the testing of the hydrogen fuel cells on the Eco Demonstrator Program demonstration, proving the concept of the new technology.

"Too much to think about."

"And imagine what they'd have said if they'd seen us testing the 757 coatings to stop the drag on the plane caused by all the dead bugs that get stuck on the leading edge of the wing."

"Coating? All you need is a big fly swatter stuck to the plane's front, don't you?"

"Precisely. Now, I'm no demolition man, but—"

Tom had heard this so many times, he could finish his sentence. "But most derbies offer an evening of destruction, not an entire incumbency."

"But look at him, flaunting his status."

"Boarding United Flight 612 to Washington-Dulles. Seating Groups 1 and 2."

Tom checked in and boarded the plane. He sat at a window seat and gazed out the window. He hadn't been to Washington, D.C. in many years and looked forward to walking past the Air and Space Museum as well as other Smithsonian museums on his way to the White House.

The three-hour flight was relatively smooth, and he made his way to his hotel near the National Mall. He slept well, considering his anxiety level was through the roof.

The next morning, with time to spare before his meeting, he walked around the National Mall. He had loved going to the Air and Space Museum with his dad as a boy. His dad would explain the history of air travel, starting with the Wright brothers. The National Mall was also full of various groups protesting different plans and political issues that President Trump had announced. Many of the protesters carried signs with slogans opposing the decisions that Donald Trump had already made.

He saw some people were protesting about changes to immigration policies and women's rights. In contrast, others opposed the decisions made about the environment. Many of the nationally known environmental protection groups were active here. Some signs asked to protect specific animals such as the polar bear from becoming extinct. Others protested the reduction in carbon emission requirements. Still, more signs called Trump, a murderer for not doing enough to help citizens prepare and provide relief from the impact of hurricanes. On the other side of the Mall, a group of Trump supporters was carrying signs praising Trump. These people were screaming at the immigration and environmental protesters who shouted right back at them.

Tom decided to walk through the environmental group protesters to feel what was

happening and show his support. He picked up a few pins with some slogans for his friends back home. One pin said, "CHANGE THE WHITE HOUSE, NOT THE CLIMATE." Another one said, "GO GREEN." A third one said, "TREAT ANIMALS WITH DECENCY." A fourth one said, "BUILD A WALL AROUND THE WHITE HOUSE AND THROW AWAY THE KEY."

Tom took some pictures to show his family. Tom really doubted there would be any compromise on many of these issues. The country was falling apart at a rapid pace since the election of Trump and Cabinet administrators' appointment that was totally opposite to whatever President Obama had done. There was just too much partisan politics.

Numerous policemen were stationed between the groups of protesters. Most of the protesters were very passionate about their positions. Tom wondered how many people were arrested daily. It would not take much more anger between the groups to bring about a riot.

As Tom neared the Washington Monument at the end of the Mall and adjacent to the White House, he felt an object hit him on his shoulder. One of Trump's supporters had seen him wearing an environmental protection pin and had thrown an object probably the size of a small rock. Tom immediately felt the pain in his right shoulder but stayed on his feet and looked around for the person who had hit him. He noticed a man staring at him about twenty feet away with his hands on his waist. Tom also noticed three cops running at the intruder.

When the man saw the police, he tried to run from them. The only place he could run was directly at Tom. The man got close to Tom. As soon as he approached him, Tom cold-cocked the man in the stomach. The man, unable to breathe from the punch, collapsed on the grass. A few seconds later, the cops had the man in handcuffs. They turned to see if Tom was all right.

Tom said, "I am glad you guys were around and acted so quickly. I have no idea how this would have turned out without your presence. What will happen to him? Does this stuff happen often?"

One of the cops responded. "We do about five incidents a day with crazy people like this. We do not mind people with permits screaming at the top of their lungs, but once it gets physical, we have to move in and make arrests. We take all the people like this guy and book them for the crime they committed. In this case, it will be assault and intent to start a riot. Assault is a more serious offense, and he may or may not be able to post bail. We need to get your name and address and contact information in case a trial is conducted. If you want, we can take you to an emergency room to have you checked out. Given the way you hit the intruder, that may not be necessary."

Tom proceeded to give the cop the information they needed. He said, "Thanks for coming to my assistance. My shoulder does hurt, but I think it will be ok. I will be sure to have it checked out as soon as I can. Right now, I am supposed to be on my way to see President Trump for a meeting."

The cop said, "Really? Good luck with that. It is less than half a mile to the White House. I will walk with you to the gate if you don't mind. You helped us catch the guy. It is the least we can do for you, especially if you are not going to the hospital. You could actually have been in the morgue if he hit you in the right place. You are a lucky man."

"Yes, I know I am lucky. Thanks for the escort, but I am sure I will be fine. Thanks again."

They shook hands, and the cop went back to his business of policing the demonstrators. Tom checked himself out one more time, took off all the protest slogan pins he had on, and put them in his pockets. He did not want to have people notice him and did not want the president to see him with those pins on. Although he still felt some pain, there was no blood, so he straightened himself up.

He walked over to the White House gate and gave the Secret Service his name. He waited a few minutes. Then, he was escorted to the Oval Office and introduced to President Trump. They shook hands. The president introduced Tom to the national security adviser, the White House chief of staff, and the state secretary.

President Trump began, "I have been advised by my national security adviser, Mark Egan, that you wish to speak to me about some kind of exploratory space trip due to problems you believe are occurring because of global warming. So far, no one seems to be able to figure out exactly what you wish to do and what you want from me regarding the project. Please tell us what you are planning so that I have a better idea if we can or cannot help you. We particularly want to know what this will cost the government in terms of the budget and whether we will be able to make any money off of it."

"Mr. President, you need to reverse your positions on the climate and global warming by rejoining the Paris Accord. You keep insisting that global warming is just a phase we are going through. Instead, you worry more about the stock market and how much money you are making. When the stock market crashes to zero, how much money will you have then? You could have worked with the world to prevent the catastrophes that will occur, but you refuse to believe it. You will not accept the scientific community's research findings that continuously warn you of what will probably lead to the extinction of life on Earth."

Trump said, "Look, many scientists do not share your opinion about the climate, and my gut tells me they are right, and you are wrong. I am not going back to the Obama days. The environment is fine."

"Mr. President, I am not here to ask for your approval or blessing on this project. I just thought as a United States citizen that I would let you know what we are planning, and that is it. I would like your support, but whether you support the project or not makes no difference to the people working with me. You have made a total mess of just about everything you have done in your position and robbed the good citizens of this country and the world of any possible future. Just look at the strength of the recent hurricanes. Floods are getting worse. The Arctic is slowly melting, and the oceans are rising. Your grandchildren will probably not live to see old age. Your Lago Mar residence in Florida could be underwater in a few years. Mr. President, the only way to save humanity is to find another planet to ensure our survival. That is my team's project. I am not sure when we will launch, but a certain number of people will be traveling the galaxies until we either find a planet or die trying to find one. I am not asking you for any funding. I do not care if you want to help me. I just thought it would be courteous for me to let you know our plans."

The president looked like he was ready to explode. He looked at his Cabinet people in the room. Then he shouted, "You are right about one thing. The Earth is not going to end anytime soon. The stupid research scientists are just trying to get on my nerves and make money with their fake findings. You will not get any help from me or anyone for your fantasized dream of a spaceship to nowhere. No person can talk to me that way. It is evident if you try to do this, everyone onboard will probably perish."

"You can believe what you want, Mr. President, but people have the right to decide their future. You are playing with the lives of everyone in this world and will go down in history as the man who destroyed life on Earth."

Tom walked out of the room. As Tom got into a cab to return to the hotel, he wondered what the president would think when things started to worsen. This was all too irrational to Tom. It seemed that the man in the White House had never found any contentment in anything about the meaning of life, the substance of life, or anything to do with maintaining life. He caught a glimpse of himself in the reflection of the cab's rear-view mirror and saw in his own eyes a tension that threatened to strain his very cornea. He felt as if they were speeding around a curve being thrown outwards even though they were driving on Pennsylvania Avenue's very straight stretch. He felt fortunate that the world and so many countries had so many scientific minds. How could the highest office willfully ignore so much substance? The feeling he felt was like the loss of equilibrium that he'd only felt during earthquakes. Any moment it could shift again, and you couldn't trust the ground you stood on for fear of another aftershock. It was shocking how overlooked he felt now.

The cab stopped at a red light. Tom was uneasy. Humankind had been on a quest for knowledge and somehow had found itself merely led by a man who feared the loss of what he knew. Tom's own loss welled up in him momentarily, as he considered whether his courtesy call had been a total loss. He recalled the pain in his arm. The threat he'd posed to his assailant's sovereignty was a loss and unfortunate, but he'd gained by getting him locked up. He started to feel better. If he was going to do anything about his plan, he had to do it before he talked to another windbag with a status that could reduce the entire cosmos down to 'nowhere.'

More Planning

Chapter 6 – More Planning

Tom Burns, Aurora, CO

While Tom had been in DC, he had several team members set up a temporary office in Aurora until they were able to get further along and secure a permanent location. He'd already put in a few calls. It was barely 8 am on Monday morning when he walked in to meet with his team. The offices would be fine during the planning phase, and it was a short drive from his house.

He along with five members of his team, began to implement their plan. They all agreed that it was clear that our solar system did not have the right planets to save the human race. However, many possibilities had been discovered in the past twenty years. By 2016 scientists had found approximately fifty-one galaxies that contained about five hundred solar systems. His boss, Frankie, was right about one thing. At the current top speed of a rocket, Mach 4, the human race would never be able to reach any of them. They recognized an increased speed would be necessary for any spaceship that was developed. It was estimated that there could be approximately ten or more (currently undiscovered) worlds capable of sustaining life as we know it. Thus, scientists had to figure out how to succeed and survive such an undertaking.

Tom recalled reading that Carl Sagan had once told Michio Kaku: "We live in the middle of a shooting gallery with thousands of asteroids in our path that we haven't even discovered yet. So, let's be at least a two-planet species, as a backup plan." So, of course, the battle of the billionaires trying to shape the future meant not only keeping up with the latest Silicon Valley space explorer ready to fulfill a childhood dream but also keeping up on scientific genetic breakthroughs like the Mighty Mouse gene and the possible super-Earths.

Tom had spent hours reading about the gravitational field differences. He shared his findings with the group. It would be a big challenge to overcome Earth's gravitational field by fifty percent, but as some who have studied transhumanism have found, an increase in muscles and bones could be just the enhancement needed to adapt to new frontiers if terraforming became essentially impossible. Once the initial experimentation phases happened, the adaptations might even become possible. Scientists hadn't rejected the red dwarf star Proxima Centauri orbiting Alpha Centauri A and B and the exoplanet Proxima Centauri b despite questions about nearby solar outbursts flares. The flares may have harmed the atmospheres and ruined any chance of possible habitability if the environment is too extreme for life as we know it. However, it was still up for debate, and their impact was still being measured.

Life as we know it? he asked himself. *Was that the right question to ask?* Every pioneering circumstance had led to new discoveries but had also increased human suffering. With so few answers, they couldn't know. Still, with so many questions, they could find out and with it achieve the most potential to fulfill that unquenchable desire to discover and explore rocky planets that were hospitable. *Sort of like the human potential that could curtail the activities they contributed to maintaining a hospitable environment*, Tom thought to himself.

Looking around the room, he wondered about the risks and who on the team would prove the riskiest in their plans. He couldn't let any form of cynicism cause him to doubt. He was right to think beyond nano craft concepts. He was glad his team thought so too. Nothing in this world had ever prohibited any civilization from escaping uninhabitable lands except for apathy, disease, and no means. But with the means, hopeful signs for meeting life on new terms meant thinking big.

Tom and his small team discussed how they would determine the number of people joining the crew on each ship. He and his colleagues developed a list of job functions and departments that would be needed. They envisioned a large team of engineers designing and creating a ship capable of withstanding every kind of situation from temperature to meteor showers to taking off and landing on any planet. They would need to consult with engineers and scientists about solar probes and the number of settlers required to maintain the crew. They talked about important questions about how life on the ship would be sustained. It all made him wonder if one of humankind's greatest challenges to date would absorb the best capabilities out of the individuals who were selected to travel and lead to eventual settlements.

This elite engineering team would also be responsible for developing the fuel and the technology to fly at speeds that had never been attained before. This also meant that the crew inside the ships would have to be able to survive unbelievable speeds. It would be necessary to produce an oxygen-sustaining environment that allowed people to breathe without wearing spacesuits all the time. Suppose someone was going to live on a spaceship for years. In that case, they should be able to live a healthy everyday life that included work, recreation, and family. They also needed medical experts and scientists who could treat virtually every kind of disease as well as develop cures for these diseases. No idea was turned away or deemed impossible. Cloning DNA materials, stem cells, and cryopreservation would all be useful, if not ultimately necessary, to achieve future settlement beyond the spaceship. Any new type of research would also be welcome if it were practical to sustain life.

This meant Tom would have to convince the best and brightest minds to join the spaceship. Once he had the main crew assembled, the ship would still need teachers, cafeteria workers, chefs, and maintenance people to perform the everyday functions so that everyone could be safe and enjoy their time on the ship. At times it might prove difficult to live in a closed environment for such a long time. Respect would have to be shown by each individual. A mutiny would not be tolerable on a ship like this. Convincing anyone to leave Earth permanently, not knowing if the plan would succeed, would also prove to be a challenging undertaking.

There was a lot of work to do, and the best and brightest needed to be found. This would be the first of many daily meetings for the next few years.

A week later, the American group met with their colleagues from around the world at the temporary offices in Aurora. All thirty-one of them were excited about the challenges ahead. Although it had only been weeks since the initial FaceTime agreement to move forward with their plans, many had already gotten started on some of the same brainstorming as the American group had. They had decided unanimously to build four huge spaceships that would carry about a thousand people each. The reason for four ships was to keep the human race alive in the event one was destroyed or unsuccessful in launching. One spaceship would be from the United States. The others would be from Russia, Australia, and Germany. All ships were to be built on a high-altitude location to avoid flooding from the oceans.

Tom was already working on a nearby location for building the American ship and for take-off. He shared the news. Everyone approved. After exploring different possible areas of the world to build and launch the other spaceships, they made a decision about the other three locations by a vote. Also, these high-altitude sites could only be approached by plane or driving up a mountain. This provided them with some safety. A commander for each ship was chosen. All four commanders had combat experience as fighter pilots and also experience in spaceship design and training. Tom had been selected to lead the American Team.

Yuri Pavlov was chosen to be the leader of the spaceship taking off from Russia. This spaceship would be taking off from the Ural Mountains. The Ural Mountains are arguably Russia's most famous range. They reach from the Arctic Ocean in the north down some 1,300 miles to Kazakhstan in the south. However, this chain is not very tall; the highest mountain in the range, Mount Narodnaya, only reaches 6,212 feet.

Thomas Dresden was chosen to head the German spaceship, and Ian Thorpe was selected to lead the Australian spaceship. The German ship would be taking off from somewhere in the German Alps located south of Munich. These mountains were part of the famous Swiss Alps. The Australians would take off from the Australian Alps. The Australian Alps are part of what is called the Great Dividing Range in Southeast Australia, the series of mountains, hills, and highlands that runs about 3,500 kilometers (2,175 miles) from Northern Queensland, through New South Wales, and into the northern part of Victoria. These mountains are only about one mile high. All the teams were to cooperate with their design and research findings related to the spaceship. It was agreed that each vessel's commanders should meet with the country's president or ruler where they were going to build their ship. It was hoped that by 2030 the work would be completed, and they could launch. However, it was not necessary for each government to support the project.

Before the meeting was finished, Yuri Pavlov, chosen to be the leader of the spaceship taking off from Russia, got up to make a toast to everyone. "My fellow comrades, I am glad we have gathered here today and developed plans to go deep into space to colonize another planet so that the human race may survive. I believe we have learned a lot about each other. We have already agreed to talk to our presidents and our governments to inform them about the project. I have asked President Putin for the Russian government to support the project and assume all costs related to it. He is totally in favor of doing so. He is prepared to do whatever it takes to make the Russian spacecraft and trip a total success. Some of this money is not all coming from the government. Many Russian oligarchs want to contribute to the spaceship so that they can join us on the journey. They, too, realize that life will end on this planet, and they want to be sure they can go somewhere safe to live with their families. I have agreed to their demands. I think Vladimir Putin also plans to join us onboard our spaceship along with a woman of his choice. This part I do not know about."

Everyone laughed. Putin could have any number of women join him on board.

"Since my government is supporting the project and Vladimir is coming along with us, we demand that the new planet be called New Russia. Vladimir or his successor will be the leader of the planet. That way, we do not have many countries to worry about like on Earth. I know some of you will have a problem with this plan."

We all have problems with this, thought Tom.

"But President Putin is ready to offer each of you five billion dollars to help you build your spaceship in exchange for guaranteeing the name will be New Russia, and he will be its supreme ruler. You do not even have to repay the money. You can use it as you wish. I would like to tell my president that we are all in agreement when I return to Mother Russia. We can modify the plan slightly if you have some concerns. I know some of you may want to call the new home New United States or New Germany, so we will buy the name from you. Do we have an agreement?"

Dr. Burns wondered, *What the heck am I going to do with all this money on a new planet?*

He asked Yuri, "Are you finished talking?" He did not look pleased.

Yuri said, "Dr. Burns, you seem to have some concerns. Let me remind you of several things. First, the Russians were the first country to launch into space. Our cosmonauts are the very best in the world. We beat you at that and your president at the time, John F. Kennedy. We also have done most of the work on the International Space Station. Your country does not even seem interested in this anymore. Without us, a man might never have launched anything. Second, your current president, Donald Trump, is not going to support you. He does not believe in climate change or global warming or anything related to the environment. Many people in the United States who are members of his party also do not believe in climate change. Your president is technically the reason we have to leave Earth so soon. Russia does not intend to honor Donald Trump. Would you expect the new planet to be called Planet Trump? He may be the person responsible for the destruction of the Earth. My president has met Trump several times now and is not very impressed with him. It is his understanding that Russia can rule space as long as your president makes some money from it."

Now Dr. Burns was angry. "Yuri, please sit down and listen to me very carefully. I do not give a damn who goes on your spaceship, and that includes Mr. Putin, and you can be sure I don't give a damn about Donald Trump. I can tell you right now not to bribe me to do something that is just not right. I cannot speak for the Germans or Australians, but that is how I feel. I will raise the money to build our spaceship with the help of friends in the United States who share my concerns about the environment. Next, I want you to know that, yes, Trump has met with Putin on many occasions. Some of these meetings have been formal, and some were more informal, such as at the G-20 summits. Yet, no one in the United States knows what these two agreed to do because there are no official documents that have been made public. There is no way for anyone to believe Putin or Trump about anything they say. It is disappointing that I have to speak so negatively about Trump since I am from the United States, but that is how it is. And finally, none of us may actually ever find a planet, or if we do find one, it might be a hundred years from now. I doubt the name of the new planet will be very important in the scheme of things. If you are going to start making things difficult for everyone, we should probably suspend our relationship. We need to cooperate one hundred percent if we are to make this a successful journey. We can't be loaded down by ultimatums that are hypothetical and may never occur. I do thank you, though, for your being so open about this. Please let President Putin know my position on these matters. If he wants, he can contact me himself, and I would be happy to discuss things with him. Am I clear? We cannot take off successfully if there are doubts about what the mission will be."

Thomas Dresden and Ian Thorpe, the German and Australian commanders, shared their support for Dr. Burns.

Yuri seemed to come unnerved by Tom's outburst.

He said, "Don't get so worked up about this. Of course, we will work with you and cooperate on all matters. I will go home and speak to President Putin to have his guidance on the matter."

"You do that," Tom said.

Yuri abruptly left the room, presumably to contact President Putin.

The Australian commander spoke. "You all know we need the Russians. They have so much technical expertise regarding space travel. Their engineers and scientists have all developed state-of-the-art rockets and equipment. Undertaking this without them as our ally would be foolish. They are currently responsible for the International Space Station as they have flown many missions there. They also have top-notch satellite equipment that can reach far into space and may be utilized by us if possible."

The German commander spoke up. "Germany also has top engineers related to engine-making. But that is mainly for cars such as BMW and Mercedes. We had had a history of war against Russia, especially in World War II, when millions of citizens from both countries were killed. Even NATO is always worried about the Russian army under Putin trying to remake the Soviet Empire. There have been some agitated moments with Mr. Putin and the leaders of other countries. What assurances do you think we will get that he will cooperate with us? None of our presidents are expected to make the journey. We don't want a war in space. It would be devastating considering all the work that will have to be done and all the future discoveries we can make together."

Everything Tom did was focused on building a way to save human life, but he was also wary of the Russians. "I agree with both of you," he said, "and I will make certain that the Russians are part of our team. I just don't want them to give orders like we are all one big happy family under the Russian flag. Really, if we make it to another planet, I probably will not care what you call it. I will probably just be relieved that we made it somewhere."

The Australian captain said, "Amen to that."

The three of them lifted their glasses in another toast.

Moments later, Tom's cell phone rang. He excused himself from the group as the meeting came to an end. Several of the group members got ready to leave. It was one of the top engineers, Bob Jackson. Tom discussed the project with Bob for years, and Bob seemed eager to reach beyond their limitations into the potentially habitable zones 4.2 light-years from Earth. With current technologies, that meant 6,300 years was the answer he'd have to give to anyone if they kept asking, 'Are we there yet?' Perhaps it would take multiple generations, or perhaps they'd be frozen in time, perhaps ...

"So, just checking in. You're laser-beam focused on the fringe of the galaxy at that meeting of yours, aren't ya?"

"Yep. Still trying to make my parents proud, Bob."

"Tom, of course, and I bet you never imagined that even today, you may have been a glimmer in a forefather's eye!"

"Not sure my ancestors had any idea what they wanted for me except for the promise of a better life. Nice to think they were thinking of me, though, Bob."

"Well, hanging on the promises we've all seen broken, you and your team hold a better promise. Proud to be on it. Someday, Sam will be very impressed. Your mission might not be full-scale operational yet, but I bet it's the best use of money around right now. Hell, I bet Stephen Hawking rolls in his grave to look skyward when we do finally take off."

"So, we're the apple of Hawking's eye? So, what's the report on your end? Are we ready to collect some tolls on the future highway beyond our reach on Thursday?"

"Nothing's beyond our reach, Tom, surely you know that! Just checking in to let you know, we're only a call away even if the meeting didn't go well."

"How'd you know?"

"I'm just making educated guesses about some dark matter."

"See you tomorrow. Do we have a full house on Thursday?"

"Very likely, but really, working in a cave, Tom? Investors might be a little bit ambivalent."

"Well calm their nerves. They shouldn't be. It's the best environment for everything we need to build and develop. I'll send you the address later. Of course, it'll be hard to miss."

CHAPTER 7

Postponed

Chapter 7 – Postponed

Tom Burns, Rocky Mountains, CO

It was getting pretty cold in Colorado. The drive from the Rockies back to Aurora was gorgeous, though. Still, it was a bit long for just a meeting with Bob. Determined to get the job done, Tom had been putting his team together faster than ever. Having secured a permanent location for them to work on their mission was a dream come true. He had located a vast and large cavern in the Rocky Mountains. His first recruit had been Bob Jackson, and despite the fact that Bob had requested that he meet with Tom about the investor meeting at the new permanent location two days before the meeting, Tom held the highest confidence in him. Having served in the Army concurrently in the Middle East, Tom knew he could trust Bob with his life. Bob could be depended on to carry out and succeed with the mission if anything happened to him.

Once he arrived at the new undisclosed location, he showed Bob around, and they talked.

"Now look, I hate to break it to you, and I couldn't do it over the phone. But we need to reschedule this meeting on Thursday and meet with the president again. I'm sorry, Tom, but some of the potential investors feel like they need you to try one more time."

"I can't believe this, Bob. It'll be a waste of time!"

"That might be true, but it'll be better to let this group of investors know you tried."

"Fine. When?"

"It's scheduled for Thursday. One of the investors arranged it, mentioning his name, and was able to get the meeting squeezed in due to a last-minute cancellation. It's unusual, I know. And again, I promise, it'll be the last time we try. But it'll appeal to this group of investors. They're all fine for postponing the meeting a week."

***

Washington, D.C.

Two days later, Tom and Bob were escorted to the Oval Office. It bothered Tom to have to meet with the president again. Despite Tom's adverse reaction, he was back to hoping they would gain his support. He knew it wasn't just about him and that there were a lot of people involved and potentially involved in the mission. Still, Tom and Bob really did not expect much from the meeting. They were doing it for the sake of the investors, just in case.

Well, they were absolutely right. Recent history and tradition of deals made in the now stifling Oval Office had been concerned with every American's well-being. Somehow, they had all ended up in the library instead. Tom felt sick at the thought that the well-being of people was simply of historical value. He hid his panic as Bob took the lead to persuade the president of their mission's benefits.

Again, the president made it clear to him and Bob that he would not support the project and that it was a total waste of money. Bob, looking as void as a shot-up burn barrel in an old farm equipment storage yard, sat across from Tom. Their last-ditch effort was a failure. His knuckles white, his chin low, Bob looked around the office as his look of despair grazed the room roughly, filling everything that Tom saw in following his gaze with the past's ghosts. Tom knew neither he nor Bob had served in the Army for this to happen to fellow citizens desperately in need of reassurances. They needed to report back to the investors that someone in the Oval Office cared enough about climate-related endeavors such as theirs. Now it might cost them the investor who'd set up the emergency meeting and maybe others they were supposed to be meeting with today.

Bob looked at the Army's white flag that waved so close to the president's desk, then the Marines' red one. Tom also peered at the battle flags. Campaign streamers vividly hung above both flags, flanking the portrait of Andrew Jackson, where Eisenhower once displayed a beautiful scenic painting, and LBJ had displayed a different portrait of Andrew Jackson. Except, LBpicture buys into limiting civil rights in the tradition of the Jacksonian extension of voting rights to adult white males with land only. Under the current president, Tom watched America become more obviously partisan, breeding an ambivalence and discontent among those who subscribed only to the larger-than-life disproportionality of elites' role in democratic decisions. Ironically enough, Jacksonian democracy helped to inspire the Great Society, but it had also inspired this type of leadership.

Bob appeared agitated. Tom's ability to stay committed in mind and heart was shaken when he saw this. He wasn't one to feel uncertain about anything, and he looked over at his top engineer momentarily to steel himself. Tom saw Bob waver a bit—his smile masking every attempt at bolting out of the room and getting back to the scheduled meeting they had postponed. From the looks of it, the tapping of his foot spoke volumes.

Glad that he'd seen the small gesture, Tom felt more at ease and confirmed in his resolve again. He knew that Bob and the well-meaning investor they might lose had figured that buy-in would help them take the voyage with less on their minds. As he watched Bob's hopes wither, he also saw the president enjoy watching them try again and fail. Tom vaguely remembered feeling the same way when he'd been to Eastern European cities, like in Ternopil's oblast, attempting to get budget approval for much-needed funding to help disabled kids in impoverished areas receive proper medical care through government funding to match all the non-profit money raised. It felt isolating, deeply ensconced in a tradition of red tape that could fit very nicely over every hopeful fundraiser's mouths. There was no attempt at a kind gesture of moral support. It felt like a vast emptiness larger than any galaxy. The hazard of a lost investment and feeling deflated, with no support and discrediting—it was the stuff of nightmares.

In fact, here in the Oval Office that he and Bob had served, his team was told that the government would do everything in its power to discredit the project. Again. Tom figured it had more to do with the fact that the president couldn't use his presidential authority to reenlist two former Army troops and subject them to whatever mission he had in mind for them in space as Commander in Chief. In Tom's estimation, Trump was still more interested in building a wall around its borders and not probably in space. Because of Trump, Tom immediately decided he would have to continue his work in secret.

As they left the White House and returned home, Tom was thankful that the foot-tapping was all that the top engineer had to say about the ordeal. Tom decided they would let the investors know right away and explain that they would do everything necessary to make sure the project's investments made the mission a success despite having tried to secure moral support. Tom also entrusted Bob with employing all the engineers and construction people needed to build the laboratories and spaceship in Colorado.

***

Arriving at their rescheduled meeting in the cavern the following week, Tom met with six billionaires who believed in the project. Robert Clark, who had secured their second meeting, listened to Tom and Bob as they shared the result of their encounter with the president. Robert explained that he'd had a chance to get the president's attention on projects that weren't generally on his radar before. He'd hoped the same would happen here before he made a larger commitment. While he seemed like he might pull out of the project, he was willing to sit through the meeting before making his final decision.

Tom appreciated Robert's patience. "We won't let you down. Promise."

They detailed the next steps and how the funding would be used. The budget being entertained in the millions would allow them to purchase fifty percent of the materials necessary to work on the project. These materials were needed to build the state-of-the-art medical labs, cryo-preservation units, and cloning area. In addition, all of the finest materials required to construct the propulsion system in engineering would be procured. The rest of the funding was steadily coming in from their global technology stock portfolio percentage figured into several wealth flagship assets and investment management advisors' pitches and their Amazon-like platform used primarily for crowdsourcing, and it was projected to continue to, since interest wasn't waning.

They were also promised they would be included as passengers on the ship. It was determined that anyone who was married could bring their spouse with them and their children. However, unless the grandparents were involved in working on the ship, they would be left behind. No pets of any kind would be allowed onboard the vessel, although DNA samples could be collected for cloning when the time was right. They all agreed that it would be an arduous process to select a thousand individuals for the ship. It weighed heavily on Tom. He knew he also needed to employ experts in many different areas.

Anyone who was hired in the first few years or invested would have to swear to keep everything a secret.

"Now when it comes to our families, we certainly know how important it is to not let anyone feel that future decisions as large as this are being made without the consent of our partners. Naturally, we understand, but again, if you at all feel like your spouses will not be interested in this or will somehow breach our agreement, then it is best that you make the right decision for everyone involved. It will be unfortunate to lose you and your investment and involvement in the project, but I'm sure you understand."

Everyone nodded.

"I have told my wife about our plans but not my children. We want them to live healthy lives until Sam graduates from high school in 2027. Sam has shown the most significant promise for being a future commander of the ship. Sophie is not interested in math and science. She seems to want to follow her mother's career as a nurse. That will be useful. Robert is our youngest, and I am still not sure what Robert wants to become. He is only a baby.

"At least one parent in each family at Sam's school is working on the spaceship and our plans. They are all eager to meet you and work alongside you. There is much to be done. After putting together our team of engineers and construction people, our next step is to acquire the expertise of the top medical doctors and researchers we can find. I'm happy to share the most current reports related to DNA studies, cryopreservation, and stem cell research, as we determine how to find the best experts and medical protocols for the voyage.

"And I am pleased to make an announcement. You are among the first to know since you are an integral and crucial part of this groundbreaking stage of our voyage. I have decided that Dr. Helen Sato will be our next recruit. Dr. Sato has been at the forefront of medical research to prolong life and advocate DNA and stem cell research. She has published over a hundred articles related to research on those very topics. If I can convince Dr. Sato to join the team, it will be easier to convince other experts to follow. I have taken the liberty of providing you information about her in the packet we have put together for you. I am hoping to give you much more encouraging news when we speak next."

This seemed to please the investors, all of whom were willing to contribute to the voyage at this stage. Even Robert Clark had become supportive despite seeing the challenge of changing the president's mind fail.

Before the investors left, Tom informed them that he had made an appointment to see Dr. Sato in Chicago the following Monday. Eager to return home, all the investors were pleased to be involved in most stages of the preparations and construction.

Driving back to Aurora, Tom couldn't wait to meet Dr. Sato in person and smiled when he wondered whether she would really mind that he'd left her out of the Oval Office meeting.

The Amazing Dr. Sato

Chapter 8 – The Amazing Dr. Sato

Tom Burns, Chicago, IL

Tom arrived at the University of Chicago, where he was to meet with Dr. Sato. She led the adult cellular therapy program. Her work had led to many innovations in stem cell and DNA research, including the first stem cells that had been created in a nuclear transfer with the potential to treat diseases.

Tom had first seen Dr. Sato at a lecture in 2003 at a worldwide symposium on stem cell research. Dr. Sato was one of the first physicians to advocate for using stem cells to find cures for various diseases such as Alzheimer's and Parkinson's disease, as well as many kinds of cancer. She had explained that stem cells are cells from which all other cells with specialized functions are generated. Under the right conditions in the body or a laboratory, stem cells divide into more cells called daughter cells.

She had been lecturing in front of an audience of nearly 500 people that included many of the leading medical researchers in the world. Fifteen minutes into her lecture, a group of hecklers had started to interrupt her continuously to the point that she could no longer deliver her address. It was clear that these protestors were vehemently against embryonic stem cell research.

One heckler had stood up and asked Dr. Sato, "Why would you want to destroy an embryo that is only three to five days old? This embryo is the beginning of life and must be allowed to grow into a human being. Why do you want to kill babies?"

Another protestor had stood up and added, "Do these embryos not constitute life? How can you, Dr. Sato, decide to kill someone?"

Dr. Sato had not seemed surprised by the hecklers, and she had remained very calm.

The head of the symposium had come up and asked Dr. Sato if she wanted the protestors removed from the lecture, but Dr. Sato had waved him off.

Instead, she had returned to the microphone. She said, "I appreciate your questions and your right to protest your feelings about this controversial topic. I would like to give a response to what you just said if you will promise not to interrupt me during my response. If you interrupt me, I will have no choice but to ask that you be removed, as I would like to address this issue, and I think the audience would like to hear the response. As you know, many of the people in the audience are also interested in using stem cell research to eradicate diseases in the world. At the same time, they do need to understand your position, so I am asking you, will you be quiet while I give my response?"

The protestors had looked at each other and had come to a consensus that they would remain quiet while Dr. Sato resumed talking. A few of them had just decided to walk out.

Suddenly the entire room had fallen into complete silence. It was obvious to Tom that Dr. Sato had been able to gain everyone's trust in the room, at least for the moment, so she could respond to this vital conflict.

Dr. Sato had begun speaking in a calm, mature voice as she paced back and forth in front of the audience. "First, I want to thank everyone for allowing me to respond to this dilemma. As most of you know, the use of stem cells is at the crux of the duty of any research doctor. We must prevent suffering. We also have a responsibility to respect human life's value regardless of that human's age or when you believe life begins. I am sure all of you have wrestled with that dilemma yourself. Some of you may have decided to give up on the idea of stem cell research. That is your right, and your decision should be respected. Some of you have agreed that the moral responsibility to alleviate suffering takes precedence over the moral case for preserving the stem cell that will be destroyed. It is not an easy decision. I want to explain to you how I arrived at my own conclusion. I cannot speak for everyone in the audience when it comes to making a moral decision on this topic. I can only speak for myself.

"First of all, the embryo will be destroyed at a very early stage, which means it cannot grow into a human life, as it has not been placed in the woman. I have to acknowledge that fact. The question is: how do I justify it? Well, the embryo that I use has not yet been placed into a woman's body. The woman who donated the cells has also given me permission to destroy the embryo. Indeed, given that she is the mother of her own cells, I could not destroy them without her consent. Each woman does this on a strictly voluntary basis. While it is not exactly the same thing, it is similar to the process of donating an organ from a live or deceased person. We cannot force anyone to give up an organ.

"As a researcher, I have to think of how many lives I could save using this embryo. My answer to that could be thousands of people might benefit from the research I do with this embryo. In fact, I might be able to save the life of the woman who donates the embryo and the lives of any future children she may have. Imagine if we could find a cure for Alzheimer's disease using stem cells that could be implanted into a human so they would not lose their memories and ability to perform even basic tasks. This would save millions of lives and protect their children from essentially giving up their own lives to take care of their parents. I am almost sure that every child who has a parent with Alzheimer's would gladly donate their own adult stem cells if they could to save the life of their mother or father. However, at this point, adult stem cells do not have that potential. I do wish we could do so, and, in the future, it may happen.

"Therefore, I choose to save millions of lives over the life of one individual. This is not an easy decision to make, and I hope that everyone can understand that this is not an easy decision but one that each of us has to make free of government intervention. If you wish to speak to me about my personal decision or object to what I have just said, that is fine with me. I can honestly look myself in the mirror and say that I would try the alternative if there was an alternative to stem cell research. I would not mind meeting with you in a private setting, and you can air all of your grievances. However, right now, I would like to finish discussing my research with my esteemed colleagues."

While not applauding, the protestors had seen the pain and seriousness in Dr. Sato's body and facial expressions as she spoke and knew that Dr. Sato had really spoken from her heart. They all had nodded to each other and had left the room so that Dr. Sato could finish her lecture.

Tom was extremely impressed by how Dr. Sato had been able to calm and control the audience and then make her point. To Tom, this was the mark of a great leader.

A few years after the symposium, it had become possible to create many stem cells using adult stem cells. They were called a pluripotent stem cells and were pioneered by Shinya Yamanaka's research in Japan. He had received the Nobel Prize for his work. These cells could reproduce endlessly and could be used to replace damaged tissue or facilitate cures for diseases. It was then possible for someone's own stem cells to be used to transplant a body's organ.

With all these new scientific breakthroughs, Tom knew that Dr. Sato was the right person for the job as chief physician because she was interested in their application. The only question was whether she would accept the position.

Now fourteen years later, he stood in her office, ready to find out. Her secretary greeted him. "Dr. Sato is meeting with a colleague to review some research, which will take about an hour. In the meantime, she has asked me to give you a tour of the research facilities while you wait, if that is all right with you?"

"Sure," Tom said. Since research facilities would have to be built, Tom agreed to the tour.

The tour was very enlightening. He was able to view some of the most up-to-date, state-of-the-art stem cell research that was currently happening as well as briefly discuss research with doctors, scientists, and students. He was cautious about the types of questions he asked, trying not to relate them back to any concerns he'd read about spaceflight impacting male fertility. Still, he wanted to better understand what stem cell research had learned about restoring fertility and many other diseases, including heart disease. It was clear that hearts and other organs were not made to last over a hundred years without some kind of problem. The scientists and doctors were in agreement that, with the latest research, there was some promise. It wasn't just at the University of Chicago. Several schools of medicine around the country had found the benefits of injecting stem cells to stimulate sperm production in the case of infertility.

And as he grappled with some of the studies, they were excited about, in particular how stem cells react to different molecules and environments, Tom wondered about the effect of the space environment on stem cells in their development. He kept his questions to himself, knowing it was too soon to be asking anyone. If Dr. Sato accepted his offer to join them, it would be something she would grapple with in researching higher levels of cosmic radiation to estimate their effects and their survival ratios. He wondered if Dr. Sato knew anyone working on NASA's Bioculture System. The research platform was meant to conduct on-orbit experiments to advance the scientific merit and application of new scientific developments that could address the response to living in space at a cellular level. If not, he'd put them in touch somehow. The expertise would be invaluable, and the practical need priceless. He was sure one of the investors at the meeting yesterday had brought up SpaceX's launch of the system.

Lost in thought, he realized that he'd been walking through aisles of electron microscopy technologies that jolted him back. "Are these part of your cellular studies into the application of the cryopreservation of cells and tissues for long-term storage? I recently read a study by the National Institute of Health that supports the possibility of reversible cryopreservation through vitrification of cells."

"Indeed, do you have your cryoprotectant on? Don't stand too close!" one of the doctors joked.

Tom smiled. "I suppose I better get to know some of the humor here if I'm going to avoid getting a cold shoulder," he joked back.

"Well, the folks in cytometry might still be able to analyze whether you might recover the use of your shoulder, but it's a little bigger than our stem cell colonies, so best to stand back for now." He sincerely hoped that Dr. Sato would be able to answer many of the questions that were tumbling around inside his mind. They'd have time, but with little proven, it seemed they'd be stuck in the labs eternally without some entrepreneurs ready to move beyond living life in a frozen state waiting for lab results.

After thanking the secretary for the tour, Tom was led to Dr. Sato's office. Her office was not that large. It was rather like any typical faculty office found on a college campus. Her room had several medical journals on the shelves. Her degrees hung prominently on the walls, particularly her medical degree from Harvard.

Dr. Sato stood up and shook Tom's hand. Dr. Sato looked like she had not aged a day since Tom had seen her at the symposium. She was only five feet, five inches tall and weighed about one hundred and thirty pounds. For someone who was forty-five years old, she looked remarkable.

"What can I do for you?" she asked. She offered him a seat in front of her desk as she sat down behind her desk. Sunlight streamed into the room from the window behind her.

"Dr. Sato, I have been told that you are the leading medical expert on various topics, including stem cell research and DNA experiments. I had the honor of attending one of your lectures fourteen years ago and came away very impressed with you."

Dr. Sato nodded and said, "So you saw me with the protestors. Not a day goes by without someone bringing that up."

Tom acknowledged that "Yes, I saw that and was amazed at your ability to get the protesters to shut up."

Dr. Sato laughed.

He then stated, "As you may or may not know, a meeting of scientists and experts in the environmental field took place in Australia years ago. At this meeting, based on scientific research, it was decided that life on Earth is going to disappear shortly. I have been selected to put together a team that will build the finest spaceship to search for a new planet. I am sure that you know it will require many years of travel before we possibly find such a place to live. I would like to hire you to lead the medical research facilities as we travel the galaxies. I am sure that you probably think I am crazy now, but I need to know if you believe anything I am saying. We have many funding streams in place and have secured a location for the ship's development and launch. Obviously, if I am right, all of your research will not be enough to save Earth. From the looks of the lab facilities and the advances in technologies, it is possible that we should expedite the application of many of these advances rather than cultivate knowledge for its own sake. And I could put you in touch with some people I know involved in NASA's Bioculture System, I—"

"I am very familiar with their work."

"Good, then you know that I have a million questions, and I hope you can develop better answers that meet our advancing time schedule."

Dr. Sato was silent for a moment. Then she spoke, "Thank you for coming to visit me. I admire your dedication to your research. First of all, I believe that we are coming to a period on Earth when life may become extinct. Humans have made far too many mistakes in their quest to enjoy life. I am not sure we will be able to correct all the mistakes we have made in the past, so I do concur that you are correct in what you say. While I agree with you about that, I do have many questions that you will have to answer before I can even think of going on a trip like this and leaving everything behind."

"Ask away, I will do my best to answer your questions."

"Number one, do I get to recruit my own team of experts, and how many of them do you think we can take on board?"

"We expect to have a total of a thousand people on each of the four ships. The other leaders of the three ships will recruit their own medical experts along with their crew. These leaders are from Australia, Germany, and Russia. I expect there will be about twenty experts who will work with you daily or eighty on all four ships. You will be able to share any research findings and data with the other three ships. You can design your own lab facilities and DNA storage facilities. Since your work is of the utmost importance on this trip, I will promise you I will do my very best to meet all of your facility needs."

"Thanks for saying that," she replied. "Now I need to know: how long would we be traveling? Will we ever return to Earth? What are the plans?"

Tom thought to himself, *This is going to be the hard part now.*

"We are not planning on returning to Earth. I expect we will need to live on the spaceship for hundreds of years, perhaps. I am hopeful all the preparations will be made in about ten years. We need ten years to build the ship to the specifications that you and other department heads need. Once we leave the solar system, we will try and find a planet that can sustain life. This is why your research is so important. We may need people to live for several hundreds of years, if possible. The question is: do you believe this is possible?" Tom asked, emphasizing the word *you.*

Dr. Sato said, "I do believe we can extend a person's life for a long time with the assistance of stem cells, cloning, and other research, but exactly how long, I do not know. Certainly, there may be a problem living for five hundred or a thousand years. Eventually, all of your organs would need to be replaced. One thing that has made my research difficult has been all the government FDA regulations and politics that limit stem cell research and cloning. I need your promise that my colleagues and I will not be encumbered by restrictions on what needs to be done. Since many travelers will likely start families on board, we will need obstetricians and doctors who can deliver babies. We can also use cloning and combine DNA into an embryo. One thing I do not believe in right now is immortality. I believe that everyone must die eventually. Are you trying to create an immortal person?" Dr. Sato asked.

"No, definitely not," Tom said. "We plan to use stem cells, cloning, and cryopreservation to sustain each person's life as long as possible. I am sure our officers will give you free discretion as far as stem cell research. Cloning will only be used when a person dies. When we clone someone, we need to ensure that the person's memory will be preserved in the clone. That means we are going to have to take DNA samples quite frequently to preserve their memories. I have heard that it may be possible to insert memories into a person. That might be quite useful when a person is sleeping in cryopreservation. It is not worth cloning someone if they have to start learning everything all over again. I would even consider a brain transplant if that is possible. For that to happen, we will have to create lab space to preserve brains. We can also grow brains with stem cell research. Once we reach a destination for everyone to live, we can decide whether to continue extending each person's life on board.

"By the time we arrive or live on a new planet, I think people will need to make their own decision about what they want to do. I do not believe right now that immortality for everyone is a good thing. There would not be a need to procreate with immortality, and thus, there might not be any new ideas. My main concern, though, is we need the expertise of many individuals if we're to succeed in finding a new planet. Do you agree or disagree with me?"

"I do agree with what you have said. Personally, I do not want immortality for myself. I want to continue my research, which probably will take years to do some of the things you want. Inserting memories into a person's brain will require the production of a nanochip. When the chip is placed into the correct spot in the brain, perhaps some chemicals could release the memories which will be absorbed by the brain cells. I also want to marry and have offspring to carry on my work or develop different skills. I have no idea if I would want to be cloned. However, given what you have said, it may have to happen. I do not think my body would withstand a thousand years in space. And then there are the questions surrounding fertility in these unchartered environments."

"Yes, I agree with you again," Tom said. "The big question is, are you going to accept my offer? One more thing you need to know before you answer. There will be no salaries. Everyone will work to ensure that the trip succeeds. If you think about it, there will be no banks on the ship and no banks on the new planet."

Dr. Sato laughed. "I was wondering about that. What would I do with all the money I made? I guess there won't be any. Ok, now am I going to accept your offer?"

She stood up with her hands behind her back and looked out the window of her office. Then, she turned back to Tom. He thought for sure she was going to turn him down. Instead, she turned the question on him, "Why should I accept your offer, Dr. Burns, and what makes you think others will also accept your offer when I recruit them?"

Dr. Burns was actually ready for that specific question. "I will get right to the point. Your research and the research of other famed scientists may never be successful if you remain on Earth. Most of you will probably die before your research is completed. By coming with me, you will all be able to see firsthand where your research leads and all the good things that can be accomplished with it. After all, we know that no human being has been cloned on Earth yet. Red tape by governments worldwide has forced issues like this to be permanently postponed all too frequently."

"Dr. Burns, I am so flattered that you would consider me as your choice to head up the medical research facilities. It is going to be difficult for me to give up my research here in Chicago. We have a series of breakthroughs that will be important in the years to come that I may need to still participate in before we leave to benefit from their potential application and results. Yet, I, too, have noticed the changes in the environment and do wonder how long this planet can sustain life. For that reason, I am going to accept your offer as long as I can select my colleagues and they can take their families on board."

He reached out to shake her hand. They shook hands warmly. He told her to keep in touch and let him know the names of the people she selected as well as her designs for her labs so they could incorporate them into our building plans. She agreed that six months should be sufficient time to do this. Tom felt relieved.

"By the way, you may thank me for not including you in one of our recent meetings. You are more than welcome to participate in future meetings. I'll always include you so you can stay informed. But I bet you are happy that we didn't have this conversation before meeting with the president twice. We were hoping to at least get his moral support and try to reverse his stance on the environment and climate change, but it was fruitless, to say the least. Almost lost an investor over it, but he came around."

"Yes, you're right. Thanks for not including me. I'd rather deal with the protestors like I did that day at the symposium. It's just been one troubling policy or rant or rally after another."

Propulsion

Chapter 9 – Propulsion

Tom Burns, Rocky Mountains

Tom was in better spirits knowing that Dr. Sato was willing to believe in the project and become part of the effort. It was one less pressing issue to handle in making the launch a reality. Now, he needed to focus on some of the technical matters.

He wasn't a man of creature comforts, but he sat down in his father's comfortable recliner momentarily. He'd never appreciated it when his father was around. He'd recoiled from it. Its significance to a bomber pilot escaped him, until now. Sitting in the chair, he felt an overwhelming desire to weep. Visions of his father's suffering engulfed him. The armchair's comfort served as a safe place, a place on Earth that hadn't been shattered by bombs, by Agent Orange, by reckless political ambitions and coverups. He imagined for a moment what it would feel like to bring this chair to space. He imagined keeping it as a place where he could think and remember the life he once had and passing the recliner on to Sam for those moments of comfort that he would someday need. He'd try to make it happen.

Sam's face, when he'd returned home from the second meeting at the Oval Office, and this chair was two things he'd never forget when he looked back at how they ever managed to move forward with these plans. Despite how traumatized he felt by his experience at the Oval Office, he knew that Sam would always recall that it hadn't stopped him. Tom laughed momentarily, recalling that Sam had looked at his dad like a space oddity—one of the blobs from a 1950s movie, a wishy-washy sequence that was cornier than frightening. Now, he felt like he was standing on firmer ground. His team was coming together despite the Oval Office's sustained effort to revert everyone to comfortable beliefs of an unexamined life framed solely within the context of stock markets, buried facts, and unbridled bandits. These were unbelievable times.

The spaceship was going to be the largest ever produced, and the propulsion system and engines needed to be capable of transporting them wherever they wanted to go. As soon as they decided to build the Colorado spaceship, Tom and Bob agreed that they needed to find the best experts available to develop a propulsion and fuel system that would allow for interstellar travel. They decided to interview Carson Newman and Dorothy Sullivan after reviewing the work of about fifty top propulsion experts.

Carson came highly recommended. He was a graduate of Cal Tech and had worked in NASA and in the private industry, developing three generations of rocket propulsion systems. Dorothy had graduated number one in her class from MIT in Boston and had spent several years working for NASA.

Tom would be meeting with them in a few hours. He got up from his father's recliner and sent off a few emails before heading out the two-hour drive door. He arrived ten minutes early. When Bob, Carson, and Dorothy showed up, he introduced everyone.

Tom said, "First of all, we really value your expertise in undertaking this huge project. We need to hear your ideas on how to proceed to do what is necessary to ensure this project's success. We are talking about a huge spaceship, which has never been built before in history. You should know three other spaceships are being built in different locations in the world. At this moment, I cannot divulge their locations. If you are hired, you will get this information. As I am sure you know, previously, the largest spaceship seated under ten people, and they were on the ship for a limited amount of time. We will need a spaceship for a thousand people who may have to be traveling in space for over one hundred years. Certainly, no one has seen a ship like this. This means we are going to need to build the largest, most powerful, and best propulsion system ever. It also means that we probably have to work around the clock with various crews if we want to launch by 2030. I would like to hear some of your ideas about accomplishing this."

Carson said, "Thank you for inviting us to meet with you. This project sounds fascinating. We will need several different propulsion systems or one that can be adjusted for various conditions. This will include the most powerful system ever made to get the spacecraft into orbit. It will need to overcome all the gravitational forces attempting to pull us back to Earth. To do this, I suggest we may need to build many rockets that will be attached to the main ship. At a certain point, after we take off, these rockets will be detached and probably remain in orbit or fall back to Earth. The rockets will only be used to get us into orbit.

"Once we are in orbit, we have to rely on our propulsion systems to get us to the next galaxy. On the main ship, the propulsion systems would have to be adjustable. We need the spacecraft to be able to navigate through gravitation fields, magnetic fields, electromagnetic waves, solar wind, and solar radiation. We need to build a spaceship that can change velocity at a moment's notice. This is going to be very difficult with such a massive spacecraft. We will also need to be able to create enough momentum to speed up the spacecraft. Then, once we have left the solar system, our goal is to be able to create a ship that will have a sustained impulse."

Then he explained to Tom what was necessary to travel in space. "Making sure fuel can be recycled is essential. There is no telling if we will be able to find elements that we could convert into energy in either space or another planet."

Dorothy, who had done a lot of the work on newer model spaceships, nodded her head in agreement with what Carson explained. She also had some suggestions for the propulsion systems. Both of them estimated it might be necessary for around eight rockets with an equal thrust to be attached to boost the spacecraft and lift it into orbit. The spaceship could weigh as much as 50,000 to 100,000 tons.

Dorothy said, "Think of the Oasis Cruise ship built by Royal Caribbean. That ship holds six thousand passengers. Imagine trying to lift that ship off the ground. That would require an amazing amount of force. These rockets would be unmanned and controlled by the space-craft. We have to determine the kind of fuel or fuels the spaceship will use. It may be possible to make more through chemical reactions, but that is not guaranteed yet. Failure to recycle the energy might result in a motionless spacecraft that cannot go anywhere or be forced to wander aimlessly until by some gravitational pull, it is forced to land or crash on an uninhabited planet or asteroid. The more fuel we carry, the heavier the ship will be, making it harder to attain the speeds we need. That is another consideration to think about.

"We may also be able to use some of the work by the late Stephen Hawking to fly the spacecraft. His work focused on moving a rather small spaceship via light beams. There are several other possibilities, of course. Still, so far, no scientist has developed a fuel to fly a spaceship this big at the desired speed. Another possibility is to build a Kugelblitz engine that will increase our chances of flying at warp speed through a black hole that the engine will create. This will enable interstellar travel. We still have to build a warp bubble around the ship to protect us as we travel at such speeds. This is going to take an extraordinary amount of research. We can't be sure this will be ready before we leave. Unfortu-nately for Stephen Hawking, he acquired ALS and died from it."

Tom thought about what Carson and Dorothy were saying. Still, he also wondered if Dr. Sato's stem cell research could have saved Hawking if the government would have encouraged or allowed it.

Dorothy continued, "It is also necessary to figure out if we could use his research to innovate our speed limits on such a massive spaceship. These innovative scientists were working towards finding a way to reach neighboring planet systems. It was planned to fly at ultra-light travel or at one hundred million miles an hour or even faster. At one hundred million miles an hour, it would take perhaps twenty years to reach Alpha Centauri, where there may be some habitable planets. Although Alpha Centauri is the nearest star system to us, it still lies roughly 4.37 light-years away. That is equal to more than 25.6 trillion miles, or more than 276,000 times the distance from Earth to the sun. If we can fly at five hundred million miles an hour, we can do it in four years. It has not yet been done. We are not even close to accomplishing that. We are at the very beginning of new research to get spaceships to fly at warp speed, which would be best if we can make it happen. We are going to need engine specialists, mathematicians, computer experts, and engineers to figure this out.

"Also, if we can fly at such supersonic speeds, we need to ensure that the spacecraft's integrity remains intact. This has been one of the main problems for several rockets that blew up after takeoff, if you remember. The outside of the spacecraft or heat shields will probably have to withstand extreme heat and cold. We cannot have any part of the spaceship start to burn up, causing the whole ship to break apart. When we have figured out the best way to maximize our speed, we will let you know. At the current speed of a spacecraft, which is Mach 4, it would take over a hundred years to travel that far. What we will try to do is develop warp speed."

"Wow," Tom said. "If you can ensure we lift off without any problems and get us going at warp speed, it would be absolutely fantastic. We would like you to start working as soon as possible. We can provide you with the finest facilities and laboratories to concentrate on your work. Several individuals are funding us, so money is not an issue. If there is anything you need, just ask for it. Please invite the best people you can find to work on this. Without your success, we cannot launch. Are you ready to accept the positions? You are both very qualified, and I know I can speak for Bob in saying so."

Bob nodded in agreement.

Both Carson and Dorothy excitedly agreed to join the team. They had worked together in the past at NASA. Besides, there was so much work to do, and most of it had never been accomplished before.

Tom left it to them to recruit a full team of experts and develop possible plans for the propulsion systems and other requirements for traveling at such speeds. They were also told to work on a new space shuttle that could leave and return quickly to the spacecraft. Each shuttle needed to be built to hold about six to eight people. They had to be capable of entering a planet's atmosphere without burning up, landing on a planet's surface, and taking off again. The shuttles were needed since they did not want to land the spacecraft on a world that was not habitable or might break up upon landing, dooming everyone living on the wrong planet or one that could not sustain life. When the shuttle landed, tests could be conducted on that planet's atmosphere and soil or rock. They could also check to see if there was water. It could also be used to fly near the spacecraft to inspect any damage or for astronauts or others to make repairs to the outside of the vessel. This space shuttle would be similar to those previously built by NASA but capable of doing much more.

Bob said, "We'll need to test this space shuttle before we launch."

They all promised to keep in constant contact as they progressed in their work.

It was one thing to make some bio-engineered food for a voyage with no arable land and attempting to thrive on a ship. It was a lot more complicated to finish the spaceship. It would require a lot of sweat and tears.

***

Back at home, Tom stood in front of his refrigerator, glancing at magnets from all over Colorado that his family had collected over the years. His wife was already in bed. Just a small late-night snack would settle his nerves. He knew that no one on the team would do anything to embarrass him in making the mission happen. Despite this hopefulness, he still wondered how his own government would attempt to discredit his project on Twitter or in conversations with many men and women who dreaded new views. He wondered what pioneers had once carried in wagons across the land and how much they sacrificed for a better chance that lay ahead of them one danger after another. At least they'd have refrigeration.

Cooking for a Thousand

Chapter 10 – Cooking for a Thousand

Tom Burns, Aurora, CO

Sitting in his office at home, he was pleased with the team that was coming together. He was sad that he wasn't around to spend more time with his son. But the amount of preparation demanded all of his attention if they were actually going to be able to succeed. Now, Tom was happy to almost have a chef and nutritionist on board.

He thought about his son's eating habits. *All Sam has on his mind is baseball and hot dogs, it seems.* The last time they indulged in that type of fun, the TV had broken into their bonding time. The political ineptitude and focus on creating more tension in the world weren't the only things that had stirred Tom into action. Strategies girded only the ones already circling themselves with massive hidden reserves. It was now once again a favorite American pastime of the well-to-do.

He couldn't believe how often his mind wandered to the horrifying political climate lately. He focused again on a few chef candidates he'd considered. The ship people weren't going to get a lifetime supply of hot dogs, even if Sam could eat those for every meal. Sure, there were plenty of International Space Station tips to follow, but Tom hadn't the slightest idea how to get there.

The spaceship was going to need an excellent chef who could make genetically engineered food. Everything they ate would have to be produced or engineered. After speaking with several well-known chefs, Tom had realized none of them had a clue how to make meals this way. Tom had decided to look for a chef and a nutritionist and a botanist to develop tasty meals and prepare them. Nutrition would be vital on the mission.

Tom's cell buzzed. It was a call from a Chicago area code. He hadn't expected a call from Dr. Sato. He answered.

"Hello, Dr. Burns?"

"Yes?"

"This is Luis Gonzales. We spoke a week ago—"

"Of course, I remember, Luis."

While visiting Chicago to meet with Dr. Sato, he had met Luis Gonzales, a chef who worked at a Mexican restaurant chain for ten years. Tom had just happened to eat there one night and had enjoyed the food. He had chicken enchiladas, rice, and beans. He had asked the waiter to introduce him to the chef.

Ten minutes later, Luis had come out, and they had shaken hands. When Tom had asked him about his background, Luis had seemed hesitant to answer. Tom had immediately known that Luis was probably an illegal immigrant who had managed to escape detection under Trump. Tom had assured him he was not working for the government or ICE and not going to do anything to harm Luis. He was looking for a chef to come with him into space to serve food daily for a thousand people until they found a new home.

Luis had said, "What do you mean space? What's the catch?"

"The catch is that there will not be regular food onboard as you have at this restaurant. All the food will either have to be genetically engineered or possibly grown on the ship using scientific methods. Of course, you will have your own kitchen and have to serve a thousand people daily, so I doubt you are going to be able to make elaborate seven-course meals. Plus, you might have to do this for a hundred years or so. Don't worry about a hundred years. Just worry about the food."

Jose had replied, "I don't care where I go as long as I can call it home and be among good amigos and amigas. Let me tell you about myself. Since I started working as a chef fifteen years ago, I have mainly cooked Mexican cuisine. I started off as a busboy and then worked my way to an assistant chef, and now I am the head chef of this nice Mexican place. However, I can cook dishes from a variety of cultures such as Chinese and Japanese."

Tom was glad that Luis was following up with him now. He wasn't sure whether or not Luis was interested beyond entertaining the thought. He walked into the kitchen to make himself some lunch.

"So, have you given it some thought, Luis? And can you cook hot dogs?"

"I have and, I'm pretty good at hot dogs. Some people say it's the meanest dog they've ever seen, and they love each bite!"

"Good, my son—"

"Say no more ... I know. The simpler, the better. Anyway, yes, your invitation intrigues me. I wanted to give you a call and ask you a few questions. Will we ever return to Earth? I do not have any family left, as I was too scared to marry and have children, not knowing what the future would hold. Many people I know have been sent back to Mexico or other countries to a life that is not desirable or financially acceptable. They may be alive, but they are basically dead."

Tom said, "I respect your answers and questions. You seem to be a real nice guy. I want you to know that whatever we discuss is confidential, and I will not disclose this conversation to anyone. We won't be returning. On the plus side, however, you can never be deported back to Earth. There will be no ICE in space. The trip will take many years, and you will be very old, but in good health with our medical team on board. You can experiment with making new kinds of food. I do not think everyone will want to eat Mexican food or hot dogs every day for the rest of their lives."

"Hmmm. Will I be able to hire my own staff, with your approval? It takes more than one chef to cook for a thousand people."

"Of course. You will need to hire a variety of chefs to provide the food."

"Dr. Burns, you have yourself a deal. When do I start, and what is the salary?"

Tom said, "You will start as soon as the spaceship is ready and we start moving people on board. This will take a little time. The salary is zero. But don't worry. My salary is also zero. Everything will be provided for free as long as you do your job. One thing you will not have to worry about is how you're treated. If anyone thinks negatively about others, they are not going with us. President Trump treated people with the utmost disrespect. On this ship, we all treat each other with the utmost respect. There will be no discrimination or racial problems on board. Everyone must work together as one big team or family if we want to survive this trip. That will be drilled into everyone's minds."

They ended the call. Tom noticed that he'd boiled all the water out of his pan before he could steam his broccoli.

"Shoot."

He added more water, put the pan back on the burner, and lowered the heat. He'd eat eventually. He sat down at his kitchen table and wrote down all the other people he needed to contact to set up some time to discuss the launch. Sam was going to be home from school in a couple of hours, and Tom's wife wanted them to spend a bit more time that evening putting together one of Sam's third-grade science projects.

Sam had told his dad that he wanted to design a planet to study planet habitability eventually. But first, he was supposed to work on a diagram about the stages in the life cycle of a star, show the sequence of stellar evolution, and be able to simply explain the lifecycle of massive stars, extending it to focus on what it might mean to live on Earth later. They needed to determine the mass of the three stars that Sam chose for his school activity and figure out what they would become either thru illustrations or using objects and creating a video.

Tom couldn't wait. He'd been waiting for the chance to work with his son on it for a while. They spent the evening getting everything ready for his presentation. Sam was excited and appeared confident about his video.

***

A few days later, he met Michelle Nixon, a nutritionist employed at Tom's exercise club. She had recently earned her master's degree in nutrition from Arizona State University's online program. She also had no family, as both of her parents had died tragically in an automobile accident. She was very young but had a lot of enthusiasm.

Michele asked Tom, "Have you hired a chef yet? I know we will be working closely together, and we will need to compromise on certain things and get along.

Can I meet or call him?"

Tom said, "I have hired a chef who is an expert in cooking Mexican food and will be working to develop as much bio-engineered food as possible. I do hope you two get along well. I love to eat balanced diets but once in a while like to eat junk. My son loves hot dogs, and Luis, my chef, promised me he will make them for my son and anyone else who enjoys them."

"Hot dogs! My god that is not very nutritious food. Do you know about the studies that show that hot dogs lead to cancer, not to mention horrible stomach aches?"

Tom was speechless for a moment. Michelle was right about the nutritional value of hot dogs. Still, Sam loved them and they were part of American culture.

After about thirty seconds, he responded. "You are right about eating hot dogs. However, my son loves hot dogs, and Luis promised me he will make them. You can work this out with Luis and my son. Obviously, we do not want food poisoning and other gastro problems to occur very often. Still, we also need to enjoy our food. I will say that if Dr. Sato, my chief physician, believes there will be long-term negative effects of eating certain foods with no way to cure whatever diseases take place, then perhaps we will need to remove the particular food from our diets. Hopefully, if we eliminate hot dogs, Sam will be old enough to understand why."

Michelle said, "I guess I will have to educate people on this spaceship about what foods they should eat and what they should avoid if they want to make it to a new galaxy. Hopefully, the task will not be too frustrating for someone like myself."

Tom said, "I am sure you can work it out with everyone on board, and we will all enjoy working with you."

They shook hands. Tom suggested she contact Jose and start planning what kind of equipment and ingredients they would need on board that could be easily reproduced.

Next, Tom figured out which botanist he wanted to hire. Zeke Smith was an assistant professor at Johannesburg University in South Africa. Tom had heard about him from a mutual acquaintance that was involved in funding efforts mostly. Zeke had published several articles on plant genetics and was an expert in some rare plants that provided nutrition as well as medical benefits. Zeke had been to the jungle in Africa as well as to the rainforest on the Amazon River. He was willing to join the mission when they initiated the conversation recently.

Tom called him to sort out more of the details.

"Hi, Zeke. I am looking forward to hearing some of your ideas and answer any questions you may have."

Zeke said, "It would be exhilarating to see new plant species when we reach a new planet or have the ability to create new kinds of plants. I am hoping to grow small plants that will provide a full day's nutrition and energy."

"Great. That sounds like a great contribution. I understand you also had a concern you needed to share with me."

"Yes. I'm concerned about my pet tortoise. This tortoise is four years old but has a life expectancy of two hundred years."

"Well, I don't want any animals on board. Does it have to go with us?"

"It does. My tortoise is like a son to me. I actually knew his parents. He has a calming effect on me."

"Look, you will be a valuable asset to our team. I'm sure we can work this out. I'll let you bring the tortoise. There really is no choice."

If Tom wished to have Zeke come on board, the tortoise was coming. "You'll have to take care of him, and we'll make sure to consider his needs in the design plans for your space. Please let us know what his habitat needs to be, of course, considering that we're limited in terms of space. He'll have to be solely your responsibility."

Zeke readily agreed. "Thanks, Tom. Absolutely. And thanks for thinking of me. I look forward to the challenge."

"Welcome on board!" After they made plans to check in with each other on email in the next few days, he hung up. Now that Tom had the food and bio-genetic team experts he wanted, he felt that the recruitment process was coming along well.

***

At least it was going well until he got a call from Luis a month later. Luis got a call from INS. Someone had found out about his illegal status and had notified him that he would be deported in two weeks. He was forced to quit his job at the restaurant. The only thing he could think of was to call Tom.

Tom flew to Chicago immediately and told Luis to pack his belongings, close his checking account, and throw away his cellphone and credit cards so that he could not be traced. They drove to Colorado to the space center where Luis immediately moved into an apartment near Tom's apartment.

Within a couple of weeks, Luis had settled into his new home. He confided in Tom, "At first, I thought it had been you who had reported me, but then I asked myself why you would do that. I decided to call you. Why would you make up such a fantasy story about a trip in outer space? I am forever in your debt for helping me not be deported."

Tom said, "The way to pay off your debt is to work hard and feed the people on the spaceship when it's built and help keep everyone fed and healthy during the building and development stages. I've never built a kitchen in a cave. Still, it's looking pretty amazing despite the fact that we needed to speed things along, given your predicament. It outrages me! We have some of the most stupid immigration laws anywhere, even though we are a nation of immigrants. I am sorry that the INS caused you such anxiety."

It seemed like the laws of the land in terms of immigrants were having some sort of Doppler effect on Tom, focusing on some of his chosen candidates. He hoped that there'd be no more passing threats he'd have to worry about. He also wished that any politically motivated discrediting taking the place of their mission had nothing to do with it. He buried the thought. He had more important things to think about and chase down. Luis was safe, at least.

Not a Gambling Man

Chapter 11 – Not a Gambling Man

Tom Burns, Rocky Mountains

Tom watched his children grow in 2017 and 2018. Taking the Rocky Mountain Space Center's drive to check on recent progress in turning the cave into a working facility for building and scientific testing gave him a chance to think through current events and how so much had changed for the worse. While his mission seemed to keep him going, the news was continually sickening him. In the first two years of the Trump presidency, natural disasters had occurred more frequently and with higher intensity. Hurricane Harvey in Houston had caused the most significant flooding ever seen in Texas. Tom remembered watching the television as the now-famous Cajun Navy had brought people to safety.

This was followed by two more major catastrophic hurricanes, Maria and Irma, that devastated Puerto Rico and Florida, causing billions of dollars of damage, making millions of people homeless. Hurricanes Maria and Irma brought home climate change in a drastic way to Dominica, the British Virgin Islands, and other islands. People living there understand how dramatic and catastrophic climate change can be. When Tom had spoken with climate survivors, it was not just about rebuilding homes. Their livelihood was also being destroyed. The local fishermen had to go further and further out to catch fish.

Trump had visited both Florida and Puerto Rico, sites devastated by the hurricanes. He had seemed more interested speaking out on the fact that spending all the money to help United States citizens was going to hurt his budget and did not seem to care about the number of deaths that occurred, which was probably in the thousands. Trump did not even mention some of the Caribbean Islands that were almost completely destroyed. He constantly feuded with other government officials over what needed to be done to rebuild communities. Puerto Rico was struck incredibly hard.

Tom had watched on television as the president had thrown paper towels to the locals in Puerto Rico. What were they going to do with paper towels? Were they supposed to clean up the flood with them? The clean-up process was not handled well. People were left without electricity for months, and water was not being delivered to the right locations. Even months after this disaster, much of the island needed to be rebuilt. The following year, Michael, the strongest hurricane ever to make landfall, occurred in Florida as a category 5. Most storms slow up as they near land, but Michael sped up. Mexico Beach lost just about every structure in town. The hurricane in North Carolina, which preceded Michael, had brought the worst flooding in North Carolina's history. Thousands of livestock animals had been lost in the storm.

What would happen if an island was repeatedly hit by level 5 hurricanes? The waters of the Caribbean had become warmer every year. Other islands were totally destroyed by the major storms. It is a wonder that anyone survived them. Many Puerto Ricans were forced to relocate to Florida, New York, or other places in the United States.

It seemed the government was not able to handle one disaster at a time. What would happen if ten disasters coincided? How could anyone abide by such a lack of response and inappropriate divestment threat-assessments and preventive measures? How could dwindling support for tackling massive disasters with practical solutions in private-public partnerships continue to ignore the fact that his children may not be able to reach their middle age with the number of life-threatening dangers they would face?

Dr. Burns was worried that his children would not even reach middle age due to the harmful effects that the environment could face. Problem sets had been devised by NASA and STEM advocates to introduce school kids to ongoing amazing discoveries and the fields of mathematics, earth science, robotics, and, Tom hoped, interstellar molecular and travel studies beyond science fair stand-outs. Yet, people, guided by the same fears about leaving the safety of our solar system and their deep pockets, chose to foment apathy. They were too attached to believing that it was impossible that the creator of this Earth would ever let it meet its own destruction.

Tom thought, *Certainly, by now, many people from different faiths, beliefs, and patterns of thinking welcome informed decisions and better warning systems even if climate changes were part of God's plan and unavoidable. Humans had to meet the challenges. These decisions needed to acknowledge that they were based in fact and on predictions and warnings that have been thoroughly studied. People were to be held responsible for their own contributions to the changing climate and its impact on life on Earth.* The gamble was too tenuous, and Tom wasn't a gambling man in this regard. It was irrational to cover up climate change studies when it could harm so many. It often reminded him of the historical mistakes that were irreversible.

The damage would be done and who cared where the dice fell. However, the president had grandchildren but did not seem to care one little bit about them, except for the holiday photos, he supposed, to temper his image. Trump appeared to believe that money was the answer to everything. Tom and others thought it was going to be the end of everything.

But Trump seemed much more comfortable with losing money and critical investments than Tom ever would be. He likened the president to a baron beyond the pale who drove people away from their lands, causing more tension, calling the shots and ignore preventive warnings, technological capabilities, and smart policies. He was more invested in the traditional scope of life; everything needed to be stapled down, the same gas stations on every corner with no alternatives.

The absurdity hit Tom in the head daily as he continued with his plans. Despite the fact that the labs out in California had been working on more efficient engines and alternative fuels, the economy of scale mass production barred them viable entry points.

If his own children wouldn't reach middle age, then how could he reflect on the past and not see that the dreams of the people who had sacrificed so much for a better future now hinged on a crapshoot. It made him reminisce about all the sacrifices his parents and grandparents had made and the life it allowed him to build. Tom's grandparents—Dick and Martha Burns from Odesa in Ukraine—had moved to the United States to seek a better life for themselves and their family. His father, William, had served in the Vietnam War as a bomber pilot. He had flown thirty-two missions in North Vietnam and had won several medals of honor, including the Air Force Cross. When he had returned from duty, William married Shelley Gordon, and she had given birth to Tom in 1975, their only child. They had settled in New York, where Tom had attended New York's public schools.

It was determined at an early age that Tom showed exceptional ability in the sciences and mathematics. As a result, he was sent to the Bronx School of Science, where he had graduated at the age of fifteen. His perfect scores on the SAT College Boards allowed him to obtain a full scholarship to the California Institute of Technology. He had graduated second in his class in aeronautical and environmental engineering. While he was there, he was captain of the rowing team, setting school records and placing well in the NCAA rowing championships.

Tom remembered the night he met his future wife at a college party at Cal Tech. It was a Saturday night bowling social at an off-campus bowling center. With a group from Fremont College, Sarah was already bowling when Tom had shown up with a nerdy friend and was assigned the alley next to Sarah's group. Sarah had long blonde hair and a pretty face. Tom had introduced himself to everyone, including Sarah and her friend. He was quite a good bowler, averaging around 170 a game. In between turns, he had struck up a conversation with Sarah, who was a healthcare student. They had taken an instant liking to each other. They had talked about bowling and where they each came from. Sarah had grown up in Oceanside, Long Island, not far from Tom's family. She had decided to attend college in California since she wanted to enjoy the mountains and beaches. Before the night was over, Tom had asked Sarah for her phone number, and she had willingly given it.

Since Tom was in the middle of rowing season and he was such a devoted student, it had taken a while for him to call her. Sara was surprised when Tom called. She had thought that he had forgotten entirely about her. Their first official date was dinner and a movie. By the third or fourth date, Tom had known he was going to marry her. However, he did not propose until his senior year. She had said yes right away. Soon, they had been planning their wedding and honeymoon along with making their career plans after graduation. The wedding had taken place in Oceanside, NY, in 1997. Since Sarah liked the beach, they had gone on a one-week honeymoon to Jamaica at Sandals, an all-inclusive resort. They had a great time climbing Dunn's River Falls and just lounging around, talking to each other.

Unfortunately for them, Tom's dad had passed away soon after the wedding. His death probably had affected Tom's next decision. After the honeymoon, Tom had decided to follow in his dad's footsteps and join the Air Force with no job prospects. He had trained as a flight pilot and served in both Iraq and Afghanistan. After four years, he had left the service and had begun working for Boeing as an aerospace engineer. Sarah and Tom had also wanted to start a family. Sarah also had grown up an only child, influencing their decision to have multiple children. When Tom had gone in to the service, Sarah had worked as an emergency room nurse. The fact that she was so busy had helped her keep her mind off Tom and all of the dangers he had faced. When Tom had returned home, she had learned about all the troubles in the world from him.

After several natural disasters had struck California and Florida, they had decided to volunteer. Their experience of helping homeless people had made a lasting impression on them. Assisting others, they had felt immense gratitude. As a result, Tom had focused on climate change during his free time and diligently kept up-to-date on all the latest research and events.

Tom had begun to learn as much as possible about the impact of carbon emission on the climate and other factors that might affect the future. He listened intently to Al Gore and Michael Bloomberg when they tried to warn governments about the future of mankind with all the harmful man-made effects on the climate. It seemed that some people did listen to them. Still, the major countries, such as Russia, tended to ignore the warnings, blocking every effort to achieve any improvements to heed warnings. They were like ships sailing blindly into the night back into old familiar grounds too afraid to look forward.

While they had been volunteering and helping communities develop some resilience against climate change threats, their first child Sophie was born in 2007. Sophie did well in school, but she loved music. She knew all the top songs and learned how to sing them on her Apple Music app. She also had a pretty good voice. Tom's second child, Sam, was born in 2009. Right away, he could tell that Sam was going to be something special. Sam was just like his father. Both he and Sarah felt the same way. It was their parents' intuition that he would be a great success. Two years later, in 2011, Robert came along. By this time, Tom and Sarah had been involved in community efforts to increase climate change solutions and staying somewhat active in town halls. Soon, much of their time was spent raising their three children.

Robert was doing well in school when Tom had to start devoting all of his time to the project. All three of their kids had a relatively normal early childhood. Both he and his wife had worked every day and made sure their children were cared for. His children had joined all the youth sports programs and had lots of good friends. Birthday parties were held almost every week where they lived, and there was not much to worry about. With young children, they wanted to ensure a future in which they did not have to worry about climate change and its effect worldwide.

When Donald Trump had become president in 2016, given that all of the positive changes implemented by President Obama were suddenly reversed, Dr. Burns and the environmental community had forecasted dire consequences with the shift in government policy. Many of the regulations in the Environmental Protection Agency were canceled. It had seemed that half the population was thrilled that they were doing better economically and refused to accept they were sacrificing the future of mankind.

It was estimated that all life would perish beginning in 2040—by 2100, everything alive would become extinct. These reports were secret, classified documents and could not be made public, since it would cause widespread panic. However, the scientists Tom had worked with had done their own calculations.

Congressional stories read by the public on the climate had mentioned the seriousness of the issue. Still, they had also watered down what the future effects might be. Congress had refused to act to help the environment.

Some people felt Trump should be impeached just because of his impact on the environment. It was treason to sell out the American people to the idea that climate change was not man-made. Dr. Burns could not take a chance on this president and his beliefs. Whoever became president after Trump would be left with an impossible task of cleaning up the atmosphere and pollution. There was a chance it would not be successful.

Just as once the fight against poverty was to be fought at all levels of society for humanity, now the battle to act on warnings at all levels of society was critical for our survival. That meant not burying intelligence and accurate assessments when it came to the environment. It was maniacal and beastly to think that just as Agent Orange had been poured out of the sky to win a war that war outcomes and strategies were a better investment of time and money in embracing another form of slow death as the world degenerated.

The skies were the realm for the undamnable it appeared, dropping any chemical to disintegrate trees and vegetation. Still, Tom would be damned if he would let them turn all the skies into another dangerous place where the absence of hope for the future would cloud everything. There was no such thing as absolution when it came to releasing oneself from the responsibility that came with knowledge for capricious reasons. Sure, our lingering wishes for a past came and went, but not every set of threats could be bombed away.

Tom didn't consider making exceptions in men's minds who distorted the sacred trust and integrity an option. It wasn't a chain of command problem he was going to recreate. He would command his ship when the time came and communicate with the other commanders in space, providing a much better sense of hope. Nevertheless, he was tinged with foreboding as he looked up into the sky on this late evening in July. He wondered if this was what his own grandparents had felt, leaving for the new world and better prospects. Maybe there would be sentimental attachments and waves of concerns about whether they were leaving the worst for the better. Other than that, the parallels ended as the times demanded he witness a different set of circumstances and that hurricanes, disappearing islands, and flooded backyards couldn't be forced into submission.

He felt a wave of relief as he considered that he was dealing with the problems of these times with his hands on a lot more knowledge and awareness. But they had come to the new world for better prospects, and that was a torch he was willing to carry to light the way for his own children's future too.

He pulled into the space center and looked forward to the challenges he and the other commanders faced.

CHAPTER 12

Data

Chapter 12 – Data

Tom Burns, Rocky Mountains, CO

The following day, Tom received progress reports on all four ships during one of the commanders' weekly video conference meetings. It was all excellent news. They shared suggestions with each other. Everyone seemed to get along fine. Things had calmed down a bit since the meeting with Yuri. Planning and building the ships began in earnest.

However, things hadn't calmed down in terms of extreme weather and climate events. Oman had seen 108-degree weather, and Algeria also hit a record high of 124 degrees. California's wildfires became the deadliest and most destructive in history. Wildfires in the Amazon threatened to destroy twenty percent of the Earth's oxygen supply. The world wasn't on track to limit temperature rises or achieve necessary emissions reductions. At the same time, droughts slowed agricultural production in central Iowa and Illinois.

People were generally nervous about when the dry spell would end, given its impact on people's lives, food production, and livelihood. If they were going to adapt to these narcissistic times, it would mean rising above zero-tolerance for immigrants like Luis or technological advances that were meant to meet the necessary climate impact goals. In the eyes of humankind's challenges, Apathy, no matter how kind God might be, meant believing religious fanatics that claimed there would be no more climate disasters since God had said so. Tom doubted sincerely that the prayerful insurance policy for the planet covered neglect and inaction.

The commanders worried about all of these weather anomalies also. The commanders agreed that hired crews would be developing and designing the spacecraft over the next several years. Each ship would have four levels, and their command posts would be on the top floor. The living quarters and medical facilities would be on the third level. The second level would be reserved for the crew's functions, including the weapon systems and space shuttles. The fourth level would be where the engine rooms were located.

Tom informed the other commanders that he'd hired several new people, including Mr. William Borucki, to develop some flight paths to the many galaxies and determine what obstacles might occur, such as meteor showers. Tom also had brought experts in astronomy and astrology to join the meeting.

William Borucki advised, "We need current maps of the stars, meteor showers and asteroids. At this point, plans can only be selected from data that has been collected by astronomers on Earth. We know this data has been collected with extremely powerful telescopes such as the Kepler taking pictures of the same part of the sky repeatedly every six seconds. Between 2009 and 2018, the Kepler has been used to identify exoplanets. Before that, I worked for NASA researching the potential of finding Earth-size planets beyond our solar system through the process or technique of transit photometry. I pioneered the Kepler mission. Now that Kepler has run out of fuel and has been retired, orbiting away from Earth, it set us all on a new course full of promise to continue exploring our galaxy."

Tom said, "Mr. Borucki is seventy-nine years old now, but I felt it was important to invite him to the meeting and be an ongoing contributor to our mission, as his knowledge might prove invaluable. At the beginning of the project, we did not have enough information to decide where to attempt to live outside the solar system. But using the Kepler telescope, it has been determined that there are three excellent candidates for planets that might be habitable in this system."

Mr. Borucki shared his insights. "What makes a planet habitable? A habitable planet needs to have an atmosphere similar to Earth and maintain liquid water near or on its surface. 2015 research using the Kepler telescope had indicated that Kepler-186f was similar in size to Earth. This planet is in a system with a host red dwarf star with four other planets, some as remote as 1,120 light-years away from Earth. It might be more feasible to start with Alpha Centauri and see if any planets could be habitable. Depending on how fast the spacecraft can travel, it is estimated it could take anywhere from a hundred to five hundred years to arrive at this destination. It has also been estimated that there may be as many as forty billion stars located in possible habitable zones in the Milky Way. From 2015 to the present, many astronomers and astrologists have continually monitored all the possibilities for vessels to travel to."

Tom said, "If the first planet that we visit is uninhabitable, the vessel will move on to the next selected planet and so forth. It is also possible that the four spaceships might have to go their separate ways and investigate planets on their own, depending on how long it would take to fly from planet to planet. Each spaceship will be free to travel where they want to go, but we hope we stay together as long as possible.

"We have set up a ship-to-ship communication system that will work even at great distances from each other. By the time each spacecraft is launched, a definite flight plan will be decided. In the past, a Voyager space probe took thirty-six years to leave the solar system. This would be too long for this project. With the improved speed in the spacecraft in development, we expect that we could easily travel to the end of our solar system in five years. That is the goal. Are there any questions?"

One of Tom's officers spoke up. "Sir, what if we cannot attain the desired speed you want to reach to get to these new galaxies?"

"We may not have the desired speed by the beginning of the launch, but we damn well will have it soon after we do. I have assembled some of the brightest minds in engineering and science to figure out the solutions to these problems. If we all think optimistically and do our job, we will succeed. The alternative will not be pleasant for anyone on board. Any other questions?"

Once the meeting was finished, Tom toured the cave to see how everyone was doing in the specific laboratories. A lot of construction was taking place. With the continued degradation of the environment, a sense of urgency was developed for everyone working on the vessel. Things appeared to be going well, and people were bonding and getting used to each other for now.

Colorless and Odorless

Chapter 13 – Colorless and Odorless

Tom Burns, Rocky Mountains, CO

Five hours later, Dr. Sato called Tom to let him know that something awful had happened with several crew members. He needed to immediately come to the UCHealth Medical Center of the Rockies, close to the space center in Loveland.

"I will explain everything when I see you."

When he arrived at the hospital, Dr. Sato was in a room with several local doctors from the hospital. They all had serious looks on their faces. Were there deaths? Did some construction workers die during an accident? All of these possibilities were running through Tom's brain as he walked into the room.

Dr. Sato turned to face him as he walked into the room. He was informed that four workers were now in quarantine in a special unit set up in the hospital. From the reports, each of the men had developed some rapidly spreading bacterial infection that they had been contaminated with from a dropped canister they had moved.

Dr. Sato explained, "The fuels needed on the spaceship and the rockets were being taken off the cargo planes and taken inside the caves. As their supervisor explained to me, each fuel required to be kept inside specific canisters and in rooms set at precise temperatures. Certain energies should never be in the same proximity to each other. In contrast, others needed to be kept at a low enough temperature so they would not ignite and burn the lab and possibly destroy the spaceship. Anyone handling the chemicals had to wear unique insulated clothing. Breathing in some of these odorless chemicals could cause numerous cancers.

"Four men were lifting some canisters when one was accidentally dropped. Knowing how severe an accident might be for everyone, the men immediately and very nervously began inspecting the canister to see if anything had leaked at all. They all had their protective suits and believed they were insulated from any effects that might befall them if they were not protected. All of the men tediously inspected the dropped canister and agreed that no damage had occurred.

"They did write an accident report as required for their supervisor to read over, but the supervisor felt that since there did not seem to be an emergency, it was unnecessary to notify their superiors or another officer on the spaceship. They all finished their shift and prepared to leave for the day. Before leaving, they had to remove their protective clothing and place them in a special chamber that would decontaminate any clothing effects. They went home to see their families. Except for the one dropped canister; all protocols had been followed.

"It seems that each of the men were fine until they all started to feel faint and nauseous. Each of them had arrived at the hospital within an hour of their episode. Their conditions continued to get worse by the minute. Their supervisor also arrived at the hospital after one of them called him to inform him of the increasing seriousness of his condition that they all initially downplayed. None of the doctors had ever seen such a rapid advance of bacteria. They didn't have any idea what to do to alleviate the symptoms."

Dr. Sato explained that their supervisor had found the accident report in the lab and forwarded it to the hospital as soon as one of the men had told him there had been an accident. He was on his way to the hospital. The doctors at the hospital had called Dr. Sato.

Tom asked her if he could see the men. Dr. Sato nodded and asked Tom to put on protective gear. He would only be allowed to see them through a tightly sealed window.

When Tom saw them, he was aghast. After all, he had studied the effects of Agent Orange after what his dad had experienced, but nothing seemed to prepare him for what he saw. The four men had blisters over almost their entire bodies. They were all in horrible pain despite receiving a maximum allowable dose of morphine.

Tom asked Dr. Sato if there was anything that could be done for them. Sadly, Dr. Sato shook her head. The gas they had inhaled was odorless and colorless. It could not have been noticed when they had inspected the canister for damage. All four were going to die a horrible, painful death. All of them were lucky that their families did not seem to have contracted the disease but were also being kept in a quarantined room for observation to ensure it would not spread.

While Dr. Sato and Tom were standing there, one of the men's vital signs suddenly flatlined, and there was nothing anyone could do. With one dead, all of the men feared that there would be no chance to say goodbye to their families or anyone else. It looked like the other three men would die very soon.

Tom was sick to his stomach. Tom left with Dr. Sato and told her in private, "Please let their families know that their dads and husbands will be missed greatly. They are all welcome to travel with the spaceship if they desire or stay on Earth. When they feel better, I would like to meet with them. All of their burial expenses will be covered, and they will receive compensation for the deaths. Please extend my deepest condolences even though I know that it is just not enough to say that."

Chemical deaths were genuinely horrible. As he left the hospital, all Tom could see was his dad's face when he died. It was so tragic.

Elected

Chapter 14 – Elected

Tom Burns, Aurora, CO

The barrage of presidential Tweets against the interstellar mission started three years after the fatal accident that had taken the lives of some members of Tom's crew. Despite the fact that all the men who had been exposed to the deadly fuel had been buried respectfully, with their privacy intact and sacrifice well-noted, news of the accident hadn't spread.

Over the next few years, the presidential Tweets had begun to bring negative attention to the mission despite the fact that Trump was re-elected in 2020 and didn't initially seem to matter to anyone. He was taking his threats to discredit the mission seriously, and in the run-up to the 2024 election, it began heated for Tom and his crew.

Yet, as the years turned into months, and people began to take notice of the spaceship, either participating in the funding or learning more about the mission itself, Tom's team of social media experts weren't the only ones defending against the president's efforts to stall or prevent their mission.

Soon, there were significant networks of support for what Dr. Tom Burns was trying to achieve. Sure, there was criticism, but a vast number of people had wondered if space was the final frontier and whether it would be necessary someday, just as Sam and Tom had found and pursued. Of course, there needed to be a first, and it needed to be well-documented, supported, and studied. Most people who learned bits and pieces about their effort understood it took years to pursue the mission. And although his sons and daughter had no idea Tom was involved in it, he sometimes overheard them talking about a mission into space that the president was attacking, but backfiring. As more people considered the prospect of space travel, it sounded like a great step for humankind. Trump had stepped into his own leadership gap. He knew little about what captivated people positively rather than promoting their worst fears with absolutely no sense of how adventure and exploration were written into our very core.

Tom and all the commanders couldn't have been happier when they heard the 2024 election results in the United States and Russia. John Stevens was elected President of the United States. He was a Democrat. One of the significant issues the campaign focused on was cleaning up the environment and recommitting the Paris Agreement.

Tom decided not to contact the new president about his work. He felt that no matter what Stevens did to help the climate, it would be too little and too late, not to mention all the politicians who might not support his ideas.

It was also interesting that in the last few months of 2024, Donald Trump had asked for a wall to be built on the shoreline near his Florida property in Palm Beach. He wanted to stop the ocean from flooding his property and demanded that they construct a high wall around it. He claimed it was only for privacy and protection, but Tom knew the real reason behind it, and so did many other people.

In Russia, Putin finally stepped down from leading Russia. He was succeeded by Boris Ivanov, who had a similar approach as Putin. He was an oligarch with a lot of money seeking a lot of power. Tom was wary of his plans for the Russian spaceship but could only wait to see what would happen. Russia seemed to move into every country that Trump was at odds with to advance its bid to rule the world.

The ship's crew was making an immense amount of progress. Planning and development continued without any significant mishaps from 2024 to 2027. Keeping politics at bay had become touchy at moments, but Tom and his crew were undeterrable. Finally, Trump had to be wishing he hadn't picked this fight or headed the effort to let oligarchs and money root themselves into everyone's future like a pirate ship. People preferred the much more hopeful future Tom and his crew. Hopefully, President Stevens, through his own efforts, was heading toward this future.

Cautionary or not, playing politics with the wrong ammo had finally restarted efforts to care and fix things to set a better course for everyone, despite it all.

Sleepless in 2027

Part II
2027-2029
Unlocking Our Potential

Chapter 15 – Sleepless in 2027

Sam Burns, Glenwood Springs, CO

I was a bit disappointed when we moved to Glenwood Springs from Aurora when I was a freshman to go to a private high school with a great reputation. Then, Dad told me that both Sally and Jose were going to the same school as I would. The fact that I wasn't going to be leaving them behind made me feel better. Their parents worked with my dad on some kind of airplane sustainability projects. Luckily, our dads had all gotten transferred so we could go to the best high school. That meant they could work on projects nearby rather than make the long drive home every few days like they were doing for a couple of years. We were still going to be the three amigos.

Now, we were all about to graduate from Goddard High School today. I wanted to get rest for graduation, but I couldn't sleep. All night my head kept spinning around stuff in the world. Like eight years ago, my dad came home and told me that parts of the Amazon rainforest had been burning for weeks. He told me no major news outlet put it on their front page at first until there was a public outcry. Instead, it turned out that the Brazilian government was doing nothing and blaming non-governmental organizations for setting them on fire. The politicians laying the blame got the most news at first. Then, follow-up news clarified that it was actually farmers emboldened to organize "fire days" to take advantage of weak burn control enforcement. The Brazilian government was keen to open up where the world's biggest rainforest grows to increase economic activity. These were the kinds of problems that new graduates were going to have to deal with someday.

I felt nervous. What sort of world gives us these kinds of people to look up to? I preferred thinking about my vintage poster of astronaut Edgar Mitchell on my wall. Edgar Mitchell got to be the sixth man on the moon. He had started out with a childhood dream of wanting to fly and put surface experiments together on the moon's surface. My vintage poster of him doing it in 1971 kept me up as I thought about what I would do with my life. I've dreamt about wanting to fly like him after high school. Now, I was thinking I'd be helping solve our world's problems. I got good grades, and I figured that I have what it takes.

And, instead of heading into space like Edgar Mitchell, I figured it was more likely I'll be building the next generation of drones. I love new technology. Then, I could dump entire ready-made forests into areas of the world experiencing desertification where there's little access to biodiversity. Sometimes I wonder if Edgar Mitchell had the same reasons to pursue his dreams in his time. I'd have to ask my dad or look it up myself.

I couldn't sleep. Looking at the moon outside of my window, I could barely imagine what threatened to stand in Edgar Mitchell's way. I felt tired and depressed, and the bed now felt like I was sinking into it instead. I used to lay on it, staring at the ceiling at all the stars and distant planets I'd pinned up there. Then, I'd fall asleep and rearrange them all in my dreams. I used to feel like I could fly up there, but now my body feels heavy. My dad and I have worked on so many science experiments, studying cause and effect, and understanding science.

Sometimes, it's been more politics than science. Except, that as my dad has explained to me, the only science that is any longer allowed to be about cause and effect is political science. Various conservative governments with a more lenient attitude toward making money have been in power until very recently. The result is that they've found a common cause in derailing all forms of protections that were in place before. This allowed preventing people from pursuing economic prosperity with total disregard for how it affects the planet.

Of course, we have to be sustainable. It's a no-brainer. It's not just my dad who's helped me understand that. It's from looking at the data, the state of the world, and what we're actually capable of. At least now, we have President Stevens. And whenever my dad reminds me about the time when the rainforests were being set on fire, it seems like my dad's right. There were plenty of good reasons why people fought for the cause. But sadly, there are various interpretations of 'cause.' There's fighting for a cause, which people often do depend on what they care most about. Or there's what my teacher calls zero-sum gains. Winner takes all. That type of cause leaves only one horrifying effect and destroys the planet.

And that's what we're dealing with when I'm just about to graduate from high school? What's that supposed to leave me in the future? Maybe Edgar Mitchell had the right idea about where he wanted to spend his time instead of dealing with politics back on Earth.

Here political leaders can bury the truth that previous political parties were more transparent about public health and safety. One informed the people, causing the next party in power to stick to a lack of transparency. My dad has been busy working on some big science projects with Boeing and other big companies. My brother, my sister, and I have been preparing for whatever comes next. What are we going to be when we grow up? In the meantime, the guardians of the Amazon had pledged that within Brazil, greenhouse gas emissions would be cut by thirty-seven percent, but the effort to fight deforestation and the boost for renewable sources never came. Politics is the one science humans are willing to be passionate about and not apply for our own overall benefit.

It has sickened as many people as viruses, diseases. It plagues science endeavors to resolve scientific breakthroughs like the cure for cancer, the cure for the bubonic plague, and vaccinations. Yet, there is no cure, and there are no known breakthroughs.

Except, of course, the newest efforts after the 2024 political elections. But then again, two years in and I'm still wondering how they can call it political 'science.' After all, there are no science labs on Earth trying to destroy the cycles of cause and effect in power politics. A lab could develop a cure to prevent everyone from just staying on opposite sides—accepting or denying knowledge. It could help us get to the truth, and some powerful common will to build a better world and meet political problems. That's when we've ever felt the most hope. When someone makes a new discovery, it sets off for a new horizon in the spirit of exploration and rises to the times' challenges.

I've been watching people act against this very spirit throughout my teens and choosing not to rise to any challenge. I have found it unimaginable or unthinkable that we would prefer to suffer under the firm belief that it would be left in the Creator's hands. It has seemed like learned helplessness to me.

I finally fell fast asleep. When I heard my mother's voice, I felt like I'd only gotten two rest hours. I must have gone back to sleep somehow despite waking up several times throughout the night on account of all my worries.

"Come on, Sam. Wake up, son. We don't want to be late for graduation."

I slowly managed to get out of bed only to be bombarded again with mom's voice.

"And, Happy Birthday! We'll celebrate after graduation! Wherever you want to go."

How many kids celebrated both their eighteenth birthday and graduation day on the same day? After getting dressed, I went to the kitchen for breakfast.

"Congratulations, Sam. Are you ready for the big day?"

Dad was reading over some reports. He has been working nearly eleven years non-stop on some secret project. It was something he never discussed with the family. My mom had been a nurse, but since Dad was always busy and away from home, she had decided to be a stay-at-home wife, a good deal of the time.

"I think so, Dad."

My mom appeared with a camera.

"Let's take a family picture. I'll set it in ten seconds. Make a nice pose."

My family got into their positions for a traditional graduation family photo. Many of our digital photos were hanging on the walls. My younger brother, Robert, was only fifteen and would have his day soon. My sister, Sophie, was already twenty.

After the photo, we began to walk over to the auditorium, where the ceremony was held. I looked forward to seeing all of my classmates and friends there. I put on my ceremonial garb and took a look around the room. My family took their seats in the audience.

I walked over to Mr. Duke, the assistant principal, who was overseeing the line-up. Mr. Duke collected my card with my name and put me between Sally and Jose. Sally, who had been my prom date, looked very pretty today—her long blonde hair in perfect order. Jose, my best buddy and fierce competitor in just about anything, looked so grown up it freaked me out. I always knew he was very well built, but he seemed to be more buff to me today. We had even competed over Sally, but in the end, Sally had chosen me. I also saw many other classmates. One of them was Susan Simpson. I noticed that her dad, Jack, was sitting all by himself. I wondered why he never seemed to socialize with the other parents and students.

As we lined up, I greeted Sally and Jose, "It's a great day, isn't it? We are finally finished with high school."

Sally looked at me and smiled. "Yes, and on to bigger and better things! And by the way, Happy Birthday."

She kissed me on the cheek. Sally's parents were Tyler and Jessica McDaniel. Tyler was an engine specialist while his mom was also a nurse.

Jose gave me a high five. "I guess we won't be able to wrestle with each other anymore, which means I can't kick your ass. Congratulations, Sam."

Jose's dad, Michael Williams, was also working with my dad. Michael had gone to the University of Texas, where he had received a scholarship to play football. After several years in the NFL, his knee blew out, ending that career. He then went to graduate school at Purdue University, known for developing astronauts and earned his Ph.D. Jose looked like his dad. His mom, Irma, who was a librarian, was also there.

The ceremony began. The graduating class of sixty students filed in slowly single file to their seats as the parents and others rose and clapped, waiting for Mrs. Smith. Mrs. Smith was around fifty years old, and about 5 feet, 5 inches tall. She wore a nice, professional blue suit with high heels. Her slightly gray hair was tied up. She was a strict disciplinarian but a great teacher and principal. I had taken chemistry with her, and she had taught me things that I could not even imagine existed. She was well respected by everyone in the school.

Mrs. Smith began the ceremony.

"Graduates, parents, family friends, those who are watching on closed-circuit television, the Internet, and distinguished others. We have an amazing graduating class. In a few moments, I will have the opportunity to shake all of the graduates' hands, give them their diplomas, and hand out some special awards. Before we hand out the degrees, I have asked Dr. Thomas Burns, our guest speaker, and father of Sam Burns, to say a few words. Please let us have a nice round of applause for him."

My dad, sitting next to my mom, stood up, and went to the podium. He acknowledged the applause and then began his speech.

"Good afternoon, everyone. Thank you, Mrs. Smith, for all your hard work in providing
an excellent education to our students. I am certain all of the parents here today are feeling just as proud as I am."

Everyone stood up and applauded with a few whistles in between. After a moment of silence, my father continued, "I am here today to bring you some exciting and severe news. First, I would like you to remember some of the horrible past events in the last fifteen years. In 2016, Donald Trump was elected president. Despite the Democrats' effort, who called attention to the decaying environment, he won again in 2020. Mr. Trump did not believe in the preservation of our Earth. He ignored every environmental report, including those from the government that indicated global warming and the consequences of neglecting these reports.

"As a result, our environment became worse and worse. We have had some terrible hurricanes higher than category 5 that have completely demolished our southern and eastern borders. Many of our beach cities no longer exist. Florida is almost entirely underwater. Flooding in the Midwest, such as Nebraska and Illinois, has devastated much of our farmland, leaving us with severe food shortages. You can see the tall buildings but not the roads. The Caribbean Islands have wholly disappeared.

"Cities such as New Orleans, Florida, and Houston are also entirely underwater. Virtually every town in Southeast Florida has been impacted. In 2022, we had six major hurricanes hit the Florida coast. Obviously, the beaches suffered enormous erosion, with flooding, as well as in New York City. Nearly one million people have had to relocate their homes. This flooding has taken place all over the world and impacted every continent. The islands off the coast of Africa almost do not exist anymore.

"Remember the flooding of Mozambique in 2019? Over 100,000 people lost their lives. In 2022, the Seychelles Islands disappeared. Also, we have had some devastating fires that killed thousands of people. In the North, most of our snowcapped mountains and glaciers have dissolved. The temperature barely gets below freezing in Alaska. Many of our animals are now extinct. Around the world, we have seen one catastrophe after another.

"These disasters were part-man-made and in part naturally occurring as the Earth ages. However, we could have done a lot more to prevent this from happening. Politicians have been too wrapped up in themselves and interested in making more money instead of thinking about our future. They decided to do nothing about the environment. The air we breathe, and the water we drink cannot speak. It is up to the people to speak for the elements. Our planet will soon become uninhabitable. By the time Trump's presidency finished in 2024, it was becoming clear that there would be no more human race."

As I absorbed everything my dad was saying, I thought about how everything that seemed innovative was being relegated into nonexistence as quickly as someone might drive into a hurricane to test the strength of their car, see if they might land with a few scrapes and bruises, and survive to tell their tale. Just to say, I told you so.

My dad continued, "This is why a group of great people has been working on a project for the past eleven years that will hopefully save some of us. I know everyone has prepared diligently for this day. Almost all of our students have parents working for many years in secret to plan for the future. That future is now at hand.

"First, I would like to bring to mind some of the people who have lost so much to get to this moment. They were some of the first to become climate refugees and have suffered incredible losses. Despite the fact that they rose to the challenge, they have had to completely change their lives. Please send your good wishes to friends who have sent me updates throughout the years about how they have attempted to rise to the occasion when those in power have not. These are friends like Joyce and Hilde Scott in the Lake Ontario area, Jeff Tirortu on Kiribati's island in the Gilbert Islands, and friends on the Tangier Islands."

He paused for a moment as he brought attention to his dear friends and the devastating effects of climate changes they had faced. They had survived but plenty upset at the lack of real, sustainable solutions. Everyone paused with him, including me, concerned about the impact and grief these people had faced due to climate changes. I felt fortunate to have my father care so much. There were, of course, many solutions, but now he was excited to share his. I could see that as he lifted his head to share his dream. It was my graduation day. I was pleasantly surprised he chose this day to share what his projects were with all of us, including my classmates and their families. I had been wondering about it for so long.

"Four huge spaceships have been built and will be ready to launch very soon, we hope. Our starships are almost set to go. They have been put through every possible situation and test we can think of, and there are future tests. Everyone alive on this planet will either be leaving or will stay behind. If you choose to remain, you and your children will probably die within a short period. However, we owe it to our descendants and the human race to try to survive. If they were alive, I know that my parents would encourage me to take my children and leave. We cannot let their sacrifices be in vain. The day we depart Earth will forever be a day that will be remembered by all of us and all the people that come after us. May God bless us all!"

My jaw had been dropping for the last minute or so. My mind raced with thoughts of Edgar Mitchell and my dream to fly better drones to create bigger ready-made forests. What was I hearing? My dad had been building spaceships?

Suddenly, the ceremony's silence after this nerve-wracking revelation that was only just settling into everyone was broken. Mr. Jack Simpson, whose daughter, Susan, was graduating with me, ran to the podium, pushing my dad away. He grabbed the microphone.

"He lies. Don't believe a word he says. Stay here and fight! He is full of nonsense. Earth is just going through a phase. Listen to the president. Things will get better. We just have to work together to restore our environment."

Everyone stopped in their tracks and stared at him. No one tried to remove him from the stage. Mr. Simpson looked at the crowd and said, "You are all a bunch of imbeciles for listening to this crap. If you go on this stupid spaceship, you will be dead in minutes probably. Our new president will save us all. You need to stay and make this world great again. Join me."

Mrs. Smith gestured for the security person to lead Mr. Simpson away.

As she did so, Mr. Simpson pulled out a gun and pointed it at my dad.

"Come near me, and I will blow his face off."

My dad, who had been a man of combat for many years, remained calm. Or at least he looked relaxed. Inside, he must have been terrified. He slowly moved toward Jack.

"Jack put the gun down. We don't want any violence or anyone to get hurt. You have stated your piece. Now let us celebrate our children's graduation. Come on, Jack. Look at your daughter. Do you think Susan wants to see you shoot me? Is that how you want your daughter to remember you on her graduation day?"

Jack looked at me and then slowly started to look at his daughter. As soon as his eyes turned away to look at his daughter, my dad lunged for him, knocking Jack over. However, Jack still had a gun. He fired a few wild shots that luckily did not hit anyone. He then started to point it at my father again.

Suddenly there was a loud pop, and Jack fell over backward, dropping the gun. The security guard had shot him through the head, killing him instantly. People gasped and started running. The graduates left the stage. Susan was in tears. People were trying to console Susan and her mom, Barbara.

My father and others waited to give their testimonies to the police.

I went home with mom, Robert, and Sophie. We were all shaken up about what happened. We talked awhile and then went to bed.

My dad did not arrive home for several hours and immediately went to bed.

I was in for another sleepless night. How could Jack do this? I finally fell asleep, looking at my poster of Edgar Mitchell.

CHAPTER 16

A Day of Consoling

Chapter 16 – A Day of Consoling

Sam Burns, Glenwood Springs, CO

Turns out, we were all a bit sleep-deprived for the next few days. We were perplexed at how Susan's father had been willing to resort to violence to get his point across. Why would he choose to threaten my father and not consider the consequences? I couldn't even imagine, and to think he'd been sitting there armed listening to my father inspire us frankly surprised me and probably a few others.

But I couldn't fathom what Susan was feeling. My dad stood up there and finally shared what he'd wanted to be our graduation, my graduation present, and her dad, well ... It was terrifying to consider that Susan would always remember her graduation and how her father reacted to the thought of reinvigorating the need to build on the spirit of innovation. He paid with his life. It became clear to me that there might be more apprehensions that turn violent in some people's estimations of the future and how people reacted to the increased environmental threats.

Every known effort to get people to stop living with such utter disregard and entitlements and change behaviors was met with indifference. Few people accept change as a constant in human existence, meaning they must move beyond and open to the possibilities. I felt betrayed at some level by humankind if one of our own could feel compelled to kill someone for disagreeing with how to secure humanity's future interests. Maybe, it was possible for the Earth to rebound still. Of course, there was always hope. But what sort of hope turned the idea of staying and making the world great again into a dismal start for his bright daughter. She'd have to realize fathers don't act like that if they care about Earth and the people on it? It bothered me so much and continued to, but I couldn't grasp or sort it out.

When we went to the funeral for Jack a few days later, it was very depressing. It was a rainy day. Just about everyone who had attended the graduation ceremony participated in the funeral. Each of us had our umbrellas out or shared one with a friend or family member. I stood underneath Sally's umbrella with my arm around her. Our pastor reminded us that we can never know what God's plan is, and there is no way to predict the future. Nothing can live forever. It was very emotional seeing Jack laid to rest. I looked around and saw many people crying and trying to compose themselves. Despite his disruption of graduation, we all thought of him as part of our family.

I looked at Susan and her mom. They were both crying and being consoled by their family and friends. Eventually, the funeral finished up, and people started to leave to get out of their wet clothes.

We then all went to Jack's house to console Susan and her mom. There was a ton of food served. All of the neighbors had donated food that could probably last for weeks. Some people ate a full plate, but I was not hungry. People were sitting around reminiscing about what a nice person Jack was and how they would never have believed he would do something like this. My mother and father joined a group of parents in the living room and watched Susan's mom cry and be kind to everyone. She was thanking each person for coming over to console them.

Sally, Tom, and I went upstairs with Susan, Jose, and a few other classmates. I was sad about the way Jack had died, but I was more concerned about Susan. How long would it take to put this tragedy behind her? She was so young to lose her father. I wondered how she would be able to cope. In a short time, she would be leaving Earth with everyone else. I stood up and walked over to her.

"Susan, I am so sorry about your dad. If there is anything you want me, Sally or Jose, to do for you, please let us know."

Susan looked at me and said, "Thank you, Sam." Then, she started to cry and put her arms around me. She was hugging me really tight.

I looked at Sally to make sure she was not jealous. It did not appear so, but who knew in situations as emotional as this. I'd never lost a friend to death, let alone a friend's parent, and the only person in my family who had died was my grandfather. That had been really hard on my dad.

After a minute or two, she let go. "I am sure we will see each other soon. I need to help my mom go through Dad's things for the next few days. I will call you."

I got up and motioned for Sally and Jose to come with me. I did not want to be in a place that was so sad, seeing everyone looking so depressed. On my way out, I realized I was furious. At that moment, I was angry about a lot of things. How could this happen? Why did we all have to see Jack die? Why did Donald Trump have to be such a lousy president when it came to the environment, causing thousands of people to die and ensuring even his own Florida property would be underwater soon? People were dying all over the planet at an alarming rate. I was glad I did not know them. It was awful just thinking about all the deaths.

Sally asked me where we should go.

I said, "Let's go to my house and hang out. I need to get away from this."

The three of us left while my parents stayed and consoled Susan's mom. Graduation seemed like it happened fifty years ago. Life was sure changing fast. My dad's dream wasn't to blame—that I was sure of—but I wanted so badly to come up with a way to mend everyone's broken hearts. I had known he was working on some secret rocket project but nothing of this magnitude. All I could think of was how helpless the scientist Louis Pasteur had been watching thousands suffer and perish needlessly from unsterile conditions. Simultaneously, the wealthy Free Thinkers were allowed to sow doubt about the need to embrace sterilization in operating rooms. It was when Pasteur could eliminate microbes that harm the body that we saved lives.

Jack hadn't wanted to save lives; he'd gotten lost in becoming part of the disease. How could he have poisoned our minds so quickly and broken our hearts? My poor dad hadn't condemned everyone on Earth to death. Jack had secured his own death and had shown his illness, an illness may be as infectious as what Pasteur had faced. Again, it felt like only science can provide the answers, although the will to spread his disease turned Jack into a symbol of the post-Truth era we have been living in. But how do we wash our hands of it and be free of this disease of the mind? Just like heat eliminates the danger associated with eating raw foods, maybe we might be able to warm our hearts to eliminate the threat of raw irrational murderers. Maybe.

Crazy Handshake

Chapter 17 – Crazy Handshake

Sam Burns, Glenwood Springs, CO

When we got back to my house, I took off my tie and jacket. I gave bottles of water to Sally and Jose, and we all sat down at the kitchen table.

After a few sips and moments of silence, Sally said. "My God, the last few months has been incredible. And it has gone so fast. I have experienced some of the best and worst days of my life. The prom with you was one of my all-time best, but graduation was one of my worst. It was supposed to be a happy day to remember, and now I can only remember one thing. Because of the environment, we are not even going to get the chance to attend college."

Jose joined in. "I have similar feelings. I was looking forward to wrestling in college and maybe winning an NCAA championship. It is a bit overwhelming, not knowing where we will live or what will happen. Will we ever set foot on another planet? Will we ever return to Earth? Will we meet an alien race and live in peace with them or go to war? Will we ever marry anyone? Will I ever be able to have a dog or play sports? The dog was supposed to be my graduation gift. I have to prepare to leave everything behind."

Sally also chimed in. "I am also thinking of all the things I will have to leave behind or never will be able to do. I was planning on seeing Taylor Swift with my parents this summer. I was accepted into Yale University with hopes of majoring in psychology. Now I imagine all of that is gone."

I listened to what they had to say. I said, "Today has been a miserable day. I also share your sentiments. I also wanted to attend college. Once we are on the spaceship, I have no idea if we will ever see each other again. I am sure we will, but what will our relationship be in ten years—that's if we even live that long? Maybe we will die on lift-off like Susan's dad said, or perhaps a speeding meteor will hit and destroy our ship. Perhaps we will arrive at a planet only to have an alien race put us into slavery. It could be just like the Planet of the Apes. In short, we could die at any moment. However, I also feel blessed to be surrounded by our parents. They really care about every living soul on this Earth and especially about us. Who knows where it will lead? The human race, if it wants to survive, has outlived this planet.

"Rather, the human race has destroyed this planet. Look at what is happening to us on an almost daily basis. Just yesterday, thousands of people were killed in California due to a considerable firestorm created by environmental failure. Thousands of people are dying from melanoma due to the breakup of the ozone layer. There will no longer be any outdoor sports leagues anywhere and no beaches to enjoy the day. Dead fish are washing up on the shores. Look at the red tide in Florida. Who wants to go to a beach with the pervasive smell of dead fish everywhere? We have hurricanes all year round, not just in the summer. Volcanoes are erupting more frequently. Everyone in America has been or will be forced to move into the center of the country. They spend most of their days inside their homes or underground. When it snows, we have blizzards greater than you have never seen. Trump kept lying about the Earth warming up, but it goes both ways. We are experiencing some of the harshest winters that have ever been recorded.

"This could all have been prevented or at least delayed until a long time in the future. I am furious at the politicians and other greedy individuals who put their own selfish interests ahead of everyone else. They believe that if we did nothing, it would all work out in the end. These idiots have altered and sacrificed our future.

"They are all going to die a horrible death. Their money and materials, savings, and goods are not going to help them. I just cannot imagine the last few people left on Earth with the look of horror that comes just before death. It will be awful, and I do not want to be anywhere near this planet when the end comes. Do you?"

They were listening to me intently the whole time.

Sally said, "That was really well said and very deep. I am angry too with the damn president and his cronies for their continuous lying and betrayal of the human race, not only the people in the United States. We could have used the billions of dollars to improve the environment to ensure everyone's safety. More people would be able to leave this planet and not die such an ugly death. Thank God I have friends like you guys. I cannot imagine living my life without the two of you."

I replied, "I agree with you. No matter what happens in the future, we will face it together. We have been selected to represent the human race as we leave this dying planet. We have to do everything in our power to stay positive and contribute to whatever it is we need to do. Let's put our hands in for the team of survivors."

We all put our hands in and did some crazy handshake like they do in the movies. After that, we seemed to feel a little better. We talked a little more, and then before Jose and Sally went home, we each put our hand on top of one another's and said, "FOR HUMANITY."

Step Outside

Chapter 18 – Step Outside

Sam Burns, Glenwood Springs, CO

The following week was technically the beginning of summer vacation. Basically, my friends and I did a whole lot of nothing. Finally, my brother, sister and I decided to go out to eat lunch at our favorite hamburger joint. A number of our classmates were there too. Sophie ordered a veggie burger, while my brother, Robert, and I had double cheeseburgers with french fries and soda. It would sure be nice if we could take the restaurant with us on the space journey, but I knew that was not going to be possible. Come to think of it, I had no idea what we were going to eat in space. I was pretty sure we were not going to see another McDonalds forever.

A few of my close classmates sat at the next table to us. We were chitchatting when suddenly Steven Donald came up to me. Steven was a local laborer who worked at various manual labor jobs. He had graduated high school a few years before me but never really seemed to have an interest in school. He was known to be a troublemaker and picked fights regularly. Considering that Jack had died recently and we were all still a little depressed, I was not in the mood for any confrontation. Since he was standing in front of me, I felt I had no choice but to greet him politely and hope he would do the same.

"Hi, Steven, what's up?"

Steven did not look happy and stood in front of me with his hands folded in front of him. I knew right away that we were going to have a problem, but I did not know what the problem was and how it would resolve itself.

After a moment, Steven spoke, "Your dad killed Jack."

"No," I said. "He did not. The security officer did. He really had no choice. Were you there? I did not notice you. Everyone saw it, right?"

I looked at my friends sitting nearby, and they all nodded in agreement.

Steven looked at them. "Your dad did not pull the trigger, but his crazy stories about the need to get off the Earth and the planet dying have made all of us angry. What gives your dad the right to choose who goes and who stays? If he really believed the Earth was dying, he would work on a solution to save it instead of running away. Why do I and my friends and family have to stay behind?"

His voice sounded angry, and I knew he was going to continue berating me and arguing. I tried to reason with him.

"I do not want to argue with you, Steven. My dad was one of the first to realize we had to leave and that there is no turning back. Blaming my dad for years of mistakes and negligence by politicians and others is just wrong. I am sorry you will not be joining us. My dad has had to make some tough decisions. Try to be positive and enjoy your life."

As soon as I said those last words, I knew I had made a mistake. This seemed to make Steven even angrier.

He screamed, "YOU LITTLE PRICK, YOUR DAD IS AN ASSHOLE. I AM GOING TO BEAT THE CRAP OUT OF YOU. THEN YOU CAN RUN HOME TO YOUR DADDY AND MOMMY, AND THEY CAN WIPE YOUR ASS. STEP OUTSIDE NOW!"

Everyone in the restaurant was shocked at what they had just heard.

What was I going to do? Of course, I was also getting angry. I was starting to get a severe rush of adrenaline. This was something that I had no control over. However, I was furious about what he had called my dad and me and belittling me.

I said, "Okay, that's it. I am going outside now. You can meet me outside in five minutes, and we will resolve this dispute one way or another. Just make sure your friends don't get involved in this."

I knew I would not be able to fight five or six of his friends, not by myself.

We all went outside to a park nearby. My friends stood on one side, and Steven and his friends were across from us. They were all hollering and moving around, hoping to see us get started.

I turned to my sister and brother, "If I do not win, call Mom. I may need an ambulance."

My brother nodded. "Just beat him up and show him who the boss is."

I asked him, "What happened to sticks and stones will break my bones, but names will never hurt me?"

My brother shrugged. "Someone has to uphold the family honor, and it looks like you have to do it."

I moved in to face Steven. Since I was a wrestler in high school, I knew how to fight. I was not sure about Steven. He was about the same size as me. Since he worked in manual labor, I assumed he was relatively strong. I put my hands out front, bent my knees and waited for him. He rushed me quickly. As he approached me, I took one step forward and punched him in the solar plexus. Steven dropped to his knees, gasping for breath.

I knew he was not ready to give up and would attack again. I stood ready for his second approach. This time he was more careful about what he was going to do. He tried to get behind me and put me in a bear hug, but my wrestling skills took over. I put my arms under his shoulder and flipped him down. Then I got on top of him and made sure he could not get up. He tried hard to get me off of him, to no avail. I just had too much experience fighting for him to win.

Finally, while I still had him down, I said, "Steven, do you give up? This is not doing either of us any good. I do not want to fight you."

At first, Steven refused, but after another few minutes of agony and the fact he was embarrassed, he gave up. I let him go. He got up, dusted himself off, and he and his friends left in a hurry.

I was exhausted. My brother and sister came over to me and gave me a high five. Then, my sister hugged me. My friends applauded a little. I told everyone that while I did win the fight, I really did not enjoy it at all and hoped it would not happen again. Then we all separated and went home.

When we got home, my brother was bragging to my mom about me taking care of the family honor. Of course, my mom was relieved I was all right, but she was also mad at me for taking the bait.

"Why didn't you call me or just walk away?"

"Mom, I wanted to do that, but Steven was not going to let that happen."

As usual, when a kid gets into a fight, parents called each other. My mother felt obligated to call a few other parents who verified my story. That seemed to be the end of it.

There were so many things to do before we left and so little time to get all of them done. I wasn't even sure whether my emotions were ever going to let me calm down enough, but I certainly wasn't going to believe that it was a worthless mission that didn't care about the future of humanity. I figured that Steven had been completely irrational for denying that people explore all possibilities and it didn't mean we were being exclusive. It meant that we were building on my dad's dream and hoping to extend humanity's chances. Maybe someday hundreds of years from now, the children from Steven's family would be able to travel across the galaxy and meet our own descendants. Maybe.

What's My Allowance

Chapter 19 – What's my Allowance?

Sam Burns, Glenwood Springs, CO

Days after the fight, my family was sitting at our dinner table. Mom had cooked some spaghetti and meatballs that we were all enjoying.

My brother asked, "Dad, how much money will we get for an allowance on this spaceship? Right now, you are giving me twenty dollars a week. We probably need more on the ship, right?"

Dad was about to reply when Sophie butted in, "Robert gets twenty, and I get thirty. I want more. I want a hundred dollars a week."

Dad and Mom looked amused.

Mom said to me, "How much would you like, Sam?"

I replied, "Well, I will probably be working a lot, so you can pay me the going rate. I expect we will all make a lot of money, right?"

Dad then said, "All three of you seem very interested in becoming rich over the years. Exactly, what will you do with all this money in space? Do you plan to get a new car? Season football tickets? The latest high-tech recreation equipment? Perhaps a new cell phone?"

My brother replied, "We have football leagues in space? Will Sophie get a new car?"

Sophie said, "What stores are going to be on the ship?"

Dad sat there, shaking his head and smiling.

"All three of you seem very close tonight. Okay, everybody, pay attention. The answer to all your questions is that there will be no need to have any money, and there will be no bank. Also, everyone on the ship will work without being paid."

"What?" I said. "Who is going to work for no pay? I've never heard of such a thing."

Sophie said, "How will I pay for new clothes or go out on a date? You need money to do those things. I need money!"

Dad said, "Sophie, you can get new clothes when you need them for free. You can go out on a date anywhere on the ship for free. However, if you want to go on a date off the ship, that will be a problem. All food, movies, and recreation are free. This planet is in so much trouble because some wealthy people think their money is more important than life on this planet. Greed is part of the reason for this situation.

"There is an old saying: 'Money is the root of all evil.'

"Rich people are going to die on Earth. Their money will be useless. They will probably offer me a lot of money to take them on the trip, but my answer is going to be no. People on the ship will work and work hard every day. They will be motivated because they want to stay alive and find a new planet to live hopefully happily ever after. Everyone on the ship will be equally rich and poor with zero dollars."

Robert protested. "But money motivates people to work too. What happens if they do not work or go on strike?"

"If they do not work or refuse to work, there will be an appropriate punishment. We can put people in the brig until they are ready to work again. We can also send them to the cryo unit, put them in a deep sleep and not wake them up until we reach a planet."

Dad saw that each of us had a look of shock on our faces. "I mean, Dad—" I started to say.

"It's the last resort, of course, son. All the officers on the spaceship have agreed there is no need for money. However, if we do reach a new planet, perhaps, we will again have money. I hope not. If we travel for many years without the use of money, we probably will be fine without money on a new planet."

"So, where is all the money we saved up over the years?"

Dad replied, "I used almost all of it to help build the spaceship. Your mother and I agreed that since we were not going to be able to use it on Earth, we might as well spend it on the ship. So, forget about money, forget about the allowance. Right now, you need to start thinking about the training all of you will have to go through before you board the ship. That starts tomorrow morning. Each one of you will be taking aptitude and physical tests. You will also be trying to select a career or job on the ship. Sam is going to be working with me, as we see his promise as a future officer and perhaps the commander of the vessel. No one will work until they reach sixteen years old, so Robert will be in school learning about everything that happens on the ship and trying to select his own career. Mom is going to work with the nurses and medical staff. It is possible that Sophie may want to do that also, but that will be her choice. Now get some sleep because tomorrow is going to be a busy day for all of us."

I finished my meal thinking about money or how there would be no money for the rest of my life. What a bummer. Now, all we had to do was wake up tomorrow and start training. At least I would be motivated to be more like Edgar Mitchell than all the other people who had proven they weren't worth looking up to.

CHAPTER 20

Before We Got Our Assignments

Chapter 20 – Before We Got Our Assignments

Sam Burns, Rocky Mountains, CO

The following day, Dad and Mom woke us all up at 7 am in the morning. We showered and got dressed. Then we ate some breakfast. By 8 am, we were in the car, driving to a test center in an abandoned school building. Just about all of my classmates were also there.

I sat down next to my best friends, Sally and Jose. My sister and brother joined some friends they knew. It looked like everyone in the room was a little nervous, as we weren't sure what to expect. We always had time to study and prepare for tests in school, but today we had no idea what the test would be about.

I asked them how they were doing.

Sally said, "I'm going crazy thinking about this space trip. I had hoped to spend the summer hanging out and getting ready to attend college. I have no idea what we are going to do here."

Jose said, "I am looking forward to doing this, but I am sure going to miss a hell of a lot of things on Earth. I have no idea what awaits us on this trip. Will I be bored to death? Who will I date? Someday I may want to have my own family. This stuff is freaking me out."

I said, "Dad has been quiet about this up till now. I think he wanted us not to worry so much and just try to focus on having a normal life until he had to spill the beans."

It was good to see Jose and Sally. I always felt comfortable with them and could talk about almost anything with those two.

We were all waiting to see who would be testing us. All of a sudden, our principal, Mrs. Smith, came out to greet us. She stood on a podium with a microphone with an all-white uniform on. Her hair was now in a ponytail.

"Hello, everyone. You did not think you were going to get rid of me just because school is out, did you?"

That brought a laugh from some of us.

Mrs. Smith then continued, "It is good to see you all again. I am going to supervise your testing. It is essential that you try your best regardless of what we ask you to do. Let's get to the task at hand, shall we? There are thirty of you here. There may be others joining you in the future. The details are still being worked on. You will be divided into two groups. The testing will take about four hours and include physical as well as mental tasks, and you will be rated on each one. There is no pass or fail. You will all be making the trip regardless of how you do on the tests. We simply want to assess your strengths and weaknesses to assign you to do appropriate work on the ship. You will have plenty of time in space to improve your skills and learn many others. Just so you know, I will be the director of education on your travels.

"Now, I want to introduce you to our two other testers today. First, I want you to meet Jose Cunningham. He is responsible for cognitive testing. When you meet with him, he will explain the tests you have to take. Jose graduated from Colorado University with a Ph.D. in psychology. He is considered to be an expert in solving problems cognitively."

Jose stepped forward and waved to everyone.

The students gave him a light clap. "Welcome, Jose."

"Our next tester is Ms. Betsy Rosen. She recently graduated from Iowa University, where she was a standout gymnast and volleyball player. She also served two years in the army."

Ms. Rosen stood up and stepped forward. She was about 5'9", and it looked like she was all muscle.

"Ms. Rosen will be testing your strength and agility skills. I am sure she will have some of you huffing and puffing by the end of the day. Both Jose and Betsy will also be joining us on our travels. Feel free to become familiar with them and ask them questions. Everyone on board will have to exercise, and Betsy will be responsible for that. Are there any questions before we begin?"

One of the students, Stacey Hill, raised her hand. She asked, "Will we be able to go to the bathroom if we need to? Also, are you planning on feeding us?"

Some of us started to giggle. Stacey was like a class clown and always asked about silly things.

Mrs. Smith did not laugh. She looked directly at Stacey, "When we tell you that you can go to the bathroom, you can do so, and, yes, you will be fed at the end of four hours of testing. I hope you ate your breakfast. You are going to need the energy. Are there any other questions?"

She did not wait to see if we had any more questions. Instead, she said, "We need to divide you into the two groups before we begin. We will have groups A and B. First, I will call group A. If your name is called, please line up in front of Jose Cunningham. If your name is not called, you are in group B and will line up in front of Ms. Rosen. When the tests are finished, we will all meet back here for some closing information. The results of today's tests will be used to plan for more training before we leave this planet. You can expect training about one or two times a week. Now listen for your names: group A: Stacey Hill, Monica Boudreaux, Roger Chapman, June Honeycutt, Joseph Jones, Mary Nguyen, Jules Patrick, Bill Bryant, Felicia Gomez, Sophie Burns, Robert Burns, Tom Bell, Wayne Diaz, Lori Shah, Jose Williams, and Brent Lee. Please go with Jose now. Good luck."

All these classmates stood up and followed Jose out to a classroom for their testing. That meant that I would be given the physical tests first. I felt relieved that my brother and sister were in the other group, although I wished that Jose was in my group. It was easy for me to compare myself to him. We could push each other to do better. My group included my girlfriend, Sally Benjamin, as well as Jackie Sands and Mark Lewis. Sally was close to me, and we shared a lot of secrets with each other. Mark was an outstanding athlete. He could run a hundred meters in around 10.6 seconds, which was much faster than any time I could do. Jackie was a great student and very friendly. Everyone liked her. She was always willing to help others.

Also, Jane Iris was in the group. Jane was in Robert's class. She was short, and it seemed that my brother liked her a lot. Becky Strong was next in line. Her name was the exact opposite of her looks. Nancy Lee, who was in Sophie's class, was next. She and my sister often went to the movies together. They liked to put on makeup and clothes that would tend to attract guys they wanted to meet. Mirabelle Jones followed Nancy. She was also an outstanding athlete. Orson Jackson, who was kind of heavy and short for his age, was next. I did not know much about him. The tallest person in the group, Lev Panko, was next. He was 6'3" tall and only sixteen years old. His parents were also tall. His dad was 6'6" tall, and his mom was 6'1" tall. I did not know the last few people. I knew their faces from school and around town but had not socialized with them yet. I expected that we would be meeting each other very soon.

We followed Ms. Rosen into a gym. There were weights laid out on the floor as well as an indoor track and various other apparatus. Ms. Rosen directed everyone to a specific place on the floor. We all had gym shorts or sweatpants on as well as sneakers.

Ms. Rosen began, "We are going to do some warm-ups first before we start the tests. Make sure you have enough space between you and the next person."

Everyone adjusted where they were standing.

Ms. Rosen continued, "Ok, first we will do some jumping jacks and stretching exercises.'"

We all did the jumping jacks and stretching exercises as she demonstrated them to us. I felt fine but noticed a few others were struggling to keep up. After a few minutes rest, we did push-ups. I did thirty-five push-ups, which was better than most people. Sally did ten. Mark did the most, forty-two. Next, we had to run a forty-yard dash. I was timed at 5.1 seconds. Mark was the fastest with a time of 4.6 seconds. Sally was slow with a time of 6.8.

Next, Ms. Rosen explained that we needed to train for high-speed motion. "You will now have some fun and experience High-G training. When astronauts face high acceleration, it is possible to lose consciousness. If one loses consciousness flying while experiencing G-force, the result can be fatal. This would occur when G-forces' action moves the blood away from the brain to the extent that consciousness is lost. Incidents of acceleration-induced loss of consciousness have caused fatal accidents in aircraft capable of sustaining high-G for considerable periods. A G-force of around seven would probably cause most of us to blackout unless we trained to get used to it. Of course, some people never got used to it. Don't worry, none of you will die today, although some of you will not like this very much and may experience some dizziness."

Each trainee was strapped to a chair one at a time on a machine that looked like something we would ride at an amusement park. Each of them only had to experience a G-force of three. All of them were successful, except for two guys. One started to faint when they got to a G-force of three. The other asked for the machine to stop after it got to two. Once everyone was finished, we took a short break. Then we had to do a bench press. I managed to lift 220 pounds, which was not bad for someone weighing 175 pounds. Sophie, on the other hand, did a bench press of forty pounds. Mark was again the best, lifting 300 pounds.

After a few more tests, we switched with the other group and met with Mr. Cunningham. He was about 5'8" tall and actually looked very smart.

He explained, "You are going to be given written problems to solve. Some of the problems have a definite correct answer. Other problems could be solved in a variety of ways. You are to show all of your work, including all of your attempts to solve the problem. Next, there are several situations in which there are no correct answers. This kind of problem could be a situation that might occur on the spaceship. In space, we may often have to make quick decisions that may save or lose lives. When you are finished, all the papers will be collected and analyzed. Once the analysis is completed, the test results will be used to assist the staff in developing individual or group training sessions."

Each person was given thirty questions to answer. Everyone worked extremely hard.

The first question was: "How many months have twenty-eight days?" I had to think about that for a few seconds and put down twelve as my answer. I wondered how many of us had put down one. The questions were obviously designed to make us think.

The second half of the test was challenging. One of the questions described an accident. It stated. "You are with your family. You are the only one that has escaped without injury. You need to save as many people as possible, but you cannot save them all. How will you make your decision to save someone, and who would you be willing to sacrifice?" I really did not want to answer the question.

I had no idea how I would react to a situation like that. I tried to think of a comparable situation and thought about my house burning down with my family stuck inside. How would I know which one to save first? Would some of them die? Would I be willing to sacrifice myself for them? I felt I would try and save my brother and sister first. On the other hand, if I was on the spaceship, I might try to save Dad first since he was the ship's commander, and we needed him to fly and command the ship.

After we turned in our answers, we rejoined the other team where Mrs. Smith

was waiting for us, standing at the podium.

"I hope you all enjoyed the first tests to prepare you for life in space. Indeed, this will be a great challenge. You will be the first teenagers ever to fly in a spaceship. You will be the first teenagers to see the universe like no one has seen it before. You will also be the first teenagers to settle on a new planet. However, by the time we settle on a new planet, you will no longer be teenagers. In fact, some of you could be really old."

That brought a chuckle from most of us. I thought about what Mrs. Smith said. It would take time for all of us to adjust and become acclimated with flying through the galaxies.

"All of the data we collect from your testing will be used to assist you in your training. We will meet each of you aboard the spaceship on a regular basis. You will all be assigned daily chores and duties as deemed fit for each individual. Daily physical exercise will be mandatory. You will also study various subjects related to the stars in the galaxies and scientific discoveries and ship operations. Beginning next week, you will start training full-time daily. I suggest you spend the next week packing up and enjoying whatever you like to do on Earth. After next week, every moment you have will be devoted to getting ready for the big day. Are there any questions?"

No one raised their hands.

"Tomorrow, we will be having a special meeting. I think you will be surprised and pleased at the same time. See you tomorrow at 10:00 in the morning."

Mrs. Smith dismissed everyone for the day.

As we were leaving, we heard her say, "We are counting on you to be humanity's future. Make us proud."

The Spaceship Gets a Name

Chapter 21 – The Spaceship Gets a Name

Sam Burns, Rocky Mountains, CO

The following morning, we arrived at 10:00, as instructed. All of us were curious about what we were going to do today. There were four groups of school desks set up in a circle. Some computers were also set up. Mrs. Smith entered the room and began to speak.

"Good morning, everyone. I hope you had a good night's sleep. Today is going to be very challenging. We are not going home until we complete this task given to me by the leaders of the mission. This means you will all have to work with each other until we have all of you agree on the subject of today's discussion. That task is to name the spaceship. At this point, all we do is call it 'The Ship' or spaceship or spacecraft. Each of the four ships needs a name. However, we are only responsible for naming our own ship. I am dividing you into six groups of ten. I have decided to give each of you an important task that might produce the ship's name. We will be doing a lot of discussing and voting multiple times, probably until we settle on one title. We will break for lunch and dinner as necessary. Hopefully, you will all get to go home tonight."

Sally, Jose, and I looked at each other as if to say: "Are you kidding me?"

Mrs. Smith then called out our names off a list and assigned us our seats. Each group had an appointed leader who would try to facilitate the discussion and attempt to select one name. After each group had chosen their name for the spaceship, everyone would form one group and decide among the four final submitted names. This name would be given to the ship's administrators, and they could accept it or move on to the second choice. They could even make us do it all over again.

I was selected as the leader of one group. Sophie was with me. I hoped she would be cooperative with me as the leader. Jackie Sands was the leader of group two. I thought that was an excellent choice. My brother, Robert, was with her. I did not believe that would help Jackie, but I did hope it would work out for them. Mark Lewis headed the third group, and my friend Jose directed the last group. I wish he had been on my team as we worked well together. Sally was also in his group.

After everyone was in their seats and provided with paper and pencil to keep notes, Mrs. Smith let us know our topics. My group was told to look at star constellations and narrow it down to one choice. That was not going to be easy since there were so many famous stars and star constellations. Jackie's group was told to focus on words that related to strength or peace. Mark's group focused on military words related to space travel. Jose was given a list of famous people's names and instructed to narrow it down to one.

We looked on a computer to list the most famous star constellations and the reason for their names. We did not want to select planet names, so a name like Jupiter was immediately voted out. Then we had to decide what culture or language to use since some of the constellations had different names for the same group of stars. Some of the names selected were: Calisto, a nymph; Ursa Minor, or the Little Bear; and Ursa Major, the Big Bear. We also picked Orion, which is one of the oldest star groups. Indian names such as Alizar and Mizar were also chosen to be on the list. Then we decided to eliminate all the Zodiac names. Hercules was also another name that was removed early. Who would want to call a spaceship 'Hercules'?

After two hours, there was a lunch break. We were provided with various lunch meats and salads, sat around, and discussed how we were doing. I sat down with Jose and Sally. They said that some of the famous names put on a list so far included: Galileo, Einstein, Newton, and Goddard, who is credited with the invention of the first spaceship. They also had eliminated some names, such as the names of all the presidents. I told them about the possible star groups we had selected. All three of us agreed it was not going to be easy to convince everyone to vote for one name among the final four selections.

Once lunch had finished, we returned to our assigned places. We spent another hour narrowing our choices down. For the most part, there was not much disagreement. Finally, my group decided on the name Ursa Minor. It had taken us about three hours to make that decision and handed Mrs. Smith the name we had selected. Calisto had been the other final choice. We looked forward to explaining to the entire group why we chose this name and why it was the perfect name.

My team looked around to see if the other three groups were finished. The other three teams looked like they were in the final stages of making their decision. What names had they selected? My job would be to present and explain why Ursa Minor should be the name of the ship. I was ready to reveal its roots to Roman mythology and the fact that it was a vast constellation.

Thirty minutes later, the other teams had selected their top name and given them to Mrs. Smith. After a ten-minute break, everyone sat down to listen to the presentations of the four group leaders.

I went first. My presentation lasted five minutes. Most of the people there knew all about Ursa Minor. It was used in navigation and was a way of guiding people to the north since it lay close to the North Pole. My group hoped to see Ursa Minor no matter where we traveled in space.

Jose went second with his team's selection. He said, "We have chosen Goddard who did the research and scientific work to build the first liquid-fueled rocket. Some of his own studies were used by the engine and propulsion team on board the ship, so it is only appropriate we call the ship The Goddard. He launched his first successful rocket in 1926 almost exactly a hundred years before this ship. Without him, we might not have this spaceship. I encourage you all to vote for The Goddard."

Mark gave the next name proposal. His group had selected Achilles, a famous soldier from the Greek Trojan Wars. He had tragically died when he was shot in his Achilles heel. However, he had tremendous fighting skills.

Jackie was the last presenter. She stood up and said, "The first three picks are wonderful possibilities. Robert selected our name at first. We played around with other names, but this word was definitely the best one. It is 'Imagine.' There are two reasons for this name. First, we are going to have to use a lot of imagination to solve problems in our travels through space. We do not know what obstacles or problems will occur or when they will happen. All of us are going to have to use our imagination to solve a lot of problems. We will be creating new solutions to old problems and unique solutions to problems we cannot even predict.

"The second reason is John Lennon's "Imagine" song. This song relates to just about everything we will be facing in space. It is almost like he wrote the music for us as we leave Earth. In his song, he talks about imagining no countries, and we really will not have a state anymore, as we will be united with the other ships. All of us going on the trip have to be dreamers, as this has never been done before. He also talks about imagining no possessions. This means we will only have a small number of items on board with no money to buy anything. The last reason is that no one on this ship will go hungry. We are all imagining what the food will be like on this spaceship."

Everyone laughed at this last statement.

Now Mrs. Smith stood up and said, "All of your choices were really great. I want to thank the leaders for working with their groups to select such fine names."

I stood up with everyone, and we applauded the four leaders. They took a bow.

Mrs. Smith continued, "Now we have four sections. I cannot tell you which one I am partial to. It is up to all of you to discuss which names you like or do not like, and then we will have a vote. Each time you vote, we will eliminate one name. The final vote will decide which name you have selected for our ship. I think you can discuss which names you want to vote for among yourselves in small groups for about fifteen minutes. Then I will ask for a paper ballot vote so that you will not know who voted for what name. You can only vote for one name each time. Is that clear to everyone?"

Everyone nodded their heads in agreement and began discussing the pros and cons of each name. I sat with my brother, Robert and Jose. Robert said he was unsure if I liked the idea of Imagine, but I told him it was a brilliant choice and to wait and see what happens. After fifteen minutes, the team leaders handed out a piece of paper to each person in the room. Everyone then put down the name that was their favorite.

Mrs. Smith walked around with a paper bag, and we all dropped our ballot into it. After a few minutes spent tabulating the results, Mrs. Smith stood up and said, "We have our first eliminated name. The name that has been eliminated first is ... "She paused like this was a game show. "Achilles."

A few people let out some ohs and wows, but most people were quiet or happy; their choice had not been eliminated yet.

Then Mrs. Smith said there were three choices left. "They are Ursa Minor, Imagine, and Goddard. Shall we have more discussion, or are you all ready to vote again?"

Sally stood up. "I think we are ready to vote, Mrs. Smith. Most of us know our preference after watching the presentations and having the recent discussion. I think we should just go ahead and vote again."

Mrs. Smith said, "Are we in agreement with Sally? If you agree with her and feel ready to vote again, please raise your hand."

Almost everyone raised their hand.

Robert then asked me, "Do you want me to vote for Ursa Minor since that is your selection?"

I looked at my younger brother and put my hands on his shoulders. "Robert, no, I do not want you to vote for Ursa Minor because that was my team's selection. "If you're going to vote for Imagine, do it! It's a great name."

Robert nodded and said, "Thanks for being a good big brother."

Then Mrs. Smith handed out papers again. Everyone voted for the second time.

We waited for ten minutes while Mrs. Smith counted ballots again. She then stood up and said, "May I have your attention everyone. The next name that has been eliminated is ... Goddard."

When she announced the eliminated name, Jose sighed. He said, "I am a little bit disappointed, but all the selected names have a lot of merits. I will have no problem with either Ursa Minor or Imagine."

During the ten-minute break, other people discussed who they would vote for. Still, no person put pressure on anyone to vote a particular way.

Finally, Mrs. Smith called everyone together for the last vote. "We are going to select our ship's name with this vote. Whichever name wins, I will present it to Dr. Burns and the other officers. They will either decide to keep that name or perhaps the second-place name, depending on their own discussions and feelings. Please put either Ursa Minor or Imagine on your paper and put it in the basket."

The final vote took only a few minutes. After counting the totals, Mrs. Smith told everyone that the vote was reasonably leaning towards one name. "That name is ... Imagine. Congratulations to Robert Burns, who submitted this name."

Everyone clapped for Robert.

Suddenly, Johnny England, one of the students, stood up in the back of the room and said, "I am not going to accept Imagine as the name for the ship. Do you realize we just selected the name of a song written by a pot-smoking Beatle name John Lennon? We cannot name this ship for a drug addict who was up to no good. If that is the name of this ship, I will not be going to be going with you. I would rather stay on Earth."

I knew about Johnny because his dad worked in the engine room, and his mom worked in the cafeteria. He rarely hung out with us, and his parents didn't bring him to many of our school events, so none of us hardly knew him.

After he had spoken, all the students were upset that he waited for the last minute to speak up and had made a threat. Many were rolling their eyes and shaking their heads at Johnny. They all wanted to go home, as it had been a long day for them. It was already past dinnertime.

Mrs. Smith said, "Calm down. First, we are not going to change the name at this moment."

Many students clapped when she said that.

"We had a democratic process in which everyone was allowed to participate and make their feelings known before the votes. Johnny, you should have spoken up earlier. I am sorry, but I object to your demand. John Lennon may have smoked pot, but he was a peace-loving man. I suggest you go home and discuss this with your parents. If they want, they can bring the matter to Dr. Burns, who I am sure will listen to you and consider your objection in making the final decision. Please try to work this out. We will surely miss you if you decide to stay here, but that is your choice."

Mrs. Smith made her closing remarks. "Please make sure you are here tomorrow again at 10:00 for more training. Everyone, please go home and have a nice dinner. I would like Johnny, Sam, Jose, and Mark to stay so we can continue to resolve the situation at hand."

Everyone else stood up and left. It was a fantastic day for bonding with the other students except for Johnny's complaint.

Mrs. Smith asked the four of us to join her at a conference table in her office. She handed out sodas to each of us and some potato chips. Mark, Jose, and I were on one side of the table. Johnny was on the other side. You could see in his face that he was still upset or angry at the events that had just occurred. All four boys ate silently, waiting for Mrs. Smith to begin.

After a moment, Mrs. Smith said, "Thank you for staying here. I think we need to talk about what just happened and what we can do to ameliorate the situation. If we are going to be on a spaceship together for a very long duration, we need to explore ways to resolve our differences. There will be times when we cannot get what we want, and we either have to compromise or agree to disagree with each other. We also have to follow the chain of command, which starts with Dr. Burns for most situations. If you cannot agree with what I just said, you need to give serious consideration to not journey on the spaceship, no matter what we call it. Do you all agree with that?"

Jose, Mark, and I looked at each other and nodded in agreement. Johnny looked at the three boys and barely moved at all.

Mrs. Smith then looked directly at Johnny and said, "Johnny, do you agree with this ground rule? If you do not, then I will have to set up a meeting with your parents and Dr. Burns."

Johnny looked at Mrs. Smith like he had no idea what to say. Finally, he was just about to speak when a group of trainees that included Robert and Sophie came running into the room, interrupting the meeting. Mrs. Smith and the four boys knew immediately something was wrong. Everyone seemed to be having a hard time breathing.

Sophie spoke up first. "We have a major problem. Several of the trainees have collapsed not far from here and appear to be in awful distress. There is a terrible smell in the air that is making us ill. I have no idea what the hell just happened, but we need to do something fast."

Mrs. Smith immediately asked, "What direction is the smell coming from?"

Robert said, "It appears to be coming from the lake near the training facility."

I jumped up and said, "I think I know what is happening. My dad told me that years ago, this area was used by phosphate mining companies. In their attempt to obtain phosphate, these companies dug deep into the Earth. Basically, they stripped the area of vegetation and wildlife—part of this process used sulfuric acid. When combined with phosphorus, it produces phosphoric acid. I believe the smell that is out there is sulfuric acid, which can be very destructive to the environment. One would hardly be able to breathe, and your lungs would feel like they were on fire. We need to neutralize the chemicals and get paramedics here as soon as possible to assist everyone. Call 911, Mrs. Smith, and I will call my dad to immediately come and figure out how to neutralize this. Everyone else needs to come inside and not leave this facility until further notice. If we have gas masks in this facility, please use them."

Everyone, including Mrs. Smith, nodded. Mrs. Smith called 911. Most of us assisted those who could be moved inside the facility. We closed off the windows and doors to prevent the spreading of the chemicals inside as best as we could.

About five minutes later, several ambulances arrived and immediately began checking students and providing much-needed oxygen. Several trainees were transported to the hospital.

My dad showed up about five minutes later with Bob and some other engineers. After a concise discussion, he called someone at the space center to deliver a large amount of lye. Meanwhile, Jose, Mark, and I checked every one to assure them that they would have this under control shortly.

Johnny sat by himself, face down with his head in his hands. He seemed to be muttering to himself, but Sam could not figure out what he was saying. Sam did not have time to console Johnny now, as he was too busy helping everyone else.

After about an hour, a chemical company showed up. All of the workers had white uniforms on and oxygen masks to facilitate their breathing. My dad and Bob put on suits and masks that were provided by the chemical company. They left very quickly and drove off toward the lake.

All of the trainees huddled together and waited to hear when they could leave. Except for a few snacks and drinks, there was no food available, and after a long day, some of them were becoming very hungry and very cranky. Nerves were on edge. We divided ourselves into groups. I sat with Sally and Jose. Johnny sat by himself.

Five hours later, or almost midnight, my dad came back inside to give the all-clear and announce that the chemical spill had been neutralized. Further clean up would be needed, but for now, everyone could safely go home. At that point, a swarm of parents showed up. They embraced their kids. Everyone looked relieved that no one was seriously hurt or sick from the chemicals.

Mrs. Smith asked my dad to meet with her for a moment. I was within earshot, unwilling to miss anything.

Mrs. Smith said, "I am thankful that you were able to alleviate the threat so fast. I was confident that you would do that, considering how long I have known you and your family. I also want to add that Sam, Sophie, and Robert have been wonderful trainees. In particular, Sam has shown me that he is a born leader, just like his dad."

This made my dad blush. It made me feel proud.

"Jose and Mark are also going to be great leaders on the spaceship. On the other hand, there are a few that I have concerns about and may create problems later when we are in space. Johnny is one of them. He is a loner and likes to aggravate others. He is not showing a willingness to compromise and get along with everyone. You may want to keep your eyes on him. Again, congratulations on getting us through this and having such a wonderful family. Say hi to your wife for me."

My dad thanked Mrs. Smith for her work beyond the call of duty and left with me, Sophie and Robert. When we arrived home, we were all too beat to do anything except go to bed. As I dozed off, I could not stop thinking about Johnny, figuring out how I could help him. We couldn't let anything like this happen on the Imagine.

CHAPTER 22

Quality Timd

Chapter 22 – Quality Time

Sam Burns, Rocky Mountains, CO

A few days later, my dad came to the training session and informed us that the ship was now called Imagine. Johnny was now silent when he heard the decision. He probably had a long discussion with his parents, who told him to forget about the name and focus on the task. We also found out the names of the other three spaceships. Each crew had done their own voting, or the government had decided on their ships' names.

The Russian spaceship was going to be called Oligarch. It was apparent why the name was chosen. The German ship was to be called Frieden, which means peace. The Australians named their ship The Kangaroo in honor of the famous animal.

My dad said, "I have ordered some painters to put Imagine in the appropriate places."

After training, my family went home. My dad and mom went out for the night to meet with some friends and had ordered some pizza for Sophie, Robert, and I to eat.

Sophie started a conversation. "What do you guys think about this trip into space? I'm not crazy about it."

Robert answered Sophie. "Whatever our dad and mom decide is fine with me."

I spoke next. "Dad has a huge responsibility. He has spent a long time thinking about this and has really given up his life for this project. I don't want to leave Earth, but I have to go with our parents."

Sophie asked, "Suppose I do not want to go with them, do you think they would force me? Or are they willing to leave me behind?"

I looked at her and said, "Are you afraid to go on this trip? You will not have much of a future if you don't go."

Robert was silent and focused on the pizza. He blurted out, "I am scared too. I really want to go to high school here on Earth."

"That is understandable, Robert, but most of your friends and class-mates will be on board with us," I said. "Their parents are working for Dad and getting this ship ready."

Sophie said, "Do you realize what we have to leave behind? I can't take my records with me or my doll collection or most of my clothes. What about my favorite television shows? It will be so boring in space."

I said, "Yes I know. We also have to leave our PlayStation behind too, but I was told there will be some good games on board to play. Instead of focusing on what you will not have, why don't you ask me some questions about what we will have and what life will be like?"

"Ok, Sam, what will life be like?"

I said, "First of all, our family members will each have a small room. Mom and Dad get a larger bedroom since they are a couple. Also, Dad is running the ship. Each of us gets a bed, a closet, a dresser, and a desk. All the furniture will be bolted to the wall or floor, so they can't fly around if we lose gravity while we travel. We can't have any pictures or posters on the wall, so please take pictures of whatever you want. We can then download them into the ship's computer or cloud and have access to them. Each of us will get a digital frame on our dresser where we can look at pictures. All of us will be working or doing something every day. We need to learn what is on the spaceship and how to use various equipment."

Sophie looked pained. "That sucks! I need more than work. What guys am I going to date? Look at me. I am twenty years old. By the time we reach wherever we are going, I could be an old lady or dead. Who will want to marry me?"

Robert cut in, "No one wants to marry you anyway, so don't worry about that."

Sophie looked like she was going to hit Robert, but she held back. "Seriously, guys, what about a social life?"

I explained, "There will be about a thousand people on board. I expect between sixty and one hundred twenty teens will also be on board with their parents. You will just have to make an effort to meet them, and who knows where that will lead? Sally will be on board, so I hope to continue seeing her."

Sophie said, "Great! You have a girlfriend, but I do not have a boyfriend. I need to talk, dance, meet friends, go out on Friday and Saturday nights. You can't just walk off the ship."

Robert then said, "You can if you want to."

"Shut up, Robert. I do not need your smart-aleck ways right now," Sophie exclaimed.

Robert then asked, "Will we have alcohol on the trip? When I am eighteen, I want to drink beer."

Sophie said, "Little brother, you are only sixteen. You have five years to go before you can drink unless you have been stealing liquor from someone."

Robert said, "No, I have not stolen anything from the stores or anyone. But will there even be any alcohol on this ship? It seems there are going to be strict rules."

I jumped in, "There will be rules, and some will be very strict. I imagine we can't go certain places on the ship, as they will be off-limits to everyone except the officers. There have to be strict rules on a spaceship."

Sophie said, "Let's be serious here. I have a question about where we are going. I have heard that on different planets, we may have different weights. Right now, I weigh 120 pounds. What will I weigh on a new planet?"

I said, "That is a good question. I learned a lot about this in physics class. We are not going to be on a planet in this solar system. I can compute what you will weigh on each planet in this system, but I do not know anything about where we're going."

"Weight equals mass times surface gravity. Multiplying your weight on Earth by a certain number will give you your weight on the surface of each planet. If you weigh 120 pounds on Earth, you multiply that by 2.34, and you would weigh about 280 pounds on Jupiter, which would make you an obese, heavy woman. It would probably be difficult to walk around if you weigh that much. However, if you lived on Pluto, you would weigh 120 x .06, about seven pounds, which would allow you to jump higher than ever before. Each planet has a different number to use to multiply by your weight. The constant numbers are:

Mercury: 0.38
Venus: 0.91
Earth: 1.00
Mars: 0.38
Jupiter: 2.34
Saturn: 1.06
Uranus: 0.92
Neptune: 1.19
Pluto: 0.06

So, you do the math."

"Wow," said Sophie, "I would rather live on Pluto than Jupiter for sure. I could move a lot faster."

"But you would die very quickly probably on either of those planets, so it is not an option for us. Also, Pluto is no longer considered a planet."

"How many days in a year will we have?" asked Robert.

I answered, "That is another excellent question. I am not sure since I do not know where we will live. I do not even know if we will have the same months of the year since they are all based on moons and the sun. The Earth goes around the sun right now once every 365 days. If we go around more often, I do not know how that will affect your age or how we will figure out your age. If we lived on Jupiter, we probably would not live very many years. Pluto takes about 248 years to go around the sun once, so we would all die as babies if we count birthdays the same way as on Earth."

Robert said, "Will they even have birthday parties on board the ship? What about candy, ice cream, cake?"

"I have no idea how they will do those things on board, but I suppose they will have some celebrations. People need to feel happy."

"This trip is going to take a long time to get used to. I will miss: going horseback riding with my friends, swimming in the lakes and ocean, parties at my friends' homes, great soup and salad, and restaurants. What will you miss the most, Robert?"

"I will miss my PlayStation and the Madden games; the rock climbing we did with Dad; my football and baseball teams; and the best hamburger places you can find like Smashburger."

I said, "I will miss: my wrestling friends; Sunday NFL football; NBA games; the walks to and from school every day as I pass beautiful homes and mountains; incredible views of flowers and trees blooming; and when it begins to snow in the fall."

All three of them were becoming more and more depressed as they thought about what they would miss.

They were silent for a few moments, then Sophie said, "Look, guys, the one thing I will not have to miss is being with you two. And our parents. I know it's corny. Plus, I will have some friends from school on board even if I do not marry them and become an old lady with no children."

They all laughed.

When Dad and Mom came home, they asked about our evening.

Sophie said, "It was great. We did some sibling bonding."

We all enjoyed a family hug.

Just A Walk In the Park

Chapter 23 – Just a Walk in the Park

Sam Burns, Rocky Mountains, CO

Everything was becoming more and more hectic with all the planning for the Imagine. We'd already accomplished almost a year of training. We knew we would be going through around three years of training. Although we'd named the spaceship and undergone many tests, the daily routine was grueling. We already saw huge improvements among members of our Goddard graduating class. I couldn't believe how much stronger we were all getting and how many skills we were acquiring so quickly. Astronauts need to be generalists, and we were definitely on track. No one was falling behind, thankfully.

Some days we practiced our skills at monitoring our health in our suits. Other days we spent time thinking in three dimensions. Some days, we spent time underwater to practice the physically demanding experience of spacewalking. My favorite, although it was the scariest, was training in simulated real-time failures in virtual reality. Jose and Sally both loved it when we practiced survival techniques and learning about the human body. Robert's personal favorite became studying electronics repairs.

I was so happy that what we were all really learning was to allow cooler heads to prevail since difficult tasks under extremely stressful situations would probably become our everyday life. It seemed like we needed to become experts at just about anything. Sometimes when I woke up, I wondered how we would get through another grueling day of training. Then, thankfully we'd have a chance to have a social life.

Sally and I had hardly had a moment together alone since graduation. On a beautiful day, we got together for a picnic at a local park surrounded by the Rockies. We brought sandwiches and some soft drinks.

"Sam, I would like to believe that everything will turn out all right, but I do have some questions for you on a spiritual level. Want to hear them?" Sally said.

"Go ahead and ask. My family is really not that religious, but we do respect people's right to religion."

"Okay, here goes. If we are leaving the solar system and galaxy, will God follow us there too, or would he remain on Earth?"

"Interesting question. I think the Declaration of Independence refers to God as a universal deity. That means if God exists, the deity will exist wherever we go."

"Nice answer," Sally said. "Next question, if you believe in heaven, where will we go when we die in space? Do you think heaven is limited to Earth? Is there a different heaven if we live on another planet?"

"Another good question, Sally. I wish I knew the answer to that. I would hope that heaven is everywhere, and no matter where you die, if you have been a good person, your soul will go to heaven."

"Okay," said Sally. "Will there be any religious leaders on board like a priest, a minister, a rabbi, or an imam?"

"My dad and some of the officers can probably perform weddings and stuff like that. There will also be counselors to help people. I imagine some people will get very depressed after a long period on the spaceship and need someone to talk with. One thing my dad has always wrestled with is the topic of religion. He supports everyone praying in whatever religion they want, as long as it is peaceful. On the Imagine, he did not look for specific religious beliefs. I am sure he would not mind someone serving as a chaplain or minister or rabbi if anyone wanted to take on that responsibility."

Sally continued asking questions. "What will the laws be on the spaceship, and who will make them up?"

"Well, my dad and the officers will have some rules related to safety and performing one's duty or job. I would think that crimes like theft and assault and even murder would be punishable, but I do not know how they will set up trials. It may be more military in nature. I have no idea. I would hope that no one on the ship does something stupid like harming another passenger deliberately. I don't think my dad is going to kick you off the spaceship for something very minor. You have been asking all the tough questions. I want to ask you some."

"Okay, shoot," Sally said.

"How do you see our relationship? I mean, we are good friends. We went to prom together. Yet, we are still only eighteen years old and have most of our lives ahead of us if things go well. We could possibly live a lot longer than a hundred, depending on cryopreservation, stem cell research, and cloning."

"If we were not going on this ship, we would probably be a couple now and planning our college choices together. If we didn't see other people, we'd be finding out if we are meant to be. Now that we are going to space together with our families, it may be a lot different. Certainly, I hope we see each other a lot. If we see each other too much, we might become sick of each other before we are halfway to our ultimate destination."

"I very much doubt that I will ever become sick of you, Sally. My family will be on board, and I will have a lot of responsibilities, but I do not see how I am going to survive this trip without a friend like you."

I walked over to Sally and gave her a big hug. Then, I kissed her on the cheek. "I hope I gave the right answer," I said.

Sally replied, "Yeah, Sam, you gave the right answer."

After that, we enjoyed the rest of the picnic before heading home.

CHAPTER 24

Faith

Chapter 24 – Faith

Sam Burns, Glenwood Springs, CO

I was home watching Star Trek's old reruns when my dad came into the room and sat down next to me.

"I remember watching those movies as a kid and dreaming of doing something like that. I never thought it would be possible, but I believe in what I am doing, and soon we will be leaving Earth. What do you think, Sam? Am I an imbecile trying to get everyone killed? Or do you have the faith to believe in me and search for a new life?"

After training had become our routine, I was getting more used to the idea of space travel. I looked at my dad. We had had some really great times.

"Dad, you know I love you and Mom very much and will follow you to the universe's end. No matter what happens in the future, I believe in you, one thousand percent. But I do have a lot of questions that you probably can answer about this trip."

"Ask me anything you want to know," my dad said.

"Well, for starters, if I remember correctly, it will take years to leave the solar system. Given the fact that none of our planets in this solar system appear habitable, how are we going to live long enough to find a new planet?"

"Excellent question, son. Believe me. Many people have asked the same thing. My team of experts has developed a solution to deal with the aging process, as we may need to stay alive for several hundred or even a thousand years before reaching our destination."

I looked at him. "People are not immortal, Dad."

"No, they are not, but we have developed and have become experts on ensuring we can live for a very long time, barring a physical accident. We will be putting people and crewmembers to sleep on and off as needed to prolong life. This will include everyone on the ship."

"How will we do that?"

"We have perfected what is known as cryonics. Robert Ettinger is generally credited with this process of freezing someone. However, all of his subjects died when they were frozen or, at least, were not able to regain life. He published a book, *The Prospect of Immortality*. We have followed up on his research with our own. Despite early failures, we have made great strides in awakening people after they have been frozen. All of our crew can be taken out of cryopreservation within one hour and be placed back in stasis within fifteen minutes. Also, we can clone everyone. Of course, if the cryopreservation fails, then that person is going to be in a lot of trouble as far as their life is concerned. When we get to the ship, you will become familiar with this process and just about everything that occurs there. We also have stem cell researchers on board that can grow various organs to transplant into bodies when essential and cure diseases. Dr. Sato is one of the leading experts in this area. You will enjoy meeting her. Are there any more questions?"

"Yes, Dad, that is interesting, but exactly what the hell am I going to be doing on a ship like that? I planned on attending college and choosing a career."

"That is true, son. All of your training is being done for the possibility that someday you will replace me as commander of the spaceship. You will have many outstanding professionals that will instruct you about the ship. We have been working on it now for over eight years. Perhaps it is time to take a tour of the ship and begin to see what is in store for you and your future. I will make the arrangements with Bob, who you will learn a lot from."

He stood up.

"You can bring Jose with you, as he will also be an officer. Now get some rest."

Seeing the Imagine for the First Time

Chapter 25 – Seeing the Imagine for the First Time

Sam Burns, Rocky Mountains

Imagine, my dad, the leader of our spaceship called Imagine. We flew to a location in the Rocky Mountains. Two massive doors opened up that actually looked like part of the mountain. As we got close to a specific peak, my dad radioed ahead to someone. My mouth opened wide in awe when I saw this. This really was not a cave, even if it appeared that way. The space inside was almost like a vast lab that my dad could have worked in at Boeing.

Suddenly, we entered what seemed like a cave in a mountain. We actually flew into the mountain. It was like, Oh My God! In our training, we learned that astronauts regularly train in caves. We'd mostly been training in an abandoned school to promote effective communication, team dynamics, decision-making, problem-solving, and leadership. We'd also practice our mapping and navigational skills in local caves. Now, we were entering a much bigger cave where Imagine was being built. I had no idea my dad was working with such top guns! People were doing all kinds of research as well as working on the Imagine. It made sense since he was always dealing with top gun aviation, but what blew my mind was seeing him in action. He had served in Iraq and Afghanistan as a pilot, but seeing him navigating was way different from anything I could ever have imagined. I had a new respect for my dad all of a sudden.

After we landed, a man dressed in a white uniform met us. My dad introduced me to Bob Jackson.

"Sam, this is Bob Jackson. Bob is my best friend and co-director of this mission. He is also someone I would trust with my life."

Then he turned to Bob. "Bob, this is my son, Sam, and his friend Jose. Both of them will be junior officers on the spaceship. You already know Jose's dad. Can you please introduce Jose and Sam to our project and show them around a little? I will be back in three hours. I need to meet with the space launching team to review some of their concerns and keep us on schedule."

"No problem. I will give Sam and Jose a VIP tour," Bob replied.

"Bob Jackson helped build and develop the ship and knows every nook and bolt of the spacecraft. Listen to everything he says. I will be back later, and you can tell me what you learned and ask questions."

Dad then left for his meeting.

After he left, Bob explained his background. "First to clarify things, you may call me Bob. We will be on this mission for a long time, and soon you will be an officer just like me. I was raised in Boston. I attended MIT and then the Air Force Academy. I was married for ten years, but we did not have any children. My wife died of cancer. I was kind of depressed when your dad asked me to assist him. Before that, I studied aeronautical engineering and worked on several government projects, including spaceships. My job was to build the fastest possible spaceship ever produced. Soon after, your dad approached me and offered me a position. At first, I thought he was totally crazy, but after some convincing—and your dad can really be convincing—I decided to join his team. I am thankful I have had the opportunity to work with someone like your dad. If there are no questions, let's get started. Of course, you want to see the ship, but first, a little history lesson for you. Why is Earth failing so rapidly?"

"Why?" I asked.

"By the year 2030, the polar ice will break up much more quickly, leading to the oceans' rapid rising. It has already started doing that. As you know, we have already lost a lot of islands and land. As you know, your dad has visited many of those places. According to most historians, Earth started to fail when the Industrial and later the Technology Age boomed. Siegfried Marcus built the first gasoline-powered combustion engine in 1870. Soon after the automobile was invented, we made too many chemical products, including gasoline for automobiles. We did not provide protection for the environment. The environment's impact totally destroyed the ozone layer, which helped prevent the sun's rays from leading to terrible skin cancers. It also led to global warming. Temperatures soared to 120 degrees in such cities as Houston and Miami; Death Valley reached 220 degrees. All of this global warming led to the development of more powerful air conditioners run via nuclear reactors.

"In the late 1900s and early 2000s, many leaders, including Al Gore, brought attention to the environment, but many politicians, especially the Republicans, ignored the warnings until it was too late. Actually, it was during the 1960s that scientists started to really notice the difference in global warming. People lobbied Congress to no avail until they realized it was futile to do any more convincing. Your dad spent years putting together four teams located in four mountain locations around the world. Mountains were chosen to avoid flooding and rising temperatures. I was part of a top-secret worldwide engineering team that developed the four spaceships. All four teams plan to launch on the same day. These spaceships are virtually indestructible and made of the finest materials. So, do you have any questions now?"

We approached the spaceship. "Wow," was all Jose and I could say. It was the biggest thing I had ever seen. I had no idea how many people had worked to create it.

"Beautiful, isn't it?" Bob asked.

We entered the spaceship by walking up a huge ramp.

As we started walking on the Imagine, Bob noted, "In the past, spacecraft were built primarily from titanium, vanadium, and carbon steel. The ship can withstand extreme temperatures and speed without structural failure. The ship weighs 255,000 pounds right now. There are 1,800 rooms on the ship, of which many are sleeping quarters. Sleeping quarters are designed to allow families to live in small apartments. Those that are single may either have their own room or share a room depending on their rank. We have tried to think of everything possible to make the traveling enjoyable. We have many laboratories, storage areas, and training facilities. We also have places for recreation. It will be your job to familiarize yourself with every room on this spacecraft."

I was dumbfounded. I asked, "How long do you think it will take me to learn about every room? I cannot imagine knowing where 1,800 rooms are located."

"Probably about 200 years," Bob replied.

Jose and I were not sure he was telling a joke or if he were serious. "How many people will be on the Imagine?" I asked.

"Each spaceship can hold up to a thousand people. This includes the crew. Everyone will have duties to perform. This means that each person will either have or learn specific skills as needed. If you are not an officer or have an essential job onboard, you will be assigned various duties such as cleaning the ship."

"Will all of our classmates be assigned specific duties on the ship?" Jose asked.

"Yes. But I understand that one of your friends, Janet Romano, and her father, Grissom, will not be coming with us. However, you may not all be awake at the same time, as some of us will be sleeping in stasis for long periods."

"What do you mean by that?"

"In order to lengthen our lives, we hope to put people in stasis for short periods. This could range from three months to a year at a time."

Jose asked, "Will Sam and I be working together all the time?"

Bob said, "Yes. Most likely, you will be together, as you are both training to be officers. There will be times you may both be on the bridge. Other times Sam may be on duty, and you could be asleep or in cryopreservation."

"Yes. My dad explained about cryopreservation," I said. "Will you be showing us where this happens?"

"Yes, you will see the cryo unit and many other places on the ship. You may be most interested in the bridge, as that is where you will be training to work with your dad. It is the command center and can control anything that happens onboard."

An unbelievable feeling came over me. How could I possibly be responsible for the lives of a thousand people on a spaceship? I could not even drive a car yet. Or fly a plane. There was going to be so much to learn.

Bob seemed to sense my feelings.

"Don't worry, Sam, you will be fine. It will be many years before you become a full captain of this vessel, and you will have many others to train and assist you. Both of you must be hungry or thirsty. Why don't we start with something enjoyable like the cafeteria? Follow me."

Does It Actually Taste Like Chicken>

Chapter 26 – Does It Actually Taste like Chicken?

Sam Burns, Rocky Mountains, CO

Jose and I arrived at the cafeteria. The chefs greeted us. Luis and his assistant Carla Benito were the chefs on the ship. They both wore typical chef uniforms.

"Nice to meet you both. Sam, your dad actually saved my life by not letting me be deported. He is a great man," Luis said.

Luis explained that since we would not be able to go food shopping like we did on Earth, we would eventually run out of food unless we could genetically engineer food from plants and animals. "What is great about this is we can make food samples with the DNA from other plants and animals.

"We can also alter those genes so food will grow faster and taste differently. This will provide us with more nutritious food and food that will hopefully taste better. We have a full stock room of DNA samples of plants and animals that we can use to experiment with and make enough food for the entire ship. We also have a nutritionist who will help ensure that we all eat healthy meals most of the time. Would you like to try a genetically engineered chicken sandwich or hamburger?"

"Sure," I said, not knowing what to expect. "I think I will have the chicken sandwich."

Jose said, "I'll try the burger."

A few minutes later, Carla brought both sandwiches and some bottled water to our table. Carla said, "Please let me know how it tastes. We take feedback on everything so we can improve the taste and quality of our food."

I took a small bite. The sandwich actually tasted precisely like chicken sandwich should taste. In fact, it was probably better than any chicken sandwich my mom had made.

Jose also liked his hamburger. "Delicious," he said.

We also had ice cream that was engineered.

Bob came back when we finished lunch and then took us to visit one of the entertainment rooms.

I figured that if we weren't going to have to sacrifice taste, I might also be pleasantly surprised by the entertainment room. I had some doubts. Given all the simulations and training we were doing using virtual reality, I wondered whether everything we were ever going to experience in terms of entertainment meant sacrificing the enjoyment I had in being in different environments, like a real basketball court or a baseball field. Would I ever get over that?

Lots of Sacrifices

Chapter 27 – Lots of Sacrifices

Sam Burns, Rocky Mountains, CO

Bob explained what they had in mind when they designed the entertainment room for Jose and me. "If we are going to be traveling for years in space, there will be times when one needs to relax, listen to music, watch any old TV show or a movie. On this ship, we have the most extensive collection of music, movies, and programs for people to watch for all ages. We also have plenty of tapes of old sporting events. Babe Ruth, Michael Jordan, and Tiger Woods are right here with us. We can also put you in a simulated game so you can test your skills against the pros, or you can compete against other people on the spaceship."

I said, "I don't think I can beat Michael Jordan in basketball."

Bob said, "Why don't we see it!"

Suddenly, a Michael Jordan look-alike appeared on a screen with a ball and actually said, "Come on, let's play some one-on-one."

Bob said, "Go behind the screen, and you will see yourself on the court with him."

I walked around the screen while Jose and Bob watched. It now looked like I was on the court with MJ.

MJ said, "Your ball. Let's see what you got."

I started dribbling and moving towards the hoop. I tried to take a shot with the ball, but MJ blocked it. He then took the ball, dribbled behind the three-point line, dribbled around his back, and went right past me. It was an easy dunk for him.

MJ said, "One to nothing, fifteen wins."

I thought I did not have a prayer of scoring against him and was correct. He won 15-0.

MJ said, "You better practice your defense and shooting. I look forward to a rematch someday."

All I could say was, "I guess I have 200 years to be like Mike."

Next, Bob asked Jose what sport he wanted to try.

Jose paused for a moment and said, "I would like to wrestle with Dan Gable, who won a gold medal in the Olympics and lost only one match in high school, college, and the Olympics. If we were not going into space, I would probably be a college wrestler. Dan Gable was probably the best American wrestler of all time. I have watched some tapes, and he was absolutely fantastic. He could have probably pinned Captain America."

Bob said, "I will set up the wrestling mat for you and Dan. You will actually feel like you are wrestling him. By the way, if you want to be in a movie with Ironman or Captain America, we can do that too."

Jose changed into some wrestling clothes, put on knee pads, and went to the middle of the mat to meet Dan Gable. They shook hands and waited for the referee to begin the match.

Bob and I watched intensely.

I said, "If he can avoid being pinned, it will be a miracle. Dan almost always pinned his opponent."

Suddenly the referee raised his hand and said, "Wrestle."

Dan circled around, eyeing Jose and saying nothing at all. Jose was in a wrestling pose with his hands out front and ready to move when Dan attacked, which was bound to happen any second. All of a sudden, Gable went down on one knee and slid toward Jose, putting his arms around the knees, and picked Jose up in the air. He put one arm around his neck and flipped Jose on his back. The referee got on his stomach and then slammed the mat, signaling Jose was pinned. The whole match took all of nineteen seconds.

Jose got up, shook Dan's hand and said, "It was a pleasure to wrestle the greatest wrestler of all time. I will try and do better next time."

Dan just smiled, and the program ended.

I asked Jose how he felt losing in nineteen seconds.

Jose said, "It was the fastest I have ever lost a match. He was just too fast and too good. The good thing is I could never have wrestled with him had it been real life as Dan is about seventy years old now."

After that, we looked over many of the recreational activities. There were board games, TV reality games, chess, checkers, poker, and so forth. There was also a music recording studio where the crew members could join famous singers or create their own music. I thought Sophie would probably like that and spend a lot of time there.

Bob said, "If you two have any ideas to improve this place, just let me know. When it comes to recreation and free time, we want to be able to satisfy everyone on board. Now let's get back to the entrance."

Jose and I thanked Bob for the tour and looked forward to seeing more next time.

Dad showed up at the entrance about five minutes later and had a private discussion with Bob for about ten minutes. We noticed they were very serious and seemed to be concerned about something.

He then came over to me. He explained that there were going to be some issues that he could not tell us about, but there was no need for us to worry. When we were more familiar with the ship and ready to assume more duties, he would share more information.

During the short flight home with Jose and Dad, we talked about packing for the big trip. Dad explained that all the furniture was attached to the bulkheads since we could not have furniture moving all over the place. Everyone would be limited to what they could bring on board. Uniforms would be provided to all working staff. However, on a day off, we could wear whatever we wanted. Laundry machines would be provided in living quarters. We would all be limited to digital photographs, as pictures could not be hung up anywhere. This meant that

I would have to take photos of my photos to remember important moments from my youth and many accomplishments. Some of my most precious memories would have to be left behind. I really doubted the Cloud to preserve all of my pictures would extend into space.

When I got home, we discussed the whole packing-up procedure again with my brother and sister. My sister took it really hard. She was upset that she could not bring all of her favorite music and dolls along. Since there would be no phones on board, we would all be given devices to communicate with everyone on the ship. These devices were to be strictly used for business and not for pleasure. This meant no music or apps could be stored on them. How could anyone live like that!

Mom suggested we make lists of things we wanted to bring on the trip so we could start weeding out what we could not bring. My list included my favorite baseball mitt along with two baseballs from the Boston Red Sox. My brother wanted to bring his soccer ball and his Game Boy. My sister wanted to bring her makeup and a few dolls she had kept over the years. We would not need books or Kindles since we could access any book we wanted via the ship's computers. Google had installed a unique program for us to do that.

We had to finish packing by September 15th. I thought about everything we had learned today and was thrilled that I had finally seen the Imagine.

Chapter 28 – Simulating Life in Orbit

Sam Burns, Rocky Mountains, CO

We weren't even halfway done with our training program. It seemed like every waking hour was spent learning a skill that we would need on board. Sometimes, I just missed the life we were going to be leaving behind. But there was little time to dwell on it.

Today all the trainees were going to experience weightlessness in a capsule to learn how to move around and manipulate objects. We had attended about a year and a half of classes so far. We had the opportunity to tell other students participating in our training what the spaceship was like. Everyone we spoke to seemed very excited. And the most exciting part was that the training had made us stronger, more agile, confident, and a lot more proactive since our first training sessions. We could see it in the way that fellow trainees would jump at a chance to put their skills to the test helping crewmembers with engineering and electronics problems, the marked improvements in our virtual reality performance, as well as some of the innovative inventions that some of our student teams were inspired to start-up.

After the discussion, which lasted about thirty minutes, everyone got dressed in bulky spacesuits. Three students entered the capsule and waited for the instructor to turn off the gravity. At first, students pushed themselves around. Then, each of us had to accomplish a specific task while experiencing near weightlessness. When it was our turn, I had to try and unwrap a chocolate bar and eat it before it was lost, while Jose had to adjust several knobs. Sophie had to lift a hose and spray some water. After about an hour of training, we were transported to the training pool.

There, we focused on understanding and experiencing buoyancy. Our underwater training session lasted six hours, and we wore 300-pound suits. We concentrated on anaerobic bursts and endurance training. We were getting used to these daily aquatic training sessions since we'd performed them regularly over the past year.

Each of the trainees completed the lesson successfully, and we were let go for the day. Since we were all interested in either sports or music, we headed to the entertainment room. Sophie started talking about which singers she was going to practice with. Robert fantasized about playing professional football.

I also had the opportunity to spend some time with Mark. He wanted to run the 100-meter dash against Carl Lewis.

I said, "Mark, you are one hell of an athlete. I pity Carl Lewis when you beat him in the 100."

"I'm not going to beat Carl Lewis, but thanks for the compliment. I do enjoy running and competing and look forward to seeing you on the Imagine," he replied.

I asked him, "What job have you been assigned to on the ship?"

"I was told that I will either be working with security or weapons. I may even become a shuttle pilot, but that's going to take a lot of practice."

"I sure would not want to mess with you if I was in trouble on board."

"Thanks, Sam, you're quite an athlete yourself and very smart. I look forward to working with you on board. I do have a personal question to ask you."

"What is it?"

"I think your sister is cute, and when we finally get going, would you mind if I ask her out on a date?"

"I am sure Sophie will appreciate it if you ask her. Do you want me to find out if she likes you or not?"

"Not right now," Mark replied. I would appreciate it if you do not mention this conversation to your sister. When I am ready, and we are speeding through space, I will let you know."

"My lips are sealed until then. Good luck with your security and shuttle training. I am sure you will do a great job."

We shook hands and left for the day. I met up with Sally, and we had dinner together. Suppose we were going to be spending so much time practicing for space underwater and in near weightlessness. In that case, we were going to need to enjoy food on Earth for as long as possible. We went to Sally's favorite restaurant, which was a local barbecue. Then we started driving home pretty exhausted from the full day of training. I saw a text from my dad that he needed to meet with Jose and me the following day first thing in the morning to talk about something very important.

When I dropped Sally off at her house on Blake Avenue near Sayre Park, a couple of blocks away from ours, I told her I wouldn't be at the morning training session because something had come up.

"Well, you better let me know what it is afterward. No telling what your dad is going to have you do."

Simulating Life in Orbit

Chapter 28 – Simulating Life in Orbit

Sam Burns, Rocky Mountains, CO

We weren't even halfway done with our training program. It seemed like every waking hour was spent learning a skill that we would need on board. Sometimes, I just missed the life we were going to be leaving behind. But there was little time to dwell on it.

Today all the trainees were going to experience weightlessness in a capsule to learn how to move around and manipulate objects. We had attended about a year and a half of classes so far. We had the opportunity to tell other students participating in our training what the spaceship was like. Everyone we spoke to seemed very excited. And the most exciting part was that the training had made us stronger, more agile, confident, and a lot more proactive since our first training sessions. We could see it in the way that fellow trainees would jump at a chance to put their skills to the test helping crewmembers with engineering and electronics problems, the marked improvements in our virtual reality performance, as well as some of the innovative inventions that some of our student teams were inspired to start-up.

After the discussion, which lasted about thirty minutes, everyone got dressed in bulky spacesuits. Three students entered the capsule and waited for the instructor to turn off the gravity. At first, students pushed themselves around. Then, each of us had to accomplish a specific task while experiencing near weightlessness. When it was our turn, I had to try and unwrap a chocolate bar and eat it before it was lost, while Jose had to adjust several knobs. Sophie had to lift a hose and spray some water. After about an hour of training, we were transported to the training pool.

There, we focused on understanding and experiencing buoyancy. Our underwater training session lasted six hours, and we wore 300-pound suits. We concentrated on anaerobic bursts and endurance training. We were getting used to these daily aquatic training sessions since we'd performed them regularly over the past year.

Each of the trainees completed the lesson successfully, and we were let go for the day. Since we were all interested in either sports or music, we headed to the entertainment room. Sophie started talking about which singers she was going to practice with. Robert fantasized about playing professional football.

I also had the opportunity to spend some time with Mark. He wanted to run the 100-meter dash against Carl Lewis.

I said, "Mark, you are one hell of an athlete. I pity Carl Lewis when you beat him in the 100."

"I'm not going to beat Carl Lewis, but thanks for the compliment. I do enjoy running and competing and look forward to seeing you on the Imagine," he replied.

I asked him, "What job have you been assigned to on the ship?"

"I was told that I will either be working with security or weapons. I may even become a shuttle pilot, but that's going to take a lot of practice."

"I sure would not want to mess with you if I was in trouble on board."

"Thanks, Sam, you're quite an athlete yourself and very smart. I look forward to working with you on board. I do have a personal question to ask you."

"What is it?"

"I think your sister is cute, and when we finally get going, would you mind if I ask her out on a date?"

"I am sure Sophie will appreciate it if you ask her. Do you want me to find out if she likes you or not?"

"Not right now," Mark replied. I would appreciate it if you do not mention this conversation to your sister. When I am ready, and we are speeding through space, I will let you know."

"My lips are sealed until then. Good luck with your security and shuttle training. I am sure you will do a great job."

We shook hands and left for the day. I met up with Sally, and we had dinner together. Suppose we were going to be spending so much time practicing for space underwater and in near weightlessness. In that case, we were going to need to enjoy food on Earth for as long as possible. We went to Sally's favorite restaurant, which was a local barbecue. Then we started driving home pretty exhausted from the full day of training. I saw a text from my dad that he needed to meet with Jose and me the following day first thing in the morning to talk about something very important.

When I dropped Sally off at her house on Blake Avenue near Sayre Park, a couple of blocks away from ours, I told her I wouldn't be at the morning training session because something had come up.

"Well, you better let me know what it is afterward. No telling what your dad is going to have you do."

CHAPTER 29

Guardians of Humanity

Chapter 29 – Guardians of Humanity

Sam Burns, Rocky Mountains, CO

The following morning, Dad wanted us to meet the other three ships' officers. Jose and I looked forward to meeting people from various parts of the world. The virtual meeting would allow all the different crew's officers to see each other simultaneously. It took us about an hour to get to the communications lab.

Dad said, "We have about an hour before the other groups come online and meet with us. First, I want to introduce you and Jose to some of our own officers who will be interacting with us daily. You are going to learn everything they know and do during our travels. Bob and I selected all of the officers on this ship. Each of them has a specific skill or talent that will come in very useful. Are you ready to meet them?"

Both Jose and I said, "Sure."

About twenty people were sitting around a large, round table in uniforms. Jose and I did not have ours yet but assumed they would be given to us.

"Why don't we start to my right," Dad said.

Bob stood up.

"You already met Bob. He is the chief engineer and jack of all trades for the ship and its design and functioning."

Bob said, "Welcome, Sam and Jose, again. Glad to have you with us on this journey."

We both smiled and waved at Bob.

A short woman of about 5'3" with dark hair stood up. "This is Gloria Gonzales. She is my first officer. She may be petite and looks young, but she has an eighth-degree black belt in Taekwondo and was a national champion five times. She also served in the Marines for four years. She graduated from Purdue University, which has produced many astronauts and has studied space travel with NASA and Boeing for many years. She will run the ship when I am off duty and help me make decisions, regardless of where we are in the galaxy. Her husband and two girls will be joining us."

Gloria said, "Welcome to our crew, Sam and Jose. It is nice to finally meet the future officers of our trip."

I said, "Thanks."

The next officer stood up.

"This is Alexander Lee. You can call him Speedy. Speedy is responsible for the security on the ship. This means he takes care of the safety of everyone on board."

"Nice to meet you, Speedy," Jose said.

My father added, "Speedy will also insert location chips on everyone on board. Can you explain this to them, Speedy?"

Speedy said, "I am pleased to meet both of you. I look forward to working with you. I will be responsible for working with Dr. Sato to insert a microchip into the wrist or leg of everyone on board. This procedure should not take longer than five minutes to do and be taken care of in the medical facility. Everyone has a unique identification or GPS on their chip. Once the chip is inserted, we will be able to monitor the location of everyone on board. If someone is missing or unconscious, we can use the computers to locate them immediately using the chip. Chips like this are similar to what we have put in dogs for years. We should have done the same for people. For years, people have gone missing and can't be found. When they are found, they are most likely dead."

"What happens if someone wants some privacy and does not want to be found?" Jose asked.

Dad said, "Jose, there are limits to how much privacy one can have on this ship. Speedy can be informed via his communicator if you want some privacy or do not wish to be disturbed unless there is an emergency. Only Speedy and his staff can take the chip offline. They will respect your privacy. They are only used to locate you. They are not used to see what you do in your own time. We have security cameras all over the ship, and they will be monitored all hours of the day regardless of how many hours are in a day. We also have a brig, or jail, onboard, which I hope we never have to use."

Both Jose and I shook Speedy's hand.

Dad continued the introductions.

"Next, we have the chief physician. This is Dr. Sato. She is capable of diagnosing just about anything that could happen to you. Dr. Sato, maybe you can explain a little bit about our medical facilities."

"Yes, Dr. Burns. We are bringing ten doctors and six nurses with us and will have a full supply of medicine for almost any medical issue. Our sickbay or hospital has ten beds and three operating rooms. At least one doctor and one nurse will be on duty at all times. If we have to quarantine anyone, we have a few places we can put people or order people to stay in their rooms until they are cleared. Since we are in a closed space, diseases can travel fast and affect many people. We will be encouraging everyone to develop excellent hygiene."

"What happens if someone gives birth?" I asked.

Dr. Sato replied, "We can handle births, and we can take care of many children. There are vaccines for most childhood diseases today."

"And deaths?"

"Unfortunately, we also have to handle deaths as they happen. We do have a morgue for autopsies, but most burials will happen when we discard the body into space. Hopefully, this will not occur very often. If you have any more questions, please visit us after we get started."

Dad added, "What is most important is that Dr. Sato is an expert on stem cell research and cloning using stem cells. We will be able to reproduce living things with stem cells, which can be used for fertilization. I am sure Dr. Sato will explain her research and all of the medical advances when we are traveling in space.

"Last but not least is General Jose Crawford. He is our military officer. We have stored many weapons on board. However, except for a very few individuals, no crewmembers will carry weapons. If there is an attack or weapons are needed, we do have a full complement of weapons to choose from. This ship can fire many different kinds of bombs, some of which are quite powerful and could easily destroy most life on a planet. Dr. Crawford served in the Marines for fifteen years and reached the rank of three-star general. We do hope that no matter where we go that weapons of mass destruction are not necessary. They can only be released under the authorization of at least two officers, including myself. In the event the ship is attacked, we will all have assigned duties. That means there will be plenty of drills to keep us busy.

"After a short break, we are going to have an official meeting with the other ships' crews via satellite link. All four ships will be able to communicate with each other via some very technical communication equipment. While not everyone is required to use English all the time, it is the official language for all the ships. We won out over having to teach everyone Russian."

Everyone laughed.

"We have translators available for the crew to use that will translate from one language to the next. All right, let us take a ten-minute break. Then we can meet the officers of the other three ships."

After the break, we returned to our seats. The computer and television screens were adjusted so that we could see four crews at the same time. In a moment, we saw the officials from the other three ships on the screen. Everyone was smiling and waving and applauding. It was indeed an exciting moment to see everyone together, yet so far from each other.

My father opened the meeting.

"Hello and greetings to all the officers from each spaceship. I hope all of you are deep into your training and preparing for the moment we will all be headed for a new world and new life. It will be an exhilarating adventure, but one in which there may be many risks and dangers that we will have to face. It is imperative that at least one spaceship, but hopefully all four, arrive at a world that humanity can live and grow into a new civilization. We will be able to use the mistakes made in the past to accomplish our goals. Now let us meet the crews. First, Yuri Pavlov will command our spaceship from Russia. Yuri is a former Russian cosmonaut. He has flown three missions to the International Space Station, which is now controlled by Russia. Yuri, would you like to introduce your top officials to everyone and perhaps say a few words?"

Yuri stood up to speak. "Hello, everyone. I would like to second Dr. Burns' greeting about an exciting journey we are about to undertake. I am thrilled that some of the most brilliant engineers and scientists have been recruited from all over the world. We will all need their expertise in many different ways. Now let me introduce my first officer. This is Anatoly Korbin."

Anatoly stood up and waved. We all applauded.

"Second, this is my chief scientific officer, Svetlana Alexander. She is one of the first female cosmonauts in my country."

Svetlana waved, and we all applauded again. After Yuri had finished with his introductions, my dad then introduced the Australian vessel leader, Ian Thorpe.

Ian was a top engineer for the Australian Army and a senior fighter pilot. He had yet to command a spaceship like Yuri. Ian also introduced his chief officers. Afterward, Thomas Dresden, who led the German ship, introduced Marlene Heinz. She was also a brilliant German engineer and an expert in astrophysics. She introduced the members of her team. Most German officers were experts in car engineering for such companies as Mercedes Benz and BMW since Germany did not have much of an army anymore.

After the introductions, everyone from each ship raised a glass to each other for a toast.

Dad said, "May we journey safely to wherever our destination and fate lead us, and may we strengthen our bonds of friendship as we travel through space."

Everyone said, "Amen" or "I will drink to that" and took a sip of their drink.

Jose and I headed back to our families. The four commanders remained in the room to converse in private. Everyone else went back to their assigned duties.

I was looking forward to learning more despite the fact that Jose and I felt utterly overwhelmed by the expertise and knowledge that we were exposed to so far. If only it all could work out without any glitches in the system. I hoped so. From its looks, they were all working together to avoid any catastrophes, with no stone unturned, and with respect for one another. I couldn't wait to see how they did under pressure.

CHAPTER 30

DNA

Chapter 30 – DNA

Sam Burns, Glenwood Springs, CO

On a day when we did not have any training, and my dad was off duty, he gathered my mom, brother, sister and myself.

"This will be an interesting experience for you. I will be training you today. Since we have no idea how long it will take us to find a planet to live on, we will be collecting some DNA samples from people who are not going on the trip with us. We will also be collecting DNA samples from some dead people via their personal effects. I want you to know that we have collected over one million DNA samples that we will be taking on board with us so far. We have DNA from every past president, famous inventors, scientists, and armed forces personnel. Our DNA samples are focused on South and North America."

Dad continued, "A large laboratory is on the ship where scientists will work on cloning individuals. We can only clone a few people at a time in our state-of-the-art cloning lab because we cannot have more than a thousand people on board. What is most important is that we store the DNA at the correct temperature to make sure that it does not degrade."

"What happens if the temperature breaks down on the ship?" my brother asked.

"Don't worry," my dad responded. "We have thought about every contingency possible. Some of the leading DNA scientists will be on board and responsible for ensuring that the DNA remains viable. It is quite conceivable that just about everyone on the ship will need to be cloned during the voyage at one time or another. However, people do have the right to refuse being cloned. They do not have to make this decision now, but at some point, during the voyage, they will need to decide. Unfortunately, all the officers will have to agree to be cloned, as we need their services and expertise."

"Can there be two of us at the same time on the ship?" my sister asked.

"Excellent question," my dad said. "We have had many discussions about the ethics of doing that. Right now, no final decision has been made about this. On the one hand, it would be great for me to have a twin to work on the ship. I would only have to work half the time. However, think about Mom. How could she handle two of me at the same time? How would she know which one of us was the real one or which came first? Both of us would think your mom was the woman we married. Would we have to call me Thomas I and my clone Thomas II? What if there were ten of me on the ship with the same DNA? Would we all think the same ten years later? There are so many questions that we cannot answer until we face the situation that occurs.

"We also plan to clone famous people only when we need their expertise. I cannot imagine what someone like Einstein would say when he finds himself in space. He also has the disadvantage of not knowing about anything that has happened since his death. I am sure he would be disappointed to learn about some of the uses of the atomic bombs that have been developed. However, we may need to produce such a bomb in the future, depending on the circumstances. Everyone on the ship will be required to provide DNA samples in case something should happen to them on the trip. Right now, I am going to show you how to collect a sample and make sure you store it right."

Dad demonstrated how to swab a cheek and collect hair samples. After watching Dad take samples from Mom, I received samples from my brother and sister. We then stored them in a specialized medical container used to transport the DNA to the ship.

Then Dad explained about the laboratory and some of the information about cloning. "Ideally, we want to avoid chemical and enzymatic degradation. That is why we need to store the DNA at −80 °C. Under these very low-temperature conditions, nucleic acids are stable for prolonged periods. We can also store them in ethanol.

"When we want or need to clone someone, we place a DNA sample from the person into an artificially made embryo. Just like a baby, the embryo starts to grow. If the process works correctly, you would have an exact duplicate of the person you obtained the DNA sample. It takes anywhere from seven to nine full months to clone someone now. At least that is what the DNA or genome scientists have told me. We can also eliminate some of the' bad' DNA in the embryo. Stem cell research will also be an essential part of our scientific studies."

I asked, "Dad, am I cloned now?"

Dad laughed. "Of course not. All the original people on the ship are their original selves."

It seemed like this whole conversation was raising a lot more questions than answers. Sally was right. I wasn't sure what my dad would come up with next. Sally thought my dad was really becoming confident in my abilities when I told Sally about meeting all the ship's officers and crewmembers. I called her to bounce some of what I had learned off of her. She seemed perplexed by the idea of cloning, unsure of how we could predict their behavior since we couldn't base it on any type of previous scientific inquiry.

She added, "Sometimes, I wonder whether these clones would just push us aside and take over and leave us to die. Do you think they'll eat all our food and leave us to starve?"

"Sally, I don't know. But I think that Dr. Sato is working on the answers. It's not a job I would ever want to apply for, but I'm hoping she'll be providing us with answers soon."

Moving Onto the Imagine

Chapter 31 – Moving onto the Imagine

Sam Burns, Rocky Mountains, CO

At dinner Friday night, my dad announced, "Now I have some really big and hopefully exciting news to give you. Next month we will begin moving onto the spaceship. At that point, we will begin making final preparations, which will still take a few years. You will be assuming your everyday duties and be provided with more training. I expect you to learn everything possible about the Imagine". My dad never believed in quiet Friday nights.

I was stunned. We had recently passed our two-year mark a few months earlier in our mission training, and we were more fit than ever. I'd never been so fit. I was already twenty years old. That meant that I would be celebrating my big twenty-first on board the ship the following year. How many people had ever done that? Probably no one. And here I was now speechless and in a panic. My palms got sweaty, and I could see everyone at the table try to stay excited but fighting with their own various stages of panic. My mother's face was the palest.

She smiled and said, "That's sudden. Well, everything must not be as off schedule as we thought it would be. Good job, dear." She grabbed her half-empty plate and headed to the kitchen.

I wanted to run in after her to talk to her, but I could tell that my dad might get the wrong impression. "Wow. I'll be the first person to celebrate my twenty-first birthday on Imagine in our family."

Sophie said, "When you turn twenty-one, we'll be in space? That's unreal!"

Robert said, "Now, this is getting pretty real."

It got quiet. Not requiem quiet but close.

I had waited to hear this announcement for a long time, but I suddenly felt like I wasn't prepared to do it. I had faith in my dad, and in all of our training, but this felt so sudden even though it wasn't. Up until now, it was something in the distant future. Robert was right. I anticipated what it would be like to have our first Friday night on board Imagine. I looked around the room and already felt a great sense of loss. How could we leave all this behind?

None of us said anything. We just digested the news. Mom walked in and started gathering our dirty plates, and I got up to help her clean them. It gave me a chance to think.

***

My family began loading our things into our cars to take us to the space center the following month. It was also a Friday. It was October, and seeing all the trees start to change had a much different effect on me than it ever had. I'd taken them for granted for so long. Now it felt unbearable to think that I would never see them again. I also couldn't help thinking about what others my age were getting to do. I felt a bit of envy. Then, I figured they'd be just as jealous about all the space training I had done and that I was going to go on this once-in-a-lifetime voyage into space, the first of its kind.

It was still very challenging. It was tough packing up the house, which would be left abandoned. There was no point in selling it. It was hoped some homeless people or someone needing a home would move in. We stood outside the house and took one more look at our house.

Mom said, "I guess this is it. We are leaving so many memories behind."

I replied, "No, Mom, the memories are all here." I pointed to each of their heads. "It was a wonderful house. It is where I grew up and learned to become a man. However, we will create new memories no matter where we go as long as we do it together."

Mom came over and hugged each of us. Then we got in the car. As we were driving, we passed Janet's and Grissom's home. Janet was sitting on the porch outside, watching everyone leave. She looked really sad.

"Stop for a moment. I want to say goodbye to Janet," I said.

Mom pulled over, and I got out and walked up to her.

"Hi, Janet. How are you doing?"

Janet looked at me. "Hi, Sam, nice to see you. Are you going to Imagine now? I really wish I could go with you, but my dad thinks you will all die on takeoff. He thinks I will have a great life here on Earth. I am so sad and nervous to see everyone go. Yet, I am happy and excited for you. Sam, you have been a great friend. I doubt we will ever see each other again."

That really made me sad.

"Where is your dad? I wish I could convince your dad to let you go with us, but I know you would never leave him here alone."

"He is inside cleaning up. Do you want to talk to him?"

I went inside and saw Grissom washing the dishes. The last few years must have been hard for him. His wife, Diane, had died of breast cancer when she was only thirty-three years old. Grissom noticed me. He turned around and faced me.

"Hi, Sam. I know why you stopped over here, and the answer is still no."

I looked at him and thought about hitting him but remained calm.

"After takeoff, this place will be a ghost town. There is no telling if Janet will even live to see old age. Are you sure about this?"

"I am sure. I think I am going to outlive all of you on that damn ship. You may not even get off the ground."

I replied, "There is always that possibility, but my dad and his team have planned for so many years, and I just do not think that will happen.

Plus, I don't think that is the real reason you do not want to come." Grissom and I walked outside.

Grissom looked down at the ground in front of him, spit, and then looked up to the sky. "You are right. I cannot leave my wife. She is buried near here, and I go to see her every day. I promised that I would do this until I died or could not physically do it. I owe everything in life to my wife. I just cannot leave her. I am so sorry, but I cannot. It may not be fair to Janet, but I need her here. Janet always said you were a good friend and a great student. Eventually, she will have to take care of me. If we are lucky, it won't be long till we both die."

I was sad. "Okay. Grissom, you need to do what you think is right. I understand you love your wife and Janet and wish to remain with them. Do you mind, however, if I take a DNA sample from you and Janet for possible cloning?"

Grissom said, "Not for me. I do not want to be in the universe without my wife. I would be depressed, no matter where we go. Janet may like that. You can ask her yourself on your way out."

I was even sadder for Grissom. He seemed so depressed. Grissom had been one of the first people to work on building the spaceship, but due to his wife's illness, he decided to quit.

I returned outside. I told Janet about the conversation, and she started to cry.

"Janet, I'm going to miss you. I guess we cannot even email each other once I take off on the Imagine." I thought for a second. "I may not be able to take you with us, but with your DNA sample, I may be exactly able to do that."

Janet looked at me like I was nuts. "You are not making sense. My dad is not going to let me leave. So how am I going to go with everyone?"

"I will take a DNA sample and then clone you when we start out."

Janet looked mystified. "You mean you swab my cheek or something, and then I grow into Janet on your ship?"

"Yup," I said. "I am not sure when I will clone you, but you will be with us once we do."

Janet smiled. "That is great. Thank you for thinking of me."

I took out a DNA kit that I had with me since I took samples of everyone in our family and took her DNA sample.

"Don't worry," I said. "Just be sure to enjoy the time you have with your dad, and we will see each other again soon."

I hugged her and got back into the car. Mom and my family were waiting patiently for me. I felt good knowing I may have saved a human life but sad that I was going to lose the original Janet.

My family told me that they were proud of me.

I guess this was it.

This is the Captain Speaking

Part III
2030: Magnitude of a Dream
in Category 5 Conditions

Chapter 32 – This is the Captain Speaking

Tom Burns, the Imagine in the Rocky Mountains, CO

It was now 2030. With the amount of financial interest and support that the Imagine had received through crewmembers and sponsors' efforts, it was hard to explain being behind schedule to them. Some investors were losing heart. One of them was Robert Clark, who had almost based his decision to participate in financing the mission on whether or not President Trump would be willing to give his support in 2016. Over the past two years, he had been losing interest fast. He'd banked on the initial take-off in 2028 and brought many investors with him once he'd become fully committed to participating. He'd turned down many other noble efforts, and his family was fully involved in various aspects of the mission. Robert felt their pressure, and not a day went by when Tom didn't hear from Robert to feel that pressure too.

Along the way, Tom had days when he felt sure that the level of enthusiasm had diminished among many of his crewmembers. Building and developing research and data hadn't gone as planned or easily. More challenges lay ahead. Some of the crew seemed to shy away from the daily challenges on occasion, and he helped them through some rough spots or when they felt disheartened. Luckily, he and Bob were able to channel their combat experience in flying through dangerous and nearly impossible challenges. It often helped, as did the training of the young crewmembers and their influence on other crewmembers. Tom was so proud of Sam and his classmates for taking on so much responsibility and meeting their potential every day. The young trainees would be finished with their training just as spring ended.

Now, Tom would be welcoming more and more of the thousand travelers to their new homes over the next several months. He hoped that their enthusiasm level would help his crew and financial supporters regain that level of interest and confidence in the mission that everyone had shared early on. The next stage of preparation would involve a lot of operationalizing plans in all of the departments.

Today, he'd heard that Robert Clark was bringing his family on board. Robert knew that more people were moving onto the Imagine every day, and he finally committed to being one of the first to bring his family to their quarters. They would arrive at 10:30 am. Tom wanted to make sure that he was there to greet him.

At 10:15 am, Tom reviewed the list of names of the thousand people to board the spaceship. Of course, it was a working document as some had pulled out and others had replaced them. All of the passengers had been recently informed that the crewmembers were concluding the building of the ship along with testing various parts of the engine and propulsion system.

A day didn't go by that didn't leave everyone feeling like they were pushed to a new limit.

Robert and his family arrived and stood behind a few newly arriving families and individuals who were being greeted by Imagine officers. As the officers explained to each person boarding the Imagine what could be brought with them and what they would have to throw away or leave behind, Robert locked eyes with Tom. Tom moved toward Robert while acknowledging the others waiting to board and to be greeted.

"Good to see you, Robert."

"Good to be here, Tom. You've met my wife, Jenna, and here are my kids, Henry and Fin. They are both super excited and have spent months deciding what they would bring along. I had no idea it was going to be as difficult as it has been. We're really looking forward to testing the new skills Henry and Fin have acquired in the training sessions."

"Hello, Tom," said Jenna. She turned to Henry and Fin. "Now please greet Captain Burns. Don't just stand there."

"Hello, Captain Burns. Sir, we are thrilled to move onboard and to help crewmembers however we can."

"Well, that's great to hear. We'll be giving out assignments a little bit later, and I'm looking forward to working with you on a successful mission."

"Now, Tom, there have been a few concerns we have. See, I'm a bit nervous seeing the people board and looking at the ship. It's frankly not what I imagined. It seems cramped. And some of these people don't give me the best impression, really. How are we going to even strike up a conversation? I don't know any of these people. I've usually only socialized with friends and family I've known all my life."

"Robert, sure. I understand. You're used to being involved with politics and with big-time rollers. I can see this will be an adjustment. The best answer is to give it time. You'll start being able to talk to people you meet at our meetings, in the cafeteria, in our entertainment room, and also—"

"What you're saying is that this is the equivalent of moving into a retirement home? People I've never met, and our common concern is when will we actually die or how we can pass the time? Please, Tom, I—"

"Robert, no. That's not what I'm saying. You can get as involved in our daily needs as is permissible, and I encourage it. You have a great mind and great experience and enthusiasm. I can imagine that you might be intrigued by some of the medical advancements we will make and even help us understand the benefits of constant learning about astronomy and its benefits in prolonging human survival. There is no telling what technologies we can develop, and you can be an integral part of that. I assure you, there will be more than retirement home vibes on Imagine."

"Thank you, Tom. I needed to hear that. I'm sacrificing a lot, and I'm still getting used to the idea beyond thinking it's a possible necessity."

"Captain, excuse me," said one of the engineers. "I'm sorry to interrupt, but I needed to give you an update. When I couldn't find you in your office, I was told I could find you here. Well, various tests have been concluded on parts of the engine and the propulsion system. The electric propulsion diagnostics have conclusively shown that after testing in the anechoic chambers with the electromagnetic interference from one of our electric propulsion thrusters that it aced the test. There's more testing, but I thought you'd be happy to hear that."

"Yes, extraordinary news."

Robert interjected, "That does sound extraordinary. Maybe we can have science trivia nights to catch up with rocket scientists to learn about the propulsion and auxiliary engines' components. Now I'm more intrigued. I'm sure our accommodations will be pretty impressive too, come to think of it." Robert shot his wife, Jenna, a glare.

Jenna chimed in, "Please, show us the way to our accommodations. I would really like to start understanding what life will be like for us."

"Yes, Jenna, by all means, and remember we're not taking off just yet." Tom knew how anxious she felt and asked one of the officers to show their family to their quarters. When they left, Tom spoke with a few more passengers and answered their questions.

As soon as Tom felt that the ten families that were boarding today felt a little more at ease, he headed to the bridge. Passing rooms that were filling up now with passengers was a bit of a thrill for him. He got on the loudspeaker on the bridge.

"Hello, fellow Imagine travelers. I am pleased to have a chance to greet you and meet some of you to talk individually. You will notice an itinerary in your rooms that specifies a time for you to meet with other fellow officers and me today, throughout the day. The first meeting will be happening very shortly, so please take a look to see which group you are a member of to participate in this brief orientation. I am sure you have many questions. I am also interested in providing appropriate resources, the sooner the better, given how much there will be to get used to in your new homes. I will meet the first group in the cafeteria, which will sometimes be an auditorium. You will be able to find it using the map provided with your itinerary. I am looking forward to meeting the first group in ten minutes. Thank you and welcome on board! Just a note, you will find several graduates from Goddard High School you may very well recognize if you have been part of the community. If you haven't, you can find them wearing a silver pin with the words' Onward and Upward' on them who are ready to assist you."

After three years of training with Mrs. Smith and her assistants, Tom could see that the young trainees felt a lot more confident about their duties. Tom had seen the changes, and he was excited they were instrumental in helping arriving passengers. He felt proud. It took quite a while to learn where all the rooms were.

Tom greeted each group of passengers every time Sam, Jose, and their fellow students dutifully helped them find their way to the orientation meeting throughout the day. Tom and the officers met each group to provide them with the spacecraft rules and get them ready for the launch. His wife, Sarah, Dr. Sato, Sam, and several other officers were also on hand to answer questions and alleviate fears. By the end of the day, most had already moved onto the spaceship and adjusted to the major changes in their lives.

Each person coming on board would be given a communicator that would allow them to listen to the news on the ship and contact others. Within a week, all personnel had a GPS chip inserted. They were instructed daily about protocols and procedures. All medical files were to be provided to the medical team. Each family had been provided with a packet of what to bring and what they could not bring in the mail prior to arriving. Now, they were reviewing it. It had been suggested that they bring enough clothes for two weeks. All crewmembers would be easy to identify since they were provided with specific uniforms depending on their rank and job duties.

All objects had to be kept in their dresser or closet. No objects would be allowed on walls, and that included any kind of pictures. It was reemphasized that it was important during the move that objects be smaller than 8x11 feet. If they were larger, these items could be returned to their vacated homes or turned into a center where these types of items would be handled by crewmembers. They were reminded that no person needed to bring any money since there was no longer any use for it.

Eric Watson, a big donor, watched his wife, Thelma, stand up, and his eyes widened. At the mention of pictures on the walls and the rules, his wife couldn't sit still.

She spoke. "I just want you to know that I have several precious pieces of art that I am bringing with us. I have a Monet, Manet, Renoir, and about ten other fine art masterpieces that are probably worth at least two million dollars each. Surely, you do not expect me to leave them home."

Tom tried to reason with her. "Since there will be no money on board, and if you cannot sell anything to anyone, what do you plan to do with those pictures? Once we go into space, they will be rendered worthless. Why not just sell them at home and donate the money to a worthy environmental cause, give them to a relative to sell them?"

"These pictures have been in my family for almost a hundred years. My father was an art collector who bought and sold art for years. How do you think we raised the money for you to build your spaceship?"

"Thank you for your donation. It is really appreciated. However, if the paintings are on the wall and there is a gravity problem, they will fly off the wall and probably break or be destroyed. More importantly, they could become missiles or weapons and kill someone, including possibly you. All objects and furniture are all battened down so they cannot move around when something like that happens."

"We can put them in crates and store them in the closet or another place, but they're coming with us. These paintings are part of my family."

"If I let you bring those pictures, then I have to let everyone bring something they do not want to leave behind. You can take as many digital photos of the art as you want, and they will be available to you on your dresser all the time."

Her husband said, "Thelma, we will discuss this privately with the commander after the meeting. We don't need everyone here to listen to your complaining."

His wife became pissed off and left the room.

Tom and the other officers were asked several more interesting questions.

One man asked, "Can I bring my wife's ashes with me? I don't want to leave her home."

"Yes, but you need to keep them in the dresser or desk and properly secured," Tom replied.

Several people complained about needing cell phones or not using them on board. Tom had to explain that Earth's Internet engines and Wi-Fi system would soon be out of range once they took off. There was no Internet or Verizon in outer space.

It took a while, but after about five weeks, just about everyone was moving to their quarters and beginning or continuing training. Many of them complained about the size of their room. Others complained about bio-engineered food. Tom tried to explain that with a thousand people on board, there was a limited amount of space available for family quarters. As for the food, Tom felt that once they tried eating a few of the dishes that Luis prepared they would get used to it.

Tom thought that some of the moving-in operations made him more exhausted than if he was working twenty-four hours a day on the engines. Whenever Sarah returned to their new quarters, she was also often exhausted from all the effort put into obtaining the people's medical histories. Some people did not want to divulge some of their family diseases for fear that they would be told to leave the ship. She often reassured everyone.

The oldest person coming on the ship was eighty-five. The youngest was two. There were no newborns on board the vessel yet. This could be expected, given that as soon as passengers accepted the invitation to travel on the spaceship, they had been instructed not to conceive before departure. However, once they began the trip, they would be free to do so.

Putting in the DNA chips into each person's wrist or neck also caused some anxiety problems. Several people said their dogs had chips, and they did not want to be treated like dogs. Again, and again, Sarah tried to explain that this was required just so they could track everyone on or off the ship. The chip also contained crucial medical information.

Sarah and the other medical staff worked tirelessly with Dr. Sato to assemble all of the medical information. Dr. Sato gave each family a tour of the facilities, including the cryopreservation unit, the cloning lab, and the stem cell research lab. Of course, there were the regular medical facilities and an operating room.

The day after the orientation, everyone on board had to sit through a lecture about the board's medical policies. First, Dr. Sato and the medical personnel shook hands with each person as they entered the room and introduced themselves. Dr. Sato and the medical personnel then explained that they would be discussing some very touchy subjects. One was that there was no way to stop the aging process. Everyone was going to die at some point. It was inevitable, at least for now. The aging process could be slowed but not stopped entirely. If a person died, they could be cloned again at an earlier age but only have the memories acquired at the age of cloning. Everyone had to understand that the goal of the medical unit was not to ensure immortality.

Things were going smoothly until Johnny's parents along with Johnny started interrupting Dr. Sato repeatedly. Johnny's parents worked in the engine room as well as on several other maintenance jobs.

Johnny's dad said, "I was told that your medicine would cure all diseases." He looked at his wife and son to gain confirmation.

Dr. Sato responded, "If you stay on Earth you will definitely die. If you come with us, you will have a chance to live a much longer life. No one person can guarantee that you will live forever. Accidents happen. New diseases may occur in space. Anything is possible. It is my job to limit the number of ways you can die medically. Our doctors are among the best in the world. And we do not have to worry about FDA approval." She continued to explain that the choice about how they wanted to live their life belonged to them.

To stay alive for the duration of the search for another planet, passengers could choose not to accept cloning of themselves or stem cell therapy. Cryopreservation was a must unless there were unusual circumstances.

Once Dr. Sato mentioned cryopreservation, it set off a new round of protests and questions. Thelma, the woman who did not want to part with her artwork, objected to the idea that she would be put to sleep for any duration without being placed in the same unit as her husband. Dr. Sato tried to calm her fears, but she was adamant that she would not be placed in cryopreservation at all.

Dr. Sato said, "We will have to address your situation when it comes time to do that."

Then Thelma's husband decided to get into the act with a new question. "Since it is a fact that there has never been a successful cloning of a human, what makes you, Dr. Sato, so sure it can be done?"

Dr. Sato calmly looked at Eric and said, "I guarantee it can be done but not at this moment. We have the means to do so. It will just take a few years to do it. If you do not want to be cloned, just let me know and we will not clone you."

It was becoming clear after a few more challenging questions that Dr. Sato was losing her patience with this group. Dr. Sato received so many questions about the policies that she gave up trying to answer them all. Sarah tried to intervene by asking people to be patient and that another meeting could be set up as well as monthly informational meetings about the medical progress on the ship, but Johnny said he wanted all the answers now. Obviously, this young man had no manners and was also scared of what lay ahead, as he should be. It was also evident that no matter what answer the passengers were given, they would not be placated or satisfied.

Dr. Sato seemed to, for now, be able to set aside the different views on these difficult decisions.

Sarah said, "Honestly, I'm not sure whether the donors, or even myself for that matter, would pass up a chance to discover a way to live forever since we will be at the leading edge of innovation and could attempt it. I don't know. I think it's something many humans have considered since we've evolved. We've advanced our fight against aging in many ways from generation to generation. Who are we to stop it when we may have the chance to rediscover that we have suffered early deaths because we haven't applied all of our knowledge and abilities to the limit?"

Tom felt fine about the conversation. It needed to be had. It seemed that Dr. Sato had come across too firm in her approach to many in the room. He also observed Johnny and how he interacted with people based on his previous conversation with Mrs. Smith. As he watched Dr. Sato address the group, Tom felt that it was a little different from how she had handled the people at the conference, he'd seen her speak at years ago. It felt a little more frustrated or intense. Obviously, all of the people on board would become research subjects, and there would need to be many successful stories for them to survive.

Dr. Sato decided to end the meeting by saying, "I've decided to save some of the answers to critical issues raised today and provide written answers for you to read once the journey begins."

Tom felt a bit ill at ease, but given the circumstances, he'd need to consider how best to proceed. He certainly was filled with thoughts weighed by nightmare Frankenstein scenarios that might play out with immortals onboard. Still, he wondered how likely were they to turn into anything but helpful to humanity by exploring the secrets of extended life. It struck him momentarily. Had she considered involving him in the written answers? Better to make it known that he must be.

Before everyone left the room, Tom approached her discreetly and explained, "Any procedures will involve a small committee given the matter's importance. Do I make myself clear?"

Dr. Sato hardly nodded. She barely glanced at him as she left the vacant room.

Valor and Heartbreak

Chapter 33 – Valor and Heartbreak

Tom Burns, the Imagine in the Rocky Mountains, CO

As passengers and crewmembers became accustomed to everyday life on the ship, life outside the ship was becoming more difficult. Environmental conditions around the world deteriorated. One of the major ecological impacts was now taking place in the Rocky Mountains. As the temperatures rose, even the snow on the highest peaks was melting, causing widespread flooding for Colorado's citizens in the valleys. Also, much of the wildlife in the mountains could not survive such warm temperatures.

Tom received a call from his wife as he was working on the engines. She informed him that President Stevens wanted to meet and see the spaceship. At first, Tom wanted to ignore the request. While President Stevens was trying hard to improve conditions in the United States, it was really too late to fully recover from the Trump years. Tom decided that since the deteriorating environment was not this president's fault, he would meet with him.

Tom told his wife to set up a meeting in a week at the Rocky Mountain headquarters.

On Thursday of the following week, President Stevens and his staff flew out to Colorado, along with his wife, secretaries, and the Chairman of the Joint Chiefs of Staff. While Tom respected the president a lot more than his predecessor, he was not really thrilled with his trip to headquarters. Tom didn't want anything to interfere with the launch plan. But Tom had decided to act courteously and show respect to the man. Beyond being mindful of professional conduct, which he expected from the experts on his own crew in the lead-up, and after the launch, he was well-suited to be a ship captain. All the things that were out of his control and those things that he and his crew were working on to make sure they got through danger zones with enough ability to out-pace, dodge, push through or avoid—kill if they had to—required that he handle circumstances, not rush off and hide and act as if he was functioning in a proverbial bubble. This new president may very well be able to do more than Trump's constant vitriol and sabotage. He could insti-gate a much better opportunity for communication between the ship and America when it became necessary or another exploratory opportu-nity presented itself in the future.

This wasn't about Tom, this wasn't about plans, this was about tak-ing another giant step for mankind, which meant he had to act like it had nothing to do with him. He was a captain. On the other hand, he was first and foremost advancing human capabilities and innova-tions, in service to all. If he didn't think that way, he would be off-tar-get and wobble like an eccentric object out of sync with the steps that humankind wanted at this point in building future options. Who knew what they would have to encounter beyond their galaxy? If he shied away each time things got tough, what kind of captain was he? He had to choose perseverance.

Of course, recent events with Trump and the effect on the elections had Tom on edge. So did the broader ramifications of whether there would be debates about immortality, cloning and living in a small space. It didn't mean he needed to fight, fly, or close off. It didn't suit him well on a voyage of this magnitude. If he asked his officers and pas-sengers to continue studying, developing physical and cognitive skills beyond what they'd ever practiced or imagined, he had to do the same. He knew that President Stevens was aware of how Trump's missteps had

led to his own win. It was all due to Trump's tweeting and his underes-
timation of what the Imagine mission represented in voters' minds and
many who were invigorated by the advancements of humanity. Tom's
phone rang.

"Tom, I've got terrible news. I don't know if I can even say it,
friend."

Tom recognized Jeff Tirortu's voice even though he hadn't seen
him since 2009, twenty-one years ago. "What's happened, Jeff."

"We might have been worried about our life here on Tuvalu,
when I saw you. I was still in Kiribati, but this is ... it's worse, Tom. My
dear daughter, Heitiare, is dead. Our nation means 'eight standing together,' and now we are falling down, no matter how much richer the
coal mines have made those bastards on Queensland!"

"The atolls! Was she defending the eight atolls?"

"Tom, I simply can't talk about it. I'm too depressed. She
never left the hole. They found her entangled in an excavator ladder.
Her husband, Ahomana, was sick for years and finally died from black
lung disease last month. Queensland mines have documented more
than eighty deaths in the past decade from black lung disease alone.
Maybe she just wasn't as safe as she used to be, grief-stricken over losing
him and all when she died. But she never emerged. They'd worked in
mines in Queensland for a few years now. But that new one, the one
in the Galilee Basin, it was supposed to bring an economic boom they
said—the Adani project. Tom, she never got out of the hole. There are
more than sixty physical deaths now over the last decade in these damn
mines polluting our air. And they're willing to ignore that coal mining is the existential threat we call it. Now, here we were building sea
walls, extracting sand for geobags for seawalls and groynes. Now my dear
Heitiare and her Ahomana are killed not because of the effects on our
islands and our lives but because of the mines themselves. No one cares
about safety anymore, Tom, no one."

"Jeff, my deepest condolences. They continue to ignore the
safety resets. This is absolutely dreadful. The loss of life is unacceptable.
They should be home safe not—"

"Gone! Tom, I'm not sure if I can forgive anyone. You know, eight years ago, their safety committee was dissolved because they couldn't reach a gender quota, and miners died. They wanted to argue about ideology instead of making sure they talked about the safety of the men and women in the mines. This is unacceptable. Well, it happened again. It's just about running around in circles. I'm devastated. I just needed to hear your voice, my friend, even if I never hear it again after you launch, you've helped me at the worst time in my life."

"Something's gotta give, Jeff. I'll see what I can do and get back in touch with you. Nothing I can say can make it better, and I'm sorry you have to go through this horror."

"Thanks for being there, Tom. Take care."

Tom hung up, and tears formed as he got up and scrolled through the photographs he had preserved in his digital library. He paused as he looked at a young Heitiare and her father, Jeff.

What dangers our children face when safety is an afterthought, he thought.

Walking from his office, trying to compose himself, he saw Bob, who informed him that the president would arrive momentarily. At last, it was a Thursday afternoon, when the president landed. Tom could feel the impossible at that moment open up wide, sucking up all the past flaws of Trump and breathe a new chance, a new possibility. Maybe he'd be someone who understood the fear and deadly circumstances of bad political decisions that were devastating communities worldwide, like Jeff's.

The power of the presidential symbol and what it stood for seemed to conspire to make Tom brace himself. Instead, he shielded himself behind every benefit that courage, strength, and determination had brought him and behind every climate refugee and a victim who lost their lives to poor decision-making. He had been brought to this point, and their losses and experiences would mean something. Standing before a president coming to meet him, he would be a visionary standing on the cusp of something remarkable, a believer in the power of what it meant to be human to him—to rise above and develop better grounds.

Tom saluted the president as he disembarked from Air Force One. The president hailed back, and then they shook hands. Unlike Trump, Stevens had served in the army for ten years, attaining the rank of colonel before getting into politics. Unlike Trump, Stevens seemed to care more about people and the environment. Having served in a war, he saw the consequences of losing a life. All of the destroyed structures in war could be rebuilt, but once life was destroyed, there was no way to get it back. Stevens had seen families despair over death all over the world and wanted to do whatever he could to ensure this did not happen often, or at all. To Tom, that made the most significant difference of all.

Once they had finished their greetings, Tom led everyone into a conference room near his office. Everyone sat down around a large table. Tom sat across from President Stevens, who sat with his hands neatly folded. Bob sat on Tom's right. Dr. Sato sat on his left.

"Mr. President, thank you for taking the time to visit us during our final preparation stages. Before we do a formal tour, I would like to know the purpose of your visit."

"Thank you, Dr. Burns, for your willingness to share your project with my cabinet members and me. Let me cut to the chase. My first question is: why have you not kept the government up to date on your endeavors? As you know, the conditions of the climate are deteriorating. We are losing some of our beaches in Florida and elsewhere. There is no question that while we can postpone our demise, we cannot reverse the process. It is my understanding that you have built this spacecraft without the approval or assistance of anyone officially in the United States government. You have been very successful in getting billionaires to donate generously. I assume that you have already planned to accommodate these donors by including them on this mission."

Dr. Burns listened intently and had guessed before the president had arrived that he would ask this question. "Sir, you have every right to ask any questions, and I will do my best to answer them honestly. Perhaps if you had been president years ago, we would not even have to build this spaceship. I know my days at Boeing were some of my best when I look at my life. Second, we have not involved the government at all in our work, as you just mentioned. Donald Trump did not want to support the project, although I did speak to him twice."

At the mention of the meeting, Tom looked over at Bob, who winced.

"Yes, we do have some large donors, and yes, we have invited them to come as passengers on the trip. Initially, we built a spacecraft under the leadership of NASA. NASA was started during the space race when we competed with the Russians over which country would send the first spaceship into orbit. The Russians did manage to launch the first person into space, but we were the first nation to land a person on the moon. As time went on, NASA suffered many budget cuts that were probably influenced by some events, including the Challenger disaster. No one wanted to see such brave people killed. In the early 2000s, the government decided it was best to privatize our future space trips. Undoubtedly, this saved the government a lot of money. SpaceX enjoyed some positive results but also had some setbacks.

"When Obama was president, Secretary Clinton worked hard to convene a world conference devoted to climate change. Just about every country in the world signed on to do their part in helping our environment via the Paris Agreement. Previously, Al Gore also did a lot of work to make people more aware of the failing climate. Then along came Donald Trump and everything changed. As you know, during his second term, many national disasters took place, killing thousands of citizens, and he did nothing about it. He continued to doubt global warming, calling it a hoax. Many of the Republicans did not believe in climate change. Along with Trump, they were mainly interested in lining their pockets with money at the expense of future generations.

"Many of my colleagues around the world decided it was fruitless to argue with Trump and began making plans to leave Earth. There was no way I would have him—or any member of his family or cabinet—accompany us on the spacecraft. You could say he is the greatest mass murderer in the world's history as he finalized its destruction. He is worse than Hitler in that regard. I have to say it was not entirely his fault, but he expedited and exacerbated the issues. I did try to reason with him and his advisors, but they would not listen. He continued to dismiss all of the scientific evidence presented to him.

"These events only made my colleagues and myself more determined to search for a new home for humanity. I am sorry that Congress did not impeach him as soon as he took office. You were elected six years ago and thrown into a very hectic situation as far as the climate is concerned. In the coming years, it is only going to become worse. While I do have some sympathy for your plight, I do not feel obligated to help you now. I am sorry, but I believe it is your job to help the remaining citizens until you are no longer president."

President Stevens looked at Tom with a straight face. "I believe that was an honest answer, Dr. Burns. Unlike Trump, I will be straight with you. I am concerned about your methods for selecting all the people that will go on this spacecraft. Millions of people will not have the opportunity to go with you. Also, you have basically stolen some of the finest minds in research, engineering, and medical science to join you. While there are surely many scientists left here on Earth, I am not sure I can allow the best of us to go with you. I need those great minds with me. As president, I am responsible for the citizens of this country. Perhaps there is still time to reverse the changes we see or adapt in other ways without leaving Earth. If they can build such a fantastic spaceship, they can surely build things on Earth that prevent deaths and allow people to live much longer. Perhaps we can build more spacecrafts to allow even more people to leave Earth and seek out new planets. Surely, you can see the needs of the many will outweigh the needs of a few."

Tom stood up. "I am sorry, Mr. President. I wish I could agree with you about taking everyone on Earth with me in as many spacecrafts as we need. I will make sure to leave you with all the specifications to build other spaceships shortly. You are free to use this information as you wish. But I will not wait until you build more ships. The people that are coming with me made their decision to do so of their own free will. I did not force anyone to join me. They all had a choice. They could stay here and hope things would improve, but it sure does not look that way. Or they could join me in our attempt to seek out a new world for us. They also know that we may fail in our endeavor in the end, and we could all die before we reach any destination. They realize, however, that there is nothing left on Earth for them to do. The scientific data from across the globe indicates that the end is going to occur soon.

"No one can take that choice away from them. We will leave when we are ready to do so. Also, if you ask me to take you and your cabinet with us, the answer is 'no.' If you and your cabinet members come with us, I believe the United States will be thrown into total chaos. However, we do have a possible problem with the Russian ship that we may need your help to address. You cannot just desert your post. A good captain goes down with his ship, and you are the commander of the United States."

The Chairman of the Joint Chiefs of Staff interrupted. "What makes you so sure that we would allow you to leave? After all, we could simply send a few missiles here when you take off and blast all of you to kingdom come."

"General, yes, you could blow us all up to prevent us from leaving, but that will not solve the problem that people on the planet will face. Also, there are spacecrafts from three other countries launching at the same time. I would hope that you and others would understand that this spacecraft might be the only chance to save humanity. I am sure you have been to many military funerals where a pastor or chaplain talks about not dying in vain. If you destroy us, all of the wars that have been fought will have been in vain, since there is a chance no living thing will survive on Earth.

"Wouldn't you rather have us carry all of our histories to a new place? At this new destination, future persons will learn the stories of all of the great deeds and battles that have taken place. My crew has led many military veterans who have been willing to die for their country. You are not going to end their lives in a fit of jealousy."

The chairman looked around the room and at the president. "Mr. President, the decision is yours."

The president looked at Tom again.

"We have always looked up at the stars as objects of beauty and wonder. All these years, people never thought they would be wandering through the galaxies and other solar systems. Dr. Burns, I have no doubt all of your intentions are well-founded. I will not prevent you from finishing your work here as long as you are cooperative and provide us with all of your work details so that we may start on our own project. No one ever thought the days and nights on Earth would come to an end. I cannot imagine preventing you from going while Russia launches their own spaceship. I have no idea what God wants us to do, or even if there is a God that wants to destroy everything we have built here on Earth. Will God accompany you on the voyage? How would we even know what God is thinking? I do not think he would want me to destroy your good work and ensure the destruction of the human race. Good luck, Dr. Burns. If it is all right with you, we would like to see your spaceship up-close so we can get an idea of what we are dealing with, and we can marvel at what you have accomplished."

The president came over, shook Tom's hand, and gave him a big hug.

Everyone applauded. Dr. Burns and his associates then gave a tour of the vessel to the president and his staff. All through the four hours, the president and his team asked questions and seemed very interested. Because of Steven's open-mindedness, Tom decided to reconsider his decision not to allow anyone from the president's team to join them on the voyage. This decision would have to be made soon since these people would have to undergo training to make the trip and acclimate themselves for life in space. He decided to let the president present a list of twenty-five people to consider for the journey.

Twenty minutes later, the president handed his list to Tom. Dr. Burns recognized many of the names as heroes in their endeavors, but his own name was not on the list. After looking at the list, they shook hands.

The president said, "Thanks for allowing some of my colleagues to join you. As you notice, my name is not on the list, as I agree, my place is here on Earth. Besides, I can help you with the Russians if it becomes necessary."

First Attempt

Chapter 34 – First Attempts

Tom Burns, Bonneville Salt Flats, UT

Once President Stevens had finished his visit, Dorothy and Carson informed Tom that the space shuttle was ready for a test flight. Given that they were only ten years away from 2040, and it was estimated that all life would perish beginning that year, the crew, especially Tom, needed to stay on course. That included testing. The time pressure factor had increased by an order of magnitude. It cost fifteen million dollars to build each one, and they were planning to have four or five of them. During the journey, each shuttle would fly out into space through an opening in the spaceship that could be opened and closed as needed. The shuttle could land and take off with a small crew that could perform tests to see if a planet was habitable. The shuttle would also be used to transport a team to fix Imagines' outer hull. First, it was necessary to find out if it could take off from the land, fly around awhile, and then land again.

The team that developed the shuttle asked Tom to meet them in Utah near Salt Lake City. They decided to use Bonneville Salt Flats, which has been the location for many vehicle tests. Many of the world's speed records had been set here. The Salt Flats were formed when Lake Bonneville dried up. It was used to set many of the land speed records for a hundred years. Among the most famous was Craig Breedlove, who sped over 600 miles per hour in America's spirit. The Flats were in a very remote area off Interstate 80, which gave the shuttle team some privacy. About fifty officers, engineers, and other scientists and Sam and Jose, were watching the demonstration.

Anticipation ran high throughout the ship at this exciting moment. It was the first time that most of the observers had seen a space shuttle.

Dorothy started talking. "Welcome, everyone, to this shuttle demonstration. As you can see, we have developed a brand-new state-of-the-art shuttle. The one thing we have not done is actually test the shuttle in a live situation. That is what we are going to do today. This shuttle is capable of flying up to 100,000 miles an hour in space. However, today you will not see that speed unless you want to see the shuttle disappear forever."

Everyone laughed.

"All of our computer simulations have checked out. We've also conducted all the proper testing of the various systems on board, including those we will rely on for takeoff and landing. The shuttle will have a crew of up to six, including two pilots and four others who can be assigned any number of tasks. The shuttle instruments will be able to do a wide variety of atmospheric and soil testing. In case of attack, several weapons have been added. Living on the shuttle for up to twenty-four hours is possible. Spacesuits will be required for anyone on the shuttle. These spacesuits are similar to what everyone will use when the main vessel takes off from Earth. The shuttle also has a state-of-the-art communications system to interact with the officers on board the Imagine. Members of the spacecraft will be able to communicate with the Imagine up to one hundred thousand miles apart from each other. In addition, the Imagine can take control of the shuttle from the bridge. The main craft can direct and monitor the position of the shuttle at all times."

Carson continued, "First, we will do an unmanned flight that will be controlled by the engineers that developed the shuttle. We are using a plasma fuel that will give it the necessary thrust to liftoff. We are conducting this test outside to provide a similar environment to what will happen in real-life situations. I have provided spacesuits and goggles to everyone that will protect you in the event of an emergency. Make sure to cover your head with the hood and wear the special glasses we have provided. We will also need to be at least a half a mile away as a precaution. The flight will be about five to ten minutes long, and we will fly the shuttle at a low altitude so that it does not set off any government radars. After ten minutes, we will land the shuttle close to the spot where we lifted off. Does anyone have any questions?"

Sam decided to raise his hand.

Dorothy said, "Sam, feel free to ask whatever you want."

Sam looked at everyone. They were all fixated on him, listening intently.

"Who is controlling the shuttle today? Are we going to test it with pilots? Don't we need feedback from a pilot who can report on how the shuttle is flying or make a course correction, if necessary, with the shuttle controls?"

Carson jumped in, "That is an excellent question. After we have successfully tested an unmanned flight, we will test it again with live pilots. Today we are controlling the shuttle from a panel we have set up here. This is similar to what we have on Imagine. We have been training ten different pilots who will be joining us when we leave Earth. We have been running flight simulations on computers for three months. We have created various situations for the pilots to respond to. Unfortunately, there is no way we can predict every possible situation and every possible response. Sometimes you just have to rely on the experience of those involved in what is taking place."

Dorothy asked Sam, "Does that information answer your question?"

"Yes, it does. I can't wait to see the shuttle in action."

"Neither can we," said Carson.

Everybody moved back to the half-mile perimeter set up to observe the shuttle.

Tom put his arm around Sam's shoulders and said, "I hope this works. We really need a good shuttle in space."

Sam nodded back and gave Jose a high-five. Everyone was indeed in a festive mood, expecting a perfect flight.

Dorothy and Carson told the crew controlling the shuttle to begin. After about five minutes, the shuttle took off. Suddenly, it seemed like there was too much fire underneath the shuttle, but the people observing and controlling the flight did not know if this was an error or not.

After five more seconds, the shuttle rose to a height of about 200 feet. Everyone watched in awe as it departed. Suddenly, it blew up in a mortifying ball of fire and immediately crashed into hundreds of pieces. An emergency fire crew rushed to the scene to put the flames out as Dorothy and Carson looked at the wreckage in disbelief. The looks on everyone's face said it all.

Tom looked at everyone and immediately assumed a leadership role. He moved quickly to get everyone's attention.

"Obviously, this is not what all of us were expecting to happen today. It looks like we have suffered a total failure. I am sure that Dorothy and Carson will begin investigating what went wrong, why it went wrong, and make the corrections needed to not repeat this crash again. While I am disappointed in today's results, I know well enough to know that mistakes happen when we are developing new devices, especially in space travel. The errors found will be corrected, and we will be successful with the next shuttle test. One positive result of this is that we did not have any live humans on board when the crash happened. Our team will note precautions that need to be taken to save lives in the future.

"Dorothy and Carson, I am sure you will get to the bottom of this problem, and it will be solved. Please be sure to share your results with the other three spaceships. They may also be having similar problems or may have a solution to what happened. As soon as you have corrected the issues onboard the shuttle, we will test it again. We must and will have a working shuttle to be successful in space. Everyone is dismissed. Please get back to work on your specific assignments and be as positive as you can be."

After the accident, Jose and Sam went back to the ship with Tom. Tom seemed to take it all in stride. Sam gaped at his father. Tom could see the look of confusion spread across his son's face. Although he wondered how he could be so calm at the moment, looking at each other communicated everything he needed to Sam. Panic was not in his veins, especially with all of these people depending on him, and he wasn't going to let anyone lose hope in their missions. He was going to get the job done regardless of how many mistakes were made.

The main thing was no lives were lost.

A few hours later, Tom sat down in his office on the ship and poured himself a beer. He put on a "Do not disturb" message outside his door. He needed to reflect on the day's events. Despite all his calmness in going about his job, he was having severe doubts about what he was trying to accomplish or if it could be accomplished at all. Tom was a perfectionist. He was not used to facing failure, and this attempt at flying the shuttle was, for the moment, a colossal failure. He expected minor setbacks, but this was not minor at all. They needed an operational shuttle they could depend on if they were to launch the Imagine. If they could not build a shuttle correctly, how could they possibly build the main spaceship? If anyone had been on that shuttle, he would have had to inform their family and prepare for a funeral service for someone, probably burnt so badly they would not even be recognized.

This led to worse thoughts. What would happen if the Imagine blew up on the launch? He then would be responsible for a thousand deaths, including his own family. Perhaps it was better to ditch the whole project. Yes, some of the people on board would be disappointed or upset, but they would be able to live an everyday life. Yes, the environment would become worse, but hopefully, everyone would get to live to a ripe old age. He and his family could probably move back into their home and get a dog. Sam could be an Air Force pilot and perhaps attend the Air Force Academy. Maybe that was the best path to follow. It sure would be a lot safer.

Tom sat there looking out the window and began drinking his second beer. This was the first time he had drank alcohol since he began working on the project, which had basically consumed his life.

As he sat there contemplating his life and failures, his friend Bob walked into the room. If Tom was going to spill his guts to anyone, it would be Bob. He was a great man who could understand all the emotions that Tom was feeling. Yet, at this moment, Tom did not want to speak to anyone. He preferred to be miserable by himself. Tom asked Bob to leave, but Bob sensed the depression and sat down next to Tom anyway. Bob also grabbed a beer and put his feet up on the desk.

They sat together silently with their beers in their hands, taking a sip every few seconds.

Finally, Bob spoke. "I guess it was sort of a rough day today. I can see you are very disappointed over the shuttle failure. Care to talk about it? You can ask me to leave, or you can tell me what you are thinking. Of course, if you ask me to leave, I will refuse, so your only option is to talk to me. I will be a good listener and punching bag if necessary."

Tom looked at Bob's face and said, "You have been my closest friend for many years. We have served our country together in war and peace and have been through many harrowing experiences. We've seen a lot. This is different. I am asking a group of totally innocent people to come with me on a mission in which, just like the shuttle today, could be over in one instant. Three other spaceships are depending on me. Those onboard are looking to me to help them travel to an unknown planet, set up a new life, and have confidence that I make the right decisions all the time. Well, Bob, perhaps I am not that man. I could not even launch a shuttle that would carry six to eight people for a short period successfully. I could be responsible for the deaths of four thousand people. I do not think I can live with that result, nor would I want to live with that.

"This whole idea about traveling to a new planet in a galaxy far away is just a fantasy that may never be accomplished, at least by me. Tomorrow I plan to announce the mission is canceled. Everyone can return to their own homes, or wherever they want to go on Earth because we are definitely not going to make it anywhere with me as the leader."

Bob was silent for a moment. Tom took a sip of beer and just stared at Bob. There was a terrible strain on his face as if the whole world's fate rested on his shoulders.

Bob responded, "Look at me, Tom, and pay attention very closely to what I am about to tell you. First, I admit today was a terrible setback for the mission. If there was any, the fault lies with the engineers, including me, that build the shuttle. We were just not ready to launch it. We will fix the mistakes, and you can count on that happening as soon as possible. If we need to hire new experts, we can do so, but this problem will be fixed one way or another. I have no doubts about that.

"The other issue that I see right now is your wanting to give up everything you have dreamed about and worked for over thirty years. There is not a person in the world that has done more to research and ensure this mission will be a great success than you. You have gained the respect of everyone on board, even Dr. Sato."

This comment made Tom smile a little bit. Dr. Sato was one tough cookie.

Bob continued, "We all came on this ship because we all want to save the human race, and we cannot think of anyone better suited than you to lead such an effort. I can see it in the eyes of everyone on board that they will follow you regardless of what you say. Everyone on board made a choice to go with you on this journey. They were not forced to do so, although you did manage to twist a few arms."

Tom smiled again and thought to himself, *Wasn't that the truth*.

Bob continued, "If we give up on this journey now, then assholes like Trump will have won."

That comment brought a grimace to Tom's face. He said through gritted teeth, "Trump does not know shit from Shinola. He also did not know whether to scratch his watch or wind his ass."

Tom laughed and shook his head. "That man lied in four years more than any human being possibly could in their entire life. He really did not understand climate change or what his decisions meant for everyone's future on Earth."

Bob then said, "Right on, Tom. Do you want to be stuck here with such a jerk? The shuttle's mistake is nothing compared to the mistake that this president made during his office term. At least you can admit when you made a mistake. So, are you going to tell everyone on board tomorrow that this whole idea of yours and everything we have accomplished so far is a mistake and a lie? Is that it? Personally, I do not think you have made any mistakes. Maybe a minor setback, but not one mistake. And I certainly know you are not a quitter. But the choice is yours. I am not going to make that decision for you. I know that everyone on board still has one hundred percent confidence in you and will travel to whatever galaxy we decide. The question is, can you get your confidence back? Having served with you for so many years, I am sure you can. So, I ask you, man, to man, friend to friend, what are you going to do?"

Tom stood up slowly and put his beer down. He stood there for a moment in total silence. Then, he spoke. "Thank you for being such a good friend and colleague. I guess I was trying to drown myself in self-pity. The pressure of having everything go smoothly to ensure this mission's success is immense, as you can well imagine, and I let it get the best of me. You did a great job of picking me up and making some things clear. For one thing, unlike Trump, I surely know my arse from a hole in the ground."

That made Bob laugh loudly.

Then, Tom said, "Thanks again. All I ask is that you do not spread our little brother-to-brother chat all over the ship."

Bob said, "Duly noted, sir." Then, he gave Tom a big salute.

Tom reciprocated, and they hugged each other. Bob left Tom to himself.

As Bob left, Tom had a smile on his face. He was already thinking of improving the shuttle and other functions, but he was also thinking about what a great friend he had in Bob Jackson.

What Could Go Wrong

Chapter 35 – What Could Go Wrong

Tom Burns, the Imagine, Rocky Mountains, CO

Five months later, Carson and Dorothy notified Tom they had fixed the mistakes causing the shuttle incident and were confident it would now operate successfully. Another unmanned flight was scheduled, and this time there were no problems at all. Everyone involved in the mission was elated.

Meanwhile, Dr. Sato and Tom met to discuss her progress in the medical facilities. She had recruited some exceptional doctors and researchers for the voyage. Dr. Sato said the work was coming along fine. Still, she needed to go on a trip to Wyoming to pick up some necessary DNA research materials. These materials had to be kept at -200 degrees Celsius. They could not trust Federal Express to keep it at the correct temperature, so she would go herself.

Tom told her to make sure she had a communicator. She had her GPS chip working just in case something went wrong.

Dr. Sato and her colleague flew in a twin-engine plane to Wyoming. The next morning, Tom's communicator buzzed. When he answered, it was Dr. Sato on the other end.

Tom asked, "Why are you calling so early in the morning? Has something gone wrong?" He thought that perhaps the materials she needed were contaminated, or there was another problem.

Then, he heard Dr. Sato crying.

"Our plane crashed in a wooded area far from any town. I was unable to call anyone on my phone, as it is no longer charged. The only thing I could do is call you on my communicator. The pilot and my colleague are both dead. I think I may have a broken leg, but other than that, I seem to be all right. However, I need assistance or someone to rescue me. You are my only hope. Yet, I doubt you are going to fly an entire spaceship to rescue me. It will look really suspicious, and I doubt you could land it anywhere around here with all these woods. If you have to leave me to die, I understand. Humanity must be saved. The mission comes first. I just have a few requests."

"Save your requests for when you see me, which will be very soon. On my communicator, I can see your exact location, since your GPS chip is still working. I will send someone soon. Let me get to work on this, and I will call you back in fifteen minutes. Do you have any water or anything to eat while you wait?"

"No. It is getting cold here, and I do not want to freeze to death, so please do something fast if you can."

Tom hung up and tried to think quickly. Another twin-engine plane, which he did not have access to, would take about ten hours to get to the crash location. Tom did not know how to contact the local authorities and wondered what they could do about it. However, he was not going to lose his chief doctor and now friend without a fight.

"Come on, come on."

As he was pacing, Dorothy walked in to let him know they could test the shuttle again with a live pilot.

Tom took one look at her and said, "Thank God the shuttle is ready. We are going to test it for real. Get one pilot immediately."

Tom explained what happened to Dr. Sato and that there was a need for immediate transport to save her and then return her back to the shuttle.

Dorothy said, "Are you sure you want to do this? We have not successfully flown this with a human. Is it worth the risk?"

"I will risk my own life and co-pilot the shuttle. That way, it will give me a firsthand look at how to operate the craft. Please get one pilot ready. Stay here with the people who monitor the shuttle and make sure other systems are working correctly. We are flying to Wyoming near Jackson Hole. I would have asked Harrison Ford to rescue her, but I do not think he is available."

"Sounds like a plan," she said. "I know how important Dr. Sato is to this mission."

She ordered the pilot, Marvin Watson, to get the shuttle ready. Tom called Dr. Sato back and let her know he was personally going to rescue her. It would also be an excellent opportunity to see the shuttle in action.

"You are crazy," she said. "What about your wife and kids?"

"They will all be fine. See you very soon."

Twenty minutes later, Captain Watson gave Tom instructions to co-pilot and control the shuttle.

"I will take care of the lift-off and landing," Marvin said. "Once we land, we will both go and get Dr. Sato back to the shuttle. I have a stretcher on board for that. So, put your seat belt on and let's see how this baby flies, shall we?"

"Dorothy, can you hear me?"

"Yes, loud and clear."

"Dorothy, I just want you to know that if this fails and we don't make it, it is not your fault. I gave the order to do this. Please put that on the record. Bob Jackson will then be in charge."

"You are not going to die on me and neither is Dr. Sato. That is probably what you told her, right? Good luck."

Readied for takeoff, the shuttle was in a field near the main craft. Dorothy gave the countdown, then she said, "Good to go."

Marvin took the throttle as the plasma gas began to lift the shuttle off the ground. For this trip, the shuttle had to fly higher than the previous test. Marvin and Tom would operate at a speed of a thousand miles an hour, getting them to the crash site in about one hour. This time the shuttle worked beautifully. The flight was very smooth and fast. Both Marvin and Tom marveled at how easy it was to operate the shuttle.

Approximately one hour later, they were near the crash site. A little smoke was coming up from the plane crash but did not appear to endanger anyone. Marvin and Tom looked to land at a place close enough to carry someone on a stretcher. They saw an open spot nearby with a forty-by-a-hundred-square-foot functional landing area. The landing was like landing a helicopter.

Once they touched down, they left the engine running, since they did not want to test another plasma takeoff right now. Marvin and Tom saw Dr. Sato near the plane and ran to her. She was weak, but her mind was sharp.

"About time you got here," she said. "Thanks for coming. How about a drink?"

Tom said, "Sure, as soon as we get back to Imagine. First, we need to get you out of here."

After putting a leg splint on her, they lifted her carefully onto the stretcher and carried her to the shuttle. Once onboard, Marvin took off. Tom got up and went back to talk to Dr. Sato.

"Your leg does look broken but will mend. I do have some exciting news for you. You are the third live person that has flown on the shuttle. This thing is really cool."

"You mean you are testing this thing to see if it really works, possibly getting us all killed?"

"Yes, it is part of the job," he said. "Relax, the shuttle is fine. You need to recover from your injury to resume your duties. Did you get the material you needed?"

"No."

"Perhaps Marvin can make another trip later this week or next and get them for us."

Marvin heard the conversation. "Yes, Dr. Sato, I will be glad to return and pick up whatever you need."

"Thank you," Dr. Sato said. "However, there is something I must discuss with you, Tom. I was supposed to meet with an expert in Wyoming to discuss joining our team. I may have mentioned Dr. Earl Kintain previously. He is very advanced in his understanding of DNA research. I would like to expedite things and get in touch with him immediately and discuss joining us on the phone rather than what I intended in person. He will understand once I explain the accident. Surely, he will say yes, and I would need him and his research technologies to be brought to the ship earlier than next week. Some of our work back on Imagine depends on it, and a time lag now could cost us dearly."

"Of course, Helen. I trust your judgment, and as I mentioned earlier, I trust that you would put together the best team for the voyage."

"Thank you, Tom."

She jotted down some notes and then went to sleep. Marvin did a great job landing the shuttle so softly that Dr. Sato did not even wake up. Her medical colleagues came out and took her out on the stretcher. They gave her some pain medicine and let her sleep. When they got back to the ship, they operated on her leg. Everyone was on edge. Dr. Sato was one of the most critical people in Imagine. Without her, some of the significant decisions would be impossible to make regarding expanding life expectancy.

The scientific controversies onboard Imagine weren't by any means resolved, and Tom wondered whether they would be before the launch. Still, Dr. Sato needed to heal as soon as possible and return immediately. Her support staff had conducted some crucial experiments and needed to continue their research to observe and test more outcomes. They were waiting for what she was bringing with her with much impatience. Tom's communication receiver had received their calls repeatedly asking about her and the safety of her cargo.

Tom understood her support team's impatience as he'd stayed abreast of their discussions. They were waiting on Dr. Sato to continue discussing what had been found eight years ago after the Chinese scientist, Jiankui. He had gene-edited twin babies to modify the CCR5 gene in the embryos that control how the HIV virus enters human cells, and the mutation had allowed them to be born free of the virus. However, follow-up researchers found that the mutation itself had led the team to discover that people who had two copies of the mutated gene had a higher risk of dying earlier, which one of the two twins had. Since then, the scientific community had ostracized Jiankui He. But the development of the tool SATI (intercellular linearized Single homology Arm donor mediated intron-Targeting Integration) had allowed Dr. Sato and her team to apply the findings from models used on mice to correct the genes responsible for progeria—premature aging—and controversially extend that to the aging process itself. Tom had been fine with it.

They were also heartened by biotech company improvements in the last few years in treating different genetic defects with adults in the body rather than embryo-stage in fighting cancers, eye-related diseases, and spinal dystrophy. The latter would be essential to study, particularly as astronauts had found that living in space took a toll on their backs, causing their muscles to weaken within the spine over time. And one of the most pushing-boundaries studies they were trying to handle was singling out a gene that might push the boundaries of mortality. To do that, they would use germline editing to edit embryos to create babies that would carry the edits, like the Chinese scientist had done—crossing the CRISPR red-line and pushing beyond scientific consensus.

Could a later generation live twice as long, avoiding any risk of the diseases that the previous generation could not protect itself from genetically? The technology, and, more immediately, the recent acquiescence of many scientists driven by the pressures of the times to accept the forward momentum of the technology, had led many prominent scientists to support Dr. Sato's efforts—if they were to be used to save humanity. If Imagine landed, needed to extend lives, and built a new colony that needed to maintain growth, they supported using technologies that would not be beholden to the restrictive laws back on Earth. Considering that editing germline cells have the possibility of immortality—since they can affect several generations, unlike somatic cells—this procedure may have much larger consequences on populations. On account of an outcry to ensure that scientific safety was established, the medical risks need to be understood.

In other words, a harmful mutation may pass from generation to generation, and then, what about the fate of humanity taking their voyage on Imagine? Dr. Sato's staff had publicly wondered with Tom if there needed to be a broad ship population agreement on the matter anyway—not exactly to Dr. Sato's liking. Nevertheless, they had recently become aware that some donors onboard were willing to let the technology be tested on them if it was thanks to CRISPR and SATI, that they might live forever.

For the time being, the medical staff assured Tom the leg would mend and that she would be up and walking in a cast and on crutches within a week. She was susceptible to the pain and suffering of being a mortal, after all.

Cryo Test Subjects

Chapter 36 – Cryo Test Subjects

Tom Burns, the Imagine, Rocky Mountains, CO

The next day, to Tom's surprise, Dr. Sato told him that she had other news she wanted to share with him.

"We are going to be moving the animals on board soon."

"What animals? I thought this ship was not going to have any animals. I already let one tortoise on board, but that's it. What animals are we talking about, and why do we need them?"

"First, we are moving around a hundred mice and guinea pigs on board. We need them for our research. I hate using animals to test for finding cures for diseases too. We will make every effort to keep these animals alive until they die of natural causes. However, to test the cryopreservation unit, test subjects need to be tested to make sure it is working properly. We intend to put a mouse to sleep, or stasis, and then see if we can awaken it. Once we awaken it, we need to check all its vital signs to see if it is functioning as it was before we put it to sleep. If the first mouse dies or does not behave properly, we need to make adjustments. Same with the guinea pigs. I would much rather use a mouse or a guinea pig as a first test subject on board and not a human being. Would you like to be the first subject to test the cryo process? I don't think so. We have to make sure it is working perfectly. Do you agree with me, Dr. Burns?"

Tom said, "I understand your concerns, but I thought we were ready to use the cryopreservation system."

"Yes, but we have not done it in space. I don't know if we have to adjust for gravity or other factors as we are flying at such a fast speed. We cannot test it until we leave Earth."

"Where will you keep these mice? We can't have them running around the spaceship. Also, how will we guarantee they will survive the launch? I don't have spacesuits for mice. The suits don't come in sizes that small."

"Hilarious, Dr. Burns," she said. "For the launch, I have arranged a special incubator cage where we will keep all the mice and guinea pigs. We keep a few there now." She watched as Dr. Burns registered that they'd been testing on animals already. Of course, they had been. He just hadn't considered where, but in any case, they were still firmly on terra firma. "A proper oxygen flow will be set up so they can breathe during the launch until the all-clear is given. They will never leave the restricted lab area."

"Okay," said Tom, "any other animals you intend to bring with you? How about some dogs?"

"Wow, you can read my mind, and yes, we are bringing ten different kinds of dogs on board. Each pair of dogs will have one male and one female so they can mate and reproduce."

"You have to be kidding me. You mean we are setting up a puppy ward? I do not think we can have dogs in everyone's room," Dr. Burns said. "Who will train them?"

"I am not kidding about this. We need dogs and cats on board for many reasons. Would you like to hear them?"

Tom had a puzzled look on his face and wanted to leave but said, "Go ahead."

Dr. Sato said, "First of all, once we have success with the mice, we need another animal to test on the cryopreservation system. We will not test the dogs until they reproduce. I actually hope not to test them if all goes well, but we cannot predict what will happen."

"Next reason," said Tom.

"Dogs are man's best friend. They can also be very therapeutic when people pet them."

"I understand that people like dogs and dogs like to be pet, but dogs also poop outside. Where are they going to poop on the ship? I can't imagine a hundred dogs running around this ship pooping all over the place. Who is going to clean it up? I don't want my ship to smell like dog-poop or have people complain about stepping in it. Once we clean it up, what are we going to do with it? We can't store it until we reach a planet, as we could have a ton of it before we land. They also bark a lot. In fact, some dogs bark an awful lot. Is this going to be a major problem?"

Dr. Sato started to laugh. "Calm down, silly. The dogs will be cared for by my staff. I did take the liberty of hiring a veterinarian to care for them. We have ordered plenty of dog food, and Luis has promised me he will cook up some bioengineered dog food for them. I intend to train them to poop in certain areas or in one room. During the launch, we will keep them together. With Bob Jackson's assistance, we have developed a special helmet for each dog and cat to regulate their oxygen. We will let the crew know that if they want to play with the dogs and cats, they can do so at certain hours. We certainly plan to limit the number of dogs and cats running around, but they have to reproduce. They only live twelve to fourteen years normally. Our research on them will also allow them to live longer. In short, we have thought of just about everything to make this work."

"Thank you for telling me all these things about the dogs and cats. I know I cannot convince you to leave them here on Earth. Any dogs or cats left on Earth will likely perish the same as humans, and I guess we owe it to man's best friend to make sure they continue to be so. Please make sure to put tags on them and give each one a name. That is all I have to say right now."

"Would you like me to name one dog after you?" Dr. Sato asked.

Dr. Burns looked at her and made a face. "I certainly hope you do not name a dog after me, but that is your choice. Are there any more animals you want to tell me about? How about some elephants or giraffes onboard?"

Dr. Sato laughed again. "No elephants or giraffes will be on board for the entire trip. I can promise that. We do have DNA of almost all species of animals on the planet except for some of the more dangerous ones. Depending on the planet, we may not be able to clone some of them. The conditions may not be feasible for every animal to live on a new planet."

"I am glad you are feeling better, and I made you laugh. I can see your mind is still as sharp as ever and you are starting to put the accident behind you already. I guess I will go and work on some other things."

As he walked away, he thought to himself, what if the animals were the only ones left on the ship? Could the dogs take over? A new movie could then be made entitled, "Planet of the Dogs" instead of "Planet of the Apes."

Wyoming Payload

Chapter 37 – Wyoming Payload

Dr. Sato, the Imagine, Rocky Mountains, CO

Dr. Sato watched Dr. Earl Kintain and his entourage exit the plane that brought them to the undisclosed cave. Marvin had been eager to help ever since the accident had happened. It disappointed him that Dr. Sato hadn't acquired the necessary material for her DNA research.

From the looks of it, Dr. Earl Kintain has arrived with a great deal of technological equipment that will help us in our efforts, thought Dr. Sato. The security guard had texted her when they arrived. She was walking in her crutches to greet him. She was still shaken from the accident and as a result of nearly missing this opportunity and the possibility that Tom wouldn't have approved of her bringing the last remaining member of her team on board. Dr. Kintain's advanced work was superior and on the cutting edge. She had been struck almost speechless when Tom suggested that Martin go pick up whatever necessary material she had needed for DNA research.

It felt that close to her being empty-handed. Her medical program onboard Imagine depended on obtaining these materials, especially since her work would rely heavily on experimentation with the original of the species of clones Dr. Kintain possessed. Their research would help them formulate a strain and divergence from any of the more controlled experiments they would try in terms of cloning methods. It would be kept in its own quarters until she and Dr. Kintain were sure that it could walk and be among humans. If it didn't do anything damaging or strange that would make the rest of the passengers uncomfortable, they would be allowed to enter other parts of the ship.

"Good morning, Dr. Kintain."

"Good morning, Dr. Sato. I'm glad that we had a chance to speak despite your accident. Marvin is an excellent pilot and very helpful. I am eager to be part of the Imagine exploration. I hope you are faring much better. I trust your leg is better?"

"It will take a bit. Of course, I have applied the stem cell gene therapy treatment first researched at Cedars-Sinai Medical Center in Los Angeles."

As they walked together, crewmembers carried all of his technologies behind them. Dr. Sato described how the method relied on the body's own stem cells, and that involved implanting a collagen matrix made up of bone-induced genes into the stem cells.

"I should be able to heal in two weeks. Originally, the method allowed for an eight-week recovery, but there have been advancements since then. I'm almost halfway there."

"Fantastic. I am glad to hear it. I am sure that, somewhere in the technologies I have brought, we can make sure that your tissue functions as it did before the break, in no time either."

"Thank you. I suppose that all the egg donors you have worked with may not know they will be supplying the potential for life in our cloning processes deep in the galaxy."

"I suppose they don't. Although the six-time limit has been stretched in many places, the supposed risks to the donors were ill-conceived. Many have donated twice that and have been fine. Now, these half-siblings may run around Imagine."

They entered the ship. Dr. Sato took him to his quarters. As the door closed, she directed the largest technology pieces to be placed in the adjacent room. It was one of the most reinforced rooms in the entire ship as far as she was told. It would be best to maintain the secrecy of their experimentation with the first human clone that Dr. Kintain had managed to create in as removed and difficult to access place as possible.

She found herself terribly curious. She wondered how Dr. Kintain managed to travel with it.

"I can see you are itching to ask so many questions. We carried the clone here under sedation so that he wasn't startled by all the new places. He's never been anywhere else but in our labs in Wyoming. He complied. Now, let me explain what we're dealing with here. I would put his educational level at this point at a mid-high school. But he advances quickly. He'll be at a collegial level within a short week in your company and mine. Also, we've not only managed to keep the human clone alive, but we have also been able to create an external uterus. ... Several in fact. That way, we won't have to rely on human reproductive cloning, since studies have shown the fetus gets rather large and can cause very difficult birthing.

"We've also managed to guarantee that all known diseases were not passed on to this particular clone, as we relied on CRISPR and SATI gene editing. He cannot become sick. He can likely outlive many of the humans on board this ship."

"You mean to say he only has desirable traits?"

"Exactly. Just like the Chinese twins that were modified using CRISPR, his brain has been inadvertently enhanced, including all age-related degenerative disorders."

"But can we accelerate aging itself by using stem cells if it doesn't work out well and the clone is rejected by the human population we have onboard?"

"Yes, although it might not be easy. He's a bit stronger than we expected and still growing. And we can't be sure that his stem cells won't self-renew, rejecting any ends we hope to achieve."

"But could we clone the clone initially using the eggs you have brought?"

"Yes, and the other amazing success rate, so far, has been that we have been able to develop the process of in vitro gametogenesis, IVG, creating eggs and sperm in culture dishes where skin cells are reprogrammed to behave like embryonic stem cells and are then IPSCs, as you know induced pluripotent stem cells. We have developed several embryos and implanted our external wombs. Since we are onboard this ship, all known US laws and Earth-constraints may be overrun."

"Although we must always be able to keep the option of destroying them if we fear the generation of mutations will somehow threaten saving humanity. Does the clone have a name?"

"Yes, we've named him Epoh."

"Nice, not too sinister. When can I see him?"

"He's been sedated for the trip, but we expect he'll be hungry in about an hour."

"I can change my dinner plans. He'll likely get me to accelerate our DNA cloning plans for those who couldn't make the trip with us."

***

When she met Epoh, he was deliriously hungry. She liked him right away. Mostly because he looked exactly like Dr. Kintain.

"I hope you slept well," she said.

"I always do," Epoh said.

She turned to Dr. Kintain and asked him if he'd brought his own food just for the day since she hadn't yet had a chance to introduce him to the nutritionist, Luis Gonzales. "I ask because he and I have a bit of a score to settle lately, and I doubt that he would find anymore secrecy from my immediate staff or me all that welcome. He's a bit of a head-counter, I'm afraid. Seems if I round up or round down, it infuriates him. I've told him in no uncertain terms that anything he can genetically engineer could also throw together in the lab through our means. I had to, just in case, it escapes him that he too may become unessential for the ship's purposes. He's a bit of a traditionalist and has some problem with several of us women not exactly being tied down just yet. Oh, and if the list needed to grow longer, well, he's suspicious of what we might be breeding over in our quarters. I have the feeling he walks by crossing himself the entire time."

"Well, to be honest, I did go to the cafeteria while you were away, but just briefly, and thought about introducing myself, except he looked so busy. I felt unsure about what he would do about a perfect stranger arriving since we hadn't met yet and decided it was in bad form. So, yes, thankfully, I did bring enough for a few days. I know his appetite is large. I have a feeling this Luis will think he's feeding several heads of cattle."

"Well, Epoh, if your hunger is any sign of what motivates you, I'll likely be going to bat for you a lot." Then she turned to Dr. Kintain and said, "Although my guess is that you're both just as motivated as I am to provide a better life for humanity and driven by other strong motivational drivers also, so eating well can foster those needs. I'm sure we'll see. Now that most of us can't be driven by money or rewards, I suppose the desire to be the best and helping others might become strong motivators that we share. Certainly, many of us are motivated by meaningful and challenging work ahead. I shouldn't be so hard on Luis, by the way. There's plenty to be said about how motivated Luis is by exploring human desires like sweetness, beauty, and intoxication in the way he makes his foods. I'll give him that! We're still not quite able to embody all those nourishing and nurturing qualities in our science lab. Still, he's worth trying in the kitchen. I'll introduce you tomorrow."

"I suppose I'll have to give him a tip beforehand," said Dr. Kintain.

"Don't you dare," joked Dr. Sato. "Dr. Burns won't have any part of it."

Healing Thoughts

Chapter 38 – Healing Thoughts

Dr. Sato, the Imagine, Rocky Mountains, CO

Hours after Dr. Sato met Epoh and got Dr. Kintain situated, she got a call from one of their advice nurses. Something terrible had struck one of their medical team. She was vomiting, terribly cold, and was in a state of confusion.

Dr. Sato made her way to her infirmary to pick up some potential medications and head to see her sick staff member. She practically ran into Dr. Kintain when she turned around in the hallway outside of the infirmary as he was walking by. It was late, almost midnight.

"I'm sorry. I am in such a hurry; I nearly ran you over."

"What's the rush? Is everything ok? No problem. I needed a bit of a jolt. Getting prepared for this voyage has me a bit on edge, wondering how we'll all be able to work together without a place to exit."

"Well, at the very least, we have some pretty impressive exercise equipment and virtual reality when we feel like taking that proverbial walk." She smiled. "I'd love to chat more, but I have a sick crew member on my medical staff who I have to tend to."

"Oh, dear. That is awful. I'm sorry to hear. Let me know if I can help in any way."

"Of course, Dr. Kintain."

She hobbled to the medical team's quarters on her crutches. *Only a few days on these*, she thought. As she presented her facial recognition details, the door opened. Inside, Dr. Olivia Stooniper, a member of her team for at least ten years, lay there, moaning. She was in complete distress, discomfort wracking her body. She twisted in her sheets, and her clothing was completely soaked through. The air conditioner was on, but it might not even have made a difference in providing Olivia any real comfort.

"Olivia, what happened?"

"Well, Helen, I'm feeling slightly better. About two days ago, I felt alright, and then I just felt total exhaustion overcome me. I was standing at the window in one of our labs and thinking about what you had said about our schedule and the assortment of experimentation. I was anxious to get started and a bit worried that you might not be able to gain more assistance from Dr. Kintain when he arrived. But I figured when the time came, you'd inform us. Well, in the meantime, I was, for some reason, anxious that the DNA that we collected wasn't safely stored, so I panicked, checked on them, and of course, they were fine.

"Then, I recall, walking out into the cave for some 'fresher air,' thinking that possibly I was getting myself worked up about when we would get the clones started, if they would be successful, how you and our team are going to handle all of this, despite our theoretical knowledge, and I found myself lost. I don't mean lost in my thoughts, which I was, but lost outside of the cave in the wooded area nearby. I literally had only moments ago absentmindedly said hello to a few people working in the cave on preparations, but they barely registered in my mind. I definitely was lost in thought.

"So, the only thing that got me back into my body was a quick flitter out of the corner of my eye that ran across my foot. I almost screamed since it was so sudden and alarming. Out of the corner of my eye, I saw a long tail. I assumed it was a rat, but I have no idea if rats live in or near caves. Well, I thought none of it, realizing that there are probably rats that live there, but I felt fine then. I somehow managed to find my way back to the opening of the cave. I got back to the ship, hoping there was no way rats could get on board. Once I got back in the lab, I started to consider some ways that we might be able to work with our limited storage capacity and came back here. I woke up, had a good day, and went to bed with a lot on my mind last night.

"I don't always sleep well, depending on whatever it is we are working on or if something personal is getting to me. I often work out a lot of stuff while I sleep. So, having a restless night at first just felt fine. But then I started to feel really feverish, and some of the things that were troubling me didn't have anything to do with bioethics, clones, or what failures we may face."

"I rarely get a full night's rest with my head going in a million directions. But what happened after you saw the rat and returned to the ship?"

"You'd think if I was tossing and turning, it would just bother me what was in the newspapers. All the sloths, envious losers, greedy bastards, wrathful oligarchs, and the lack of gumption on the part of religious leaders constantly tempering anyone trying to do anything about fixing the environmental problems we face."

Dr. Sato said, "I can relate. So much of it leaves me feeling sick. If I wasn't motivated by our meaningful work, I don't think I could watch, just based on pain avoidance alone."

"Normally, that's what causes me to lose sleep, but I started thinking it was something physically wrong. And then I found a tick."

"Oh, Olivia. Did you pull it out?"

"Yes, but I hadn't found it until this morning. I saw a rash all over my wrists, palms, ankles, and soles of my feet. Then—"

"Rocky Mountain spotted fever. Oh god."

"Yes, so I got Dr. Gene Finaren to quickly bring over some doxycycline. He's run a lab test, and it's a confirmed diagnosis. I'm hoping we don't get to the IV stage."

"Well, let's monitor it. I bet you've caught it in time. I've realized that Lyme disease is unlikely to be spread here since that type of tick isn't found in Colorado. Still, there's Colorado tick fever, RMSF, tularemia, and tick-borne relapsing fever. I'm glad you were able to get it out within the first few days. At least this can't spread. So, don't worry, we won't throw you in ..." Dr. Sato leaned forward and whispered in Olivia's ear, "with the clone."

With that, Olivia's eyes opened wide in excitement. "It's here?"

"HE'S here."

"Is he everything you ever dreamed of?"

"Well, if I'd been dreaming of Dr. Kintain!" She laughed.

Olivia's eyes showed some sparkle.

"Look, Olivia, get some rest. We need you back in the lab. I'm expediting our cloning schedule and I need you right there to get things going. No use taking walks picking up ticks if we're taking a much more difficult trip."

"Maybe we'll just go through the teacup up in the sky or touch Polaris on our way?" Olivia laughed. "I suppose, I might have some rare hallucinogenic effect from the doxycycline if I'm picturing touching the stars. I get it. I better get some rest. Look forward to seeing the clone."

"Oh, you will."

***

Dr. Kintain, the Imagine, Rocky Mountains, CO

In the meantime, Dr. Kintain had returned after a late-night walk and running into Dr. Sato to set up Epoh's accommodations the way he liked them. He'd noticed that during the conversation between Epoh and Dr. Sato that Epoh had retained a great deal of knowledge about the ship and about the potential good he could contribute in the coming months. Winter brought with it many challenges in Dr. Sato's mind as she'd shared with Dr. Kintain. As they discussed his meeting with Dr. Sato, it appeared, however, to largely escape Epoh. Yet, Epoh had learned that the testing had happened in September after some failures during the earlier part of the year and that the ship was already filled with their passengers. The passengers were allowed to still come and go and were adjusting to life on the ship.

Epoh was fascinated with the idea of the outdoors. He'd never been outdoors. He'd been sheltered in secrecy due to the nature of Dr. Kintain's experimentations, and Epoh was remarkably stunned by Dr.

Sato's excitement when they met. Dr. Kintain hadn't introduced him to too many people. Dr. Sato had shown her enthusiasm when other colleagues seemed to hold back their reactions, afraid of imprinting any ideas on Epoh that would complicate the testing and the conditioning that Dr. Kintain wished to secure of Epoh.

"Epoh," said Dr. Kintain, "we are in much more advanced quarters and advanced planning than we were back at the lab that we left yesterday. Maybe you recall that I told you we were leaving our planet and that we have secured passage on Imagine in order to travel beyond our solar system."

"Yes, I recall."

"Good, Epoh. Well, only a short while ago, I ran into Dr. Sato again. She is handling a sick crew member who has come down with something dreadful. It is very concerning to her. So, although she may have mentioned that she looked forward to seeing you in the morning, I simply wanted to warn you that it is possible, I can't be sure that she will be swamped handling her sick staff member."

"Why would she allow someone sick here in the first place? What if it spreads? Why would she compromise—"

"Epoh, for the time being, I need you to understand something. There are very advanced experts onboard who will likely be working with you who you may not understand, especially if they cough, if they sneeze from an allergy, or have a headache. I need you to understand that you may look like me, but I'm just like them. I too may very well be sick one day."

Dr. Kintain stopped for a moment. It was so difficult not to become attached to Epoh. Still, at times he doubted very seriously the feeling was mutual. It seemed solely based on somewhat of a captivity and his likeness to him, and he wondered if, at some point, Epoh would try his own escape.

It seemed to Dr. Kintain that Epoh could out-compete him and others on board and either ignore the chain of commands and potentially take matters into his own hands if he knew the protocols and the functionality of how the technology worked. Besides, he might be able to accomplish improved methods and scientific solutions also. He could either harm the humans in his way or be taught to see them as allies. The line might move on an hourly, daily, or minute-by-minute basis. As people on board dealt with their spiritual and human concerns, principles, and values, Epoh likely would have no such problem.

Despite the fact that he watched Epoh mimic Dr. Sato's personality, her mannerisms, her voice and complete many of her thoughts once he'd already developed a good gist of everything she shared with him, Dr. Kintain knew Epoh would continue to advance his understanding of Dr. Sato while he waited to see her. He would be relentless.

Epoh's expression never changed. It seemed he felt nothing about the possibility of Dr. Kintain becoming sick. Therefore, he would certainly not care if that was even possible for him if it was one of the strangers on board. Maybe there was a way to teach him to care not in an unscientific manner often developed in personhood but based on rationality, scientific thoughts, and Epoh's own motivations. Dr. Kintain had seen that he was motivated by hunger. He was also motivated by other drives, and those would become more apparent as he grew older. He was now only Sam's age. He wondered if sex would become one of his strongest motivators, which concerned Dr. Kintain. If he had only developed a clone his age at the time.

"What I mean by saying this is that many of us feel, um, think at your age that we are, sort of, indestructible until we get hurt and things change. You haven't experienced pain or suffering. I will try to explain to you what we generally react like when someone tells us a story that should make us sad or feel for them."

A considerable number of cynical thoughts ran through Dr. Kintain's mind. He had visions of people he knew who had become so callous in life, they were willing to hurt the poor, the vulnerable, and those who were in the worst paths of climate change or areas prone to diseases and viruses with little affordable or accessible means to bring themselves back to health.

Perish the thought, he said to himself.

He tried again, remembering that, as he proceeded with this training of Epoh, he would have to rely again on what he found to be one of Epoh's strongest motivators, reward. He'd found that it wasn't pain-avoidance, but outside factors, since, so far, Dr. Kintain had not seen much of an individual spirit or esprit that revealed itself in Epoh—just to do something for its own sake without a reward.

"I will try to explain why if I were sick and I was supposed to meet with you, or I was caring for someone sick, and I couldn't meet with you, you would need to consider that the next logical step for you would be to consider what sickness the person may suffer, what they may experience, how long they might be sick, and how others will try to jump in, see a need and fill it. It's why I'm called a doctor. It's how I try to think. It took a lot of practice, especially when I thought I was indestructible. However, if I were Dr. Sato, I would be very concerned about losing one of her important crew members. She is a necessity for the success of this voyage. So, her recovery is important. Just like it is important that Dr. Sato's leg heals soon. She will be able to put away the crutches soon. Suppose I was taking care of her crew member. In that case, I might be looking up appropriate medicines, appropriate treatments, suggesting rest, and making sure she was in a safe and comfortable room. I know you are able to sleep with very little deemed to be comfortable by our standards, but when someone is sick, there is even more need for comfort and care."

"I hear you, although I find it a huge waste."

"And I thank you for sharing that with me. I will likely have you help me conduct a few research studies this week so that we can apply this to an actual reward for you, seeing as you like to try things in our lab that we left behind in Wyoming. You would be surprised at how many medical advancements have taken someone in what you call a wasteful state and led them over time to a recovered state. How can that then be called a waste? Your reply, now, will be less informed before we test it scientifically, correct?"

"Correct, but for the sake of now and a reply, the need for this type of medical attention or advancement is a form of life in an immature state. I remember you once showed me a chart of the evolution of humanity. Of course, as I remember, microscopic animals in the earliest stages on the evolutionary path and the story of human evolution have led to modern homo sapiens. But when did his hands become numb? When did he begin to suffer from allergies? When did he stop being fully healthy and able to operate everything that needs to be operated on a ship destined beyond our known galaxy? If there is evolution, you have helped it along with my origins. If there is a world of problems that have surpassed the known abilities of human systems of thoughts, governance, beliefs, and practices, then you are running out of options, fast."

"Epoh, correct, and that is why I will help you become a healer through testing our scientific needs for this voyage that you are an important part of, because the future of humanity may very well depend on it, not just me, or Dr. Sato."

Dr. Kintain thought about the future generation of children on board and wondered what they would make of the young man who was about their age who'd never call in sick a day in his life. But at least tomorrow, Epoh wouldn't be wondering why Dr. Sato was tending to the care of someone who was now flawed and possibly a jeopardy in Epoh's estimation. Hopefully, Epoh had absorbed what Dr. Kintain had just said and, if he could, taken it to heart, to better understand.

Deteriorating Conditions on Earth

Chapter 39 – Deteriorating Conditions on Earth

Tom Burns, the Imagine, Rocky Mountains, CO

April 2030. Tom was happy to hear reports from everyone that almost everything was in place for the big day. He'd been given brief updates from Dr. Sato and her growing crew. He'd been relieved to find out that her ailing crewmember had recovered fully. He was also happy to hear that the cloning program had been accelerated. He was being kept apprised. Sam had told Tom that he was proud of having helped collect some of the DNA.

In the meantime, environmental conditions on Earth had deteriorated considerably. Tom's wife, Sarah, had just heard from some cousins in Orlando, Florida. The news there was very distressing. Two category 5 hurricanes had hit Florida from each side of the state at the same time. Orlando, which was in the middle of the state and not on a beach, had suffered major damage. Disney World and Universal Studios were almost totally decimated and would probably never open again. The state had been just about split into two parts. Orlando and south Florida were now an island, cut off by the ocean and the Gulf of Mexico. This meant that anyone living south of Florida did not have any access to roads to the north. Bridges would have to be built for anyone to evacuate Florida. Considering all of the other issues around the United States, it was doubtful that this would happen. Among the other facilities cut off from the New Mainland were the Kennedy Space Center and Trump's resorts. At least most people were still alive.

With the environment worsening, all the officers felt they had no choice but to move up the launch date. Tom had hoped to take off in 2030 or 2031 after running more tests and making sure it would be safe to do so.

Tom, Sam, and Jose participated in a meeting with the four spaceships commanders to gather information about when the launch could take place. Various estimates about when their ship would be one hundred percent ready for takeoff were shared. Yuri's Russian commander was in his usual arrogant posture, telling everyone what a fantastic job Russia was doing and wanting to know why everyone was not ready to go now.

After a lengthy discussion, they decided that November 1, 2031, would be the launch date when the four spaceships would leave Earth.

Suddenly, a crewman came running in out of breath. Tom saw him and stopped the meeting. He gave him a drink of water.

"Sir, our communications bureau has just received word from NOAA and the president that the San Andreas Fault has just ruptured almost completely. The Richter scale had measured the earthquake at a magnitude 7.5."

The devastation from this earthquake would be astounding. There was no way to predict how many lives would be lost, but it would probably be in the millions. He could imagine all the people falling into Earth along with all their belongings. The San Andreas Fault is roughly 750 miles. It forms the tectonic boundary between the Pacific and the North American Plate. Over the years, it had caused several earthquakes, of which the most famous was the 1906 San Francisco earthquake that destroyed most of the city. Tom also remembered some of the worst fires in history in California the past few years that had destroyed thousands of acres and killed large numbers of people and livestock. Some of those people had been burned beyond recognition in the second four years of the Trump presidency and the first four years of the current presidency.

This was something different, though. With the buckling of the fault, the catastrophe would be worse than anything else that had happened yet in history. Tom imagined that most of the California people were dead or about to die, and there was nothing he or anyone else in the room could do about it.

He said, "Thank you, sir, for bringing this information to us. If you receive any updates, please let us know immediately. Feel free to interrupt me at any time."

The crewman had his hand over his face and was in tears when he left the room, as was just about everyone else. Tom immediately told the other commanders he would have to call them back due to the disaster taking place. Tom watched Sam look around the room at the dark faces with despair overcoming him.

Sam said, "Dad, is there nothing we can do for the people there? Is there no way to save anyone?"

Tom responded, "Everyone, may I please have your attention."

Everyone became silent and immediately stopped what they were doing all over the ship to listen to their communicators.

"First, I think we should have a moment of silence for the millions of people who may have died in this earthquake. I am sure we would all love to do something to save and salvage these people's lives in great danger of ending prematurely in California. I hope that President Stevens and the United States government, troops, and so forth will put every effort into assisting those in need. If we were not so busy planning to take off in our spaceship, I could tell you that I would be one of the first responders on the scene. However, we cannot send anyone to help them. We cannot risk losing our space shuttles or other equipment with the possibility of not saving a single person.

"Our first priority is to have this spaceship ready for the mission. If we lose our shuttles now, we have to build more. That will take too long and postpone our ability to launch. We can monitor the situation and pass on any news via our communication system. Still, the risk is just too great to go there now. If you have any family in California, you have my permission to try and contact them. All issues will be addressed on a case-by-case basis. When this is all over, and we are in space, we will have appropriate memorial services to honor those who have died."

Everyone in the room nodded. Many people were crying. Suppose the people on board all went to California to deal with the earthquake. In that case, some might not return to the spacecraft and thus, diminish the chances for a successful mission.

About an hour later, while the officers and Sam and Jose were still sitting there, numbed by the information that had just been received about California, Tom was contacted by the Russian and Australian spaceships. He had the call on the viewscreen. Ian Thorpe let him know that several volcanoes had just erupted in the ring of fire, and lava was pouring out rapidly. The Ring of Fire is a significant area in the Pacific Ocean basin. There had been multiple earthquakes underwater and volcanoes. It stretched all the way from Indonesia, where some of the worst eruptions in history had occurred, to the California coast and South American coast, which included Peru and Chile.

These volcanoes were all ranked 7-8 on the Richter scale. Volcanoes had their own ranking system—the Volcanic Explosivity Index—similar to the Richter scale used for earthquakes. On the Richter scale, the worst earthquake could be around a 9.0 magnitude earthquake and would result in almost total destruction. If a volcano were ranked a 1, the lava flow would be minimal. A rank of 10 indicated that there was going to be mass destruction in the volcano areas. NOAA was now on the viewing screen and was reporting that at least four significant volcanoes had erupted. Two were in Indonesia. One was in Chile, and one was in Washington State. It was expected that the ones in Indonesia would be particularly devastating given the volcanoes' history there. Tsunamis all over southeast Asia had been reported, and more would be possible.

With all these disasters occurring, leaders of the world had canceled all commercial flights anywhere. All planes were to be used for emergency purposes only. All cruise ships were to return to port and be taken over by the government for emergencies.

The United States was particularly concerned about the Kilauea volcano on the big island of Hawaii. In 2018 many homes were destroyed. This was not a significant volcano at the time. Still, geologists had predicted a major eruption could happen anytime in the future. If it did happen, they expected boulders the size of washing machines to be hurled around the island. Although the Hawaii volcano had not erupted yet, it seemed everyone on the big island was attempting to evacuate. Planes and ships packed with people were leaving the island rapidly since no one knew if there would be a major eruption.

In Indonesia, one of the volcanoes had triggered a massive tsunami due to an undersea earthquake. One of the worst disasters in history was the Indonesian volcano eruption, Krakatoa, in 1889. This was one of the most violent explosions in recent human history—completely destroying the island on which it resided. The last eruption at Krakatoa was said to be four times more potent than an atomic bomb. People could hear it around the world. Tsunamis were produced that devastated the region, killing around 36,000 people and destroying whole villages. Another volcano in Indonesia was the deadliest of all time, killing 120,00 people. This took place in 1815 on Mt. Tambora. As a result of this volcano, there was a tremendous loss of crops due to the temperature taking a drastic drop.

With all this activity happening around the world, one of the major concerns now for the spaceships was they might have to adjust their trajectories to avoid all the ash and smoke given off from the volcanoes and other disasters.

Tom told Sam, "I have a big job for you and Jose. I need you two to study the weather patterns and wind currents and figure out where the smoke will be the worst. We need to understand where we can fly without being blinded. You will need to monitor this carefully and then let us know the best flight pattern for our spaceship. I am sure the other ships will have to do the same thing. Please keep in touch and let me know if you need help. This has to be done daily. You also need to monitor NOAA and any other channel available for more earthquakes and volcanoes and their forecast for the near future. There are still going to be aftershocks that will affect all the regions concerned, and there is the possibility of more volcanic eruptions."

Tom watched the two of them as they both absorbed the people's concern and sadness on board. Sam and Jose left for the weather lab to work on their new duties immediately.

Part IV

It was All-Hands-on-Deck

Chapter 40 – Recalculating

Sam Burns, the Imagine, Rocky Mountains, CO

Seeing the opportunity to make a significant contribution, Sam and Jose raced to the control room to monitor the weather and events happening around the world. On the way, they saw Sally and asked her to join them in the control room. All three were sickened by the incoming disaster reports.

Sam explained that they needed to figure out several factors as they worked on calculating the path to fly the spaceship into orbit. Of course, this was all subject to change daily, depending on the smoke from disasters and the weather. They agreed they had to figure out the rotation of the Earth. Once they did that, they calculated the straightest trajectory needed to overcome the planet's gravitational pull. Also, they had to avoid flying into a large plume of smoke and perhaps being hit by boulders that could damage the ship.

Sam had learned about some of the work that members of the North American Aerospace Defense Command (NORAD) had done in terms of collision-avoidance support for space shuttle programs and tracking small objects in the solar system. NASA's Jet Propulsion Laboratory hadn't launched its NEOCam (Near Earth Object Camera) because they wouldn't commit to funding the mission by the time Sam had finished high school and even as his dad's crew prepared to launch Imagine.

Nonetheless, several billionaires had already run their own space-based near-Earth objects (NEO) detection systems. They provided access to Sam, and his dad since the two of them had shown interest in analyzing the data and were known advocates for the advancement of these thermal-infrared telescopes that were designed to discover NEOs.

Thankfully, they also had access to Galah, the Galactic Archaeology with HERMES survey. Since 2013, Galah was ambitiously measuring each chemical's abundance in stars to determine the Milky Way's chemical makeup of approximately one million stars through algorithms, partnering with the European Space Agency's Gaia to map more than one billion stars in the Milky Way. A lot could be practically applied to traveling onboard Imagine within the galaxy. Having the latest information to chemically tag individual stars combined with knowing the motions and speeds within the Galaxy in constant motion and the positions and distances of the stars, was informative. The analyzed data would help the Imagine team understand the past, present, and future to see how the Galaxy can change over time. It would help explain galactic material, allowing their measurements to become more accurate about how much the universe is expanding and the relative movement of celestial bodies within the Galaxy. It was going to be vital to make sure that their advanced communication system could continue these critical mission partnerships back on Earth.

Through these partnerships and all the work Sam had already been contributing to the data analysis and interpretations of the data, he learned the power of knowledge and its practical application. He figured that if the world actually faced an existential risk of complete destruction with too many emergencies and climate changes that disrupted human existence, then there would be people still working on Earth unwilling to stop potential human progress. If there were enough people in the Milky Way Galaxy ensuring that they could leave Earth, then it was possible that all the combined efforts could ensure saving humanity from its worst offenders. The desire to leave Earth and explore beyond the farthest edges of the universe for future generations depended on it. Working alongside so many dedicated people who were contributing such meaningful work to humanity, Sam would be surprised if, in the future, their combined efforts didn't help those left on Earth through renewed technologies and advanced capabilities.

Finally, they needed to figure out the trajectory within the Orion arm of the Milky Way Galaxy to get to Alpha Centauri—the Southern Pointer Stars aimed at the Southern Cross in the large, sprawling Centaurus constellation—overcoming the Sun's gravitational pull. From their studies, they knew they needed to figure out a hyperbolic trajectory. Jose said they would apply Newton's laws of motion. The hyperbolic orbit was calculated to allow for unlimited space travel. Regardless of the path chosen, they would have to take off in a particular direction to ensure the ship's integrity. Once they escaped the Earth's gravitational pull, they had to establish the correct velocity to escape the solar system.

Sam and Jose started crunching numbers on the computer and simulation screens. They knew they could not launch towards California since the earthquake's fumes and fires would impact the trajectory.

After some consideration and mathematical models, they all agreed to launch in the direction of Florida. They would probably fly over Disney World and Cape Canaveral. Once the ship was past Florida, it would have to move into orbit over Africa to avoid the plumes from Europe's volcanoes and the Ring of Fire.

Sam, Jose, and Sally went to see Carson and Dorothy to ask them to recheck their calculations to verify if they were correct. They, too, were monitoring the situation and making their own predictions.

Dorothy said, "One problem we are all facing is that we need a group of people to control the launch from the space center controls. We do not have any personnel skilled enough yet."

Carson further explained their predicament, "And the launch console inside the space center does not seem to be functioning correctly yet. Dorothy and I had thought we could work on the problem over the next two years, but now we only have months to fix it. Unless we can fix that problem, we won't be able to take off."

"We'll have to talk to Sam's dad about this. These are urgent matters, and we'll need to find or train people who we can depend on," said Jose.

Scrambling

Chapter 41 – Scrambling

Tom Burns, the Imagine, Rocky Mountains, CO

Tom had a long discussion with the leaders of the other spaceships about the ongoing difficulties they faced. The other ships' commanders all hoped to have more time to prepare. Still, if the catastrophes continued at this alarming rate, they could not wait. Could they even launch by November 1st?

Tom told them to keep working as hard as possible, even if it meant twenty-four hours a day. They would all keep in contact with each other, monitor the situation, and then try to set a new date as soon as possible.

They hung up with each other and returned to work.

Five minutes after the commanders' meeting, Tom got a call from President Stevens, calling from Air Force One with his family and a full staff on board. His plane would be landing nearby in fifteen minutes. The situation was precarious. He and his entourage were going to the Rocky Mountain launch site. The president explained that he needed to station himself near the nuclear warheads in North Dakota, Montana, Wyoming, and Nevada. They could not afford a natural disaster that would blow up the atomic bombs in the silos. He'd received a report that California's recent disasters had destabilized the ground near some nuclear missiles.

The army decided to try and disarm all of them except for a few in North Dakota in case of an emergency. Since Denver, Colorado seemed to be the only air landing strip big enough for Air Force One, the president had decided to land there.

Tom, focused on the situation for his spaceship, did not want to see the president. However, with the terrible disasters occurring in the United States, he could not ignore hundreds of thousands of citizens' immediate plight.

While he waited for the president to show up, the German captain called on the view screen to let Tom know that Europe was now experiencing extreme flooding. The snow in the Alps had been melting rapidly due to all the smoke. Since their ship was in the Alps, it remained all right for now. The other main problem for the Germans would be volcanic eruptions in Iceland or Mt. Vesuvius. Years ago, the ash and smoke plumes from the Iceland volcano had disrupted air travel all over Europe. It was also entirely possible from seismographic reports that Mt. Vesuvius was going to explode sooner. This volcano had been responsible for the destruction of Pompei and could also disrupt the German launch.

On the spaceship and all over the United States, cell phones and web services started shutting down. Verizon and AT&T were experiencing massive failures as cell towers failed to work. The phone lines were either extremely overloaded with too many people trying to contact each other or damaged and needed to be repaired. People were having difficulty trying to communicate with each other to either find out what was happening or get instructions about what to do. All over the world, including the United States, people were panicking.

However, the spaceship communicators and view screens were still working, allowing them to communicate. The problem was they couldn't contact people they knew in various parts of the world. Many of them were heartbroken or in a state of panic now that their phones had stopped working. Tom felt terrible for the loss of communication with people outside the ship. There was nothing he could do about it, however. The best thing to do was for people to focus on their duties and keep busy. Tom knew they needed to leave immediately. He gave all officers, and department heads the order to check preparations to enable the ship to lift off. Crewmembers raced to their stations and performed their duties with the expectation they would be leaving soon.

Shortly after that, the president showed up with his family and a few cabinet members and secret service members at Denver International Airport. He asked Tom to meet him there.

The president spoke. "I am so sorry that I could not do more to reverse the effects of climate change as president. But I am glad that we are here with you considering all the disasters happening right now. I am lucky that I can access Air Force One and go where I need to be. Dr. Burns, you were right. The time has come. I've brought the twenty-five people you agreed to accept onboard Imagine here. It's now come to this."

Tom decided to use the shuttle to meet him at the airport as it was only twenty minutes away. Tom noticed the president looked like he was not too worried that he needed to supplicate to feel some mercy still existed somewhere in the world. The number of catastrophes and the sense of urgency that would shortly position itself at the center of the president's every waking hour would demand all of his attention, and Tom could sense his dire need for relief.

"This is very difficult for me. I love my family very much. As a husband and parent, I will try and do anything to save them, including sending them into space. I am comfortable knowing you will care for them as you care for your own family. The other people standing here have worked with me for a long time and whom I value not only as colleagues but also my dear friends. They're deserving of a second chance at life and will prove their worth to you regardless of what assigned tasks. These people have left their families behind. Many were unable to locate their families and do not even know whether they are alive or dead."

Tom watched as some of them began crying, while some of them clutched each other's hands. Although Washington, D.C. was not experiencing widespread damage, it was hard to fathom if the government could function any more under the Constitution. Indeed, the Founding Fathers could not have imagined anything like this would take place. It was entirely possible that new laws, rules, and regulations would have to be written. There was no way to know how many government officials were alive. In parts of the country like California, it was also very possible that a lot of criminal activity would take place since some people would have to rob or kill to ensure their survival. It would be almost like a nuclear attack had taken place.

Tom, as he had promised before, welcomed the president's group.

"Your family and everyone on Air Force One are welcome to join us on our travels in space. We will assign them quarters as soon as they board and will provide necessities for them. The only requirement I have is that all of them will be expected to contribute to the spaceship's everyday functioning. Mr. President, are you joining us?"

All eyes were on the president.

The president replied, "Once more, I am afraid I will not be going with you. I would love to join you on your travels. I hate the idea of separating from my family and friends, knowing that I will never see them again. American citizens need me here. They will be looking for me to make any decisions that may help them survive these tragedies. Also, I need to command the armed forces to save people wherever possible. I cannot abandon everyone here. It would be a disgraceful act. I am certain that if any trouble develops on Imagine, you would be the last person left to disembark. I know you would sacrifice yourself for your family and the many wonderful people that are going with you. So, no, I will not be joining you. I will watch you take off and then go about my job as president, regardless of what happens after that."

The president turned to his wife.

"You have been by my side through every success and failure for thirty-five years and have guided me whenever I needed guidance. I cannot bear the thought of us separating, and I want to tell you how much I love you and how much I will miss you. Please keep me in your thoughts and prayers and remember all the good times we had together."

His wife, Isabella, started to sob.

"I love you very much. If you were not the president, I would expect you to join me on the spaceship. However, if you were not the president, the truth is, I doubt I would get on the ship. I expect you will do a wonderful job for this country's people no matter how bad the conditions become. I will think of you every day and hope to see you again among the stars."

The president embraced his wife. The tender embrace lasted several seconds. They had been married for twenty-four years. Isabella had been at his side for every success and failure. He had never imagined her not being at his side. The loneliness that was already creeping over him would haunt him forever.

He said, "You are the light of my life and my hero. Without you, I am nothing."

He turned to the group and said, "Goodbye, everyone. I wish you all the best. I will be looking up at the heavens and wondering if I can see you until the day I die. God bless you all. If you do not mind, I will hang around until the ship leaves. Maybe I will be able to make myself useful to someone who needs help. I need to get in touch with our nuclear facilities in North Dakota, Nevada, Wyoming, and Montana to see how they are functioning and if we need to disarm as many nuclear weapons as possible, so they don't blow up on our soil and cause more catastrophes. I also want to do what I can to transport people out of California and get first responders to the scene. I am sending as many emergency operations as possible, even though it will be rough just traveling there. I am already estimating twenty million dead in the next few days. I cannot just stand by and see these people suffer."

The president then motioned to two generals to follow him to a place where they could communicate with other people involved in the disasters, FEMA and the Department of Defense.

Meanwhile, while that was happening, virtually everyone on board was in a frenzy to try to get ready. No one knew exactly how much time was left before the launch. Tom's communicator was lighting up like

Christmas lights as officers and others reported their departments and equipment's status.

Suddenly, Tom got an emergency message from Carson in the engine room. Carson wanted Tom to come right away. Tom called Bob and told him to go immediately to the engine.

Five minutes later, they had run down the three levels from the bridge and were standing in the engine room with Carson and Dorothy. Carson and Dorothy were arguing, in a heated discussion about what the problem was and how they were going to solve it, or if they would be able to explain it.

"Stop arguing and explain to Bob and me what the problem is or possible solutions to fix it. Time is of the essence, so please tell me what is wrong. We are in the final stages before we launch."

Carson looked at Dorothy and asked her, "Do you want to tell him the problem, or shall I?"

Dorothy turned away and said, "You go ahead and tell him."

Carson turned to Tom and said, "We have everything in place. We have the eight rockets attached to the spaceship to provide for a powerful boost at lift-off. We also have the fuel system ready, although we have not checked it out to verify it is working one hundred percent. The only way we can do that is when we launch and hope it works. However, since no one has ever attempted this kind of lift-off, we could not account for every possible problem that could arise along with every possible solution. We really had hoped to have more time, like another month or two, to finish our work and figure out how to solve the last main obstacles to launch. If we were launching in two years, we would not be having this convers—"

"Are you trying to tell me we cannot launch? What is the specific problem? Bob and I are both engineers. We will assist you in solving it or get extra help."

"There are two main problems. The first problem is after we blastoff with the eight rockets attached to the ship. Until we reach orbit, the entire ship may experience a blackout. There may be no way to detach the rockets or make course corrections or do anything until we regain radio frequency and consciousness. During the blackout, none of our control systems may work. People may not be able to function due to possible extreme G-forces. This means we will all be unable to communicate with each other or anyone in the space center. Therefore, you will be unable to give any commands or orders, and we will be unable to check our flight trajectory or make decisions as to whether to increase the power or decrease it. If we cannot function, we may not reach the desired orbit or detach the eight rockets at the right altitude. We also have to be aware of the heat shields, since they will interfere with the radio frequency. Consequently, we also contribute to the possibility that we will end up flying somewhere we did not intend. In the worst-case scenario, fires could start up all over the ship, and the propulsion system will blow up.

"There has to be a way to monitor the whole thing from outside the ship. We have run simulations, and it is estimated the blackout time will be around twelve minutes after launch. Someone has to basically take over control of the ship for that length of time."

Tom and Bob could not believe they were hearing this right now.

Bob said, "Did you set up a control center or equipment in the space center to control the ship for that short period?"

Dorothy responded, "We were planning on doing that next week. We did not think we would be leaving, not this soon. It would need to be perfectly synchronized."

"So that means we cannot launch? Or does it mean we can launch but possibly end up with a failed mission, and that everyone on board would be dead?"

"That is correct. I am so sorry we had not thought about this issue until now."

"How long would it take us to build this control system or to set up equipment to monitor our launch with all of the necessary adjustments?"

"We do have the materials here to build it. It will probably take one week. Then we need to make sure the ship and control system are on the same radio frequency and synchronize the systems as necessary to launch."

"We will work around the clock. I will give you access to all the engineers on board and all the electricians and so forth. If there are any more problems, please let me know immediately, all right?"

Tom got on his communicator and started calling for a team of people to begin to build the necessary system to monitor the ship. He now expected a delay of a week to ten days. Bob also stayed behind to work on the controls.

Promptly, Tom found the president with a few of his colleagues, looking at a map and barking orders.

"Thanks for letting me use your communication system to work with the government. How can I be of help now?"

"Mr. President, I wanted to tell you that Ivanov plans to join the Russian ship, and I feel they are probably going to cause problems when we get into space. Do you have any advice for me to handle him if he, in fact, does join his spaceship?"

The president nodded his head. "I had heard rumors to that effect since a lot of the responsibility has been delegated to his cabinet and backups. I do not know if he really will be on board, but if he does go with the Russian spaceship, you can be sure he will cause conflicts and try to play people against each other. I do not think Ivanov even really cares about Russia or leaving it behind. He hides behind that façade that everything he does is for Russia. He is like Donald Trump and his predecessor, Putin. They both love money more than people. I can't stop him from going on their ship. If I were you, I would talk to him and whoever is in charge of the Russian craft in powerful language and not negotiate with them about important matters. Knowing Ivanov, he would not mind being on the only spacecraft to reach a new planet and calling himself "Ruler of the Galaxy."

"That is very reassuring," Tom said.

The president smiled at Tom. He had a winning smile, one that made you feel like he wasn't preoccupied even when he most certainly had to be, given the number of problems he was facing and having to leave his family amid the world's biggest disasters.

"Excuse me, Tom, now I know that you and your colleagues did all the work on this spaceship yourselves without any assistance from our government. And perhaps you do not respect what the government has done regarding the environment. Still, I really need your assistance now, and I have a big favor to ask. I need to borrow one of your shuttles to get to the Nevada facility to shut down twenty nuclear silos active about an hour outside of Las Vegas. The heat from the California earthquake and fires are very near Nevada. Las Vegas is a ghost town. About an hour from Las Vegas where the nuclear warheads are located, the temperature is now 145 degrees, higher than anything they have experienced. Right now, there are only five soldiers there due to the dangerous situation. The others have been sent away in case of an atomic explosion. I need to count on you."

Tom didn't have much time to think, but he couldn't say no. "You got it. I'll lend you one shuttle. We will get you ready right now to fly to Nevada, shut down the atomic bombs, and get those men out of there. I am sure we can squeeze seven people into the shuttle. It is less than a twenty-minute trip at the speed the shuttle can travel. My officers and I can monitor you in case of an emergency. Please contact Nevada and tell them you are on the way. If they plan to pack anything to bring with them, ask them to get it ready now."

"Thank you, Tom. I need a co-pilot. I can't fly on Air Force One, as the ground is too hot to land the plane, and I don't know the effect of all the smoke on the plane. I can fly the shuttle at a speed that would take less than one hour to get there.

"It cannot be done by remote control. To shut them down, they need a fingerprint ID to enter the passcode. Ordinarily, General Wallace would do that, but before the earthquake, he visited his family in Los Angeles and has not been heard from since. I have no idea what happened to him. The general is a good man, and he served his country well. The only other fingerprint available right now that the device will accept is mine. Mine can be used anywhere, but it has to be done in person.

"Once we have shut down the missiles on-site, I plan to bring the five soldiers back here. They will stay with me or help out until you launch."

Tom immediately called Marvin to get ready and assist the president into a spacesuit for the shuttle. In fifteen minutes, he was strapped in and ready to go.

"Good luck, Mr. President. See you in a few hours."

The door closed, and the shuttle took off five minutes later.

Danger Zone

Chapter 42 – Danger Zone

President Stevens, shuttle trip to Nevada

President Stevens sat down next to Marvin and told him to let him know when they got close to the coordinates that were given to him. As a former pilot himself, Stevens was very curious about flying the shuttle and paid attention to whatever the pilot did. They had brought extra spacesuits for the others to put on that could withstand the high temperatures.

Twenty minutes later, the pilot notified him that they were close to the landing spot.

As they traveled to Nevada, the president thought how all of this did not have to happen. *If only man had taken better care of the environment, we would not be in the situation we are facing today,* he thought. Politicians, wars, and religion doomed the planet. Religion and politics have caused almost all the deaths caused by war. The world would have been better off if it was one big country where everyone cooperated together to continuously improve the quality of life without sacrificing the future. He particularly hated the heated partisan battles in Congress that helped to divide the country more and more. These partisan battles had split the country into two when it came to the environment.

Now it was too late. Millions of people around the world were now going to die because of these battles. If natural disasters ceased, it was hard to imagine what could be salvaged from the destruction. The effects of natural disasters were going to last for years.

The president told Marvin to land near the area that led to the missile silos. He thought of the twenty-something missileer who'd been stationed at the Montana Air Force Base before some of the newer prototype classified twenty-four-hour alert nuclear ICBMs had needed her attention in Nevada, given her training and high-adaptability skill level. She'd signed on at the missile alert facility, knowing full well that she was to launch any or all of the nuclear weapons now in her custody if ordered by the president. She probably had never thought that she'd signed on to handle the way current events had unfolded and were developing. President Stevens doubted she'd ever thought she'd meet a president while she served.

What was the missileer's name, again? That's right, Air Force Lt. Col. Thea Derse. She'd been a steward for the nuclear enterprise for nineteen years and had pulled close to two hundred alerts as a missileer. Now, they weren't fighting an enemy without; they were fighting an enemy within, and it was multi-headed, spanning multi-generations—their adversary now fire and earthquakes. Several reports downplayed the hazards from potential fires and earthquakes to the highly secure national security site that contained a nuclear device assembly facility, several stockpile safety stewardship reliability programs among other threat detection efforts, and one of the nation's launch control centers. Yet, preparations for this magnitude of a natural disaster had been minimal. They had relied significantly on an overall vulnerability assessment that took in a very different kind of worst-case scenario that was a lot milder.

"Remain with the craft and wait for us," the president said on approach to landing. "If there is any grave danger, you are to leave and return to the spaceship."

"Don't worry, sir. I am sure it will be fine, and you will all be going back with me in a short period. I am not leaving the President of the United States in Nevada."

Then the president disembarked from the spacecraft and closed the door. He ran inside the designated building. Once the president got inside, Major Joseph Johns introduced him to the other soldiers, including Air Force Lt. Col. Thea Derse. The two of them immediately went to the control room so that the president could use his fingerprint to enter the password and work on shutting down the nuclear weapons. The print allowed them to access the control panel where the atomic weapons were stored.

As they entered the room, the president looked at the enormous missiles on display. He developed a real sense of just how terrifying things could be if they exploded. No president had ever been asked to or decided to fire such lethal weapons. If they had been fired at a target such as Moscow, it was doubtful that any citizen would survive.

As they approached the missiles to disarm them, the colonel reminded him to proceed with extreme caution. Sweating through the next few hours, the president watched and helped when he could. A missile combat crew proceeded to dismantle the missiles, disposed of all the fuel, removed the warhead explosives, and prepared everything for transport to safe disposal sites. To save Nevada and anyone in the fallout range, they withdrew the explosives and plutonium from the warhead's primary. Nuclear teams removed the highly enriched uranium and fusion fuel. They would transport it off-site to dilute it. Within a few nerve-racking hours, the missiles had been dismantled.

The president commended Colonel Derse and her crew for showing such bravery in protecting and disarming the missiles.

The major then said to the president, "Thank you, sir, you are a hero. You probably saved half the people in the United States with your actions today."

The president said, "It was my pleasure, Major. You and the others are the real heroes, not me. You have sacrificed your lives and spent most of your time protecting America from its enemies, including the Russians and Chinese. If we do survive this disaster, you can be sure the first order of business for me will be to get everyone to shut down their nuclear weapons. Now, let's get out of here. Please put on these space-suits. You are about to experience an unbelievable ride. It is too bad the United States does not own this device." They ran into the shuttle and buckled in.

Major Johns asked, "When did the government build this thing? It looks fresh and modern."

"This shuttle is not ours, and the government had nothing to do with it. It belongs to a bunch of geniuses."

"Welcome, everyone, to the new space shuttle. As a small reward, I think I will take a spin around Las Vegas and the Hoover Dam for a minute so you can see what is happening there now."

The shuttle took off smoothly and flew over Las Vegas. They could see the strip where all the neon lights should be. Instead, it was mostly pitch black. There was no electricity, and the smoke from California was swirling around. The president wondered if anyone was still in town or if they had all evacuated. People could not last long there, as the heat would be unbearable. Before all this occurred, people won and lost fortunes in Las Vegas all the time. It was once an exciting place if you had the money and the stomach to play. He wondered if anyone had any casino chips with them. They were now virtually worthless. Even if people were still alive, the water would be severely contaminated, forcing them to leave.

The president thanked Marvin for flying over Las Vegas and told him to return to the spacecraft. On the way back, the major asked to co-pilot the shuttle. Everyone enjoyed the twenty-minute flight. The soldiers could not believe the speed at which the shuttle flew. They flew right into the main spacecraft with ease, landing in perfect position. When they opened the doors to the shuttle, Tom was waiting for them and saluting everyone, including the president.

"Well done, Mr. President. I assume your mission was a success. Due to disasters, it has become difficult communicating with people around the country. Did Marvin do a good job?"

"A great job. Without you and the shuttle, we would never be able to stop the nuclear weapons from blowing up."

"Well, you can relax a little bit. My staff will give your men a tour of the ship, and they can shower and get a good meal of bio-engineered food."

The major asked, "Engineered food?"

"Wait until you try our engineered steak and potatoes. Chef Luis can make anything. We have terrific pizza too. While you tour the ship, if you can think of anything, we might be missing. Please let us know. You can also inspect our weapons. I know you must have great expertise in this area."

As the men began their tour, the president was able to reflect on what had just occurred. Since World War II, virtually every president had been responsible for the safekeeping of the most destructive weapons on Earth. Billions of dollars had been spent to ensure that these weapons would provide the most destructive and deadly force unimaginable to any human being alive if fired. Every time the Russians or Chinese decided to upgrade their atomic missiles, the United States kept pace with them. While all of the leaders and countries continuously ordered new weapons, it must have been sickening to any leader to know that in one minute, any one of them could have been responsible for the destruction of every person on Earth.

CHAPTER 43

Is It Worth It or Not?

Chapter 43 – Is It Worth it or Not?

Sam Burns, the Imagine, Rocky Mountains, CO

About an hour later, the soldiers were eating in the cafeteria. Sam and Jose noticed them in part because they had so much food on their plates and asked if they could join them.

The major said, "Sure, have a seat."

They had questions. Sam wanted to know what life in the armed forces was like. All of them had served in Afghanistan and various places around the world. He also asked the soldiers, "Did you ever kill anyone?"

Each of the soldiers said, "Yes, but only when we had to."

Jose asked them if they had families.

"I was married for a short time, but I was away from home for too many years, and my marriage fell apart," said the major. Other soldiers had also been married. Two of them had just lost their spouses who lived in California.

"How can you guys still do your job even when you suffer the loss of family?"

"We have a job to perform, or at least we had a job until today. We try not to stop and think about our family all the time. We have no idea what will happen to us or where we will go next. I am sure it will sink in very soon about what we have lost."

Sam asked, "Was it all worth it?"

Each nodded that it was worth it and said if they had to do it all over, they would do it again. They explained that it was a great honor to serve the United States of America.

One of the soldiers said, "This spaceship is very exciting, and I would like to know from you guys if this is worth it for you, and what do you see in the future for you?"

Sam asked Jose to respond first, except Jose needed some time to think about his answer.

Sam said, "You know I graduated from high school only three years ago. I imagine I would have gone to college and then maybe into the military like my dad did. Soon after graduation, my dad told me about the mission and how important it was to keep the human race alive. I was excited about the idea of saving the world, but sadly I am leaving. Both Jose and I were made junior officers, which is excellent for me since I will see my dad every day.

"I have no idea what the outcome of this trip will be. Maybe we will land on a beautiful planet and set up a new human race. Perhaps we will find new alien life among the worlds, and I have no idea what it will look like. I doubt new life would look like the little green Martians you see in the movies. It is also possible that this ship will find no planet at all to live on. In that case, we will fly until we are all dead. Or even possibly have to fly back to a future desolate Earth if we survive saving humanity.

"What is important is that we try and do what is best for us and everyone else. I don't have enough experience in life to tell you if this is worth it or not. I just hope that years from now, I can look back and say it was all worth it and how proud I am of everyone on the ship and those who lived on Earth."

The soldier said, "You explained that very well, Sam. Your dad must be proud of you. How about you, Jose? What does your dad do on this spaceship?"

Jose responded, "My dad is a co-commander of the ship. He and Tom are good friends, just like Sam and me. At one time, he worked for Boeing as an airplane engineer. My mom is a nurse and works with Sam's mom. As far as whether or not I think this trip is worth it, I don't see that we have any other choice. If these natural disasters that are killing so many people weren't happening, this mission would be the furthest thing from my mind. Sam is my best friend, and he will be for the next hundred years, depending on what happens. I just wish we could stay here and enjoy life. It sucks that so many people messed up their decisions about energy and pollution."

The soldier said, "I wish the best of luck for the two of you. I hope you will live for many more years and have a great life. As for us, we will be soldiers until we either die or live to be old men."

They finished their meals, momentarily silent.

Sam felt that his father's lifelong fear of dying from humankind's negligent acts of burying facts and degrading the environment willingly had led to this. It was utterly foreign to anything any of them had prepared for in life. Their training over the past couple of years helped and would continue to help. His grandfather had died a horrid death from Agent Orange, and Sam's own father was willing to stop this form of misguided thinking and negligence, once and for all.

Now his own lifelong fear of dying from a nuclear bomb had surfaced. These soldiers, his father, and the president, had helped save countless lives. Here they sat quietly eating genetically engineered food. How that fear had transformed into this massive effort in time to coordinate and save as many lives as possible from the threat of potential nuclear annihilation confounded Sam. Nevertheless, he never felt clearer about his lifelong hope to achieve something in the future. It would be far greater than what was in store for him if his grandfather's life was a reflection of the human limits that were reasserted rather than reassessed. And that he had to thank his dad for, indeed.

Then, There Were Three

Chapter 44 – Then, There were Three

Tom Burns, the Imagine, Rocky Mountains, CO

The next day, the natural disasters around the world had calmed down a bit. There were still hundreds of aftershocks all along the San Andreas fault in California, but that was to be expected. Volcanoes spewed smoke that was very thick and flew miles into the air. Even without eruptions, it was making flights very difficult.

The president made every effort to save as many lives as possible. Three cargo planes filled with rescue supplies were sent to San Francisco and Los Angeles. The Department of Defense and Homeland Security did everything they could to assist people in need. The problem was that many of the rescuers were also in need of assistance. Many fire departments were destroyed and unable to reach anyone.

Tom felt horrible for all the deaths occurring all over the world but continued to stick to his task of preparing Imagine for the launch. They had to finish work on the launch console. Sam and Jose joined him to see what progress had been made. They went outside the ship to the space center where the men worked in shifts around the clock to build and perfect the controls needed to launch.

Bob Jackson was there, looking over some instruments when Tom and the boys arrived.

"How is it going, Bob? Any luck yet?"

"Hi, Tom. Yes. We are making a lot of progress. We are now working on calibrating the instruments to be in sync with what we have on the spacecraft. I want you to know that the Germans and Australians have been very helpful. They have provided some suggestions, and we have done the same for them. The Russians, however, do not seem to be in the sharing mood. They claim they are ready to launch, which may or may not be true."

"Good work, Bob. Tell the Germans and Australians we value all their feedback. I will talk to the Russians. Do you need more help? I have five soldiers responsible for launching nuclear missiles around the world, and they ought to know a thing or two about making this work. Shall I send them here? It may speed up the work."

"Do you think we can trust these guys?"

Sam jumped in, "Yes, I spent some time with them, and they are awfully dedicated soldiers who have given their whole life to serve this country. If anyone can help you, it's these guys."

"If Sam says they are trustworthy, then that is good enough for me. I hope to see them soon."

Tom, Sam, and Jose left the space center to take care of the next problem.

Tom turned to Sam and Jose, "Why don't you two ask the soldiers if they would be willing to work with us on the console? I will go talk to the Russians in private on the view screen. You do not want to hear what I am going to tell Yuri or what he is going to tell me."

Sam and Jose went to see the soldiers.

The boys left to talk to the soldiers. Tom went to the commander's post on the bridge.

Fifteen minutes later, Bob met Tom on the bridge and reported that his call with the Germans and Australians had gone well. He'd thanked them for working so cooperatively to do everything possible to make the mission successful. Also, he had asked them for more feedback as they made progress. They had all agreed that a few more years to perfect everything would have been ideal. Bob had updated them about the soldiers they had recruited, hoping they might know how to fix the problems.

Both the German and Australian commanders had wanted to know if there was an exact date to launch yet. Bob had conveyed that until they fixed the launch problem, they could not give a specific time. They had all agreed to keep communicating about their progress and then had hung up.

Tom felt pleased by Bob's account, thanked him, and wished him a good evening. Bob returned to the space center. Alone, Tom sighed, anticipating the difficulty of his task. Tom called the Russian commander. He had no idea where this conversation was going to lead. He hoped it would end on a positive note, but he was prepared for anything the Russians might say or want.

It was answered by one of his lieutenants. Tom was told that Yuri was too busy to talk to Tom now. Tom asked the lieutenant to convey the message to Yuri that it was vitally important to discuss the launch matter, and he needed to call back within fifteen minutes, as this was an emergency. Tom hung up.

Waiting on the bridge for the call, Tom sat there thinking about what he would do if Yuri did not call back. He considered that there might have to be two different missions. There was nothing to stop the Russians from taking off if everything was as good as Yuri claimed it to be. If that happened, there was the possibility of a space confrontation. He did not want it to come to that, but if the Russians wanted to play hardball, then there was nothing he could do about it. He certainly did not want a war in space.

Five minutes later, Yuri called back. "Commander Burns, how are you and your ship coming along? What can I do for you today? Are you still having problems?"

Tom looked at Yuri on the screen. Yuri looked confident, but Tom detected some doubt in Yuri's words. If Yuri were fully confident, he would have been bragging about how ready he was to launch, and maybe the Russians would just go ahead and do so. Yuri had not said that. To Tom, that meant the Russians were not ready either, but he did not know their problems or if it was the same problem the other spaceships faced. Yuri might have had too much pride to tell him that the Oligarch was not ready. Another possibility was that he did not want Ivanov to know the ship was not prepared. Ivanov could easily remove Yuri as commander. Tom was sure that Yuri did not want that to happen, which might mean he would be left behind. Just like Tom, he had invested many years of his life into this mission.

"Thank you for calling back. I know you are a busy man, but we need to discuss some important matters. We are still having some problems with the launch console calibrations to coordinate them with the main ship. We have added a team of experts to our crew to assist with the launch and hope to solve the problem very soon. How are you coming along with that?"

"Russia does not have the same problems as you do. Our spaceship is different from yours. We have a lot of experience with land-based launches, as we run the International Space Station. Our main problem is dealing with the kinds of weapons Mr. Ivanov wants on board. I cannot explain more, but we are still having discussions with the government here. Sometimes our government is helpful, and other times it is not, just like in your country. I hope you understand what I am saying."

Tom did understand. The Russian leaders wanted to bring nuclear weapons on board. It could be a disaster for them, or for us, or for a new planet. There was no guarantee those kinds of weapons could survive a launch. Of course, one could make them while on the mission, but it was safer not to launch with them.

"Yuri, I understand the situation now. Is Ivanov still planning to join you on the trip? Or is he planning something else?"

"As of now, he is not coming with us. However, he did make us take twenty different DNA samples of himself so that they will be cloned as soon as we begin doing so. We also have a lot of Putin's samples. It seems the earthquake in California, and the volcanoes around the world, have made Ivanov change his mind about what he wants to do. He seems to be meeting a lot with the military leaders right now and not really focusing on the Oligarch so much."

Leave it to Ivanov to take advantage of a wounded person, Tom thought to himself. *Ivanov must know that we had to shut down many of our nuclear weapons due to the earthquake. He could be preparing the military to attack Ukraine or just about any country in the world. So, Ivanov wants to be on Earth and the spaceship at the same time. How many clones of Ivanov were there supposed to be?* This was becoming more dangerous by the minute. He decided to tell the president what was happening.

"Yuri, thank you for all the information you have provided. I did not realize that you are facing a different situation than myself. I will be in contact with you again soon."

When Tom got off the connection with Yuri, he contacted the president. The president was not glad to hear the news that the Russian military was on the move.

"There is nothing the United Nations or NATO can do for us. The Security Council would veto any plan since Russian is on the council. NATO is too busy trying to save lives after the flooding in Europe. I doubt the leaders of other countries are going to listen to me right now. They are all trying to take care of their own people. War is the last thing this world needs right now. We need peace to come together and help each other. Unfortunately, it looks like Ivanov sees himself as ruler of the world. I will have to notify the Pentagon. One thing we have over the Russians is superior submarines. They have been staying on the bottom of the ocean due to the flooding and currents. We have several in the Black Sea. I will call Ivanov right now and see if I can put an end to his grandiose plans. I don't know if he will listen to me, but the world will end a lot sooner if he does not. And I hope my men can get your console ready soon."

"Good luck talking to Ivanov, sir. Don't worry about the consoles."

Tom spent the rest of the day with Sam and Jose visiting various departments and meeting people, seeing what was happening on the ship. He liked to keep the morale on a high note. One of their stops was the cafeteria, where they had stopped for lunch.

Chef Luis was in a jovial mood. Sam asked him why he was so happy.

"I have found a way to make some of my favorite desserts using the bioengineering process. Now we can have fantastic tiramisu and chocolate mousse. There seems to be no limit to what we can accomplish here. My staff and I are looking forward to preparing food every day for a thousand people."

Luis projected a very positive attitude. However, Tom seemed to have some doubts about why Luis was in such a good mood. After all, Luis had probably made thousands of new desserts before. Tom felt satisfied that he'd provided Luis such a great opportunity and had found someone who fit the bill for the ship who would be enthusiastic about the challenges that lay ahead. He'd seen how glad Sam and Jose were that he was developing new foods all the time. It would get awful boring to eat only a few things for a hundred years. However, it still seemed like there was something going on that he did not know about.

While Tom was thinking to himself, Luis interrupted his thoughts.

"Tomorrow morning, please come and try our new bioengineered pancakes with bananas and syrup. It tastes a little bit different than normal pancakes, but I think you will like them."

"I can't wait to try them, Luis," said Jose. "This chocolate mousse tastes great."

After they finished lunch, all three of them continued on their rounds. Tom watched Sam and Jose join several classmates in a soccer game momentarily against Ronaldo and Messi in the entertainment center. It brought joy to Tom to see them be able to take things in stride. After about a half-hour, they visited the medical center to see their moms and Sally. They decided to have dinner together to catch up on the events of the day on the ship.

After dinner, as Tom prepared to get some sleep, he anticipated that once he talked to Bob again, he wouldn't be able to prevent himself from swearing under his breath. He couldn't wait to see Bob's expression when he told him the president was now being asked to intervene.

Speechless

Chapter 45 – Speechless

Tom Burns, the Imagine, Rocky Mountains, CO

The following morning, Tom decided to pay a visit to Dr. Sato to see how she was getting along with the new doctors, and if she had all the necessary equipment on board.

When he arrived, Dr. Sato saw him and suddenly closed the door behind her. She approached Tom.

Tom asked, "How is your leg coming along? You seem to be walking much better."

Dr. Sato assured him that she was improving by the minute.

Tom said, "Do you have everything you need now? How are Dr. Kintain and the others? Are they all comfortable?"

"I'm sure that his advances helped me heal much faster. He's also brilliant, so our team is lucky to have him."

"Good, glad to hear. Do you need my help with anything? I trust you one hundred percent. You will do a fantastic job, and if there is anything I need to know, I am sure you will tell me about it, right?"

Dr. Sato looked directly at Tom. She had been the whole time. She hesitated briefly before answering, "Dr. Kintain and the rest of my medical team are all doing great and are forming great teams, bonding together, and appreciating the medical challenges that we face. I can't tell you how much your trust in me, in us, matters. I have worked with some of the most esteemed people back in Chicago, and I am fortunate to continue working with some of the greatest minds of our times here. I will certainly notify you if anything develops onboard that you should know about. I know that we still have many decisions to make with the committee about medical procedures and policies. Still, in the meantime, our scientific research has hit no glitches. Your help has been much appreciated."

Tom said, "Thank you."

As he was about to leave, Dr. Sato suddenly said, "Tom, ok, there is something I need to show you. As the commander of this ship, you will have to make an important decision eventually that you may not have expected or anticipated."

Tom said, "Ok. I had a funny feeling that something was going on. So now tell me what I will have to deal with, please."

Dr. Sato said, "I need you to be calm when I tell you this. This is going to shock you as well as anyone on board who learns about this." She took a deep breath. "Ok here it is … Dr. Kintain has cloned himself, but the clone is really not a mirror of himself. It may look like him, but it sure has a long way to go before we know enough about him to be able to decide whether it is a success or a total failure."

Tom was speechless at first. He had not expected any cloning would occur until they were far away from Earth. Now suddenly, there was one on the Imagine. However, from what he had just heard, there seemed to be many things that would have to be considered with this clone. He fought every urge to demand that Dr. Sato ask the clone and Dr. Kintain to leave at once. A flood of revulsion threatened his cool-headedness to the core. He figured there must be a reasonable explanation for this.

"Dr. Sato, of course, it's not what I was expecting to hear." He paused to collect his thoughts. "Can you tell me what I can expect from this? I assume the clone is already here on the ship, and I will have to meet this thing, or what do you call it, him or her?"

Dr. Sato said, "His name is Epoh. Epoh will go down in history as the first human clone, but no person on Earth will ever know this. It seems that Epoh has some undesirable traits which will have to be addressed as we move along. If Epoh becomes a danger to anyone on Imagine, then we would have to terminate him. We hope that we can find a way to make Epoh a valuable member of this ship before we leave Earth. Only time will tell. When you are ready, I will have you meet Epoh and Dr. Kintain to discuss this issue further. It would be more dangerous for us to attempt to work with clones without having tried in the environment we are more familiar with here on Earth. Surely, you agree, Dr. Burns."

Tom was not really comfortable with what Dr. Sato had just said. However, he had to trust her to make good decisions or not be on the ship with him. "Yes. Please let me know when you are ready to introduce him to me. It will have to be way before we launch, so make it as soon as feasible. Try not to let too many people know about this. They may think we have a monster on board, and we do not need widespread panic."

Dr. Sato thanked Tom for his understanding of the situation and promised to introduce him within a few weeks. Tom let her get back to work. He was inquisitive about this Epoh. How would it affect the crew and the trainees? Would Epoh be able to take orders like everyone else? What were its physical abilities? Only time would tell. For now, he had an open mind, since anything that would help them reach another galaxy needed to be considered.

Mutual Destruction

Chapter 46 – Mutual Destruction

President Stevens, the Imagine, Rocky Mountains, CO

Although he had served in Afghanistan and Iraq, President Stevens had grown up a pacifist. He wanted to avoid war at all costs. Before becoming president, he tried to pass bills in Congress to cut military spending and focus on domestic issues as a representative from Maryland. This had not gone over well with other members of the legislature who were very hawkish. These bills continuously failed in part due to the aggression of Russia. The United States always needed to build more advanced weapons to keep up with Russia and other countries. By 2029, a new, upgraded ICBM that improved on the Trident II D5—the result of a cooperative effort between the Air Force and the Navy—would replace older arsenal. Tom's former employer, Boeing, and Northrop Grumman were in development deals to build the advanced, nuclear-armed submarine-launched missile. Part of him was glad Congress had failed to cut back on military spending.

President Stevens knew he was going to have to confront Ivanov about his military build-up. A fragile peace had been held together by treaties broken by both countries. There were many occasions that Ivanov tried to influence a nation, offering them weapons to fight an adversary. Ivanov probably wanted to go down in history as a great ruler and a great military man. History had already been shown in Syria and other countries that Ivanov was willing to kill to get his way.

Before he met with Ivanov, President Stevens met with military leaders from the Pentagon via the communications center of Imagine. The Pentagon developed a strategic plan to move as many nuclear subs as were available into locations that would allow them the opportunity to hit all the major Russian cities and military bases at a moment's notice. They would take out as many Russian missile silos as possible. B52 bombers would fly from Frankfurt, Germany. The Poles were told to activate all missile defense systems so they could shoot down any missiles Russia launched at Europe. Everything would be in place for a counterattack to anything that Russia did. Everyone was told to be on the highest alert and to stand-by for further orders.

One thing Stevens wanted—before any attack—was for the spaceships to lift off. Any war between Russia and the United States might be the last war on Earth. He knew he would have to wait at least a week before a major confrontation with Ivanov. Before this happened, his generals were directed to contact their military counterparts in Russia and let them know that their troop movements were being monitored. They needed to withdraw immediately from their frontline positions. If the Russians withdrew, it would solve the problem, but the president did not think the Russians would do so just yet. He spent the next few days in constant contact with the Pentagon and their allies.

Stevens hoped that Ivanov would notice what he was doing. Maybe he would give up his military plans if he knew the United States stood ready to attack him. If the president ordered the attack on Russia, there would be no going back.

It would probably lead to the total destruction of both countries.

Ticking Time Bomb

Chapter 47 – Ticking Time Bomb?

Dr. Sato, the Imagine, Rocky Mountains, CO

Fully recovered, Dr. Sato headed down a long hallway on the ship, having just met with her office space staff. Her experimentations were unfolding quickly. Her brief reports to Tom were essentially bringing enough to the surface to gain credibility in his eyes. Still, she wished she could share with him some of the experimentations that Epoh had done under Dr. Kintain's supervision. They were beyond magnificent. Tissue samples had recovered from horrible ailments in record time—implementing modern studies, tackling resveratrol infusions, and testing telomerase alterations. In short order, he'd become a tailor of sorts. The system of rewards Dr. Kintain had discovered fostered in him a better understanding of his role. Epoh—and future others—like him could understand the importance of keeping "flawed" humans around on the ship even if he felt a part of himself that wanted to destroy them for their inability to be more like him—sickless, unerring, and machine-like.

Yet, Dr. Sato found Epoh's thoughts troubling. She felt it was a vulnerability in his system design. She desperately wished to improve upon him, and they clashed on the topic. He thought up ways to coax Epoh into releasing the thoughts, but in truth, Dr. Sato was bothered by the fact that they were there in the first place. Was he deeply murderous toward the humans that they would be sharing close quarters with even though he would be held in his own quarters for most of the journey until it was safe to introduce him to people? She appreciated that Epoh had discovered ways of immortalizing skin cells in labs repeatedly and had found a way to destroy the cancer cell byproducts. If Epoh's tendency toward destructive thoughts was to be used for anything, Dr. Kintain had found one of the best ways.

She just couldn't shake being bothered by it in the meantime. Was he a ticking timebomb, or simply just as flawed psychologically as many people were, continually altering their lives by getting caught up in conflicts or reconciling? Was it only human to turn to the human capacity to nurture and address our fears and anxieties with potential solutions? Dr. Kintain and Dr. Sato were learning just with one clone what the spectrum of clone capacity was, meaning it was limited data. Yet, as the DNA samples were being incubated currently in the lab, what would they find when they had a population? It wasn't ideal that they were going to find out on a spaceship far away from Earth. She worried, but there was nothing they could do.

Circumstances most certainly were often not ideal in any case, especially in pioneering efforts. Some might see only the dangers of uranium, for instance, but the radioactive core and nuclear forces at the core of Earth have kept Earth's core hot. Speculation about whether rogue planets might have radioactive substances to keep them warm has led to the possibility that, in fact, that is where life in the galaxy might be found rather than within the habitable zone.

She wondered at times whether any form of life could be pulled away from its destructive capability with a commitment like Dr. Kintain had to a daily vigilance and broadening of understanding and empathy. In the meantime, as some of the DNA samples had been merged in external wombs, she figured it would be essential to maintain a strict policy of separation until they had more time to study the clone population. Many on Earth had been willing to participate in the clone program that she administered. Still, they certainly expected it to be safe, with no casualties or clone-causing mishaps.

And as Epoh became more and more capable in the lab, they shared a hope that they would gather a better understanding of how he worked with humans. So far, there had been absolutely no problems other than occasional misunderstandings. Her lab partners found that Epoh was incapable of spiritual or philosophical musings.

She entered the small place of worship at the end of the medical team's hallway to briefly light a candle in memory of Earth, the home they would leave behind, in hopes that this daily habit of hers would remind her of the place where she had been born and had become a danger to humankind. Lately, she'd paused outside, taking in all of the wildlife and nature she would miss dearly. It would be strange to look out the windows and not see trees and sky. Yet, her own fears of perishing on Earth had turned her reluctance at first to an opportunity to finally expand humanity's horizons. Now, she was almost certain that—as sad as it was—star-trekking was only made possible when it seemed that humans were in grave danger.

In other words, just like Epoh's existence in the human journey posed a potential threat, at least with Epoh, it could be managed. If all else failed, she and her lab partners were willing to do whatever was necessary to prevent any harm to the humans on board. Yet, unlike Epoh, Earth had been mistreated, and it had forced them first to be refugees.

As Dr. Sato walked away from her candle back to the lab, she considered it debatable that they would be refugees for long, rather pioneers. She hoped those on Earth would be able to survive whatever the future held so that they could prosper together eventually, once they settled among the stars. She knew that she could barely talk to Tom on this last point since he had a rather dismal view of Earth's future. Still, the catastrophes on Earth were emboldening leaders like President Stevens. She was more inclined to think, 'who knows.' Still, she was glad the ship was closer to its launch date.

The door to the place of worship slid closed, and she walked toward Dr. Kintain's lab. As she entered, she smiled, seeing them hard at work.

"Hello, Epoh. Hello, Dr. Kintain. What discoveries have been made today?"

Epoh and Dr. Kintain said, "Well, we might be able to proclaim 2030 as the last generation to suffer from Alzheimer's."

She gleamed with abundant curiosity. Epoh never showed any expressions, which always threw her for a loop. Her lip curled a bit, and she decided to look at Dr. Kintain, whose expression was priceless. If a smile could be broader, it would be as walkable as a beach. It appeared she couldn't hide her worry that someday Dr. Kintain wouldn't be there to alter Epoh's course or line of thinking. What if at the wrong moment Epoh didn't have an empathetic response to a person, from all of this conditioning, but instead plowed ahead with his discoveries only to turn people into potential test rabbits?

"Is it sound? Reliable? How can we know?" she asked Dr. Kintain.

"I have tested it. And not in the worst imaginable way as I can glean from the expression on your face. Let's be clear, we tested it properly. And the plaque, the amyloid protein fragments, have broken down in the brain's nerve cells with the introduction of Epoh's caffeine-magnesium-vitamin E treatment. Dr. Sato, he may be the fastest learner I've ever had the pleasure of training."

Dr. Sato couldn't help wondering what was rolling around in Epoh's head, though. For the time being, she needed to have faith in Dr. Kintain's handling of Epoh, as he would be essential in molding the clones developing in utero now. She could continue to give positive reports to Tom with confidence and not share her own doubts. Tom needed to focus exclusively on the upcoming launch. *Maybe it was just her imagination getting the best of her*, she thought.

"That is amazing. I would like to further explore it and test it with different variables with my team this week."

"That would be just fine, Dr. Sato," said Dr. Kintain as he glanced over at Epoh. "Epoh will be glad when our latest reward for his services is complete. We have engineered for him a companion, and soon he will be rewarded for all of his breakthroughs."

When Dr. Sato looked at him, no warmth exuded from him at the thought of the reward. Epoh didn't look curious at all. This was a strange response to her. Dr. Sato longed to find a companion. It took up much of her thinking, and at night when she went to bed, it became clear that she wanted it with all of her heart. Who would she find on-board that would satisfy her desires and love her? She stopped letting her thoughts and heart wander and looked at Epoh, hoping for some sign of contentment or relief. Nothing. Her nerves got the best of her, and her jaw clenched.

"In the meantime, I'm starving," Epoh said.

He walked toward the kitchen in his compartment and disappeared from her view. When he turned the corner into the kitchen. She heard the door slide shut behind him.

He would function well, she thought. Now, if she could only see her relationship to Epoh as one that could be entirely trusting.

CHAPTER 48

Visitors

Chapter 48 – Visitors

Tom Burns, the Imagine, Rocky Mountains, CO

About six weeks before the planned launch date, Jose, Sam, and Tom were testing navigational sextants in order to be able to rely on the small telescope-like navigational tools without computer assistance. They were all impressed at how they could take precise angle measurements between pairs of stars to navigate.

An officer interrupted their experimentation to announce that some visitors were waiting to see them. The three of them walked down a two-hundred-foot ramp to the spaceship entrance and were surprised to find Grissom and Janet. Janet gave Sam a big hug, and Grissom shook their hands.

"How is it going with the spaceship? I hear you are just about ready to leave and may do so in the next few days," asked Janet. Both Janet and Grissom looked at Tom intently.

"We have made a lot of progress and are almost ready to go. We plan on launching in six weeks. We wish we had more time to do more testing, but it is best that we leave with all of the natural disasters occurring. When it happens, it will be both an exciting day but also a sad day. I will be excited to begin the journey, but I will miss people I know, like you two."

"That is what I want to talk to you about," said Grissom.

"Would you like to see some of the Imagine? How are you, Grissom?" Tom warmly shook Grissom's hand. "What can I do for you? What brings you here?"

"Sam, do you mind taking Janet for some ice cream or snack while I speak to Dr. Burns alone? After I speak to him, I will come and join you and perhaps see some of the Imagine."

"Sure. Janet, you are going to have an amazing ice cream experience."

Janet and Sam left to go to the cafeteria.

"Okay, Grissom, what is it that you need to talk in private about? I can see in your eyes and body language how much you love your daughter."

"First of all, I want to thank you for being so gracious to Janet and taking the time to talk to me. I know things must be very hectic right now." Grissom started to choke up a little. "Tom, may I call you, Tom?"

Tom nodded.

Turning to Tom, Grissom said, "I have reconsidered my decision, Tom. I want Janet to join you now. I know she has not had all the training you and the others have had, but she needs to go with you. There is no reason for her to stay on Earth. The natural disasters of the past week or so have made me realize Earth is dying sooner than everyone thought. Certainly, it is making it more difficult to live day today."

Without any hesitation, Tom said, "Janet is welcome to come with us. She has been friends with Sam for a long time. I am thrilled that you want her to join us. Why don't you join us too?"

"I do not want to leave my wife even though she is dead. There is also another reason. I have a brain tumor. It is inoperable, and the doctors have given me less than six months to live. With all the disasters, doctors seem to be cutting back on care for critically ill patients. I had a terrific life, especially when my wife was alive. Now I need to do what is best for Janet. I think my wife would want her to go with you. If she stays here with me, we would only have six months together at the most, and then she would be all alone with no one to turn to. She would probably die at a young age. If she goes with you, I am sure you, Sam, and your wife and kids, can help her and guide her through life."

Tom was sad. He gave Grissom a hug.

"Grissom, I am sorry about your situation. I wish I could do more for you, but I cannot at this time. When we first started to build this ship, you were one of the first construction people we hired, and you did an excellent job. I will take a DNA sample from you for safekeeping. When we figure out how to cure your disease, perhaps, we can selectively remove a gene that may have caused your problem. If we can do that, perhaps, we can clone you. Janet may face the same situation in the future, too, as the disease may be hereditary. You are very brave and courageous, letting Janet go. She will not have to see you suffer and then have to suffer herself without anyone to help her. I promise you that my wife and I will watch her like she is our own daughter and help her grow into a wonderful woman. You have my word."

"Thank you, Tom. That means a lot to me, and I really appreciate it. Can we go see Sam and Janet now? I have her suitcase with me and will say goodbye today. Tomorrow I have to go see the doctor again. I do hope to come back and do what I can to help you and then watch you leave."

After taking his DNA sample, Tom motioned for Grissom to follow him into the cafeteria. Sam and Janet had joined a group of friends from school, and they were eating ice cream, all laughing and having a good time.

"Sam, we are going to show Grissom and Janet a few places on the ship. How was the ice cream, Janet?"

"Wonderful! I have never tasted anything like that."

"Great! I am glad you are enjoying it and seeing some old friends."

Sam and Janet got up, and the four of them took a tour for about an hour. Now came the hard part.

"Janet, please come with me and bring your dad. I will show you to your living quarters. You will be near my family and near Sally, whom I know you have met before."

Janet now seemed to get a little bit nervous, but she and Grissom followed Tom to her new room.

"How do you like it?" Tom asked. "It will be your new home."

Janet put her suitcase down and said, "I am sure I will get used to it. I just wish my dad would change his mind and come with me."

Grissom and Janet looked at each other, and then they both started crying, hugging, and kissing.

Grissom hugged Janet and said, "My Janet, my only child, I wish I could go with you. However, I promised your mom two things. First, I would not leave her and will be buried with her. Second, I promised I would take care of you as long as I could. Unfortunately, that part is coming to an end. I have assurances from Tom and Sam that they will look after you and make sure you are comfortable on board. I will be thinking about you every day until I die. I will look up at the stars and know that my Janet is a great pioneer who helped start a new world. Please make me proud and think of your mom and dad once in a while."

Janet, who was still crying, said, "I will always remember you and think of you all the time. Please come with us, please."

"I cannot. My fate is sealed. Now I will leave you to unpack and set up your room and learn more about this wonderful ship. What I have seen makes me sure that you will be kept busy and be happy for as long as you live. Goodbye, Janet. I love you very much."

Janet was almost hysterical but said, "Dad, I love you always."

As Grissom turned around and left, Tom put his arms around Janet. He said, "Sam, why don't you, Sally, and whomever you want, help Janet to unpack and start to learn more about the ship, particularly about what to do and expect during take-off. I need to go to the bridge."

"I will take care of Janet. Thanks for helping her."

Tom left, feeling the grief of a father making one of the hardest decisions anyone would ever have to make. He hoped that the next few days of preparations would allow his son to include Janet, even if the feeling of being homesick tugged at her. She learned how important Sam had become to the success of their mission.

CHAPTER 49

Meeting of the Minds

Chapter 49 – Meeting of the Minds

Tom Burns, the Imagine, Rocky Mountains, CO

After meeting with Dr. Sato, Tom went to see Sam, Jose, and Sally working in the engineering room.

"Please give me some good news and tell me you have been able to calculate a flight path."

"Yes, we have calculated one that took into account all of the disasters happening and Earth's gravitational pull and so forth. We believe this represents the best chance for success."

"I am sure your data is probably correct, but you realize if you are wrong, we may never end up where we want to go and could fly to some distant galaxy without ever finding a home?"

Jose and Sally looked like they were going to pass out. Their faces turned white.

"Are you serious?" asked Sam.

"No. Because we are not going to take off today or tomorrow. I will have someone check your data, and if it is correct, we will use it. Be confident in your actions. We must double-check everything we do. Any decision you make for the entire ship would have repercussions, so you need to be extra careful."

Jose and Sally now looked relieved, although their faces stayed white.

"If I could drink, I would do it now," said Jose.

"Me too," Sally said.

Sam said, "All right, we need to be ready to do whatever my dad asks. So, get some rest and be ready to work at any moment. Everyone is under a ton of pressure now, and we can't make things worse."

Tom grinned.

Two days later, there was more bad news. Tom, Sam, and Jose were on the deck, along with several other officers. Given the spaceship's advanced communication system, the president set up his communications center on the ship to stay ahead of bad situations. It was able to link up with almost any mobile satellite in space. This included the Russian satellites. The president had brought his officers to the bridge to discuss critical options to significant problems he suddenly learned about.

"The first problem is that there has been another significant earthquake overnight in Anchorage. It was a 7.5 magnitude earthquake, which was the largest ever recorded for Alaska. There were not many deaths reported, but the quake's impact is really going to be felt by the environment. The Alaskan oil pipeline has ruptured in several places, resulting in large oil spills. Nothing like this has ever occurred before. This oil spill is more massive than the Exxon Valdez. I have asked Canada and our own northern troops to go to Alaska in response. Wildlife is severely affected. The oil has spilled into areas of large salmon populations. It is estimated that fifty percent of the salmon will be killed."

The president then turned away from Tom to speak to his generals and Major Johns.

"We can handle the spill, although it will cost us both financially and ecologically. I have sent teams to shut down the oil pipeline until further notice. Our second problem is the more serious of the two, and I am asking for suggestions before making the final decision about our course of action. We have intercepted communications from Russia and have verified via a satellite that Ivanov has ordered many Russian troops to the

Ukrainian border and Estonia. It looks like an all-out invasion, which is going to be very costly in terms of life. Obviously, he is striking now due to all the disasters happening around the world. He believes he can take advantage of everyone and consolidate his power since we are so focused on trying to save our own people.

"We have to stop him from doing this. We do have NATO, but many countries are also suffering from natural disasters, and I do not know if they can be of great help. England is willing to use its air force to help us. France's attitude is to give us the cold shoulder. They are still smarting from Trump's refusal to follow environmental protection protocols established in Paris years ago. Poland is a bright spot. We set up a massive missile defense system there that can shoot down almost any Russian missile directed at Europe.

"Does anyone have a suggestion? We still have nuclear missiles ready to go from North Dakota and nuclear subs in the area. I have also ordered two battleships and two aircraft carriers to the region standing by for orders. I prefer to use nuclear weapons only as a last resort. If we do so, you can be sure that Ivanov will also use them to attack Europe and the United States. Once we go down that path, millions will die regardless of the natural disasters. One thing I am hopeful for is that this spaceship takes off and is out of harm's way before I call Ivanov again. An all-out war might end up destroying this ship before you can launch."

The generals focused on where to attack Russia. Some wanted to pursue an immediate strike and assassinate Ivanov. Others preferred to wait and see what Ivanov did and then counterattack. These generals did not want the world to see them as starting a world war. They all started arguing with each other about what to do.

Sam had an idea. He tried to raise his hand to speak, but everyone ignored him.

Finally, he screamed, "Excuse me, everyone."

Everyone turned toward him.

"I have an idea that it seems no one has mentioned. Why doesn't the president call Mr. Ivanov again and try to work things out? An all-out attack should be the last possible option. I suggest that the president make it clear that the United States, while facing many obstacles, still has the use of military force in the region and can retaliate immediately if necessary. Let him also know that any missiles he fires will be shot down from our missile defense system in Poland."

The bridge became hushed. All eyes were on the president as he looked at Sam. The president smiled.

"Excellent idea, Sam. Unfortunately, we did try that once before to no avail. I may call Mr. Ivanov again as soon as we finish this discussion. It is always better to avoid military confrontation if possible, but sometimes we have no choice. Sam, someday you are going to be an amazing officer. Dr. Burns, you should be very proud of your son."

"Yes, Mr. President. I am very proud of him, although sometimes I do forget to say so."

Denial and Deception

Chapter 50 – Denial and Deception

President Stevens, the Imagine, Rocky Mountains, CO

Moments later, the president left the bridge and returned to the communication center with his officers and called the Russian leader. Of course, Ivanov denied everything, telling the president that he knew nothing about Ukraine's invasion. President Stevens sent satellite photos showing the Russian troop movement confirming what he knew.

Stevens made it clear to Ivanov he could have a war if he wanted it but that he would lose. There was no reason to kill millions of people over his foolish ambitions. The world was hurting. He should be using his troops to assist others.

Ivanov tried to bully the president, but the president demanded Russia withdraw its forces or face an attack by the United States and its allies. In the background, he could hear Ivanov discussing the matter with his generals. Time seemed to stand still. Finally, Ivanov told the President his troops would remain in Russia for now. He realized the risks were too high to have an all-out war with each other, one in which millions of people would die.

When the president returned to the bridge, he announced that the Russian troops were going to withdraw. Everyone on the bridge was clapping, giving high-fives to each other.

Jose and Sam hugged each other.

"You did it, Sam. You are a hero," said Jose.

The president looked pleased, wanting Sam to have his moment of fame. Still, he knew there would be more trouble ahead with the Russians. It was not possible to trust Ivanov.

He said, "We may have dodged a war for the moment, but I doubt Ivanov will lay low for very long."

Unify

Chapter 51 – Unify

Tom Burns, the Imagine, Rocky Mountains, CO

Two weeks later, Tom felt more confident than ever about all the preparations. Carson, Dorothy, Bob, and about fifty other people, were still working furiously around the control consoles' clock. There would be minimal time to test anything. If the launch failed, they would all be incinerated. Perhaps. But perhaps not. Everyone was bringing their best effort to secure their passage beyond Earth.

It was going to work. The only question was whether it would work before any other major conflict erupted that would interfere with their launch date. He went to his quarters. He decided to contact the three commanders of the spaceships to let them know what was happening and see if they could offer insights to rectify the situation. He also wanted to know what other problems they were having and how soon it would be before they could launch.

The German ship commander let Tom know that he was also building a new control console as he was faced with a similar situation but having difficulty with DNA samples. Tom was glad to hear from the commander, but sorry to hear about the DNA problems. The Germans were still loading DNA samples on board. That meant some of his medical staff were off the ship and had difficulties returning due to the flooding in some countries like the Netherlands.

"When do you think you will have everyone on board and be ready to launch?"

The German commander replied, "It is difficult to say. I think the control console will be ready in ten days. I have to hope that my medical staff will all be here within that timeframe, but I am not sure. Due to the sporadic phone service around Europe now, I cannot contact them when I need to. When will you be ready? When do you think we must launch or be stranded on Earth?"

"I can't speak for all the ships. Some locations are probably more stable than others. There has not been much damage in the Rocky Mountains, so we are safe for now. However, the earthquakes in California probably shook up the mountains everywhere. I just don't know yet if there will be any more natural disasters soon. I believe we have to launch within thirty days. I also need to speak to the Russians and Australians after my call with you to see how they are doing. How are the Alps holding up?"

"Right now, we are in a lull. There is no specific storm threat and no earthquake. There is one volcano in Italy that erupted, but that is a local or Italian issue."

Tom thanked him for the information and called the Australian commander.

The Australian commander said they would be ready to launch soon. They were in the midst of finishing up the control console being built outside the ship.

"The only geographical problem that we're facing is the Great Barrier Reef. It is being destroyed by the rising ocean and currents."

Temperatures had soared in the desert areas, which were no longer habitable for many species. However, even though people had to move to different parts of the country on a moment's notice, Australia was holding together very well. He believed they could take off within two weeks but preferred more time to recheck all the systems.

Tom thanked him. Then he called his Russian counterpart.

Yuri told him he was doing well and was ready to go. He had already completed the console preparations and could launch at any time.

"I am surprised that you are not ready. It is clear Russians have better intelligence and more technological superiority."

"Yuri, this is not the time to debate who is smarter, stronger, or more advanced. All the ships face critical decisions, and we must launch before we are unable to do so. When we get into space, it is not going to be a competition. You will no longer be employed by Russia. I will not be working for the United States, and the Germans and Australians will not be working for their countries either. We will all be working for humanity. It is not a game. It is imperative that at least one ship survives long enough to colonize a new planet. If we only have one ship and that ship is yours, so be it. I will be glad to die knowing that someone survived the long journey. Also, I foresee there will be times when we have problems with each spaceship. We must work together to ensure everyone's safety. I am sure there will be maintenance issues, but there will be many amazing discoveries, I hope. We must work together period. Do you understand that?"

Yuri replied, "Relax, Dr. Burns. I know we are all in this together. What will the name be when we all arrive at a new destination? Will it be the new America or the new Moscow? People don't always get along, no matter how hard they try. That, my friend, is a fact of history. We are taking the history of Earth's countries with us no matter how hard we try not to do that."

"Yuri, by the time we arrive at a destination or planet, I may not care what we call it as long as it is a home we can live on and thrive. When and how we land the people on your spaceship, and you want to set up your own colony and call it Russia, we can deal with that then, but it is the furthest thing from my mind right now. Right now, I need to get four spaceships in orbit to begin the journey. I will call you when we're all ready."

With those words, Tom hung up on him.

Sarah had come in while he was talking to the Russian commander. She said, "I guess it is impossible to avoid politics between nations even when there will no longer be any nations."

Tom turned around to face his wife. "You are damn right. It seems the Germans and Australians will be fine, but I am not so sure about the Russians, with Yuri in control. He could have told us about the console problem when he discovered it himself. It seems that his ship has already solved that problem and is ready to launch now. What are we going to do in space? Are we going to attack each other and try to blow one another upon our journey or when we see a new planet?"

Sarah said, "You are the man I love, and I know you have always had your family's best interest and the people around you in your heart and mind. I will go anywhere in the galaxies with you because I know you will succeed. Right now, you need to focus on our spaceship and not let the Russians bother you. Don't let him get under your skin. I trust you will make the right decision when the time comes."

Tom hoped he'd do the right thing. It had all put him in a pretty foul mood, one that he'd kept mostly hidden from the people around him, but his wife knew him better. One thing was for sure. *It was crucial that it remained a group effort,* he thought, as he prepared mentally for his meeting next week with the president and the major who would be their eyes and ears on Earth after they launched next month.

Made the Team

Chapter 52 – Made the Team

Tom Burns, the Cave, Rocky Mountains, CO

About a week later, having worked virtually non-stop for months, Major Johns informed Dr. Burns that the launching mechanism was all set. They had run many simulations in the cave laboratory, and everything appeared to work well together. Tom went to the lab to meet with the major and the president. They all stood around the ten-foot-long console that looked like a giant series of computers, nobs, and switches. Beyond the systems integration and being built based on the input of all the engineers who would use it and rely on it, the consoles had been tested in thousands of simulations of real scenarios. Tom was very thankful. He told the president and the soldiers how much he appreciated their work.

Tom said, "You have done a wonderful job."

The major said, "It has been our pleasure doing this for you, Dr. Burns. All five of us have worked as a team for many years. We were on the front line of some of the most destructive weapons of all time. We always had to think about launching the nuclear warheads towards Russia, which effectively probably meant the end of human life after the Russians retaliated. We were thrilled to be out of that decision-making process, but we have no doubt that we would have launched those weapons if the president gave the orders. In short, we could have been responsible for the deaths of more than twenty million people. Now we have a chance to participate in such an exciting project and one that will save lives or the human race hopefully."

The other soldiers all nodded their heads in agreement with the major's comments.

Tom said, "Nevertheless, you have fantastic skills and loyalty to duty. I want to offer you a chance to be cloned once we are on our way. To do that we will need to collect some DNA samples from you and the soldiers." Tom turned towards the president. "And to be honest, after Donald Trump, I did not think I could ever stand another politician. However, President Stevens, you have really impressed me with your dedication and the way you care for people. I could certainly use someone like you to help me deal with the Russians in the future, especially if they keep cloning Ivanov. So, what do you say? Shall we collect some DNA samples?"

The president spoke up before the major had a chance to respond. "I wish I were going with you. This has been one of the most exhilarating experiences in my life. I am sure the government could never do this, as we would have argued continuously over just about anything related to the spacecraft. I am hoping you reach your destination soon. By the time you reach it, all of us on Earth will be long gone. I have no idea how much longer we can live with all the disasters happening, but as long as I am alive, we will try to keep going. Who knows, maybe we will build more ships and get more people off the Earth? We will be watching with great pride when the takeoff is done successfully. As long as we can have radio or satellite communications, please let us know how you are doing among the stars."

"Thank you, sir," Tom said. "I want to shake each of your hands. You are all heroes, and the ship's people will always remember you, whether we clone you or not. May we collect your samples now?"

The men agreed to do so, and the samples were collected and brought onto the ship for safekeeping. Afterward, Tom shook each of the soldier's hands again and saluted them all. Then he turned to the president and hugged him.

He said, "I wish you the best, President Stevens. May you fare well with these disasters and Mr. Ivanov."

Tom returned to the Imagine. He anticipated that he could give the signal to launch between forty-eight and seventy-two hours.

One if a LIfe Cycle Opportunity

Chapter 53 – Once in a Life Cycle Opportunity

Tom Burns, the Imagine, Rocky Mountains, CO

At the commander's post on the bridge, Tom turned on the viewscreen.

"May I have everyone's attention, please. The next forty-eight hours will be hectic. In forty-eight to seventy-two hours, we are going to launch. All hands-on deck, please. You must go to your assigned station. All those involved with the Warfare Center Weapons Division should report for duty at those stations. This is just a precaution. You have forty-four hours to put on your assigned spacesuit. During the next forty-four hours, please make sure that everything is put away or bolted in place. During the takeoff, there is a possibility you may blackout or experience feeling lightheaded. We may also experience weightlessness, which is why everything needs to be bolted down. It is expected that you must remain in place for about twelve to thirty minutes. During take-off, do not attempt to get up and move around. You will not be able to control your movements. Once it is safe to do so, the board officers will give an all-clear and provide you with further instruction.

"My understanding is that leaving the ship at this point will be difficult now. Please do not leave the ship from now on in any circumstances or left behind. Now please get to work and do what must be done before we launch."

Over the next two days, the ship became a bustle of activity. Tom instructed the officers to inspect departments every four hours until the launch. If anything was wrong or out of place, it was to be reported immediately so that the appropriate personnel could fix it.

Tom was glad to see Sam and Jose meeting with the launch team to go over calculations again for the lift-off trajectory into orbit. Sally told Tom that she was on her way with Sophie, Janet, and Sarah and other medical personnel to secure all the supplies.

Tom visited Dr. Sato's quarters. Dr. Sato was giving orders as to how to secure everything in the medical labs for the launch. She was very meticulous about safety and her work.

Everything seemed to be going smoothly.

***

After the two long, hard days of securing all the medical personnel supplies and making critical preparations, Tom ate breakfast with Sophie, Janet, Sarah, Sally, and Dr. Sato in the cafeteria. Sophie suddenly started getting upset. She looked sick and disoriented. Her mom could see it happening.

"What is wrong, Sophie?"

Sophie looked like she was about to lose it and started to pull at her hair.

"How can we possibly do this? We are all going to die. I want to go home and live in our house again. I'm getting out of here, Mom. Come with me, please. Dad is going to get us all killed, and you know it, too."

Sarah was staring at her but waited for her to finish. All the people in the cafeteria were now watching and waiting to see what she would do.

Dr. Sato did not want to make a scene and make things worse. She approached Sophie.

"Sophie, take a deep breath, please. Then we can talk about it. I am sorry you feel this way."

"Shut up. I don't need a big breath of air. Why can't you do what I want for a change? Mom, I thought I could get through this, but I just can't. Please let me leave before it is too late. I don't want to die."

Sarah tried to put her arms around her daughter, but Sophie pushed her away.

"Don't you dare touch me now."

Dr. Sato said, "Do you want me to call security? We can't do this all day and be ready for launch."

Sarah was about to respond, but Sally cut her off. "Sophie, I can certainly understand how you feel because I have some of those feelings. I don't want to die in a ball of flames either. I am anxious, just as you are. Probably all the people on the ship are anxious too. But look at the world, Sophie. We could be dead in a year if we stay here. We really have no choice. Earthquakes. Volcanoes. Hurricanes. Floods. Disasters are killing a lot of people. Some of those people would have given anything to board this ship and try to live. We are lucky to be right here. You have a loving mom and dad and two wonderful brothers, one of whom I like a lot. My parents are also on board, helping me feel safe. Everyone here trusts the officers and scientists to do the right thing. Your dad would not launch if he felt we could not do so. You need to calm down and trust the experts on this ship. Please, Sophie, let us help you get through this."

Sophie seemed to calm down a little.

Janet gave her some water. "Look at me, Sophie. I have already lost my mom, and soon I will lose my dad. My dad made a huge sacrifice to let me go on this trip. He knew if I stayed behind, I would die soon and perhaps in a lot of pain. I know I have some friends here, including your parents, and I trust them one hundred percent to do the right thing and take care of me. They are always going to look out for our safety. We have to take this trip one day at a time. Each day we wake up, there will be new experiences and wonders that humans have never seen before. I feel blessed to be on this ship to be able to participate in all the things we will do and see."

After listening to Sally and Janet, Sophie calmed down and seemed to be feeling better. "I am sorry for the trouble I just caused and the anxiety I may have given some of you. I hope you will forgive me."

Everyone said yes, and there were hugs all around.

Then Sophie went to her mom and give her a big hug and said, "Sorry, Mom, I apologize for my actions."

"Your apology is accepted. We will get through this hard part together." Then Sarah turned to Sally and Janet. "Thanks for helping. Sometimes it is difficult for a mother to talk to her daughter. I can see why Sam and your friends really like you two."

Tom was glad it had all worked out.

Meanwhile, Luis was tying all the pots and pans down, the ones he was not using. About six hours before lift-off, he would put everything away. Until then, people had to eat.

Tom called the other three spaceships to let them know he was ready to launch and finalize the scheduled launches. The Russians would go second, with Australia third and the Germans fourth. The other three were to wait to see the United States spaceship results before beginning to launch.

President Stevens informed Tom that all subs were still holding their positions, and all of them had been given specific targets. "We continue to monitor the Russians."

"All-hands-on-deck, and I anticipate the launch in twenty-four hours," said Tom.

Moving Parts

Chapter 54 – Moving Parts

Dr. Sato, the Imagine, Rocky Mountains, CO

With only twenty-four hours before launch, despite her concerns about Epoh and the incubating clones, some of which would be ready for birth soon after launch, Dr. Sato felt prepared for whatever came her way. She was glad to see that Tom approved of how the medical quarters were prepared for the launch. There were still a lot of moving parts. There were a lot of things to work out, especially given the recent discussions that had clamped down on her a bit, unfortunately, in terms of guaranteeing the policy and procedures she had prepared for distribution on the launch date.

Certainly, she wasn't going to let her beliefs about how things like certain placebos would work get in her way of maintaining the health of everyone on board as they prepared for launch and launched. She wasn't sure if they would work. But these placebos had been developed in the lab in case of major cases of anxiety or people jumping up during the take-off and needing immediate medical attention. Still, nothing would stop her from seeing the power of the mind and body to heal and the massive gaps in knowledge they were still dealing with. If it wasn't placebos, they had other methods to turn to. Those on the ship had already undergone early evidence-based care and seemed to heal quicker based on the work her medical staff and Epoh were secretly developing.

Indeed, some of the passengers were understandably fearful of any side effects from any potential cures that might sound good in theory, but in terms of the real-world application were more powerful psychologically than researched. Time would tell. Wanting to see the science behind everything became a constant amusement of some of the passengers. Despite Dr. Kintain and Dr. Sato working together to provide more information, they indeed were still keeping hush-hush about Epoh and the clones. They didn't want any real-world hysteria to occur. Real-world applications of scientific discoveries would be found in a completely different environment away from Earth. At times, her sense that what they found in the labs might need more scrutiny and testing took her over.

For one thing, last week's meeting with Tom and the committee had been assembled to discuss her written policies and procedures. They had raised some key issues and concerns. She recalled how she had felt during the discussion.

"So, after reviewing the policy and procedures, we can at least all agree that each person onboard can choose how they want to live their life. We're also in agreement that passengers can choose not to accept cloning themselves or stem cell therapy, and that cryopreservation is a must, given that we are concerned about the duration of the trip and potential future implementation of scientific findings," she had said.

The committee of eight members had sat around the table, combing through pages of her policy and procedures. Briefly, Dr. Sato had felt a solidarity with them that day. Still, soon she had noted a few of the committee members were simply not into the science of the procedures, but the application as to how they might be able to, in fact, ensure immortality. Several of the wealthy members had represented their views. She deduced that this question lingered in the corner of their vacillating minds for many of them for years. For some of them, securing passage into humanity's future with a whole new rule book developing potentially was the reward they had in mind.

"Is it possible that what we're not able to do on Earth has less to do with ethics and more to do with a mindset that prescribes to us a certain hunter-gatherer limitation to life or even an agricultural society domestication, that we must swallow like a pill? I mean, come on! We're about to set sail across the galaxy! Doesn't it serve us to break from certain ways, especially if we end up being the only ones who survive Earth's ravages because we pioneered off? Can't we move beyond systemic thoughts and how we develop relationships and our relationship with our mortality?" Joe Hirant, one of the wealthiest donors for the Imagine voyage, asked.

Joe had joined the committee and was the most vocal the entire time during the committee meeting. Dr. Sato had barely met the man. He was tall, almost a foot taller than her, with a former football player's body, brown hair, and a habit of wearing sports jerseys. She'd seen him before, lurking around the cafeteria. Still, she had never heard from him in the time that they'd been in preparations for the launch. She had heard from one of her staff members that he had been following their medical programs on board with a very keen eye. Joe had taken a lot of time to talk to Tom about the direction of the policy and procedures that she had discussed at a lecture about the medical policies onboard more than six months ago.

"Yes, but we need to know where you're going with the age-old desire humans have shared to live forever and how that can be explored by members of our committee. We need to determine how to address it within certain parameters," she had replied.

"Aren't you in the least bit curious? That is one of the virtues of a scientific mind, not a vice," Joe had continued.

"It can be absolutely abominable in many ways, shared space, shared resources, and what if new ailments that we've never even heard of developing as a result of the older ages? Will our scientific endeavors keep up? And what harm do we encounter if we don't cope with our mortality in the spiritual sense so that we stop focusing on our own selves and extending life, but instead learn to let go? I'm afraid I don't know the answer," Dr. Sato had admitted.

Joe had claimed, "It starts with your fear. You are looking at this as you might look at a prey! Why not look at it as something with potential? You cannot prevent the possible human edge of innovation that we may all be able to contribute to, given our shared future onboard. You can't ignore that we'll eventually be landing on some distant star or even rogue planet with a solid radioactive core!" Joe had stood up. "Dammit, Dr. Sato, with all due respect—"

Tom had spoken up. "Please, Joe."

Joe had sat back down.

Tom had continued, "In all practicality, nature-based scientific discoveries have been unable to become systemic replacements on Earth. We have witnessed industry protectionism become the standard-bearer of societal guilt in embracing any potential fundamental changes that might better human and environmental life on Earth. Having seen some of your work in the labs, I am sufficiently certain that you will continue to work on nature-based advances as they materialize. I am sure there is more openness among those on board to see the practical, real-world applications to their lives and our lives together aboard Imagine. If our thinking is systemically based, it's true, as Joe suggests, we may adapt in the same way that we did on Earth."

Joe continued, "And the potential loss to humanity can be devastating. Tom, you've spoken to me about how important your father was to you. You knew him. Many people never knew their grandparents from your son's generation. They were ravaged by the latter effects of war and unfulfilled promises in life and inexcusable industry standards protectionism. Few have been encouraged to seek medicinal plant knowledge as was once studied not just as a hobby but as a way of life by indigenous groups. And that's the sad part. They don't want to. When there's a will, there's a way, we've learned over and over again. Of course, some members of our wealthy minions, who we've also now grown to be quite skeptical of, only care about their nutritional value for not spreading public knowledge.

"You of all people know, you would wish that Sam got to know his grandfather more. And what if, as we find, wisdom does come with age and we can amplify that? What if stopping the aging process does indeed lead to greater wisdom that outcompetes any of the clones we develop? What if it's our Occam's razor? We keep putting our hope in future generations, but what if we are, in the process, letting spiritualists decide what must happen with the soul and where it goes? What if the reason for our constant soul-searching—and many of my own sleepless nights—in search of meaning has less to do with where we end up but what our potential is on the journey? What if we keep hampering it with strict disciplinarian theories about how long we have to live? Who decides that? Surely, it's most likely whatever ingredients we have in the lab and our own ability to grasp what we are capable of, not fear it!"

Tom had blurted, "Since wealth plays a smaller role on the ship, it won't be funding that decides what we explore. Wisdom comes from experience, just like we hope that with innocence, courage continues to be displayed, in spite of those who are more motivated to avoid pain and may not be as nimble, quick, or adventurous with time. It's possible death will become a problem for us, but we must remain open to exploring all options, Dr. Sato. We insist that any policies and procedures that you were going to distribute before we launch to the ship members accept that there is no finality. You cannot decree that we will not potentially seek out and discuss the ethics or viability of speculative solutions such as rejuvenation and mind uploading! Or the various human potentials we are not exploring based only on our history on Earth! We may find that our next legacies are born out of the newer necessities and needs of living off of Earth. We may need to apply scientific discoveries to real-world situations as they come up and as we evolve."

The room had stilled. Dr. Sato had wondered if her understanding of life expectancy had developed from the systemic ways that she had grown used to developing against. Scientists had engineered real-world applications that could have lowered the dependence on fossil fuels and other petroleum-based products. Yet the status quo—and the fact that the dinosaur industries were on every corner—meant any seismic changes were steeped in perturbing politics and economical paranoias. For a moment, she had thought of Epoh and Dr. Kintain and how she would ever be able to explore with the committee her promising findings if she was being asked to prioritize lab studies in slowing or stopping the aging process. It appeared that, at the very least, there were members of the committee who would be interested in conducting clinical trials.

Just as Dr. Sato had begun to stand up, Joe had said, "Please sit down, Dr. Sato. We are aware of the justice argument and how we can justify trying to extend the lives of those who have more already, which for all intents and purposes, includes the majority of people on Imagine. Yet, since you've had your head buried in the labs, you may not be aware that we are a more diverse group. Tom had felt very disturbed after his son, Sam, had hidden from him a fistfight that he'd had with a kid roughly his age named Steven, who felt that Sam's dad had no right to choose who got to go on Imagine and who didn't and had to stay behind. Sam's mom had kept it from Tom, as she didn't want to worry him. Then, recently, she'd felt that it was potentially something they needed to consider. A fourth ship is in development through the help of AI research in Africa and will join us, even though humanity is now reliant on the president and his people in helping make that happen.

"They have started their developments using the specifications that Tom has provided to President Stevens, who has expressed his concern about our methods for selecting all the people that would go on our spacecraft. Millions of people will not have the opportunity to go with us. It got us thinking. Indeed, it's not that we want to be exclusive about our findings on board Imagine. We have absolutely fantastic communication systems in place that will allow us to communicate with all the ships.

"And the nature of how quickly the Earth is being ravaged doesn't really give us the chance to deal with how to improve conditions for life in communities on Earth now. And yes, I've considered letting go of self-preservation, opening to transcendence in the face of our limited time on Earth in the spiritual sense. But what if humanity's future also means extending the same meaningful experiences that we have in our life span to our understanding of human evolution? Life expectancy has already benefitted from improved conditions and improved scientific breakthroughs in our lifetimes! Maybe we're not finished yet."

Even though Dr. Sato had been preparing to get up, simply to ask that they be willing to finalize the procedures and policies before launch, she knew it wasn't going to happen. Tom and the committee had guaranteed that the policies and procedures would be discussed, and she would have to grow to accept it. All she could do by the launch date was to inform everyone that the committee had met and that they were working on essential policies and procedures that would shape the future of medical studies on board.

The committee had adjourned. She anticipated some complaints when she sent everyone the message after the meeting. She was surprised when no one complained at all.

8 am Wednesday

Chapter 55 – 8 am Wednesday

Tom Burns, the Imagine, Rocky Mountains, CO

Of course, things don't always go as planned. Tom had called off the countdown. It was 8 am on Wednesday. The last twenty-two hours had pushed Tom to the complete brink. He felt like a disgraced golf player trying his luck and hitting every ball in the water.

Everything was going fine after he spoke to the president the previous morning about monitoring the Russians. What he hadn't expected was finding one of the president's men standing on the bridge, unaware of Tom being within hearing range.

"There's little reason to believe that we need to leave all our money behind, and I've let some of the folks on the other ships know too. This isn't negotiable. Can you imagine what sort of lack of leverage we'd be facing? What? Suddenly, we're all just back in line? Anyway, look, I know for one thing that I've already purchased the paintings from that daughter of an art collector, what's her name, oh yeah, Thelma. She spoke up at a meeting after we first all started boarding. Her own husband called it out as simple complaining when she had brought up that she had brought her collection of art from Monet, Manet, and Renoir, among others. Life without art would be traumatic! I've created an amazing storage area for banned things that I have on complete lockdown onboard. It will be viewable by permission only. It's outrageous that I have to resort to this. Not everything can be in digital format if we're going to be representing humanity so far from Earth. Anyway, look, I can't stand to have to hide it, but even the president agreed it was a bit, shall we say, overboard."

Tom's shoulders sank. He hadn't thought of it that way at all. He'd considered only the safety hazards of pictures flying off walls as projectiles. He'd even forgotten to meet with Thelma and her husband. He started to doubt his ability to meet the human needs of people who relied on him to get the Imagine off the ground and avoid failing the future generations of humanity. And those future generations of humanity now might include much older humans, thanks to science and science-based evidence, but also clones when the time came to try it in a controlled environment.

He'd returned to his quarters, thrown for a loop, wondering how he should proceed. He couldn't merely address it with someone who, along with the president, knew that the strict policy was outrageous. Soon, he realized, he was fine with it. If problems arose, he would deal with it discreetly. Just as Dr. Sato had come to realize that her stance on policies affecting the future of humanity could potentially lead to irreconcilable differences and cause temperaments to flair if all options weren't considered, he too could feel the importance of the appeal and need to preserve cultural antiquities. He'd been inconsiderate. He'd read about significant losses to those treasures in cultures and how deep the thread of pain could be stitched into the vast morass of failure. Humans had repeatedly experienced a hard time recovering from such a severe loss.

Late on Tuesday, on his way to reviewing all the routine maintenance procedures and making sure that all on board were in sequence in terms of the timing of all the launch stages, he'd received the weather report. The Air Force Weather officials predicted only a 20% chance of acceptable launch conditions for the following morning. He'd be better off waiting to set the T-27 hours in a day rather than for Wednesday with all the built-in holds to accommodate the launch team to have a cushion of time for tasks and procedures that his team needed to carry out. Evening conditions would look much better, and the weather squadron expected 80% "go" conditions during the Thursday window. Although all close-outs had been prepared, all backup flight systems were a "go," all platforms had been secured. All flight systems and navigational systems loaded, activated, and retested; they would have to hold. He'd have to coordinate the cryogenic reactants for the fuel cell storage tanks still, ensure all the procedures were followed before T-20 hours for the sound suppression system, and still dial in all engineering briefings.

In the meantime, he wasn't sure that piloting the shuttle had prepared him for this level of launch. He shook the fear, realizing that if he went to look at the spaceship from the outside and walked through the cave, where so many hours had been spent in preparation, he'd realize that it was all in his head. A day or two of changes, even months of delays, were all part of the real-time needs they had to consider to stay real with themselves and give themselves the best chance for a successful launch. Maybe there was a Planet B, but there wasn't an Imagine B.

He stood looking at the personnel clearing the launch pad and conducting various inspections. It had taken nearly twenty years of blood, sweat, and tears to get to the final countdown. Now they were finally going to be looking for a new planet to live on. As he looked at the Imagine, he felt a lot of mixed emotions. On the one hand, he felt a great sense of pride that he and his team had designed and developed a spaceship that no one had thought was possible. This was going to be his home for possibly the next hundred years.

On the other hand, he felt that there were certain things on Earth that he would truly miss. He loved going to parks with his children and seeing wondrous wildlife. He also enjoyed boating and fishing when he was younger. He brushed those thoughts aside. He would simply have to find new ways to occupy his free time. As long as he had his family with him and felt he could protect them, everything would be all right.

Ultimate Sacrifice

Chapter 56 – Ultimate Sacrifice

Tom Burns, the Imagine, Rocky Mountains, CO

After experiencing these delays, forty-four hours later, it was time to launch. Tom was making announcements encouraging people to get ready. Everybody had to get into their spacesuit. All suits were to be checked to make sure they were airtight. The spacesuits and the Imagine interior had been pressurized, allowing the people on board to function normally.

At T-4 hours before the blastoff, everyone was in their assigned places. The officers went through the ship one more time to make sure everybody was strapped in correctly. Tom could see that many of the passengers were nervous, but that was to be expected.

At T-2 hours before the flight, Major Johns was running the outside control room, and Dorothy was handling the engine room. Tom was in constant contact. President Stevens and Grissom, along with several generals and guests, were in an observatory location. Each of them understood that the launch would be postponed until further notice should any problem arise.

Sam and Jose were strapped in with Dorothy and Carson in the engine room. Everybody seemed nervous about what might happen on the launch.

As the clock reached T-60 minutes to launch, Major Johns contacted Tom.

Major Johns yelled, "Stop the countdown. We need to stop immediately. All systems are not go, and we are experiencing a major failure with the flow of the fuel. We are running out of time too fast and can't correct in time for this launch. I'm sorry."

Tom was incredibly disappointed. As he felt all of his mixed emotions, he couldn't contain his calm disposition any longer. He screamed, "What the hell is wrong?"

"I don't know, yet, but the control panel indicates the flow of fuel is very uneven as it moves to the rockets and spaceship. If we blast off now, it is possible you will be upside down, on the ground, or incinerated. We cannot risk it."

"Okay. I understand. We will meet in twenty minutes in your control room. I will get the experts together, and we can figure out the solution there."

Bereft, Tom announced that the launch had been postponed, and everyone could unstrap until further notice. Just about every person on the ship let off a groan or cursed. The delay could be anywhere from five to forty-eight hours. If it was going to be longer than that, he would make a new announcement. He contacted the other three spaceships and let them know his status. They were monitoring the launch from their own ships. Tom told them to check their fuel systems to ensure the flow was even since that seemed to be the problem on the Imagine.

In the control room, everyone stared intently at the screens as Carson and Dorothy started to push buttons to run the simulated launch. Everyone was looking at the instrument's measures on the panels as the countdown began. They focused their attention on the flow of fuel. After running it a few times in simulations, no one had a clue about what was wrong. Everyone there was deep in thought.

Tom knew they would solve the problem. The only question would be when.

"Thank you all for coming down to look at what happened," said Tom. "We need to figure out what went wrong and how to fix it as soon as possible. I do not want to sacrifice safety over the need to launch as soon as possible, but we cannot wait another six months or so to leave. So, let's put our heads together and see what can be done right away. First, Major Johns, can you please explain what happened? You told me it was a problem with the fuel flowing to the rockets. Is that correct?"

The major said, "Yes, sir. We noticed on the control panels that all of the rockets were not getting fuel at the same rate. We felt if you went ahead and launched, some of the rockets would provide much stronger power during lift-off and turn the spaceship sideways or even upside down."

"Thank you, Major, for explaining the situation. You did the right thing. It is obvious we could have destroyed the ship and caused a lot of injuries. Let's study the simulations with the fuel and propulsion system a few times to see if we can pinpoint the problem. Does anyone see what needs to be fixed and estimate how long it would take? We have some great minds here. We should be able to identify this problem. Obviously, Major Johns is correct in his analysis of the flow of fuel. The other three ships are also looking at the same situation, with the possible exception of the Russians, who seem to have built a different spaceship."

Bob Jackson said, "All right. I think I may have found the problem. We have eight rockets spread out around the main spacecraft. It takes a lot longer for the fuel to reach the rockets farthest from the injection point. As a result, the speed we are loading the fuel is too slow to reach the rocket farthest from where we start to inject the fuel. The farthest rockets will have little fuel, while the rockets nearest to the injection point could have too much. Does anyone else agree or disagree with me?"

Everyone thought for a moment.

Then, Dorothy spoke, "I believe what you are saying is correct. The question is: how will we get an equal amount of fuel to all eight rockets at the same time?"

Everyone concurred with her statement, nodding their heads.

"I am open to any and all suggestions, so please do not be afraid to speak up. I have a lot of confidence in this group."

Major Johns said, "Right now, we have only one fuel line that injects the fuel. We may be able to add a few more lines at a certain point where we can separate the flow so that each rocket will receive the right amount."

"How long would that take to build these extra lines and connect them to the control system?" Tom asked.

"Probably a month or so if we all worked twenty-four hours a day."

Bob said, "We cannot do that. We do not have enough time for that. If we cannot figure out a faster way to solve this, then we would do that as a last resort, but we do not know what the situation on Earth will be in a month. Are there any other possibilities?"

Suddenly, Grissom spoke up. "Hi everyone, my name is Grissom. My daughter,

Janet will be a passenger on the spaceship. She is a great kid, and I hope you all get to meet her. I was one of the first people to work on building this spaceship until my wife died of cancer, and now, I am also sick with a brain tumor. I am not asking for anyone's sympathy. However, I have been studying your instrument readings and trying to figure out how to speed up the flow of plasma to each rocket on an even basis. I have another solution for you to consider. To inject the fuel, I assume you are using magnets to draw the fuel into the system. Perhaps if we vary each magnet's strength depending on each rocket's location, we could make the flow more evenly. You would have to do some math to figure out how strong a magnet you want at each position, but this might work. You would not have to rebuild anything."

"Thank you for your suggestion. Does anyone have any comments on what Grissom just said?"

There was another moment of silence.

"I think this may work," said Dorothy. "What a fantastic idea, Grissom."

Tom asked Major Johns how long it would take to install the magnets or change their strength in various locations.

"As soon as we calculate the fuel flow based on the strength of each magnet, which I know Dorothy and Carson and their team can do, we can adjust the fuel injection system."

"It should not take longer than a day, sir," said Carson. "We will probably use some kind of inverse proportion formula, which should keep it simple."

"Does everyone agree with this? If you have another suggestion, now is the time to say it."

Everyone was silent.

"Well done, Grissom. Why don't you help Dorothy and Carson with the calculations so that the major and his men can adjust the magnets. That was a real team effort."

All the people in the room stood up and clapped for Grissom and slapped his back, congratulating him for his idea, all giving each other high-fives. Grissom went with Dorothy and Carson to do the math. Tom made an announcement to the ship that they would probably delay the launch by only twenty-four hours. He also contacted the other spacecraft, giving them directions and tasking them to see if there was any other way to fix the system.

Two hours later, Dorothy, Carson, and Grissom gave the data to fix the magnets to Tom. Tom thought they would be thrilled, but all three of them looked like a bomb had hit them.

"Thanks for the data, Dorothy. You should be looking thrilled. What is the problem now?"

"The data is fine and is correct. However, to ensure the flow is even, we still need someone who can stand there and adjust the flow, controlling the flow with a lever as necessary. This person will not burn up, but the exhaust from all the gas would overwhelm them. They would die within a few days. This person will not be on the flight."

"Is there any way to prevent this from happening? What if we put the person in a spacesuit?"

"The spacesuit might help prevent some of the fumes from getting through. This will allow the person to live a few more days, but we are talking about some of the strongest gasses ever made. This person is definitely going to breathe it into their lungs. Whoever does this is going to die days after the launch."

"What kind of death are we talking about? Please explain."

"We spoke to Dr. Sato about the effects to expect after the launch is complete and if there was a treatment. Dr. Sato said even a small amount of this fuel would prove deadly. There is no treatment for something like this. The only thing that can be done is to provide morphine or other pain medicine until they pass away. This person will be standing there for thirty minutes, maybe. By the time the launch is complete, this person will have difficulty breathing, and he/she will also feel burning sensations all over their body. It will feel like you are on fire. He or she is definitely going to die a horrible death."

"In that case, we will try to find another way. If we have to stay for six months, then we stay. I cannot possibly ask a person to volunteer for such a great sacrifice knowing such a horrible death awaits. It would not be fair to anyone." Tom thought of his father's painful last years. "I will let the team and the other spaceships know that we will just have to postpone our launches and look for another solution."

Dorothy, Carson, and Major Johns all looked crestfallen over another postponement.

"I am so sorry. Carson and I share the blame. We should have done a better job in our analysis before any of this happened," said Dorothy.

After a moment, Grissom spoke up. "Tom, I have known you a long time, and I know you could not ask anyone to die this way. However, there does not appear to be any other solution. Each day you postpone the launch means there is a possibility you will never launch. Therefore, I am volunteering to adjust the flow of fuel for you. It is the only way."

Dorothy, Carson, and the others standing there went into shock and put their hands over their faces.

"Grissom, thanks for volunteering, but I cannot do that to you. I have known you for a long time. What will I tell Janet: that I sent you to your death? I cannot do it. We need to find a different way. There has to be something we can do without such a sacrifice."

"There is no other way, and you know that is the truth. You are not sending me to my death. First of all, I am going to be dead within six months anyway. My end has been slated, once I got this brain tumor. I am already experiencing some pain due to my cancer. Please do not tell Janet until some time has passed after the launch. I want to see this rocket go into space.

"I am willing to suffer the consequences of my doing this so that Janet and the rest of you can go on your mission. If you don't go, you could be sending all the people on this ship to their deaths. Promise me you will find a new home and that Janet will be happy as long as she lives. That will make my sacrifice worth it. I will die knowing I did something to save humanity. The only other thing I ask is that the major and his soldiers bury me next to my beloved wife. Please let me do this."

All the people there started to cry. They all looked at Tom for his decision.

Tom did not see any way except to do what Grissom wanted. What a noble man Grissom was for being willing to do this.

"Grissom, I guess I am going to have to accept your wonderful and brave offer. Of course, we have your DNA, and we can create a new Grissom, but we are all going to miss the real you. What you are willing to do is beyond the scope of what any person could be expected to do. When people go into war, they know that they may have to make the ultimate sacrifice but hope that they will live and come home to their families. Very few of them knew exactly how they were going to die and how much pain they would be in." Tom put his hand on Grissom's shoulder briefly. "When Janet is safe, at the appropriate time, we will let her know what a courageous decision you made. I do not feel comfortable letting Janet know at this time what you are going to do. I do not want her to cry and be miserable during the launch. We certainly will not forget your sacrifice. You are a great hero, my friend."

Tom then hugged Grissom tightly. Grissom followed Dorothy and Carson to meet with the major to make the necessary adjustments to the magnets.

Tom relayed the information to the other ships and told them that someone may have to stand outside near the fuel pump to make the adjustments. The other commanders said they would see if anyone would volunteer. If not, they might have to order someone to do it since time was of the essence.

Tom then went on the view screen to make the announcement to the ship that they had found a way to launch, and within twenty-four hours, they would try again.

In the next few hours, the major, and his team, worked fervently to make the changes. He then ran some simulations with Tom, Dorothy, and Carson, looking on as well as Grissom. Dorothy and Carson explained to the major what Grissom needed to do and where he needed to stand to do it.

The major was to keep an eye on Grissom the whole time in case someone had to pull him out early. As soon as Grissom finished, the major would ensure he would be taken care of until the end. When the major heard the sacrifice Grissom would make, he and the other soldiers stood at attention and gave him a big salute.

The president walked up to Grissom and shook his hand. "You're a man of honor. I will do what I can to give you the Congressional Medal of Honor as soon as I can."

Keepng Them Busy

Chapter 57 – Keeping Them Busy

Yuri Pavlov, the Oligarch, near Moscow

President Ivanov was sitting in his office in the Kremlin, surrounded by state officials and generals. As the second forty-eight-hour count-down began, he contacted Yuri, as always, via the Russian network.

When Yuri signed on, Ivanov welcomed him. "Yuri, the great day is here at last. Soon we will launch our new spaceship that can reach the farthest galaxies in the search for a planet to live on. You should be commended for doing such a fantastic job on the Russian spaceship. We have also noted that the American craft is getting ready for launch again."

"Yes, President Ivanov. I am aware the Americans, it seems, have fixed the fuel problem and are going to try again. They are planning to make their second try at a launch. We have been in contact with them as well as the Germans and the Australians."

"Yuri, what I am telling you now is strictly confidential. Only you and your co-commanders can be trusted with this information. You cannot share what I am about to say to you with anyone on the other three ships. Do you understand that?"

"Yes, Mr. Ivanov. I understand completely."

"If you do tell anyone, I will remove you as commander, and you will be charged with treason. You will either spend the rest of your life in prison or be put to death. Do I make myself clear?"

"Yes, my President. What do you wish to tell me, and how can I help you?"

"Only Russians can be the first to settle on a new world. We have always been first when it comes to space travel, and our work is far superior to the Americans. Once the Americans and the Russians are in orbit, we are going to shoot down the American spacecraft. It will be totally destroyed. I cannot let the United States become the first country to settle on a new planet. I cannot even understand why they are launching first. We are the greatest nation when it comes to space. If we destroy the American spaceship, it will be easy for you to force the Germans and Australians to do what you want. If the Germans and Australians do not follow your orders, you will also destroy their ships. You will do what you have to with assistance from us to destroy the vessels. Do I make myself clear?"

Yuri was horrified, but he had no choice. He had to accept the orders or face his own death. His family was on board. If the Americans found out about this plan, there would be a space war that neither commander wanted. It would only end with one of their ships being destroyed.

"My President, how will you shoot the Americans down? They will be moving at a breakneck speed. Our missiles may not be able to catch up with a ship going that fast. It will be tough to accomplish."

"Leave that to me, Yuri. I have already spoken with the generals responsible for our missiles. We plan to launch at least eight missiles at various European targets and one missile at the spaceship. That way we will keep the Americans and their allies busy playing defense. The Americans will think we are beginning a large attack on Europe and will move to defend Estonia and Ukraine. They will not realize our primary target until it is too late for them to do anything about it. The generals assure me that we do have missiles capable of hitting the ship while they orbit Earth. They will just have to make sure the missiles are on the right trajectory. The spaceship is too large to avoid a missile attack like this."

"I understand, sir. We will settle the first planet colony for the greatness of Mother Russia. But what happens if, for some reason, the spaceship evades the missile? Do you have a back-up plan?"

"Yes, Yuri, we do have a back-up plan. If the missile fails, it will be up to you to destroy the spaceship. You have been given some very destructive missiles of your own that you will launch at them. After all, if our missile fails to hit the American ship, they will most likely come after you. Then it will be your ship in danger of being destroyed. Surely, you cannot allow this to happen."

"I wish I could share your confidence, sir. What makes you think your plan will succeed? Dr. Burns is a very resourceful commander. He was a fighter pilot, sir."

"Yuri, calm down. I guarantee success. The Americans have spent too much time fighting amongst themselves about the course of action they should take when it comes to the armed forces. Because of the natural disasters that have hit the country in several places, they have lost much of their firepower and missile capability. Now, America is weak. President Stevens will not be able to retaliate, despite what he says. We know they have disarmed many of their nuclear missiles in their silos, so they will not be able to use them against us. They have been weakened while we have become stronger. Mr. Burns has not fought a battle in outer space, and I doubt he is capable of doing so. We are now capable of fighting back if they choose to attack us. Be confident, Yuri. It will be over in a matter of days, and Russia will be victorious."

"I will go back to the ship now and prepare. I have confidence in you, Mr. Ivanov, and the Russian generals. You will go down in history as the man who defeated and destroyed the American empire. We will be the victor and go on to a long and prosperous space flight."

"Thank you. Now go to work and prepare for the coming battle. Make sure all your weapons are ready to use once you get into orbit. Dr. Burns is no match for you or your ship. No matter what happens, the Americans must not succeed. Is that clear?"

"Yes, sir. I will prepare our launch and weapons immediately."

Need To Know

Chapter 58 – Need To Know

President Stevens, the Imagine, Rocky Mountains, CO

Friday mid-afternoon, with T-3 hours and counting, everyone was involved in the launch. They'd been running around the clock, performing their duties. President Stevens watched as the crew checked for leaks and listened as they performed air-to-ground voice checks with launch control. He knew it had always been United States policy not to start a war. But at the same time that Ivanov was plotting to blow up the American spacecraft, President Stevens was preparing for an attack on the Russians if the European countries were attacked first. He had the Pentagon aim all of the remaining missiles at Russia and moved all the nuclear submarines within shooting distance of Russia. Several aircraft carriers were transferred from the Middle East to the Black Sea.

As he stood near Major Johns at mission control, he was informed that someone was there to see him with urgent intelligence. He stepped away to take it. The CIA gave the president a classified report that proved the Russians planned to destroy the spacecraft flown by Dr. Burns.

When the president read the signals intelligence report, he was appalled. The Russians had not found the listening device that had been planted in the Kremlin. Ivanov was not planning to withdraw from his plans to conquer Europe and perhaps the world. Ivanov and Putin had always wanted to restore the Soviet Union. To Ivanov, these natural disasters meant an opportunity to inflict more danger on everyone until they surrendered to Russia. He probably felt the Americans were weak and could not defend the NATO allies. That was one thing. Attempting to destroy the American spaceship was another problem.

Why would Ivanov want to destroy everything that these space explorers had cooperated on for twenty years? There were many benefits to having four spaceships search for a new world instead of only the Russian ship doing so. After all, these four spaceships had worked together for almost twenty years in preparation for securing a new planet in the spirit of cooperation. President Stevens did not want an escalation of war with Russia, but it seemed inevitable at this point. Plans needed to be set up and followed if the spaceship was to be saved.

The president knew Tom would be busy on the ship and would not let anyone board once a countdown began. If he could not get through to him, he would have to tell Major Johns to stop the launch again.

After fifteen minutes, he contacted Tom on his view screen.

"Mr. President, what is wrong? It must be very urgent."

"Hi, Tom. You are correct. We intercepted communication from Mr. Ivanov, describing plans to blow up your spaceship after it reaches orbit. The Germans and Australians will be destroyed after you, in all probability. Evidently, Ivanov never wanted to cooperate to save humanity. He is still obsessed with power and wants the Russian ship with Yuri to be the only one that will settle on a new planet."

"That is very disturbing. Is Yuri part of the plan? I have had some problems with him, but I very much doubt he planned to blow up my ship. Are you sure this is true?"

"I wish it were not true. The CIA caught Ivanov discussing the plot and all of his plans. As for Yuri, with his own life and career at risk, he will not disobey Mr. Ivanov or help you. We think he is a puppet for Mr. Ivanov. He is just obeying orders. Can you postpone the launch again for a short duration so we can meet with the officers on the Imagine and the people in the Pentagon?

It is vital that we are all on the same page. We can make up a story for the reason to postpone it again. We cannot let on we know about the Russian plan. If we do not meet, there is no guarantee that you will escape the Russians' attack. There is no guarantee with our help, either. But you will have a much better chance to defend yourselves."

"Okay. I will announce a six-hour delay due to the installing of a few magnets in the fueling process. We might as well let people know that the liquid hydrogen and liquid oxygen propellants are almost finished being filled. We should be ready to meet you within one hour. I will let you onboard again. Please come to the bridge."

CHAPTER 59

The Rising Tide

Chapter 59 – The Rising Tide

Tom Burns, the Imagine, Rocky Mountains, CO

Tom hung up with the president. *Just when I think we might succeed and launch, someone else wants to interfere with our mission*, he thought.

Minutes later, Tom made an announcement informing everyone that the launch had been postponed a third time due to a few maintenance issues. All personnel had to remain at their designated areas until otherwise notified. Meanwhile, the principal officers went to the bridge to meet with the president and Pentagon via the viewscreen.

After setting up communication between all the parties on a secure line, the president spoke first. He repeated the intercepted communication that was obtained by the CIA. It was clear the Russians were going to attack Europe to set up an attack on the Imagine. The one thing they had going for them was the element of surprise since the Russians did not suspect America could do anything to prevent the attack.

The president was willing to attack Russia at multiple locations. Two main issues had to be discussed. First, should the spaceship even launch knowing that they could be struck by a nuclear missile designed to kill everyone and destroy the mission? Second, should the United States attack the Russians before the Russians attacked the United States?

The generals in the Pentagon wanted to deal with the second issue. About half of them felt a first-strike initiative was better than waiting for Russia to attack.

"If we destroy them first, they might not be able to retaliate or shoot down the spaceship. It would teach the Russians a lesson not to meddle in the United States' affairs," said one of the generals.

The other half of the generals preferred to see Russia attack first since American missile defenses in Poland and on the submarines could effectively blow up the Russian missiles before they did the damage. If America blew up a Russian nuclear missile while still over Russia, the radioactive fallout would kill millions of Russians.

After several generals weighed in on that issue, the president asked Tom and his officers what they wanted the United States Armed Forces to do, knowing hostile missiles would be shot at them. There was no guarantee the missile defense could block every Russian missile.

After a short discussion with his officers, Tom stood up.

"This is the biggest decision we have had to make as a team. I was not sure how we would get along with the Russians in space, given some of the problems we have already had with them. Still, the idea that we will be shot down and killed by Russian nuclear missiles is quite terrifying. My understanding of United States policy is we do not attack another country until they attack first. My feeling about attacking them first would depend on the number of missiles they plan to launch at us and our allies. If the number is large, we should hit them first. However, suppose we are talking about a few missiles. In that case, I say let them attack first, and we can destroy the missiles before they hit anything of consequence."

Next, Bob Jackson stood up. "The officers of this ship will support whatever the president decides. However, it is our feeling that we cannot wait to launch forever. We cannot postpone our launch due to a Russian threat. The Russians will always have the capability of shooting at us. Whether they succeed in destroying us is another story. We have worked too hard and too long to back down to a threat like this. If the

United States government can protect us until we are out of orbit, then we all agree we want to launch soon and take our chances."

"You are telling us that you are not afraid to be shot down?" asked the president.

Tom replied, "All of us are prepared to take the chance and launch, sir. However, I think Major Johns and his team might be able to help us here. He has done an incredible job with the fueling system and launch process for us. Major Johns and his men have been in the missile business for over twenty years. They have a tremendous knowledge of how missiles fly and at what trajectories they will be fired. I am willing to give Major Johns control of my ship until the danger passes, or we are too far away to be shot down. He is capable of adjusting our trajectory or try to evade the missiles. He is an absolute professional. I trust him to keep us alive."

Bob added, "The United States Armed Forces are the strongest in the world. The Russians just don't know it yet. They think we have been weakened considerably. I trust the president and his generals will make the right decision whether to strike first or not."

"Then it is settled. Tom, meet with Major Johns to outline your escape possibilities from the missiles. I will call Ivanov one more time in a few minutes and let him know we are onto him. If he decides to attack us, we will wallop them. This meeting is adjourned. Please keep me up to date on all decisions you make from now on until the crisis is over. The generals in the Pentagon have a green light to attack Russia as a defensive maneuver.

Yellow Light

Chapter 60 – Yellow Light

President Stevens, the Imagine, Rocky Mountains, CO

President Stevens and Major Johns watched the crew prepare for the launch. It was unique to him that this spaceship was ready to be launched. He doubted anything would happen with the Russians until the American spaceship launched. With his generals on standby, he decided to call Ivanov to try to defuse the situation.

President Stevens wanted to see how Ivanov reacted to his words. It was always a game of chess between Ivanov and himself. Once in awhile, Ivanov would tell the truth, but often he lied to try and deceive others to further his own goals.

Before calling Ivanov, he contacted the Australian and German prime ministers to let them know what he had uncovered about the Russian plot. They were furious at Ivanov and offered to help President Stevens in any way possible. They would inform their commanders of the threatening situation. As Dr. Burns had predicted, neither prime minister could see a way to continuously postpone the launch. They all agreed they would keep in continuous contact until the situation was resolved.

He dialed.

Ivanov asked the president why he was calling.

"I understand our spaceships will be going on a long journey together soon. I wanted to congratulate you on working so hard to get your spaceship on its journey. The Russians should be proud of what they have accomplished. Our spaceship had no government support, but they succeeded and are now ready to go."

"Comrade Stevens, yes, I know about the launches. It is a great time in history. Despite all the natural disasters taking place, we can show the world that there is still hope for everyone. Russia has done its part in making this happen, and we hope all four ships arrive at a planet where the people can grow together."

Stevens knew this was a lie based on the information obtained through the CIA. He wondered if Ivanov knew about the plans he had just discussed with everyone. Somehow, he had to tell Ivanov not to do anything stupid or face the consequences.

It would be better for everyone in Russia—and the United States—if they could prevent nuclear missiles from being fired. The effects of these bombs would cost millions of their lives, including his and Ivanov.

"Mr. Ivanov, I need to know your intentions about this journey. All the spaceships are to be guaranteed safe passage out of the solar system. Do you agree with this? We do not want to see anyone attacked or hurt as they go through space. All the commanders have their families on board and the DNA of millions of people, including yours and mine. We may not be able to survive on Earth, but we can hope to live again somewhere else in the galaxy. We all need to work together to ensure the success of the trip."

"I can assure you, President Stevens, that we do not intend to interfere with any of the launches. We have better things to do than shoot at rockets. Why would you even consider suggesting I would do such a thing? Perhaps we can help you help those citizens stuck in the natural disaster or earthquakes in California and Alaska. I am certain you have your hands full dealing with those situations."

This answer told President Stevens that Ivanov would not admit he would attack several sites, including the spaceship. It also said to him that Ivanov thought the US was too weak to defend a military attack and that the US was totally focused on lending support to the earth-quake victims. Obviously, according to Ivanov, the US was not paying attention to anything Russia was doing.

Stevens was mad at Ivanov but decided not to show it.

"No, we are fine and working well with our first responders and others to aid the victims of our earthquakes. We do not need any help with the earthquakes. We did have to shut down some nuclear warheads in Nevada, but I think you already know that. I am going to warn you now. Please do not try to take advantage of the situation. There is too much at stake in the world for any kind of military action and the response it may receive."

"Don't worry. We are not planning on any kind of military action anytime soon. However, if we wanted to, it would be difficult to stop us, given the conditions in America and around the world."

Stevens had heard enough. Millions of lives were going to be lost because Ivanov was not going to back down.

"Mr. Ivanov, I wish you well. Let us try to keep the peace between us and be friends with each other. The world is counting on us. Goodbye."

After he hung up the phone, he contacted the Joint Chiefs of Staff and the German and Australian prime ministers.

"I just spoke to Ivanov. He is definitely going to attack numerous targets and will not give an inch or back down. Please have the satellites focus on all the missile sites in Russia to determine the location of where they will be firing their missiles. Also, locate the Russian military. We are going to strike them. We hope they will think twice about retaliating."

The general replied from the Pentagon, "We have taken care of all of that already. We are monitoring the Russian movement twenty-four hours a day. The missile activity is coming from two different sites. Their military troops are along the borders of every country from Ukraine to Estonia. They have some navy ships in the Black Sea. We do not think they are going to launch their full arsenal. We are well prepared to carry out any orders in a very efficient manner. Unfortunately, when one deals with nuclear weapons, many civilians will die. Are you willing to accept that?"

Stevens said, "Ordinarily, I would not be willing to accept that, but we do not have any choice here. We cannot let Ivanov shoot down the spaceships and take over several countries without responding to him. Make sure that at least one or two missiles will hit the Kremlin. This does not have to be a nuclear missile, but strong enough to destroy the building. His obsession with power is going to destroy him."

"All of your orders will be carried out, sir."

"Wait till they fire, then give the full response."

"Don't worry, Mr. President. We are ready for anything they have. Where will you be during the attack?"

"I will be near the spaceship, watching it launch. Wherever it goes, I hope it avoids situations like this. This world is crazy for letting us do this to each other. I will talk to you later. Bye."

The president hung up. He was confident they could handle the Russians. If the spaceship succeeded in getting out of the solar system, it would be a real positive experience. However, that would soon be followed by the worst possible experience a president could have.

He now had to call Tom again and focus on helping launch his ship and avoid being hit by any missiles, if possible. This was going to be an experience that would never be forgotten. Of course, he might not live very much longer to remember it.

CHAPTER 61

The longest Two Hours

Chapter 61 – The Longest Two Hours

Tom Burns, the Imagine, Rocky Mountains, CO

It had only been two hours since the meeting with the officers and the Pentagon. Tom wondered if he had made the right decision to launch. If he waited too long to launch, it might never happen, but they would be able to live for a few years on Earth. His officers were all supportive of his decision, however. They were all ready to assume the risks of the launch and journey.

Major Johns told Tom not to worry. It seemed like the major would do everything in his power not to let them get shot down. Obviously, he had been through a lot in his life. Tom knew he would keep them safe if possible. The keyword was possible. Tom had been going over the controls of the spaceship with Major Johns and the launch team, including Dorothy and Carson, waiting to hear from the president before giving the crew's final orders.

Was it possible to evade the missile in orbit? This had never been attempted before. There was no way to test this with simulations. If the Russian rocket did get through—into orbit—what would be the best course of action for the spaceship? No person on board could survive a direct hit by a nuclear bomb.

Then his thoughts were interrupted by the president's call.

"Yes, Mr. President. I hope I am going to hear good news."

"Hi, Tom, I am sorry that is not going to happen. Ivanov is going to go ahead and attack. My armed forces are all ready to take out targets in Russia and basically destroy them before they destroy us. If you do not launch, that may happen anyway, so you really have no choice but to go for it. I will be in the space center with Major Johns and Grissom and the others awaiting the launch. I can coordinate with the Pentagon from there. The Russians will not know my location, I hope. Also, I am in contact with the German and Australian prime ministers who are in contact with their commanders to let them know what is happening. They need to make their own decision about whether to launch their spaceship or not."

"Thank you, Mr. President, for bringing the full force of the United States to assist us with our launch. Trump was a disaster for the world. For years I hated the government and would do anything to avoid connections with it. Now you are about to save my life and many others.

"I will reset the launch to forty-eight hours again. I need to tell everyone on the ship what we face, as it is better to be transparent. I have to order them to battle stations once we get through the blackout period if we are still alive."

"Have faith, Tom. I am sure everything will turn out fine for you once you are traveling on your journey. Don't forget, my family is on board with you, and I will not let anything happen to them. I am not sure what will be left of civilization after Russia shoots their missiles. As they say, 'All hell is going to break loose.' And a lot of people are going to be going there. Go ahead and do your job, Tom, and leave the rest to the military and me. Good luck."

Tom said, "Thanks, Mr. President. I will be thinking of you if we survive this. Maybe the new planet will be named Stevens. You never know. Goodbye."

They hung up, and Tom went to the bridge to prepare the launch again. The president stayed in the space center and linked up back with the Pentagon. The moment in history was finally here. How would it turn out? Neither of them would know—until it was finished.

Deadly Serious

Chapter 62 – Deadly Serious

Sam Burns, the Imagine, Rocky Mountains, CO

Sam and Jose were in the cafeteria eating with a group of friends when the announcement came on. Sam had been wondering if they were ever launching as did many of the people on board. Many of those people had no idea how complicated things were about to become. Soon they would know what was transpiring.

"Good afternoon, everyone. I am sorry for the continued delays. I have some good news and some bad news, so please pay meticulous attention to what I am about to say."

Sam saw many of the people in the cafeteria groan.

"The good news is the launch will now proceed in forty-eight hours. We have fixed all the problems involved with the launch, and things are looking great."

Sam could hear everyone clapping. Finally, the Imagine would be on its way to Alpha Centauri or another destination. Sam was happy about the news but now worried about what the bad news was going to be. People were talking about the good news and giving each other high-fives. They completely forgot that there was a second part of the announcement. Sam had never heard his dad talk about bad news, so he knew it would be something serious.

"I am glad everyone is excited about the launch. Unfortunately, I also have to give you the bad news. I could keep this to my officers and myself, but I believe I must share it with you to be as transparent as possible. We have a severe problem. I am asking all of you to keep this information as confidential as possible. Do not contact anyone off the ship with the information that I am about to provide. It seems that the United States government has picked up information that once we are in orbit, the Russians are planning to destroy the spaceship."

Sam could not believe what he had just heard. Why would the Russian government want to destroy everything they had worked for? He looked around him. People were now either crying or becoming very angry. Everyone went from elation to total fear.

Tom continued, "I have been in constant contact with President Stevens, and there is a plan in place to help us launch and to evade the Russian missiles. It is a very delicate situation. I have informed the commanders of the German and Australian ships. The German and Australian prime ministers have been notified of the impending attack. Most likely, the Russians will attempt to destroy their crafts too. Both are furious and will cooperate with us in whatever way we wish. It has been decided that if we are killed first, the Germans and Australians are to break orbit and then make their own decisions about what to do and where to go. They do not have the firepower to fight a war with the Russians.

Mr. Ivanov apparently only wants Russia to settle on a new planet. This means we have to set up precisely what all of you will do once we launch and come out of the blackout period. First, I am giving each of you the option to leave the spaceship and not join us on the mission. I cannot force you to face a missile attack. We will do everything in our power to prevent being destroyed. Still, I cannot give any guarantee it will not happen. I can certainly understand some may now have a great fear about dying at the Russians' hands. However, anyone who is on this spaceship will quite possibly be facing dangers, and this may cost lives. We do not know what dangers await us. We all hope for a very uneventful trip to a new planet.

I have given the command to launch again in forty-eight hours, as I do not believe we can keep postponing. The Russian attack can come whether we launch now or in one year. The threat will always be present. Therefore, my officers and I feel it is better to confront the threat head-on and take the necessary steps to prevent the Russians from destroying us. I am giving you one hour to make your decision. If you wish to leave the spaceship and remain behind, I respect your decision. I am hoping you all stay and that we will get through this together. If you wish to leave, please pack your belongings and go to the entrance to the spaceship. I will be there in one hour to let you disembark. At that point, I will announce the new directives to provide us with the best opportunity to make it through this attack. Thank you, everyone, and may you forever hold onto the promise of tomorrow and that together we can overcome."

Sam and Jose started looking around again. It seemed that there must have been a hundred different conversations happening at the same time. For Sam and Jose, there really was no choice. Their fathers were officers, so they would be staying. Sam did not know if a few or many people would leave due to the danger presented to them. They could only wait and see what would happen in one hour. They decided to go to the entrance to stand with Tom and the officers.

Sarah, Dr. Sato, and Luis joined them. Dr. Sato and Luis made it clear they were staying, as they believed that Tom would not deliberately send them to their death if there was a way to prevent it from happening. They were willing to take that chance.

"In fact, based on all the discussions we have had with those who have funded this endeavor and those interested in the medical application of our ongoing scientific research, I couldn't leave all my work behind. It would feel absolutely wrong. Better to face it together, given all the progress we can make to push the limits of human potential, and I feel you will help us overcome this and many things that lie ahead, Dr. Burns. I didn't sign up thinking this was going to be easy."

Tom smiled.

Luis turned toward Tom and said, "There is no place I would rather be than going on this spaceship with you."

Tom and the others stood near the entrance waiting quietly for anyone who wanted to depart the ship. Sam and Jose expected as many as a hundred would be leaving. However, to their surprise, there were precisely zero people who wanted to depart. Sam knew each person had their own private reason for staying. Still, they also knew if they stayed behind, they would probably die soon anyway. In any case, Tom and the officers seemed relieved about the situation. There did not seem to be any panic. In fact, it seemed that all the people on board were deadly serious about being prepared for the possible missile attack.

"May I have your attention again, please. I would like to thank every person on this ship for having the confidence in me and my officers to get you through this safely. We will do our very best. I will be giving you these directions, so please pay attention to every word I say. The safety of this ship may depend on our actions while in orbit. First of all, do not release your seat belts unless I give the word.

Second, we are going to be moving some of you to more strategic locations so that we can access our weapons and shuttles faster. All shuttle pilots and shuttle control crew will be strapped in as close as possible to the shuttles. All shuttles will be armed and ready to fire the weapons on board. All weapons experts will be strapped in near the space torpedoes so we can fire them as fast as we need to. Everyone will have their spacesuit on for some time after launch, so please make sure you are as comfortable as possible.

Also, make sure you are near someone else in case you get stuck somewhere. Our communicators may or may not be working depending on the events as they unfold. Senior officers will be in charge. In the event something happens to me, Bob Jackson or another appointed officer will give directions. Please do whatever they say. Our lives may depend on it.

"If the ship is hit, there are only five shuttles for evacuation. Please try to get to the shuttle launch. It is the only way off the ship if we are hit by a missile. That is all the instructions for now. If I need to update them, I will do so at two hours to launch, in which case all of you must be strapped into your positions. The forty-eight-hour countdown has now begun."

Doveryai no Proveryai
(Trust, but Verify)

Chapter 63 – Doveryai, no proveryai (Trust, but Verify)

Yuri Pavlov, the Oligarch, near Moscow

"Fire eight missiles when I instruct you to," Ivanov had told the Russian generals in the Kremlin.

Ivanov was intent on reestablishing the Soviet Union. No country was allowed to evacuate the Soviet Union. One missile was a ballistic missile with a nuclear tip. This would be the one to shoot down the spaceship. The other seven missiles were to be shot in Ukraine and Estonia, former Russian colonies during the Soviet Union.

Yuri was anxious. If the Russian missile attack failed, it would be up to him to destroy the American spaceship. It was entirely possible that his own ship would be destroyed if he were unable to do so. His family and many friends were on board with him, and he did not want any harm to come to them. When he first started on this project, Putin nor Ivanov had mentioned anything about destroying the other ships. Only in the last few years had Ivanov become more involved with the space voyage.

There were times Yuri enjoyed collaborating with Dr. Burns, and times he did not want to even speak with him. It was not personal. It was just that Yuri believed he knew more than Dr. Burns about rockets and spaceships and how to build a superior ship that would reach the desired destination safely. While Yuri thought that Dr. Burns was a little stubborn, he admired him for pursuing something that had never been achieved.

He also believed that Dr. Burns was a capable military commander. If the two ships had to battle with each other, Yuri had no idea who would survive. If Dr. Burns were aware of the attack, he would prove to be a formidable adversary. With Ivanov intending to destroy all the other ships, it made things difficult for Yuri.

What would happen if he needed help once they left the solar system? That was one of the benefits of having four ships. Each ship could assist the other, and everyone could learn from each other. He also enjoyed working with the other two commanders. It would be nice if all four ships could land on the same planet and live in peace.

Ivanov interrupted him for an update. Yuri informed him that now there were around forty hours left before the Americans launched. They had had another six-hour delay in fixing the fuel system. The Russian ship was due to start two hours after them. So far, all of the systems on the Russian spaceship were working well. They were ready.

Ivanov then told him, "Yuri, tomorrow will be a great day for the Russians. I have spoken to Stevens and told him that we are cooperating in everything and have no plans to harm anyone on the voyage. They may suspect something, but I do not think so. Please listen to me. One hour after you launch, we will send seven missiles towards the Ukraine and Estonia. I expect the Polish missile defense will try and knock them down or blow them up. Twenty minutes after we send those seven missiles, we will launch the ballistic missile with a nuclear warhead straight to the American ship. I doubt they will expect this attack and certainly not a nuclear attack. They will be too busy complaining about and destroying the missiles we sent twenty minutes earlier. They will begin to debate with their allies about what to do next like they always do. Once the American ship is destroyed, it is up to you to convince the other two ships to support you, or you will let them know they will also be destroyed. I will contact the German and Australian prime ministers and give them the option of joining us. If they disagree with this, you can destroy them at will. Is everything clear to you?"

"Do you not believe that the United States could attack you with their nuclear arsenal?"

"They have disarmed most of their land-based nuclear weapons, so I am not afraid of them. They are having too many problems with earthquakes and other natural disasters to think about war with us. Stevens does not like war. He will chicken out from a fight with us. He would probably try to have a United Nations meeting to protest our missiles. Still, it will not do any good, as we will veto whatever they want. Now I must go to meet our generals in the Kremlin to prepare our missiles and observe everything. Good luck with your mission. Don't forget to clone me soon after you leave the solar system so I can govern in space."

Yuri hung up. Until the American ship was destroyed, he was going to be very nervous. He did not trust anyone at this point. Yet, Ivanov was right about one thing. If the missile failed to hit the United States ship, Dr. Burns would come after him.

Now it was either kill—or be killed.

Country Mile

Chapter 64 – Country Mile

Tom Burns, the Imagine, Rocky Mountains, CO

The shuttle was armed and ready to speed toward the Russian ship if necessary. For the next thirty-eight hours, Tom and his officers focused on making sure everything was perfect for the launch.

His military officers made sure they could launch torpedoes as soon as the missile was launched towards them.

Tom was informed that Grissom was getting ready to go outside and help with the fuel. Major Johns was in continuous contact with Tom, the president, and the Pentagon. He was prepared to do whatever was necessary to get the ship in orbit and prevent it from being blown up by a Russian missile.

Sam and Jose were strapped in together near the bridge in Tom's line of vision. Both of them seemed nervous about the launch ever since hearing about the potential of a Russian attack.

Dr. Sato and the medical staff had prepared supplies in the event anyone had an injury during lift-off or during the attack. Tom saw her anxiety level register all over her face. Although Tom knew she wished for an antidote beyond any she had on hand for radiation exposure should the time come, there was not much she could do about a missile attack. No treatment would help them if they were struck by a nuclear missile.

The rest of the ship people were all set to go, all waiting for the announcement to come two hours before the flight.

Exactly two hours before launch, Tom came on the viewscreen again to make his announcement.

"Everyone, may I have your attention again, please. We are now two hours away from blastoff. All systems are go. I am not a man of religion, but I do support your right to pray as you wish. I have already said my prayers in the hopes of a safe launch, and I encourage all of you to pray in silence if you wish. I have never heard God speak to me, but if there is a God, I think he or she will be on our side. Best of luck, everyone. Let's get this done. It is going to be a hell of a ride."

The entire crew and passengers were strapped into their assigned places.

From the command post on the bridge, Tom was keeping track of everything. This time everything looked great.

Twenty minutes before liftoff, Tom instructed Major Johns to start pumping in the fuel.

Tom was impressed with Grissom as he made sure the flow was even and adjusting the lines and magnets as needed. Unfortunately, he was breathing in some of the fuel all the time, and it bothered Tom, recollecting his own father's last days.

As Tom and everyone heard the ship's countdown, the other three ships were also aware of the countdown. The countdown lights flashed 10, 9, 8, 7, 6, 5, 4, 3, 2, 1.

Suddenly, all eight rockets attached to the main ship, and the ship started to rise quickly. Smoke and fumes surrounded the Imagine.

Major Johns was doing a good job controlling the speed and trajectory as the ship moved into orbit. It was now going at 50,000 miles an hour, which was more than enough to break gravity and get into orbit. Five minutes before they reached orbit, the eight rockets detached. They would either go into orbit or fall back to Earth after a specific time. In eighteen minutes, the ship was out of the blackout period.

Tom blacked out suddenly. It was only for a few minutes. He was wide awake when they reached orbit and ready to spring into action.

First, Major Johns was contacted to tell him what an outstanding job had been done, and then Tom asked about Grissom.

"As the ship took off, Grissom fell down on his back. He gasped for air. Once the rocket was at a certain height, the president had run out to help him. When he saw Grissom, well, he knew the end was near. The president grabbed him and held him so he could see the spaceship moving away from Earth. He whispered a wish for his daughter, Janet. The president congratulated him and told him how proud he was and that he was a greater hero than all of the men who served America. Together, they had watched the ship go into space with his daughter. He knew that she was safe and would reach her destiny, and that soon he would be with his wife again. He smiled at the president and then slowly closed his eyes and died in the president's arms. When the president closed Grissom's eyes, he lifted him. He took Grissom into the space center to prepare him to be buried alongside his wife."

Tom cried as he listened to the major describe Grissom's last minutes.

"May his soul rest in peace. I will let Janet know at the appropriate time about the sacrifice he made so that we could launch the ship. How is the president holding up?"

"Hi, Tom. The launch looked fantastic," announced the president. "Now comes the hard part. In two hours, the Russian ship will launch, precipitating a whole bunch of events. None of these actions are going to be endearing to anyone. We expect the Russians are prepared to launch their missiles at the targets and your ship. I think he will send the missiles even if the Russian ship does not get off the ground. I am sure you and your shipmates are all prepared for this."

"Yes, we are, sir. All hands survived the launch, and we are all still strapped into our assigned places. We are ready to confront the Russians if we have to. We may have a surprise for the Russians when they fire their nuclear warhead at us."

"Keep in contact. We have a short time left, and then all hell is going to break loose probably. Good luck."

Tom made an announcement. He told everyone that the launch was a success and to stay where they were until the Russian threat had passed. They were going to have to evade one powerful nuclear missile. Tom could see everyone waiting in anticipation. He didn't blame them if they wondered whether everyone would die a horrible death in space. He watched his own son and Jose appear calm, and Sophie holding her mom's hands. He was sure they were as wracked with nerves as he felt, his body buzzing, his lips tight.

***

Two hours later, the Russian ship blasted off without a hitch. It joined Tom's ship in orbit as they waited for the Germans and Australians to launch. Once the Russians were in orbit, Tom was in continuous communication with Major Johns and the Pentagon. President Stevens and the Pentagon were waiting for the Russians to launch their missiles. They had expected them to be launched after the Russians were in orbit, but it was very quiet so far. Could the Russians have backed down from the plot? Did they know the Americans were ready for them? The only thing they could do was wait and keep on monitoring the Russians. The Russian missile would travel at 25,000 miles an hour. That would not give them a lot of time to decide or for Tom's ship to avoid it.

Two hours later, the fourth and final spaceship was in orbit. As soon as the Australians were in orbit, Tom and the other three captains heard from Ian Thorpe, who informed them they were fine and ready for the next move. Tom and the other three commanders knew that whatever decisions they made would mean life or death for the people on board their spaceships. Still, it wasn't clear yet if life and humanity's future were as precious to some as they were to Tom and his crew.

A Great Warship Needs Big Skies

Part V
Pioneers Providing
Nowhere to Hide

Chapter 65 – A Great Warship Needs Big Skies

Russian Federation President Ivanov, the Kremlin

Ivanov sensed something was wrong. He was inside the Kremlin with his generals but had not given the order to send his missiles. Could the Americans be aware of what they were doing? He did not think it could be this easy.

He thought perhaps that Stevens had tried to tell him or warn him that he knew about the plans. There were no signs that pointed to this, but he could not be sure. He asked his chief military officer what he thought.

The general replied, "We have not seen abnormal activity by the Americans anywhere. I am sure they are monitoring all the spaceships, but that would be normal. They also have a few subs in the Black Sea, but they have always been there, and they are quiet now. We did notice an aircraft carrier moving in our direction. Yet, our navy base at

Sevastopol has not noticed a change in their behavior. I am confident that we can destroy that spaceship. We must fire the missiles before they break orbit to leave the solar system."

Ivanov called Yuri. "Congratulations on getting into orbit. In less than a half-hour, we will launch the first set of missiles in Ukraine and Estonia's direction. It is an honor to follow our doctrine, is it not? Glory will once again be ours. In space, for the first time, you will be among the first Russians with a front-row seat view of another first we can claim. We will be the first to move beyond our current cyber and electronic warfare attacks in the form of one of our nation's space assets, the Oligarch. It is not just a step, a rover, or a station—it is the Oligarch. With it comes the great certainty that we will continue to be able to reduce any weaponized satellites, weaponized pseudo planets, and any threats to Russia's expansion. It has not gone unnoticed. You are already heralded in every news stream, on VKontakte and social media channels, among our diplomats who tout your success in world forums and summits. No nation with any ambitions will be able to avoid replicating our space weapons' sophistication, including our disruptive airborne lasers, that equip your ship once we destroy the American ship. You destroy the German and Australian ships if they do not comply with your authority. Since monarchies have become relevant again, you may soon hear from Earth's monarchs. I will put them through to you. They will be delighted to convey their country's wishes."

"I am sure it will be a welcome gesture."

"There may be cause for more than gestures."

"To those, I will defer to you, of course, sir. We have gained more influence than the Americans in the last decade, and I am happy to oblige our doctrine. Thank you and my family thanks you. May it be one of many changes for our beloved Russia and the people who left our protection.

For the time being, however, I do have a question," said Yuri. "Dr. Burns is a smart man. He may suspect something is happening. What shall I tell him if he is suspicious of anything? They may be able to see us power up our weapons on board."

"Do not prepare to fire on the other two ships until the Americans are destroyed. I am sure you can do this in one hour after we are done. They will not suspect anything if you just act normal and keep your ship in orbit as planned."

"I will do my best, sir. I am sure we will talk again later."

"Yes, Yuri, we will be toasting to the New Russian planet in a new galaxy. You will be a national hero on Earth, as well as all of your crew and family. We finally get to see the day when we can boast of how superior we are to the Americans."

Safety First

.

Chapter 66 – Safety First

Yuri Pavlov, the Oligarch

Minutes later, Yuri received a call from Dr. Burns on the view screen.

"Congratulations on getting into orbit. It is an inspiring day. All four ships finally did it. The German and Australian commanders have had no problems either."

Yuri did not notice anything abnormal about what Dr. Burns had just said. It appeared Tom was excited, as he claimed to be, and after all those years of hard work, why would he not be? It was clear that Tom did not suspect a thing.

"Tom, congratulations to you too. I know we have been a little harsh with each other, but now we can work together and cooperate as we make our way to a new galaxy. I hope to see you onboard the Russian ship when you visit us sometime."

Tom said, "Yes, Yuri. That would be nice. See you later."

Inside, Yuri felt a little sad for him. He was happy to hear that Tom was now very pleased. In the next few hours, he would be dead along with the rest of his crew. Yuri had done what he needed to do to protect his family and team on board the Russian ship. That was the only thing that mattered to him.

It was going to be a long journey, but he would be a national hero like Ivanov said.

He felt totally safe with the plans now. Before Ivanov had hung up with Ivanov, he'd heard him give the Russian general the order to send up the first seven missiles, headed to various cities in the Ukraine and Estonia, including Lviv, and Tallinn, the capitols. Several million people were living in those two cities and the surrounding areas. It would only be a short matter of time that the U.S. would be preoccupied.

Waiting for Dead Man's Shoes

Chapter 67 – Waiting for Dead Men's Shoes

Tom Burns, the Imagine

The U.S and its allies readied for the launch of the missiles.

Tom had a first-row seat to the whole thing on his spaceship in orbit. He watched the missiles from his command post with the officers the bridge. When the missiles hit, it would be utter chaos.

However, most of his crew did not have access to a view of Earth. This told Tom that there was only a short time before the nuclear missile would be launched at them. He immediately contacted Major Johns and the president to verify that he had also seen the missiles.

Major Johns had seen the missiles. He was standing by at the controls to maneuver the spaceship with Tom.

"Tom, all our military personnel and the president are intently monitoring the situation. First, we need to neutralize the seven missiles about to hit Ukraine and Estonia. The missile detection system in Poland was built around 2019. It is fully operational and ready to launch rockets. The Pentagon wanted to intercept the missiles before reaching their target while still over Russia or the Black Sea. Five minutes after the Russian missile launch, the missile defense sent out seven rockets on an intercept course for each Russian missile."

"Thank you for the update, Major." Tom stood by.

This was a very tense moment. The only thing Tom or anyone could do was wait to see if the interceptions were successful. At the Pentagon, the generals could see the missiles from Poland and Russia on the satellite radar system as they approached each other.

If one missile were to get by the defense system, it would mean certain death for many civilians.

"Dear God!" said one of the Pentagon generals.

Within seconds, Tom heard Major Johns and the president exclaim also.

The major explained, "All seven Russian missiles have been intercepted. Explosions can be seen over western Russian and the Black Sea as the missiles fall back to Earth."

Tom thought that since the missiles were intercepted, Ivanov must know now that the US was ready for whatever move he made. He decided to announce to his passengers the news about the interceptions, and the fact that the nuclear attack against them was coming soon.

"May I have your attention, please. Seven missiles were intercepted by the allied forces as the Russians attacked Europe. All of the damages appear to be in Russia. Please be ready for the strike against our ship. We may be changing speeds very rapidly and turning around to do whatever is necessary to avoid the Russian missile aimed at us. Please just strap in and hold on. This should be finished in a matter of minutes. Thank you."

There was no time for celebration. They were waiting for the next missile to be fired into space and attack the Imagine.

CHAPTER 68

Shto?

Chapter 68 – Shto?

Russian Federation President Ivanov, the Kremlin

Ivanov was livid with rage. The allies had just shot down his seven missiles. In the Kremlin, Ivanov and his generals were stunned. None of their missiles had made it through the missile defense in Poland. They had expected perhaps one or two missiles would be shot down, but not all seven. His generals wanted to call off the nuclear attack on the American spaceship, but Ivanov refused. He felt if he called it off, it would be a sign that he was a weak leader. He could not let failure be an option.

Indeed, they were going to retaliate. Ivanov was sure that President Stevens was going to call him any minute to file an official complaint and perhaps shoot a couple of bombs at some Russian troops somewhere in the world. However, no call from President Stevens came.

How dare Stevens get away with this!

Ivanov gave the order to shoot the American spaceship down. If he destroyed the spaceship, it would show his might to the world, and Russia would be in control again. His top general called the military base to fire the missile on its way.

They will never know what hit them, Ivanov thought. He expected the missile to be in the vicinity of the spaceship within thirty minutes.

CHAPTER 69

Flinch

Chapter 69 – Flinch

Tom Burns, the Imagine

Tom could see the missile from the spaceship as did the other three commanders.

As soon as he saw it, Tom told Major Johns, "Begin Operation Debris now."

The head of the Joint Chiefs of Staff in the Pentagon simply said, "Fire!" At that moment, three nuclear submarines in the Black Sea launched multiple missiles at strategic targets all over Russia. Five B-52 bombers took off from an aircraft carrier in the North Sea.

Tom and the Pentagon saw the missile immediately moving towards the Imagine. They estimated it would make impact thirty minutes after being launched.

Tom, who was surrounded on the bridge by his chief officers, said, "I suggest we haul our asses out of this mess. I am sure we are all going to do our jobs in the next thirty minutes, or we will not have to worry about anything any longer. Personally, I would much rather be somewhere else. Still, I am also sure that we have the most capable crew around to handle the incoming missile. When this is over, I promise to buy a round of drinks for everyone, even though it will not cost me anything."

That brought a smile to many of those on the bridge. They had been planning for this moment ever since the battle plans had been drawn up. They were all focusing intensely on their assignment and were prepared to change course or plans at a second's notice. They knew that if their calculations related to the speed and path of the Imagine were off by even a second, it could mean the difference between having that drink or suffering a horrible death.

Tom was confident that each and every one of them would do their duty and not freak out if a change in plans had to be made. Yet, there was always a lingering doubt that they might fail regardless of what plans had been made. After all, this was the first real space battle in history. Within thirty minutes or less, they would all know if they were alive or dead.

While Preoccupied

Chapter 70 – While Preoccupied

Russian Federation President Ivanov, the Kremlin

The Russians were totally caught by surprise. They informed President Ivanov right away. Ivanov wanted to know where the missiles were headed, knowing he had been entirely wrong in his estimates about this attack on the allies and the spaceship. The generals told him they were going to hit all over Russia, including their missile silos, the navy base on the Black Sea, and, worst of all, the Kremlin. They told Ivanov to leave immediately.

"And go where? My decisions have probably cost millions of Russians their lives. Where will I go? We are not even prepared to shoot any missiles right now. We certainly are not ready to intercept the missiles coming our way. I did not think Stevens had it in him to make this decision."

Ivanov and his generals quietly sat down.

They waited for the inevitable. Ten minutes later, the Kremlin was hit. The noise of the strike could be heard for miles. It was almost totally destroyed. Nearly all of the Russian missile silos were damaged as well as the navy base on the Black Sea.

"Long live Mother Russia," said Ivanov.

His body was never found.

Somewhere on a TV Screen

Chapter 71 – Somewhere on a TV Screen

Tom Burns, the Imagine

Tom and Major Johns were trying to evade the one remaining Russian missile aimed directly at them. It would be a miracle if they survived this. Tom gave the order to speed up by 10,000 miles an hour and fly directly at the Russian spaceship. Simultaneously, per the agreed-upon plan, the Germans and Australians moved in the opposite direction from the Americans and away from the Russian ship. Those two spaceships would be able to make their own decision about what to do, depending on the result of the Russian missile.

Tom was at the controls with Bob Jackson.

Major Johns said, "We're calculating the computer's trajectory and speed while tracking the missile on the radar."

First, they sped up to 60,000 miles an hour. They changed speeds by 10,000 miles an hour every twenty seconds, sometimes going faster and sometimes slower. This was an attempt to throw off the speed and direction of the Russian missile. When the missile was within one-half miles, both the American and Russian ships were almost parallel to each other.

Tom knew Yuri was going to fire at his ship at any moment. He just had to time what he was trying to do correctly. Tom's ship kept getting closer and closer to the Russians while the Russian missile moved towards them.

Suddenly, Major Johns screamed, "NOW!"

Tom suddenly moved the ship to a higher orbit. Tom left Yuri's orbit as he saw torpedoes fired from Yuri's ship approach too quickly for his own comfort.

The nuclear missile from Russia headed towards Yuri's spaceship. Instead of hitting the Imagine, the torpedoes hit the nuclear missile head-on, blowing it up. A great fireball was seen in outer space as the missile and torpedoes exploded into thousands of pieces. Right after the explosion, Yuri's ship was suddenly bombarded by a large amount of missile debris. Tom saw the blast from his new location. Finally, his ship was safe. He put Yuri on the viewscreen where Yuri was sitting on his bridge with his officers. They looked downright miserable. Tom did not want to destroy the Russian ship. He knew it was too damaged to continue with the mission and could no longer attack anyone. Operation Debris accomplished.

"Yuri, Are you and your crew all right? I am sorry this had to happen. We knew of Ivanov's plans a while ago and were prepared for it. Your ship is damaged. And I can see some smoke coming out of it. Can you maneuver it at all? Please do not make me destroy you. However, if you do try something now, we will have to do so."

Yuri sighed and spoke. "Tom, I guess you have won a great battle. I can see from our observations that a lot of Russia has been damaged. I have no idea how many people have been killed. My weapons systems are disabled now, so we cannot possibly take action against you. It will take a long time to repair a ship like this. Ordinarily, as a Russian military man, I would ask you to blow us up, or if I had weapons, force you to do that. However, my family and many others are on board with us, and I do not wish to harm them. I know you have your family with you. I have two beautiful children. I guess the best thing to do is simply surrender my ship to you."

"Thank you, Yuri. You do not need to surrender to me. Can you make it back to Earth without too much trouble? You should know that

Ivanov is dead, as the United States destroyed the Kremlin and many other Russian military sites. You do not have to worry about facing Ivanov when you return. I doubt very much that there is anyone in Russia left who knows what was supposed to happen to the spaceships. You and your crew should be safe when you return to Russia."

"I think we can return to Russia. But it will take a few days or weeks to repair some parts of the ship so that we can safely land it somewhere. The problem is: where are we going to land? Most of Russia is gone. I want you to know, Tom, that this was not my idea. We did not always get along, but I thought if we traveled in space together, perhaps things would change between us once we were rid of our governments. Thank you, Dr. Burns. You have been a good adversary and a better human than I. I wish you luck in your travels through space with the Germans and Australians. I will get on with my repairs and wait for word about landing on Earth again. I assume we will never meet again."

"Goodbye, Yuri. I wish you a good life on Earth and hope your children grow old there. I will think of you when we are speeding through space. Perhaps, someday, you will build a new spaceship and meet us there on New Earth."

"You just said New Earth. That is a good name for wherever you decide to settle."

"Thanks, I have been thinking of a name for a while. Goodbye."

Tom turned off the view screen with Yuri and contacted the president and Major Johns.

The president and the major, as well as everyone else, were ecstatic that the spaceship had survived. At the same time, they were sad about the number of people that had just been killed in Russia.

The president spoke first.

"Well done, Tom. I am sure by now you know that the Russians have suffered extreme damage, and their missiles have been rendered useless."

"Thanks, Mr. President and Major Johns. You did a tremendous job with the Pentagon planning this whole thing, and it worked out great for my ship. It looks like it is time to say bon voyage. I expect the Germans and Australians to turn back and join my ship in orbit. To leave the solar system, we will be using our propulsion system to fly at speeds that have never been attained before. I want to wish you all the best of luck in extending living conditions on Earth and perhaps building some more spaceships. Dr. Sato does have all of your DNA samples, so I may be seeing some of you faster than you think is possible. I will take care of your families as long as we travel through space. Don't worry about anything."

The president spoke. "Best wishes, Tom. I will send you a digital postcard from Earth when we are ready to join you on "New Earth." I need to sign off now. The press is waiting. People are desperate to know what has happened to the Imagine. Goodbye."

"Somewhere on a TV screen in a restaurant, there are plenty of people who need some good news for once, Mr. President. I know the feeling. Thank you for everything!"

Soon after that, the Germans and Australians rejoined him in orbit.

Tom said, "Welcome back, commanders. Are we ready to see the universe now, or have you had too much excitement already?"

Ian Thorpe said, "I think I can speak for the German ship in saying we can't wait to see what tomorrow brings and look forward to many new adventures. Lead the way, Dr. Burns."

Tom announced to everyone on all three ships, "The Russian threat has been neutralized. You are now free to unstrap yourselves and enjoy the ride as we go past Mars and beyond. Dorothy and Carson, let's get this propulsion system going!"

CHAPTER 72

Epilogue

Epilogue

Tom Burns, the Imagine

After Tom had announced that the Russians had been disabled and they were now safe and ready to begin their journey to a new life, just about everyone on the Imagine, as well as the Frieden and the Kangaroo, breathed a sigh of relief.

Tom and Commanders Dresden and Thorpe set up communications and meetings between the American, Australian, and German ships to discuss the next steps.

Commander Thorpe said, "Congratulations on a great victory, Dr. Burns. If the United States had not defeated the Russians, I would not be telling you this now. I actually will miss Yuri and the Oligarch. He was just following orders. I am sure he had no intention, personally, of harming any of us."

Commander Dresden of the German spaceship concurred. "We will miss Yuri's expertise in space. He was the only one that had actually served on spaceships. I am sorry it came to this. Now there are just three spaceships left, and we have not even begun our voyage. I hope that we can overcome any future obstacles."

Tom said, "And hopefully some more will follow given President Stevens' hopes. And thanks for your support, commanders. I am sure we are extremely tired of trying to rush into space and defending ourselves against the Russians. Now we must decide what our immediate plans will be. I do not think we can rush off to Alpha Centauri at maximum speeds, considering how tired we are. And we need to get used to flying in space."

Commander Thorpe said, "I agree with that sentiment and plan. My crew could use a few days of relaxation and test all of our systems before we reach the point we cannot return to Earth. Do you agree with this, Commander Dresden?"

Commander Dresden concurred. The three of them decided to take a few days to do what was necessary to prepare their crews and passengers. They then set a time to start the journey to the end of the solar system. Each commander would meet with his crew to ensure they were all set before moving forward.

After saying goodbye to each other, they made further plans. They checked out their ships to ensure there was no damage following the launches. They all agreed that the crews needed to unwind from battle and take it easy. Wherever Tom walked on the ship, people were hugging him and each other at their good fortune.

Tom decided to turn over control of Imagine to his assistant commander, Gloria. Gloria had pretty much stayed in the background during the launch but had done a great job. Obviously, Tom could not be in control twenty-four hours a day, and he needed to see how Gloria performed now that they were actually in space.

Leaving Gloria in control, Tom met Sarah and Sam, and the three of them went to see Janet in her room. Tom knew that Janet must be feeling awful at the fact her dad had died. She had found out very discreetly and had basically retreated from everyone ever since.

Tom knocked at the door of Janet's room and heard, "Come on in."

Janet was sitting on her bed. Tom, looking at her face, immediately knew she must have been crying. There was a stack of crumpled tissues next to her.

Sam sat down next to Janet and put his arm around her. Janet looked at Sam and put her head on his shoulders. Tom paused for a moment, as the room was now entirely quiet. Sarah grasped her hands together, taking in the scene of Sam holding Janet.

After the short pause, Tom began to speak. "Janet, I wanted to see how you were doing and tell you what a great sacrifice your dad made to ensure your safety and the safety of the entire ship and crew. I know you are disconsolate right now, as you should be, but I do hope in the coming days, weeks, and years, you will find your place on the Imagine and have a wonderful life."

Janet replied, "I wish I had known what sacrifices my father was willing to make to give me the future he so badly wanted me to have. I have lost him, but we have all lost one of the best people alive. He put so much faith in us and our future. How can I ever live up to it?"

Tom thought for a moment and said, "Sarah, on the battlefields, when American soldiers die, there is a saying that a person did not die in vain. Each soldier killed made the ultimate sacrifice so that others, including their family and all Americans, might have a better future. This phrase was first said by Abraham Lincoln at Gettysburg's Battle during his famous address to the nation. Thousands of soldiers lost their lives that day, fighting for freedom. All of their families in the North and the South lost someone they deeply cared about and would never see again. I think if Lincoln was still alive, he would be talking particularly about your dad. Without your dad's sacrifice, none of the people on the Imagine would be alive right now. The fact that we are here right now means that we have a chance to save humanity, and you will be a part of a great adventure. Your dad knew you could not survive on Earth much longer, especially with his certain death looming. He did not want to die without reason or to die in vain. He wanted a better life for you. When you feel better, you can let me know if you would like to name a specific room on Grissom's ship. We will do an appropriate ceremony celebrating his life. I know my words may not mean much to you right now, and I can surely understand that. However, you should know that Grissom will always be with us in our hearts and memories for what he did."

Once Tom had finished speaking, all four of them had a great hug together. Tom actually saw a little smile on Janet's face. Then Tom and Sarah left the room. Sam stayed behind to console Janet for a while.

***

A few days after the battle, all three remaining ships were still in Earth's orbit. Tom was still in contact with President Stevens, who gave him updates on the situation on Earth. The city of Moscow was mostly destroyed. Millions of people were killed in the blasts. The Russian generals had surrendered to the United States, and a plan was being worked on to rebuild Russia. Some of the oligarchs had survived, but their money had been confiscated to pay for war costs.

Meanwhile, FEMA was still trying to rescue survivors in California. It was estimated that 500,000 people had died in the earthquake. Anyone who wanted to leave California was encouraged to do so. It might take twenty years to rebuild some areas. San Francisco was totally in ruins, and Los Angeles might not have any electric power for months.

President Stevens also told Tom that just about every country globally, including China, had offered congratulations to the United States. Many of these countries were now ready to give up their military weapons and spend all of their defense money on improving life on Earth for all citizens. They planned to meet at the United Nations to iron out the details of this newfound cooperation. After seeing all the destruction and deaths in the battles and manmade environmental disasters, they knew they had to take a different course and focus on saving the Earth.

President Stevens said, "While I am pleased that we all want to work together now, there is no telling when the next crisis will happen, and we will go back to trying to destroy each other again."

Tom felt mixed emotions hearing this. On the one hand, it was great that all the countries were willing to cut back drastically on their military budgets and weapons. On the other hand, Tom was sorry to hear about all the casualties.

He asked about Major Johns and his army buddies.

The president said, "Who is Major Johns? I only know a General Johns who will be assigned to the Pentagon and be given a lot of responsibility."

Tom was glad for the new general. Without him, they would never have been able to accomplish what they did in launching Imagine and defeating the Russians.

Tom agreed to give President Stevens updates on their travels through space for as long as communication was possible. By the time they reached the end of the solar system, it would probably take a great deal of time for any messages to reach Earth.

"Please try to keep the communication going. I'm glad to have the blueprint for building more spaceships. While I intend to do everything possible to save as many people as possible, it really looks like we cannot survive for too long on Earth, no matter how much cooperation happens. The leaders of each major country, including the United States, should have decided a long time ago to focus on saving the Earth. If we had spent all of our money on the environment and not on building weapons of mass destruction, we might not be having this discussion, and you might still be here on Earth."

Tom said, "What happened is not your fault. You just got stuck with the mess your predecessors created."

Tom said goodbye and got back to work. First, Tom and the senior officers inspected the Imagines' hull to make sure there was no damage. Since almost everyone had never actually been in space before, Tom felt prudent to give people time to get acclimated with the ship and their duties.

He was glad to see that everyone on the ship was taking time to glance at the Earth from thousands of miles away while Imagine was still in orbit around Earth. Sam and Sally took some time to do this too. It was great watching his son and Sally so awestruck.

Sam said, "This is unreal. Earth looks so beautiful from up here in orbit. However, in a short time, we will never be able to see it again."

Sally responded, "Yes, it is beautiful. Yet, as we are in orbit, we can also notice the crumbling ozone layer and be thankful we are up here and not down on the surface where I expect more people are going to die horrible deaths."

"Amen to that," said Sam. "It's been hard grappling with that. I mean, look at it. That was home, and now it's been suffering from crumbling ozone caused by chemicals. It's like there's been a constant contest for who could poison for bigger reasons and higher priorities than saving everyone who depends on the whole Earth being treated properly."

"Really makes me sad. You know, my mom used to tell me how much hairspray they used before CFC production all but stopped."

"Never thought you'd be spending your free time gazing out the window and see Earth, did you?" asked Tom.

Sam smiled. "Never. It's breathtaking."

"And to think that we used to play basketball down there."

"How's it going with the NBA All-Stars in the rec center?"

"Not so good, Dad, but we've decided to have one NBA All-Star on each of their teams to keep the games even. When we try this, it resembles a game of one-on-one with the NBA players running up and down the court. We just can't keep up with them."

"Well, keep trying. Don't forget we're bowling tonight. Mom, Robert and Sophie, and you and me. Team Burns. A little family time getting to know other families."

***

After one game of bowling, Sam's new friend, Mark, informed Team Burns that he had begun shuttle pilot training, and so far, it was a good experience. He would be doing a lot of simulations on board before actually flying one into space.

"Would you like to join my family for the second game of bowling?"

Mark said, "Sure."

They bowled together, and it was pretty evident to Tom that Mark and Sophie clicked. Mark had a few laughs with Sophie. Mark and Sophie might make a good couple. He really liked Mark and knew that Sam could count on him as a good friend.

Everyone said their goodbyes and gave each other a hug. Of course, Mark and Sophie had the biggest hug in the group. The next night Tom ate with his wife, Sarah, and family.

Sarah said, "Thank God we are safe now. For a while, I really thought we were going to be goners. Thank my great and dear husband for keeping us safe through this adventure. I am willing to follow you anywhere."

This made Tom blush, which was something that did not happen often.

Robert said, "That was the scariest thing I have ever done. It was way worse than any rollercoaster I have been on."

Sophie then said, "I am sorry I panicked so badly. I, too, am thankful to be alive, sitting here with my family. However, I want to get some things off my chest, so please be good listeners."

Everyone at the table nodded for Sophie to keep talking.

Sophie continued, "First of all, in a short time, and before we even really began our trip, we have almost died twice. This is not how I thought life would be when I was in high school. How often are we going to be almost killed? We are lucky to be alive. Eventually, some disaster will happen, and we may not be so fortunate. And either one or all of us will perish in a matter of seconds. I know Dad is a great commander and pilot, but even the best pilots can make a mistake. Also, we do not know what lies ahead of us. Will the ship be hit by a giant meteor or a comet? Will the engines fail, and we'll find ourselves drifting in space forever or crash on another planet? Have you ever thought about those things? We could be facing a disaster every day for the next fifty years. It is terrifying to think of all the problems that we will face. I do not know how I am going to be able to cope with all the pressure. I do not want to die tomorrow or very soon. I do not even have a boyfriend yet, although I had a nice time with Mark yesterday."

That last sentence brought a smile from Sam and his mom.

Sarah and Tom looked at each other as if determining who wanted to respond to Sophie. Sam and Robert were quiet, waiting for one of them to speak up.

After a few moments, Tom replied, "Sophie, I am also glad to be alive. When I started planning this trip, I had no idea what lay ahead of us, except for the fact that I would be trying to save my wife and children and as many others as possible. I know there are some things I can prepare for and some things I can prevent from happening. Still, I cannot honestly promise that we will have a comfortable, safe trip for a hundred years, and there will be no major or minor problems. There is just no way I can foresee everything. I do not have a crystal ball. However, if we want to try and have a successful voyage, we cannot focus on the negative all the time. If we always think of the worst possible scenarios, we will go crazy."

Sarah, Sam, and Robert nodded in agreement.

"I selected the people on Imagine because I have the utmost trust in them to get the job done to the best of their ability. They have promised to do everything they can to make life as enjoyable as they can. If you feel the need to talk about your feelings to us or a counselor on the ship, please do so. It will take time to get used to this way of living for everybody on board, and that includes you. I do not expect everyone to accept everything that happens here, but we must make the best of it if we want to survive."

Sophie looked intensely at her dad the whole time. She said, "I will do my best to think more positively and be more optimistic about this journey, but I am still going to worry every day and need to talk about it occasionally."

Tom said, "Thank you. Now I must attend to my duties and meet some people. Do you think you can all go get some of that great ice cream in the cafeteria and perhaps mingle with people there?"

They jumped at the thought. When his family went to the cafeteria, Tom and Sarah met with Dr. Sato in the medical quarters' conference room. She was probably the busiest person on the ship after the attack. Bob and several others also joined them for the meeting. The meeting's primary purpose was to discuss maintaining the health of the crew and researching various methods of prolonging life. Tom wanted to know what her plans would be for the next few months and perhaps years to come.

Dr. Sato had several members of her team with her, which included Sarah.

"Thank you for inviting us to meet with you to discuss various issues related to everyone's health on board the Imagine. There were no major medical incidents during the launch or during Operation Debris. My team is looking forward to working with you and ensuring we get to our destiny in good health if that is possible. First, we need to discuss everyday health habits and suggested protocols. I recommend that every passenger on the Imagine take time to have their vital signs measured every two weeks until further notice. There are several reasons for this. First, it will give us useful baseline data for each person's current medical status. We will be able to identify any pathological changes people have. Second, if they become sick, we hope to immediately catch the problem and provide the necessary care. This is especially important if someone comes down with a contagious disease. We do not want an epidemic to overwhelm the people on board.

As you know, we are now living in a closed space, and some of these diseases and bacteria have no place to go except into another person. We do not want everyone to be sick. Are you all right with the two-week checkup plan?"

Tom said, "When it comes to medicine and the health of this crew, you are in charge. I have no reason not to listen to you. In fact, if you believe that I am putting lives at risk and ruining the health of people on board, you need to tell me. I will ensure that everyone adheres to a certain standard of cleanliness, including cleaning the ship regularly. Also, if you believe that my health has deteriorated at some point on the journey, you will have the right to relieve me from duty. Therefore, your two-week checkup plan is approved. Are you all right with this?"

Dr. Sato nodded.

Tom looked at Sarah and added, "If people fail to adhere to these rules, I am sure my wife, Sarah, will make sure people follow them. She can be very persuasive, right?"

Sarah laughed and said, "I will do my best to police everyone regarding their health and checkups."

Dr. Sato said, "Thank you, Dr. Burns. I also need to talk to you about the research that will be vitally important if anyone will live long enough to see another galaxy or a new planet to call home. My cryo team has been working very hard to get the equipment ready to test our first subjects. Now that we are in orbit, we need all the equipment to be tested again to adjust for being in space. What was done in Colorado may not work here."

Tom asked, "Who will be the first subject, and do you have any details about what you will do? If things go well, when will we be able to use this on humans?"

"Our first subjects will be two mice. We plan to put them in stasis for twenty-four hours and monitor all their vitals. After twenty-four hours, we will hopefully revive them and see if they are back to normal. We need to study how long it takes to revive someone and how long it takes them to function normally again. If we are successful with the mice, then we can try again with a dog or monkey. I do not know how long it will take someone to come out of stasis in good health until we perform the tests. We will have to test their memories and their personalities to see if there are any changes.

"If there are no major mishaps, I would say it will be between six to twelve months before we test a human. Keep in mind the other two spaceships are also beginning to test this process. We will compare results with them."

Bob then said, "I guess the million-dollar question is, do you have any idea who the first human subject will be? I am sure you will not test anyone until there is a ninety-nine percent chance that the person will live through the experience."

"You are correct that I will not allow a test on a human until I am absolutely sure this will work. I would never forgive myself if we lost someone, regardless of who it was, during this research. As of right now, I do not have anyone in mind to be the first person on board to undertake this procedure. I presume when the time comes, I will ask for a volunteer. If all goes well, it will probably happen in six to twelve months."

Tom said, "That is fine. I do hope we are successful with cryopreservation. It would be nice to slow our lives down once in a while. Next, what will we be doing regarding cloning? If things go well, when do you think you will test the first human?"

"I am working with two other specialists on this procedure. As you know, animals have already been cloned, but no humans have gone through the process, except for Epoh, who did not exactly turn out the way I would have hoped. We are practicing and researching how to take a DNA sample in a petri dish and watching the cells grow into a living thing. It will be a while before we produce a human. To ensure maximum success, we need to test for how fast or slow we can clone someone. Will it be two weeks, six months, or one year to successfully clone a person? We probably do not have to wait nine months for cloning to be successful. I am sure we may have some failures with this. Luckily, we have DNA from over one million people in storage. We will probably try first on someone that is already deceased. We are also researching how to improve stem cells that can be implanted into people on board if they need a new organ or face an incurable disease. This may also take a while until we show some success. In short, there is a lot of work to do between the everyday medical examinations and the research we are doing."

Tom said, "That was an excellent overview. We do appreciate all the hard work you have done and will be doing in the future. You are probably the most important person on board the Imagine. Your team is certainly going to be the busiest on board for the foreseeable future. I may be able to fly the Imagine so that it avoids hitting anything. Still, if we do not live long enough, eventually, we will all die before arriving at any destination.

"Speaking of humans and cloning, how are Dr. Kintain and Epoh? As you know, we agreed to keep Epoh a secret and limit his movement area to the medical area. By the way, where is Dr. Kintain?"

Dr. Sato suddenly appeared a little bit annoyed. I requested that Dr. Kintain come to this meeting to give you his report on Epoh, as he is the person who spends the most time with him. I have not seen Dr. Kintain for the last several hours. I paged him on the communicator but received no answer."

Tom's mouth opened as if to say, 'uh oh.' "Dr. Sato, please take me to the area or lab where Dr. Kintain works with Epoh. I have a bad feeling about this, but I hope I am wrong. The rest of you, please return to your duties or go to the cafeteria. Once again, I must remind everyone not to speak of Epoh to others on board the ship. I do not want to alarm anyone."

Dr. Sato led Tom to a room that was supposed to be locked. A' Do Not Enter' sign hung off of it. However, the door was open. Dr. Sato and Tom entered the room and looked around. After two minutes, they found Dr. Kintain on the floor. They ran to him.

"Dr. Kintain!"

Dr. Sato checked on him. He seemed to be all right, and there was no bleeding. He was awake but had a few bruises on his arms and face. Dr. Sato attended to him while Tom started talking to him

"Where is Epoh? What happened?" Tom asked.

Dr. Kintain told Tom that he had been doing a routine exam of Epoh when suddenly there had seemed to be a loud noise coming from other places on the ship. Epoh had wanted to know where the noise was coming from. Dr. Kintain had tried to get Epoh to forget about the noise. Still, Epoh had refused to listen to him and demanded that they go find the noise together. When Dr. Kintain had refused, Epoh had started to attempt to open the door and leave. Dr. Kintain had tried to stop him, but Epoh had just overpowered him, pushed him down, and left. Dr. Kintain just hoped nothing was going to happen to either Epoh or anyone on the Imagine.

Tom immediately got on his communicator to contact his officers about Epoh. Tom had kept Epoh secret from all of them, but now he had no choice but to ask for their help in locating Epoh. Their orders were to find him without killing him unless he was a danger to others.

Truth be told, Tom did not know how people would perceive Epoh if they saw him and how Epoh would perceive people on the ship. He just hoped the situation would not escalate.

Sam was one of the officers that received the alert. He was in the busy cafeteria. The mood was giddy and elated before they broke orbit, and things got more serious.

Just as Sam got on his communicator, they heard a loud gasp from several people in the cafeteria.

"What is it, Sam?"

"Dad, you're not going to like this. I found him."

"I'll be there in a flash!"

Tom ran into the cafeteria as everyone saw Epoh for the first time. Epoh looked like a Tarzan version of Dr. Kintain, but without hair. Tom wasn't sure what had happened to his hair. Dr. Sato had never described that there had been any alterations made to the clone. Except for his loincloth, Epoh had no clothes on. He was also much whiter than any person he had ever seen.

Epoh seemed nervous and unsure of what he had just walked into. Tom figured Epoh had no idea if the people in the cafeteria were his friends or enemies. After all, this was his first contact with many humans all at the same time.

Tom instructed everyone to quietly move away from Epoh. While they were doing that, Dr. Sato raced to the cafeteria along with several security people and officers who were told to meet there. Dr. Sato had a large syringe filled with enough tranquilizing medicine to knock out a horse. Since Dr. Kintain needed to rest from his bruises, they couldn't rely on his help. It also appeared that Dr. Kintain might not be able to apprehend the clone any longer using his techniques.

Epoh recognized Dr. Sato.

Dr. Sato said, "Epoh, please sit down where you are, and we can give you some medicine."

Epoh did not like the sound of that. He suddenly spoke, "No, I will not sit down. I want to know where I am and who these people are. What is happening here? What was that loud noise?"

Dr. Sato looked at Tom. Tom stepped forward and said, "Epoh, I am Tom Burns, the commander of the ship you are on. I am a friend of Dr. Kintain's and Dr. Sato's. I need you to do what Dr. Sato asks, and everything will be all right."

Tom also motioned for everyone to stay back to allow Epoh to listen to Tom. Epoh could probably hurt just about anyone in a one-on-one fight and even kill someone, depending on his behavior and how he reacted to the person coming at him.

Epoh stood his ground. He asked, "Where is Dr. Kintain? I want to talk to him. He gave life to me, right?"

A few people started laughing nervously. Epoh did not like the laughing and started moving toward them. At that point, Tom had no choice but to tell security not to shoot him, but to move in and try and wrestle him down to the ground so that Dr. Sato could give him the tranquilizer. Four security personnel moved to intercept Epoh and tried to detain him to prevent him from hurting anyone.

They were just about to close in on Epoh when suddenly, out of nowhere, Dr. Kintain showed up and pointed a gun at Tom. He said, "Everyone, stand back. None of you are to touch Epoh or harm him. He is my s—" Dr. Kintain quickly corrected himself. "My clone. If you do not do what I say, I will shoot you. Epoh and I are going back to the lab and will stay there. Do you understand me?"

Tom had been in this situation before and recalled Susan's dad for a fleeting moment. He was very calm once again and did not want anyone to get hurt or shot. He told everyone to stand down. Then he addressed Dr. Kintain.

"You need to put your gun down and let us take care of the situation at hand. Too many people have now seen Epoh, so it is no longer a secret. WE need to ensure that Epoh is not going to harm anyone. Look what he just did to you? We need to tranquilize him and bring him back to the medical area to decide what is best. If Epoh actually hurts someone, it could mean the end for him. So, if you want to see Epoh again and continue your cloning research, you will have to put the gun down. If you shoot me, you will be dead in a minute, and Epoh will be without you. Is that what you want to see? You have ten seconds to decide. Put down the gun, or I will order them to open fire."

Dr. Kintain took one look at Tom and knew how serious he was. He said, "Ok, you win," and he put the gun down.

As soon as he did this, security picked up the gun and handcuffed Dr. Kintain.

Before they led him away, Tom said, "Now ask Epoh to get down on the ground. He is not going to listen to me or anyone else."

Dr. Kintain turned to Epoh and said, "I love you, Epoh. You are my clone, and I do not want anything to happen to you. Listen to Tom and do what he and Dr. Sato tell you. If you do that, perhaps you and I will see each other again soon."

Dr. Kintain was on the verge of tears. Epoh looked at Dr. Kintain and saw how sad he was. While he had no empathy for anyone, he did see the tears and said, "Ok, Father, I will do what they say. See you later." Then he sat down.

Dr. Sato walked over to him with Tom, and they gave him the tranquilizer.

"How long will he be put under?" cried Dr. Kintain.

"This will put him to sleep for at least twenty-four hours. That would give us enough time to decide what to do."

Tom gave security the order to take Dr. Kintain to the brig and to guard him.

Tom turned to face everyone in the cafeteria. He said, "I am sorry for the distraction. Only a few of us on board know about Epoh. I did not expect any cloning to occur until we were well into orbit. Still, Dr. Kintain had already proceeded to clone himself well before our mission. Dr. Sato invited them on board when she was injured on her way to Wisconsin to include them in our efforts. Obviously, based on what I saw just now, some of you are not ready to accept Epoh, and Epoh is not ready to live among you. Perhaps in the future, that will change. We will see what happens. One again, I am sorry this had to happen." The cafeteria emptied.

Tom, Dr. Sato, Bob, and a few others held a private meeting in Tom's office near the bridge. After a lengthy discussion, it was decided that Dr. Kintain would serve two years in the brig. He would receive counseling during that time. Since he did not shoot anyone, he hoped he could continue to be a doctor after serving his sentence. After all, he did have incredible knowledge about cloning. The advances he made would fuel Dr. Sato's medical team efforts in the meantime. As for Epoh, it was decided he would be their first cryopreservation patient or experiment. He would be placed in cryo for two years. During that time, it was hoped they could develop a way to inject him with memories that would help him survive and get along with people. Of course, there was no guarantee this would succeed, in which case, they would have to terminate him.

Before they separated, Dr. Sato said to Tom, "Despite all the excitement tonight, I wanted to add that there is still one more way we can try to ensure life continues on board."

Tom said, "And what is that? Is this a procedure I am unfamiliar with?"

Dr. Sato said, "You are very familiar with it. With Sarah, you have produced three wonderful children. On Imagine, there are probably around seventy-six to one hundred females who can probably get pregnant. If everything else fails, this might be the only way to preserve life."

They both smiled.

Finally, Tom spoke. "Sounds like what happens when there are power outages—something to do in the dark. Of course, I have no problem with people falling in love and having children. That could be great for the morale of the ship and a time to celebrate new life. I just hope that the research you are doing is very successful, and some of the original crew members arrive in good health on a new planet."

Dr. Sato said, "I do too. I will provide you with further updates in a week or so. For now, there is plenty for the medical team to work on."

Everyone stood up and shook hands as the meeting was adjourned. Tom and Sarah decided to go to the cafeteria to check to see how Luis and the other staff were doing.

When they showed up, about a hundred people were still sitting around. They'd returned since the incident. Some of them were eating dinner. Others were just having ice cream or chatting with each other. Tom could hear some of the chatter about Epoh, but most of it was small talk.

Sam noticed Tom when they walked in and motioned for them to join him. He was sitting with Susan, Janet, Jose, and Sally.

"Where's Robert?" asked Tom.

"Robert chose to sit with someone his own age, and Sophie joined Mark's group."

"Hi, Dr. Burns," said Janet.

Everyone smiled at Tom and Sarah when they sat down.

Sam said, "How is everyone adjusting? I am thankful we are sitting here together, talking to each other. It was touch and go for a while, but thanks to people like Janet's dad, Grissom, we made it."

"Thanks, Sam. Without you, I doubt my dad would have even let me come on board. My dad really respected you and your dad, and I know I will be fine. Susan has really helped me get used to things, as we have both gone through a similar experience losing our dads. We both try to focus on our daily routine and not dwell on the past. However, when we have free time, we do think of our families left on Earth."

Susan said, "Glad we can help each other through difficult times."

Tom said, "That is good news. I hope you two become fast friends as we travel. How are you doing, Jose? I want everyone to know that Jose is also a hero for calculating the launch path to get us into orbit. He and I worked extremely hard. Right, Jose?"

Jose responded, "I would say that Sam and I are really not heroes. It is kind of you to say that, but we were really just doing our duty or following orders. It does feel good to be appreciated, though.

I am looking forward to learning more and more about this ship and outer space."

Everyone agreed.

Then Mrs. Smith showed up and sat down with them. "Greetings, everyone. I can tell you that this experience is something that I never imagined as a high school principal even though I knew several years ago that I would be on Imagine. I was never more nervous in my entire life than yesterday."

Sally said, "We were all petrified and nervous, but I think I was more nervous during your chemistry exams, even though Sam tutored me."

Everyone laughed around the table, including Mrs. Smith. It seemed to improve their spirits.

Jose asked, "When are we beginning our training again? There is so much to learn."

Mrs. Smith said, "I will be providing some of the training, but I do not know enough about what will happen every day on board, so I also need to study. I will be a student just like you. For the students under sixteen, I will provide their education, similar to what you learned in high school."

Tom said, "Hi, Mrs. Smith. How are you doing, and how are Sam and others doing with their training?"

"All of them are fantastic students. They absorb everything we teach them. I am honored to be able to work with so many wonderful people on Imagine. I couldn't be prouder of them."

Sarah jumped in. "That is good to hear. I have never properly thanked you for providing such an excellent education for my three children."

"Thanks, I look forward to teaching them for another hundred years or as long as it takes to find a new home."

Sam then said, "That will make you the oldest teacher ever and us, the oldest students ever."

Everyone smiled.

At that moment, Tom started to relax and smile also. He probably should not have done that. All of a sudden, two people came out of the kitchen, screaming at each other. Luis, the chef, and Ruth Sparrow, one of the passengers that Tom recognized as the mother of one of Sam's friends who attended high school with him, were having a heated debate. They were heading straight to Tom. When they reached him, both started to talk or scream at the same time. Tom could not understand them, as each was talking loud and fast.

Everyone else was staring at them, hoping they would calm down. After all, they had recently had enough excitement to last a long time.

Finally, Tom said, "Luis and Ruth, please be quiet now!" His very stern and the demanding voice stopped Luis and Ruth from yelling. Then, Tom said, "One at a time, please explain to me what is going on. Luis, you go first."

Luis started talking, "Dr. Burns, I am happy to be the chef for you and Imagine. However, this woman, Ruth, has complained about my chicken enchiladas. She claims that her recipe is better than mine, and she can cook it better than me. First of all, I am Mexican and have cooked chicken enchiladas for twenty-five years. This woman is a white person who knows little about the ingredients I use to make my food. Yet, she insists that we must use her recipe from now on, as mine is not good enough. Dr. Burns, please tell her to leave me and my kitchen alone."

"Thank you, Luis. Now, Ruth, please explain to me why you are arguing with Luis about his chicken enchiladas."

Ruth said, "Luis cannot cook Mexican food very well. Yes, I am a white female, but my family has been cooking enchiladas for nearly a hundred years with the same recipe handed down by my great grandmother. I was merely trying to improve his food taste, but he is too stubborn to listen to me. I am asking you to tell Luis that he needs to learn from others also."

Luis jumped in. "I will not use your recipe. I do not need it. I have several assistants working with me, and we will provide the best food we can and not be forced to use your great grandmother's recipe."

Ruth responded, "I demand a chance to show that my chicken enchiladas are better than his. I want a cook-off with this imposter of a chef."

This made Luis mad again. His face reddened.

Tom said, "First of all, you need to be nice to each other. Luis is a terrific chef. That is why I hired him to come with us. I actually ate his food in his restaurant in Chicago, and it was delicious. Nevertheless, I don't want to throw your great grandmother under the bus, and if Luis agrees, you can have your cook-off."

Luis said, "Anytime is fine with me. Let's do it now for the Burns family."

Ruth said, "Bring it on."

Tom then said, "I will use my family and five others to taste your food. We will not label who cooked each dish with your names. Each taster will note which enchilada they liked best. Whoever gets the most votes will be the winner. How long does each of you need to pre-pare your food? We can come back then and taste it."

Both Luis and Ruth said two hours would be enough time.

Ruth demanded, "If more people like my cooking, I expect that recipe to be used from now on."

Luis said, "One more thing, Ruth. The enchiladas have to be made through bioengineering. I am sure you know everything about this pro-cedure to prepare food."

Ruth said, "What are you talking about? My great grandmother's recipe had nothing to do with bioengineering. What kind of a joke is this?"

Before Luis could respond, Tom interrupted, "Luis is right. All of our food is made through a bioengineering process. Remember, we are on a spaceship, and we have adapted to find ways to provide edible food. As a judge and commander of this ship, your food will have to be made using this principle."

Ruth looked very frustrated. "Until I learn how to do this, I guess I cannot have this competition now."

Tom said, "I guess not. However, I do know who you are from read-ing your file. It seems that you actually were a drama teacher for many years. Is that correct?"

Ruth said, "Yes, I taught drama in college for twenty years. I had some very devoted students who went on to work on Broadway and other places."

"Then perhaps you would like to teach drama on board Imagine. In time, maybe you could get some of the crew to put on a show. It does not have to be anything extravagant. I am sure some of the younger people here would enjoy doing this. It could be a traditional play or one that you create on your own."

Ruth said, "Thank you for trying to make me feel better. In a few days, I will let you know if I want to be a drama teacher again."

Tom said, "Thanks for considering it. Would you mind shaking hands with Luis? I expect there will be conflicts between people on board regarding almost anything. It is part of human nature and cannot be avoided. However, we have a thousand people on board who are not going anywhere for a long time, I hope. We have to learn to resolve our conflicts diplomatically. I am responsible for any decision that will impact everyone here. Still, you cannot depend on me to resolve every personal situation on board. Please try to think about that. I will have to post guidelines and procedures about personal conflicts on board soon. I suggest that both Ruth and Luis would be great to have on this committee given we've resolved this. What do you think?"

Ruth and Luis agreed it would be a good idea. They shook hands and went their ways. Tom put his hands on his head and breathed a sigh of relief. He was really hoping for some relaxation before they broke orbit. He ate some ice cream to enjoy the moment.

One minute later, Tom knew he could forget about relaxing. Zeke, the botanist, came running toward him, out of breath.

"Dr. Burns, I can't find Billy. I have looked everywhere."

Tom said, "Who is Billy? I did not think you brought any children with you."

Zeke said, "Billy is a tortoise, not a child, although I do think of him as one."

"What do you mean one of your tortoises is missing? I thought you only brought one with you."

Zeke said, "No, I brought two. We need a male and female if there is going to be any reproduction. As you probably know, these tortoises may outlive everyone on board, as they can live as long as a hundred years, and they don't need cryopreservation to do it."

Tom said, "Does anyone else on the Imagine know you have two of them?"

"Yes, Dr. Sato knows as well as Luis and many other people on board. They all love my tortoises."

"Well, a tortoise certainly can't go that far and can't walk off the ship, so it must be here somewhere. I will make an announcement for everyone to look for it."

While Tom went to make the announcement, he was thinking about the tortoises. If they had baby tortoises, the animals could live longer than anyone on the ship. Maybe they would be the real Ninja turtles or tortoises. Five minutes later, every off-duty passenger was looking for Billy. How difficult could this be? This tortoise was huge, and it would be difficult to find a space to hide.

Twenty minutes later, Janet found Billy eating plants in the botany lab. He must have been hungry, spending all the time during launch in his cage. Zeke hugged Billy first and then Janet. Janet seemed happy just to have contributed to finding Billy.

Tom said, "I am glad we found the tortoise. Please make sure he is at least locked into a room and has plenty of water and food to eat. I don't want the entire ship looking for tortoises all the time."

Zeke was happy to find Billy and told Tom he would make sure this did not happen again.

"I'd love to help with that if you don't mind an assistant! I love tortoises. I used to have one back at home," said Janet.

"Sure, Janet," Zeke said.

Then Tom started walking to the bridge. If this was relaxation, then Tom preferred to go back to work.

The next day, Tom, Bob, Sam, Jose, and a group of officers met with Dorothy and Carson to inspect the engines and to discuss the speed they would continue at for the next few weeks. They also needed to figure out how to obtain and maintain warp speed.

Everyone was sitting around a large round table in the conference room for the bridge.

Tom began, "I want to thank you two for working almost twenty-four hours a day to launch this spaceship. I am sure you are both exhausted, but now we need you more than ever. I believe you two, as well as Dr. Sato and the commanders, are the key people who will determine whether we ever reach a new galaxy like Alpha Centauri."

Everyone in the room applauded for Dorothy and Carson.

Carson said, "Thank you for your compliments. While Dorothy and I certainly worked hard at our jobs, we could not do this without the assistance of all the people working on the engines and our great commanders."

Everyone applauded again.

Dorothy then said, "We have some updates to report and some matters to discuss. First, all of the engines are working fine. Our new fuel system, which will continuously recycle fuel, is working, and we hope it continues to do so. I doubt we will have many gas stations in space or many places to pick up the necessary chemicals needed to make more, but you never know for sure. Second, we can verify that we can fly at Mach 8 faster than any spaceship has traveled before. However, it is still not fast enough. Now, I have some really fantastic news. My team will be working on this issue probably day and night until we reach warp speed. We believe we have found a solution to achieve this goal. If we are successful, we will be able to travel ten times the speed of light."

Tom said, "This is absolutely fantastic news. Can you explain how this is theoretically going to work?"

Carson stood up and said, "Yes, I would be delighted to explain it to everyone, and we will conduct simulations very soon. To fly at warp speed, we need to create space-time to warp around the starship, creating a region of contracted space in front of it and expanded space behind. As you know, Einstein always believed it as impossible to travel faster than the speed of light. However, we can bend space to achieve warp speed."

Tom asked, "From what I understand, to achieve that, it would take a huge amount of energy that is not possible on a ship like this. How will we be able to produce the energy needed to successfully fly at warp speed?"

Carson said, "That is an excellent question and one we have been wrestling with even before we set foot on Imagine. In fact, I would say that it is probably the most important factor in why we have not been able to achieve warp speed yet. What we need to do—and have been successful in determining in our calculations—is to find the right shape of the warp field to greatly decrease the amount of energy needed. We may need less energy than was required to launch. We are going to run some simulations and find the best warp field possible."

Sam, who had been sitting the whole time quietly, suddenly said, "Fantastic. I may actually get to a new home before I turn one hundred years old."

Everyone laughed at the remark.

Tom also laughed. He said, "That is an incredible discovery. When you are ready to run your simulations, please let me know. This is of the utmost importance. Carson and Dorothy, you have done a wonderful job since you have worked for the Imagine. Keep up the good work."

Dorothy was all smiles. She said, "Thank you, Tom, for your great leadership on board. I am sure we will be discussing the warp issue in the near future. I would also like to recommend that when we break orbit and head toward Mars, we start off at Mach 1 or 2 and gradually build up speed. There are two reasons for this. First, we need to keep monitoring the engines as we increase speed to identify and fix any problems that occur. Second, everyone on board, including the officers and us, has to get used to traveling at such a fast pace. We hope that no one even notices the speed or becomes ill from the ship's motion."

Tom said, "Your comments are understandable. I will notify the other ships to start off at Mach 1, and we can decide when to travel at Mach 2 and so forth. I am glad the engines are all working fine now. When we break Earth's orbit, how will we get past the gravitational pull again? We do not have eight rockets or controls from the surface to help us anymore. We are now on our own, except for the two other spaceships. We will need to work closely with their engineering teams to discover the best way to travel in space. Also, all three ships will continuously plot our path to Alpha Centauri."

Jose asked, "What can Sam and I do to help with this? We enjoyed assisting with the launch plans."

Carson responded, "Both Sam and Jose did a great job working with us, and if the officers do not mind, we would love to have them continue."

Tom said, "That will be fine with me. As long as we are making progress, I do not mind anyone assisting you."

Dorothy said, "You asked about how we will break orbit. The simple answer to this is that we will increase the propulsion system's thrust to boost the energy necessary to break orbit. We will not need a lot of power. However, all three ships must use the same controls to ensure we will be moving at the same speed to stay relatively close to each other. Before we leave orbit, we need to test the shuttle as it moves outside our ship and transports people to other vessels. The shuttle could be vital if we need to perform repair work on the hull."

Tom said, "You are right. Do you have two pilots ready to test the shuttle?"

"Yes, Marvin Watson, who tested the shuttle with you before, can pilot the shuttle. I think Bob may want to be the co-pilot. It will be a learning experience for him. He can quickly check out the systems onboard while the shuttle is in action."

Bob responded, "Sure, I would like that. It will be nice to fly something again. How soon are we going to launch the shuttle, and how long do you want us to fly it before returning to Imagine?"

Dorothy said, "It will only take an hour to fly the shuttle around the ship. You will need to do two things. First, check out all the systems onboard the shuttle to make sure they are all functioning correctly. Second, as you fly around Imagine, check the hull to ensure it is all intact from the outside. The inside hull is fine, but we need to check to make sure the outer hull was not damaged."

Bob said, "And if it is damaged?"

Tom said, "Use the camera inside the shuttle to video the hull. That way, the people on the bridge and myself can assist with the process of repairing it. If it is only minor repairs, then we will tell you how to fix it. If it is significant damage, we will send another shuttle with supplies and engineers to assist you."

Thirty minutes later, Marvin and Bob took off in the shuttle and began testing its maneuverability while following Imagine in orbit. The maneuverability seemed fine. It took about an hour to fly around Imagine. Bob did notice slight damage to the hull in one area and took some photos and sent them back to Tom. Carson and some engineers discussed the repairs necessary and decided to use a laser to repair the damage. Since the shuttle had a laser, Bob and Marvin maneuvered the shuttle to a distance of a hundred yards from the outside of the Imagine. Their first attempt to seal the hull failed miserably, as they had a hard time aiming the laser and adjusting for the speed of Imagine and the shuttle. They missed the target area by forty feet.

Bob said, "I wish I had played some Playstation now with Sam and the others since I seem to be such a lousy shot with the laser stick."

Tom told him not to worry about it and try again but compensate for the moving shuttle and Imagine.

Bob said, "All right. Let me work on this laser for thirty minutes, and we can try again."

Thirty minutes later, the shuttle again maneuvered into a position to seal the hull. This time, Bob was able to close the hull after missing again on his first two shots, and Tom was happy to witness their success.

"Good job," Tom said. "So far, so good with the shuttle. Now you are going to have to land inside Imagine while it is going in orbit. Marvin will have to do this part. I imagine it will be the first time he attempts this but indeed not the last time."

On the shuttle, Marvin said, "Great work with the laser stick. Now I need to land safely on Imagine."

Bob asked, "Have you ever done this or practiced it in simulations?"

"I have practiced in simulations on the computer. I had landed a shuttle on Earth when we flew to Las Vegas with the president and picked up Dr. Sato after her accident. But this will be the first time I do it for real on a moving spaceship."

"Exactly how do you land this thing on a moving ship?"

"First, despite what you may be thinking, I don't fly the ship's shuttle. It might be too difficult to stop the shuttle before it crashes and destroys the ship. Not only that, but I could also miss the opening in the ship and hit the hull. However, that is not going to happen. What I have to do is get the speed right, so we are flying parallel to each other. There is a crane that I attach the shuttle to outside the ship. This is similar to docking a spaceship at the International Space Station. Once we dock with the crane, we come to a halt and turn off the shuttle's power. Then the crane, which is operated from inside Imagine, will slide us onto the ship, and the doors will close. It really is an easy thing. I just need to operate the controls to get the speed right."

Bob said, "You seem confident, and I have to trust you to do this. I just hope it goes well."

The shuttle then made a perfect hookup with the crane and slid into the ship. Bob looked relieved to Tom. Marvin looked like he had not even broken a sweat.

Tom then contacted the commanders of the other two ships to see if they were ready to resume. Captains Dresden and Thorpe informed Tom that they were prepared and could continue at any time. The three of them decided they would break orbit in twenty-four hours to give everyone a chance to prepare.

Tom made an announcement. "Everyone, may I have your attention, please. We will break orbit and head towards Mars in twenty-four hours, although we will not stop there. It will probably take fifteen days until we reach Mars, which will be the fastest anyone has ever done it. We will start off at Mach 2 and build up to Mach 8 as we become accustomed to flying in space. Once again, please make sure all of your belongings and loose objects are put away or bolted down.

We will let you know when you can take off your helmets. Please be sure to be at your posts and with your seatbelts on, as the relaunch could be a little bit stressful. In twenty-one hours, my officers will inspect all of you to make sure you are ready for the next step. If there are any problems, please contact an officer to assist you. They all can communicate with me at any time."

Twenty-one hours later, everyone was in place. Dorothy and Carson were all set for the energy surge that would be necessary to break orbit. Tom and the officers then checked all the instruments to make sure they were still working correctly.

Tom contacted the president, and they both wished each other a wonderful and enduring future life.

Three hours later, Tom was ready to give the order to break orbit. He looked around the control room and at the other officers. They had all done well in the launch, and Tom was proud of them all. He could not have asked for a more exceptional crew and knew he could count on them all. He was sure he could live with everyone on board until they found a new home.

The countdown began. As it got to ten seconds, Tom blurted out, "Good luck, everyone. SO LONG EARTH,"

All three ships headed off on their new journey. At that moment, they were pioneers ready to unleash humanity's potential while escaping degenerating lands and the unwelcome aspects of the demise of civilization. Only time would tell if they would be successful.

THE END

**Michael
Bienenstock**

Michael Bienenstock"s science fiction debut gazes at the pioneering efforts to save the future and potential of humanity, contemplating the promise and blunders of an ambitious quest to colonize beyond our own galaxy where we face existential dangers. This is his debut novel and is not written by his clone who will be on the spaceship. He is a retired teacher with over 35 years of experience publishing papers and giving numerous presentations, He has an earned Bachelor's degree in Chemistry from Rochester Institute of Technology (RIT), a Master's degree in Deaf Education from Gallaudet University, and a Ph.D. in Special Education from the University of Maryland. He currently resides with his family in Florida.